HEARTED

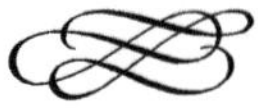

KENDRA THOMAS

ISBN:

Hardback: 978-1-7350153-5-4

❀ Created with Vellum

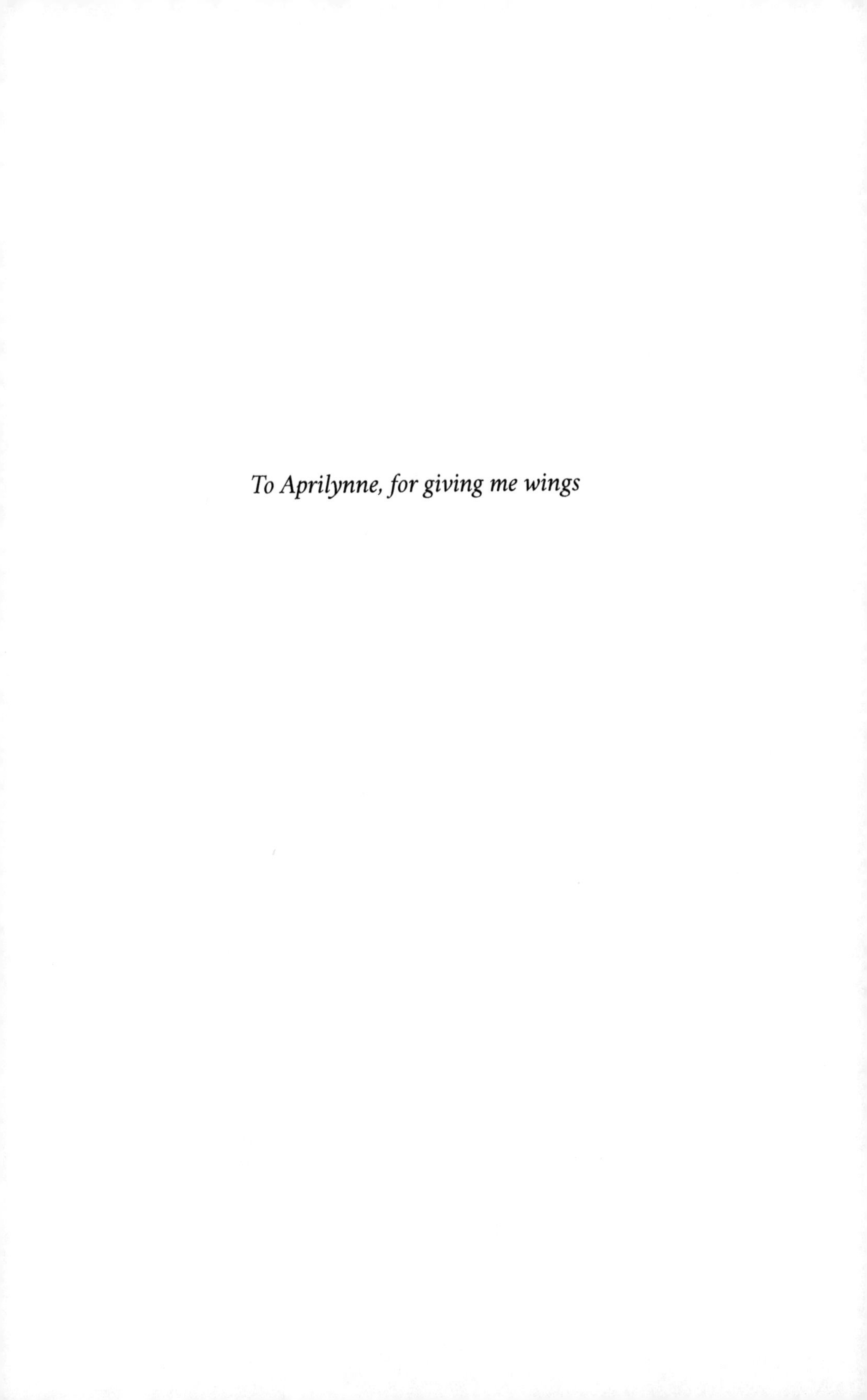

To Aprilynne, for giving me wings

Stables
Field
Envoy
Academy
Drego
The Comission

ONE

Burning in the flames of the Spirit Tree, I had succumbed into a dreamless vacancy. At first it was peaceful, a brief reprieve from the constancy of chaos that I'd left behind. And then the nightmares began.

Obsidian's malevolent black eyes, fire consuming Aveladon, a polar bear's mighty roar.

Emerald-scarlet eyes accompanied the near constant burning sting that never seemed to leave my skin, and I ached for relief.

A faraway voice urgently hissed in the darkness, *"Wake up!"*

Dizzily I opened my eyes. It was hot. Little beads of perspiration formed on my brow and dripped onto my nose and lips. I appeared to be in an empty room, an upgrade from the filthy, leaking cell I'd awoken in some days before. The walls were a chaste white, meeting against a thick stone floor. It was the sight of the chains around my wrists that solidified the reality of my situation.

"No . . ." I moaned into the empty room.

I could hear my heavy breathing. I was acutely aware of the way my chest rose and fell, the pinch of the metal chains against my newly born skin, and the scratchy material of the brown prison clothes I'd been forced into. I could hear the rain pattering outside the room that was absent of windows, giving no view to the outside world.

My eyes zeroed in on the dust particles on the leg of the plain wooden desk, then to a miniscule crack in the far wall. I could taste the tangy humidity in the air as it seeped into the brick crevices.

I breathed in another deep breath, amazed at my heightened, meticulous Stone-Hearted senses. I looked down at the golden light in my chest.

The amulet that usually hung around my neck was gone.

Panic instantly seized me.

What happened to it? Did someone take it? My heart beat escalated. A worried nauseousness built in the pit of my stomach, and just when I thought I might vomit, I heard shuffling outside the door, and then someone walked into the room.

A man in sleek black clothes and combat boots strode inside. He took a seat on the edge of the desk. He had short brown hair with a single streak of brassy blonde that fell into his intense green eyes. He had a regal looking tattoo on one side of his face. The edges of the black design penetrated into his eyebrow. He crossed his arms over his chest where a blue light pulsed, followed by his ankles. He looked at me with an emotionless expression and didn't say anything for a while as he observed me.

"Where am I?" I asked, breaking the stagnant silence. My voice sounded hoarse and scratchy from sleep.

The man raised his tattooed eyebrow, pushed himself off the corner of the desk, and paced in front of me.

"You're in the Sethen Courts." He continued walking. "You've caused quite a stir of commotion burning down the Spirit Tree."

I didn't say anything. I felt it was essential not to provoke the man. He stood with a power and an authority that was unmistakable.

I knew I was in captivity, but the reality that I was in the Sethen Courts created a distubred knot in my core. I vaguely remembered waking up in a dark cell and a man, probably this man, asking who I was. It was a question that wouldn't have been asked unless in ignorance. I didn't feel it was safe to tell him who I was. For some reason I doubted sympathy to be one of his qualities. *And on what grounds would he even believe me?*

"We've had to keep you under high-level security waiting for you to wake up."

"How long have I been asleep?"

"You've been in and out of consciousness for four days."

Four days? My eyes widened. But I was ignorant to what occurred during transitioning to a Stone-Hearted. I could only assume changing into my new identity had been the result of my exhaustion.

"Somehow you were rescued from beneath the remains of the tree, completely unharmed. I've had my soldiers observing you, trying to understand how you survived." I could hear the confusion, the animosity in his voice, but he hid behind an impressive, emotionless expression. "What are your powers?" he suddenly demanded.

"I don't know," I whispered. And it was a terrifying reality. Somehow I had survived the burning of the Spirit Tree and emerged Stone-Hearted. Yet, I had no knowledge of the power I had been granted. I began to feel nauseated again . . .

"We have ways of getting information, and trust me, it will be easier to tell me."

I glared at him, hating the way he threatened me. "I told you. I don't know what my power is."

"Fine, have it your way." He leaned in close to me, his face coming inches from mine. I could feel, and smell, his hot musty breath on my face when he spoke again. "Don't say I didn't warn you." He straightened up, and I flinched as the heavy-metal door slammed behind him.

The guards returned not long after. They were big burly men, both wearing intimidating black clothes and boots. I could see a variety of weapons fastened to their belts and didn't even think about trying to make an escape.

They took me back into the hallway that was just as dull as the room we had come from. We winded through many long hallways, passing white walls, and the occasional metal door placed with heavily armed guards. It was eerily quiet and blistering hot. Our footsteps echoed off the plain, thick corridor and soon we came upon a set of metal stairs.

I tried to remain calm as the guards forced me down the steps. I knew I was returning to the dark, abysmal cell I'd first awoken in. The thought nearly froze me with terror, and I suddenly realized the severity of the situation.

I had burned down the Spirit Tree. An unpardonable crime according to the laws of the kingdom. And I would be continually interrogated by these men that had captured me and taken me to the Sethen Courts. I was in a prison. The most vast and terrifying prison in the entire realm. I was Stone-Hearted without knowledge of what my power was, why I had changed, and to add to everything, I was completely alone.

I tried not to think about my family or Mid because I knew if I did, I would surely be unable to stay composed. I took another shaky breath and forced my heart to steady from its rapid pulsing. It was then that we descended to the bottom of the stairs.

This hallway had the same horrible stench I vividly recalled when first waking up. The guards led me past a series of cells identical to mine. It was dark, nearly pitch black, and extremely wet. My feet sloshed through hot rain water and other debris. I kept my eyes down, not wanting to see the faces of the other prisoners. I could hear them. Some wailed, others shouted viciously as we passed. My presence was obviously riling up the other residences of the dungeon, and I was grateful when we reached my cell, the one at the farthest end of the tunnel. They locked me into another familiar set of rusted chains before shutting the cell door behind them.

I wilted like a flower the moment they left. Tears leaked out onto my cheeks and I silently allowed myself to cry, moving into a state of numbness. The only thing keeping me from truly believing I wasn't in a dream was the pinching of the chains against my wrists and the intense hunger I felt.

For what felt like days, I watched the light from the small window fade until the night returned and I could resist sleep no more.

A dim room appeared with an intricate sitting room sofa on one wall and a blazing fire on the other. Several individuals stood inside the room. A blurriness concealed their faces. I tried desperately to clear the image, but to no avail. I couldn't see who was in the room, but I could hear them arguing, and a familiar sense of dread filled me.

"How could you do this?" I heard someone say.

"It was the only way," another voice chimed in. I felt fear, terror, and most of all heartache when I heard this other voice. But I couldn't put a face to the voice speaking.

"You're not going to get away with this," another person said. And then the fighting began. I watched a group of what appeared to be guards enter the sitting room, their faces also concealed. The fighting erupted, and I raced to hide behind one of the sitting room sofas.

But my hiding spot wasn't enough to conceal me. I heard the screeching of the sofa legs as someone shoved it out of the way. Something knocked me over. My head slammed into the wooden floor, and then I woke up.

~

When I awoke from the dream, it was from the sound of the screeching of the metal latch being unlocked on my cell door. My heart nearly beat out of my chest when I startled from my cramped position on the dirty cell floor. I gasped for air and retrieved only humid mist into my lungs.

For those several days I'd been asleep, I'd dreamed of nothing. At first the dreamlessness was peaceful, but it had quickly become suffocating. This was the first time I'd dreamed of anything so solidified. I didn't have time to unravel what it meant, didn't have time to question it because the guards had returned to retrieve me again. I numbly allowed them to drag me behind them out into the corridor and past the other prison cells. I stumbled on the wet, slushed floor as we traveled. I couldn't remember the last time I'd had something to drink or food had replenished my body. The wet heat penetrating the air made me swallow thickly. And despite the humidity, my throat felt like sandpaper and burned every time I swallowed.

Once we made it up the metal stairs, the blank pale walls returned. And after traveling through endless hallways that seemed to go nowhere, we finally came upon another door. The guards unlocked the latch and quickly shoved me inside.

The room was much larger than any other room I'd been brought to so far. In fact, it was unexpectedly extravagant. Compared to the plain, unembellished prison room I'd previously been interrogated in, this room was absolutely magnificent.

Hand-crafted, slate gray granite, tiled the floor while a massive skylight covered the entire length of the ceiling. I had to squint at the unexpected light that poured in.

Ten throne chairs lined the wall across from us. And Ten Stone-Hearted men and women, all dressed in the same attire as the man who had interrogated me the day before—black, sleek, and entirely intimidating—occupied each chair. The men wore black shirts and trousers; the women wore black dresses with long ebony skirts that cascaded down the marble steps. Cloaks that usually symbolized a kingdom were absent from their shoulders.

They watched me with judgemental, disapproving eyes. It wasn't hard for me to realize I had become the enemy. The man with the tattoo breaching across his forehead was in the very center, already standing to greet me.

The guards that held my chains released me and shoved me roughly. I pitched forwards onto the hard-stone floor. I didn't make a sound and just embraced the cool surface as it met my cheek with a thick smack. It took me several moments to sit up, and I ended up in a submissive kneeling position.

"It seems you've been redeemed," the man said sharply, obviously despising the words he had to spit out. "The council has decided to release you into royal hands," he explained.

Confused, and not really grasping what he was saying I looked up, perplexed. *Had someone come to save me? Did they know I was the princess?*

"The Commission should really hold her for further questioning." The man was no longer talking to me. He turned to someone, another individual suddenly walking into the room.

"I told you, the girl is nothing but a rebellious child." The voice was familiar, and entirely unexpected.

When our eyes met, I could barely stop myself from breaking into emotional pieces.

"She doesn't seem like a child to me."

"Please, Vayel, you know I wouldn't be asking if I didn't know."

Shar's green eyes met mine and it was as if we were meeting again for the first time. His expression was stone cold—heartless. He was dressed differently. He too wore dark clothing and the same black combat boots as the man who's name I now knew was Vayel. He wore short sleeves, and tattoos covered nearly every square inch of both his arms. I had never seen Shar without sleeves on, and I was shocked to see the intricate inkwork covering his skin.

"What are you going to do with her, if I let you leave?" Vayel asked bitterly.

"I plan on putting her in the Galloway. Seeing what she can do."

"And then what will you do with her?"

"Then if she proves herself, I'll take her with me on the journey to Obscurum."

"The blood will be on your hands if she fails you," Vayel said, and he walked over to take a seat in his empty throne on the panel.

"She's not going to be trouble," Shar said roughly.

Vayel didn't look convinced. "I hope you're right, for your sake." The two nodded to each other, and then with one last pressuring look from Vayel, Shar took me by the arm, and led me from the room.

TWO

I could feel the need to stay quiet and didn't dare speak while we walked.

Shar guided me back into the prison corridor, then with several guards on our trail guided me through the blank white maze of hallways. We passed soldiers guarding the doors, their expressions emotionless at the sight of us.

I longed for freedom and the suspense was almost too much to bear. We walked for what seemed like hours, until we finally came to a lone metal door. Shar waited patiently as one of the guards following us pulled a key from his pocket and inserted it into the handle. With a resistant squeal from the metal hinges and a gentle shove, the guard pushed the door open.

Shar tugged me outside into the morning light, and I squinted against the bright sun. The guards behind us didn't follow. The door closed, and suddenly it was just me and Shar.

Finally, I let myself speak.

"How did you find me?" I asked, my voice in a near panic. "What happened—"

"What happened was you were completely irrational and reckless," Shar spat.

We looked to be in the front of the prison building I'd been locked within. The prison was a giant gray stone compound. Thick metal lattice snaked around the building like a net. It sparkled in the sunlight and gave the winding architecture a spider web appearance. Atop the building were two large spires that penetrated the sky. The tall spikes were also a glaring silver.

Giant slate walls surrounded the entire length of the prison compound, with sharp wire on top. It blocked all view of our location. A paved road stretched out from the prison, leading to a large silver gate up ahead. It seemed to be the only point of exit. Every couple seconds the gate would open, letting guards pass in and out of the compound.

"Do you have any idea what you've done?" The waves of fury rolled off him, hot and rapid.

"Shar I—" I didn't get to continue, he cut me off again. He motioned for me to be quiet and then I noticed a prison wagon coming up the road toward us. It was being pulled by a pair of giant white wolves. My eyes widened, and I took a step back when they came near.

Shar gave me a pointed look then proceeded to talk to the guard leading the terrifying canines. I'd never seen anything like them. They were nearly taller than me, their fur glistening like freshly fallen snow. Their ebony eyes were focused forward as they tossed their heads against the harnesses. I gazed in awe at their graceful, anxious marching, as they waited for the commands of their owner.

"We need transport to the Drego," Shar demanded. The

guard was much like the others, menacingly built with dark clothes, and sloe tattoos. He nodded at Shar's request and led us to his prison wagon. It was essentially a rectangular box, bars on all sides, made for transporting prisoners.

"It's good to see you back here, Envorydian," the guard said.

Shar nodded curtly to the guard then handed him a set of coins from his pocket. The guard's cloak was also missing, along with every other guard I had seen. I had yet to see a kingdom signifying cloak on anyone.

Shar proceeded to take off the chains that were binding me, and gestured for me to take a seat in the wagon. His face still indicated I shouldn't speak. I took a seat on one of the benches, and Shar sat beside me. The guard locked the wagon door, and then we rolled toward the gated exit.

I rubbed back the feeling into my wrists, wanting to ask a million questions. Where I was? What happend to Ethydon and my family? Where the amulet might be? But, I could tell this was not the time. I scratched at the itchy prison clothes chafing at my arms and legs and tried to analyze the scenery around me, telling myself there would be time for questions when we arrived wherever it was Shar was taking me.

It took only moments for the guard to tell the gatekeeper to let us through. We passed out of the prison walls, and the paved road eventually ended and turned into a small dirt path. We were quickly immersed into a sea of trees where there was nothing except tropical jungle. I was sweating in my heavy prison clothes. The humidity was much thicker in the depths of the dewy palm trees. Watery plants and vines dripped with blistering precipitation. Nothing seemed capable of escaping the hot wetness.

I could hear the song of birds in the branches and even

spotted a monkey scurrying down a thick green vine. I stared in wonderment at the beautiful flowers that bloomed on the bushes, the colors more vibrant and vivacious than the flowers we had in Aveladon. After about an hour of this jungle path, we finally emerged onto the edge of a hill. I could suddenly see a clear view of a city and the massive walls surrounding it.

I was momentarily confused when seeing the enclosure. The vast circular barricade was a hundred times larger than any city walls I'd ever beheld. It surrounded everything, and encompassed within this giant enclosure were acres of jungle and in the very center, a city. I realized then that the building with the heavily guarded doors and spiked outer walls wasn't a part of the Sethen Courts, but was inside of it. All the things I'd dreamt the Courts to be, this was the least of my imaginations.

We traveled down the hill, and I reached out to grip the bars of the prison wagon, gazing in awe at the peculiar scenery before me.

It didn't take long to descend into the city, and it was immediately louder when we emerged onto the busy streets. They were bustling with commotion, unlike anything I had ever witnessed. Wagons, animals, and Stone-Hearted moved in every direction, so close to one another, it was impossible for them not to brush against one another. The people were going about their daily business, free of chains.

Each edifice was fashioned with jagged metal casting and alloy roofs. Lopsided pieces of tin, copper, and other mixtures of metals plated the exteriors. They were shocking, the glittering of the hardware, somehow standing with its ill-fitting, haphazard construction. The ancient, vintage pieces of rubble and waste were put together, creating a rummaged scrap heap known as the Drego.

The animals were it's other defining contrast to the other kingdoms I'd seen. Animals I'd never before encountered wandered the streets, creatures that would have been prohibited in the kingdoms. I saw winged horses, fierce lions, and jungle cats. I caught sight of a man riding a tiger. A fox on a curious woman's shoulder. A Crykon colt glittering beside a young girl, and a giant black bird perched outside a tarnished metal window.

"Where are we?" I whispered. I couldn't hold in my questions any longer.

Shar wasn't focusing on me, instead he was fumbling through a satchel at his side.

"What was that place we just came from?" I pressed, hoping he would say something, anything. "Where are we going now?" I persisted. "Are you going to tell me what happened in Ethydon?"

He finally looked up from his rummaging, an irritated look on his face.

"We are in the Drego, the main city of the Sethen Courts. The place I just rescued you from is called the Commission, the Sethen Courts headquarters. The people inside that building govern everything here. As for where we're going, it'll be somewhere safe while we figure out a way to get you back home." His eyes flitted to the wagon driver to see if he was listening. "As for what happened in Ethydon, we'll talk about it later."

Shar pulled a canister from his satchel and handed it to me. Suddenly remembering just how thirsty I was, I put the rim to my lips and drank it's entire contents. I gasped for breath after watering the rough desert of my throat.

"Why didn't you tell them who I was?" I asked.

"Let's just say the Sethen Courts aren't very keen on the royal society. And though I'm acquainted with the Commission officials, I'm still only a Captain in the Ethydon Royal Guard, not high enough to demand your pardon. We'll need someone of higher rank to ask for your release. And until we can figure out who that is going to be, we are going to have to keep you out of sight. " He continued rummaging through his bag again and pulled out my mother's amulet that had been missing from my neck.

"My amulet . . ." I reached for the necklace, relief filling me. But before I could grasp it, he quickly tugged it away.

"Not so fast, princess."

We stared at each other, both our expressions filled with irritability and distaste for one another.

"Here's how it's going to go. I'm keeping the amulet in my possession to make sure it stays safe. We must keep the facade that you are indeed a criminal and I your holder. No one can know who you are, or why you are here."

I nodded, reluctant to listen to him, but responding to the seriousness in his whispered tone.

"Fine," I relented.

He slipped the amulet around his neck and then looked up ahead at the street. I wondered if he had my mother's book too but then realized I had left it in the saddlebag on the dapple gray steed outside the gates of the Spirit Tree. The book had to be either burned or lost by now. I felt my heart sink at the thought.

"When we get to the house, you'll be able to eat and wash up. There will be a set of clean clothes there you can change into."

I self-consciously looked back down again at the prison clothes I was wearing. I knew I must've smelled terrible. The conditions of the dungeon I'd been kept in had quickly soiled my clothes. I had gotten used to the stench by now, but I assumed it was unpleasant for anyone who got too close.

“Where is this house exactly?” We had dispersed out of the lively center of the city and had come upon a quieter part of town.

“On the outskirts of the Drego.”

“And might I ask who’s house?”

“A friend of mine.”

THREE

The house we stopped at was a fragmented metal flat. Tall and thin, a similar scrappy tin contraption as the buildings in the main part of the city. Shar thanked the driver as he pulled away, and then it was just the two of us. We walked up to the door, a wobbly ill-fitting aperture. Shar knocked several times. A loud thunking noise echoed with every pound of his knuckles.

"Coming!" a muffled voice called from inside. Then the door went swinging open and the man behind the door took up the entire frame.

"Shar? What a pleasant surprise!" The voice startled me. He had a deep bellowing timbre that vibrated through my entire body when he spoke. The man looked to be about Shar's age, which, on the outside, appeared about thirty years old. But he could've been a hundred for all I knew. He had a thick head of brown hair, and a beaming smile on his face that wrinkled the corners of his carmelly-brown eyes. Underneath his white shirt was a faint green light indicating he was Stone-Hearted.

"Sorry to drop in but—" Shar began to explain but was quickly cut off when the man spotted me. The man reached out his hand, ready to greet me, and that's when I realized his arm was made completely out of metal. His brassy fingertips twinkled, and almost in awe, I reached out and clasped his cool bronze hand.

"I'm Theon, and who might you be?" He gave me another beaming smile, and it softened the harsh appearance of his jagged face tattoo by his eye.

"Ehren," I said softly.

"What a pleasure it is to have you here, Ehren." He winked at me, and I smiled shyly at his greeting. I immediately liked Theon. He had a lighthearted, relaxed personality that quickly put me at ease.

"We need a place to stay. Do you mind?" Shar quickly asked, before he could be interrupted again.

Theon instantly opened the door wider, motioning for us to enter. "Of course old friend."

As we walked inside, the smell of food instantly wafted to my nostrils and my stomach growled.

"You two must be hungry," Theon commented as he led us into his house. The interior looked as mismatched as the exterior. The living room had an old couch and a ragged rug no doubt peppered in soot from the fireplace next to it. And the floors creaked and whined as we walked across them. The kitchen was a rather shiny room. A large bronze piece of scrap metal functioned as a table, and each chair was made of copper. The pots and pans hung from the ceiling, and something cooked in an open wood burning stove.

"You're just in time for lunch," Theon said, scooping something delicious smelling from a large pot.

Shar and I took a seat, and Theon passed us each a bowl filled with rice and potatoes. I quickly started on the food, nearly starving from being in a prison cell for so long.

"So what brings you to town, Shar?" Theon asked, and I could hear something behind his tone. *Was it worry?* I almost sensed hesitancy, but he did well to hide it.

"Business," Shar said bluntly.

"This have something to do with the war?"

"Something like that."

Theon looked at me from across the bar. His face went serious for a moment, thinking. Then as if shaking himself from the spell, another smile grew across his face.

"Why do I have a feeling it has to do with this little lady?"

Seeing my bowl was empty, Theon kindly refilled it. Shar grumbled something under his breath, but it was too quiet to hear.

"Theon, I promise I'll tell you everything soon enough. Would you mind giving Ehren and I some privacy for a moment." An unsaid conversation passed between them, and Theon nodded. When he left the room, Shar turned to me, and the look of exhaustion on his face was suddenly very apparent.

"Are you going to tell me what happened now? " I asked.

Shar sighed then nodded his head reluctantly. "After you disappeared, the castle and the entire city were attacked. The wedding was raided, so the betrothal was compromised." I was helpless to stop the feeling of relief that threaded through me.

"So what does that mean for Ethydon and Aveladon?"

"Alliances through betrothal is a formality. It's simply a better way of ensuring alliances last. But with everything that had happened, the need for such precaution has diminished. I would say at this point, there isn't really a need to have them married. Aveladon and Ethydon are allies, and the blood that was shed on that battle field was enough to prove that."

"So they aren't getting married?"

"Not anymore, at least that was the decision when I left. And Mid and Jasper were both fine with that outcome," Shar explained.

I was immediately confused, remembering how much Jasper seemed to like Mid. But maybe there was more to the story than Shar knew. I was about to press for more but then remembered his last words and asked him something else.

"What do you mean, the blood that was shed?"

"The fighting lasted all night and into the next morning. We pushed back the best we could. Eventually, Obscurum retreated but not before nearly taking out the entire Ethydon and Aveladon people." He stopped and looked to be thinking back on the memory for a moment.

"Did the others survive?" I whispered. He seemed to know I was referring to my family and the Knadians. I was worried to hear his next words, terrified of the pending truth.

"Everyone is fine," he paused, "except for Embrosine." He looked up at me with a pained expression.

I couldn't hide the shock and heartache that crossed my features. "No . . ." I said, covering my mouth with my hands. I imagined the worst: her lifeless body on the floor of the music room, her heart drained of the beautiful azure color. "She can't be. . ."

"She's not dead." Relief flooded my body. "But they did kidnap her." The relief was short lived, and I felt an ice-cold anguish pierce my chest. "One of the guards saw her being taken from the castle during the raid. He couldn't reach her though, and they got away."

"What?" I asked in disbelief. My mind was unable to comprehend the news. I sat in shock for many moments. For some reason that reality seemed far worse. "This is all my fault," I finally said, tears filling the corners of my eyes. Memories of my fists pounding against the music room door as she sacrificed herself for me filled my head. If I had just had a power, some sort of extra strength, I could've helped her. But I had been useless. I tried to reason that she had ordered me to take her daughter, and I had gotten Sunn to safety. But the thought did little to ease my guilt. *It should've been me,* I thought to myself.

"You couldn't have saved her," Shar said gently. And for the briefest of moments, it was almost as if he was showing an emotion toward me other than sarcasm and contempt. "There are people looking for her as we speak. We'll find her."

I sat wide eyed, still trying to grasp onto the news.

Shar cleared his throat and continued. "When the fighting ended, we all met back up together to regroup and talk about the plan to search for the tokens. You and Sunn were nowhere to be found. And we assumed you had taken Sunn to the docks. Everyone started to get worried. Then the tree burned down and the curse hit."

I looked up at his mention of the curse, suddenly breaking from my state of shock. "What's happened? Have you noticed a change?"

"I can feel my powers are weaker already. Everyone felt it." Shar stretched open the collar of his shirt and showed me his glowing purple heart. The color was pulsing, but it was a much weaker glow than what it should have been emitting. "All I know is something changed when you burned down the tree."

I thought back to Elsmith the Reminant who had helped me meet my mother. He had seemed to know what was going to happen. I wondered if he escaped the clutches of the fire. I could only hope that he and the nurturers had made it out safely before the tree had burned. The guilt would be too much to bear if something had happened to them at my hand. I told myself when I returned to Aveladon, I would inquire what happened to them as soon as I could.

"What about finding the tokens?" I asked, trying to push images of the burning Spirit Tree from my head.

"We decided to stick with the original plan. A message from Ashelor arrived a couple days later, confirming that you had indeed taken Sunn to the docks. But you had yet to return, so we assumed the worst. . . that you were dead or captured. So Jasper and Ruby decided to stay and keep searching for you however futile, while helping with the remaining survivors."

The thought of Jasper ripped through me just as intensely as the news about Embrosine. I thought about our last conversation. She had gotten upset about her lack of involvement with the curse and she'd stormed away from me. More guilt weighed on my heart, and I felt at any moment I would sink with the feeling.

"Then the rest of us went searching for the tokens. I left to the Sethen Courts and was shocked to find they had a prisoner in their midst who apparently burned down the Spirit Tree." He looked over at me. "You." He ran a hand through his hair and tugged on the tie, setting his blond locks free. His hair fell into his eyes, the expression on his face tormented. "At first I didn't know if it was you. You looked much different Stone-Hearted, but once it was confirmed that the amulet had been found along with you, I knew I wasn't mistaken."

I watched his eyes flicker to my glowing golden heart. And then he asked the question I feared to have to answer.

"Sabeara, what happened to you?"

It took me a moment to think of how to explain it all to him. But anyway I put it, it was going to sound insane.

"I know it may sound crazy but. . . I felt that I had too." It sounded pathetic coming from my lips, but I didn't know how else to say it. My lame explanation only caused his anger to return.

"You didn't have to do anything, Sabeara. Getting yourself locked inside the Sethen Courts as one of the most wanted criminals was *not* a necessary part of the plan!" His green eyes pierced mine, and I couldn't help but be afraid of his rage. I knew he was right, but I didn't want to admit I'd caused such chaos. "You've put the entire kingdom at risk by being here. And put a huge obstacle in my plans to find the other tokens."

"Shar, please. Will you let me tell my side of the story?"

He stood from the stool and paced the kitchen floor. I swallowed back the lump in my throat, and continued.

"I left the wedding." As I began, memories of that night flooded back to me. They were just as vivid as the day I experienced them. I didn't think I'd ever be able to forget. "When I left, I went into the music room to get some air. Calm myself down. But then, Obsidian was in the room with me. He was talking about how he had burned down Aveladon and that it was the Obscurum king's plan the entire time." I felt the nausea return. "He told me he was my cousin, that we were family."

I watched to see Shar's reaction. But he just continued to pace.

"Then Embrosine came into the room, she was worried and had come looking for me. Then it all happened so fast. I was trying to push her out the door, not wanting her to get hurt. But then she told me to find Sunn and shoved me out into the hallway . . ." I trailed off, despising the memory as it burned inside my head. "So I went to find Sunn, I took her to the docks, and her father took her to the Isles. I was about to return to Ethydon, but then I had this realization." I let out a shaky breath, knowing the next part would sound entirely deranged.

"I couldn't return to Ethydon. I had to do something, and when I went to the Spirit Tree, I talked with my mother, and she told me to burn down the tree. She said our realm needed to experience the flames, so that it could live again. Whatever that means." I sighed and felt the tears begin to leak down my cheeks. "I don't really know why I did it either. I just felt I needed to listen to her, that it was what I had to do. I had no idea I would survive the fire, become Stone-Hearted, or that I'd be taken to the Sethen Courts for what I did."

Shar halted his rampant pacing and came over to me, placing both his hands on my arms, he shook me slightly. "Sabeara, you —" he paused, his eyes searching mine. I didn't bother to hide the tears now, and he noticed. A mix of emotions passed across his features: anger, fear, disbelief, uncertainty.

He suddenly sighed, and like a broken fever, he finally simmered. "Midennen would want me to get you back home. So that's what we are going to focus on. We'll figure out the rest later." I felt the sting at his words, realizing he was only dealing with me because of Mid's love for me.

"I don't need your help," I snapped, and his familiar patronizing chuckle followed.

"Oh yes you do. The only way you're making it out of here alive is with my help." He glared at me, and I glared back.

I wasn't in much of a position to argue. And even though I

wanted to insist that I figure this out on my own, I knew it was impossible.

"Fine," I finally spat, not thinking of a better comeback.

I had nowhere to storm off too. So I just turned and stared at the empty bowl in front of me, refusing to look at him.

Shar left the kitchen, only to come back several minutes later. He set a stack of clothes in front of me, letting them fall carelessly onto the metal table.

"Your room is upstairs. Follow me."

I grabbed the clothes and reluctantly followed after him through the strange little house. We passed through the living room and started up a twisted staircase to the second floor. Theon was nowhere in sight, and I wondered where he had disappeared to.

The little staircase was barely big enough for one person to travel up at a time. So I followed closely behind Shar's heels until we emerged onto the second floor. We were immediately greeted with a hallway, and Shar gestured for me to continue down to the very end. He opened the final door and led us into a little room.

The roof slanted, and at some parts, I had to bend over so as not to hit the ceiling. The room had a small bed with a haphazard set of sheets and a pillow. A dainty armour and mirror stood in the corner, while a lone flickering candle sat aflame on the nightstand. Beside the window, that gave view to jungle trees and iron houses was a small basin filled with water.

"You can wash up here." He started for the door. "You should get some sleep. Your body will be drained from your changing." The way he lectured me was different from Oli. He was hard, like the captain of an army directing one of his foot soldiers. Everything he said was rigid, and emotionless.

The thought of my guardian, and his soft golden curls and peridot eyes was almost too much. Oh how I wished I could have talked to him right then. I had to force myself not to break down until Shar left the room.

"Don't do anything reckless," he added, just before closing the door behind him.

I growled under my breath. I was frustrated, slightly angry, and most of all, heartbroken. All the fervor I'd felt before I'd burnt down the tree was gone. And everything Shar had told me about Embrosine, about Aveladon and Ethydon was now beginning to hit me as I sat alone in that foreign little room. I was beginning to question all my decisions.

I took a seat on the edge of the cot for a moment and buried my head in my hands. I finally allowed myself to cry. I had caused Embrosine's kidnapping. She was now somewhere, who knows where, captive at the hands of Obsidian, or worse, the Obscurum king. Obsidian was my cousin, and he had a deep grudge against my family because of something that had happened in the past. My family was safe, but the kingdom was in ruins, and I could painfully imagine Ethydon crumbling to the same fate as Aveladon. To add to everything, everyone I loved thought I was captured or dead, and I had left most of my relationships in pieces.

I allowed the image of emerald-scarlet eyes to fill my head, and that's when I felt the unimaginable stabbing pain in my heart.

I clutched my chest, gasping for breath. *What have I done?* I thought. And without permission, my mind began to replay memories of him. The festival in Ethydon, playing arches, him holding me in the tent during the hunt, the kiss in the rose grove. . . leaving him at the wedding.

Shaky sobs began to wrack my body, and I desperately wiped the salty droplets from my cheeks. I didn't want to face the feelings.

For what seemed like hours I lay on the little bed, trying to ease the ache in my chest. Eventually I ran out of tears and could but lay silently on the quilt feeling empty and numb. It would be easier to try and feel nothing. Burying my feelings seemed the only option.

I decided I could at least change my clothes before trying to fall asleep. I'd already slept so much it seemed, but Shar was right, I still felt drained. I used one of the blankets on the bed to cover the small bedroom window. I abandoned the soiled, ugly prison clothes and used a small towel I found in the armour to rinse myself of the grime and dirt on my skin. It was a slow process. I never seemed to get dry. The humidity kept me in a constant state of wetness. Giving up, I reached for the stack of clothes Shar had given me and put them on.

I looked in the mirror after I had changed and wondered if he'd made a mistake. I felt nearly naked. The shirt was sleeveless, and my shoulders were showing. He'd given me a dainty midnight blue tank top, and a matching pair of loose, baggy pants, that met at to the middle of my shins.

I wasn't used to such simple, depraved clothing. I'd worn many gowns, ones that flaunted my bare shoulders and seen many other women flash scandalous swooping necklines. I had even worn trousers while in Ethydon. But somehow this seemed very different. Yet the freedom of the scanty attire left me much cooler with the humidity and I couldn't fathom putting on more layers.

I gathered my black raven locks and twisted my hair into a braid down over my shoulder. Looking at my reflection, I did not recognize the person staring back at me. My eyes were red and puffy from crying, and I gently reached up and touched the tear stains on my now perfected cheeks. I then traced the golden light shining through my chest. I wondered what power was pulsing inside of my now gleaming heart and how much of the curse had tainted its power. I didn't feel weak, or that my power was waning, but then again, I'd never had anything to compare it to. I stared at my chest and the glowing heart I'd so longed for and tried not to think about the power weakening with every passing day that the curse went unbroken.

I looked back at the stranger in the mirror and gazed into her watery sapphire eyes and couldn't help but feel uncertain if it was really me standing there.

Once again, I felt the estranged awed feelings that accompanied my new reality, and I couldn't help but ask myself once more.

What have I done?

FOUR

The same dream occurred that night. The one in the dark sitting room. I would see the sofa and the fire, and then the shouting would begin. The faces remained blurred in the dream, and I was unable to depict who was speaking. It was frustrating and terrifying.

When I woke up, I was just as affected as I had been the first time I had the dream. I could immediately feel I was drenched in sweat. I peeled the bed sheets off my skin and urgently went to open the small bedroom window. I did my best to shake off the nightmare and stuck my head out into the morning air and breathed in a deep breath. Most of it was thick and moist, but it was better than the stifling temperature and humidity now in the loft.

I left the window and went to check my appearance in the mirror. My eyes weren't as red and puffy as the night before, but the clothes were still unnervingly thin and slim. Otherwise, I looked well enough. I stepped out into the hallway and made my way down the stairs to the kitchen.

Just as I was halfway down the steps, I heard voices and quickly picked out Shar's. He was talking to Theon, and instinctively I stilled on the stairs. I couldn't help but listen in.

"I'm heading to the Envoy. I have to talk to the others about the Galloway fight."

"You think they'll listen?"

"Do you really think they will say no?" There was a moment of silence between the two of them.

"Are you going to tell me who she is?" I heard Theon ask quietly.

"Trust me, it's best if you don't know," Shar said. "And she'll be gone before you know it. I'm sending word to have her retrieved from the Courts."

"You have the power to do that?"

"I don't, but I know someone else who does."

"How did you get her out anyway?"

"Vayel trusts me, and I may have been pushing that trust by asking him to let me take her, but I didn't have an option."

"Are you sure you want her to leave? She could help you retrieve the tokens."

"She's not a fighter, Theo. She isn't meant for this kind of thing."

I'd heard enough and made a point to walk noisily down the stairs so they could hear I was coming. Their conversation immediately ceased as I descended onto the main floor. I locked eyes with Shar who was obviously just as stern and grumpy as the day before.

"Good morning," I said easily, trying to seem innocent.

"You're up early. Care for some breakfast?" Theon gave me a

big smile as I came to take a seat at the table. He was mixing something in a bowl, his metal fingers carefully clutching a wooden spoon.

"I'd love some."

Shar started for the door, and began fastening a variety of weapons to his belt.

"I'm heading out. I'll be back later tonight. Watch her for me?"

"Wait, where are you going?" I asked hurriedly.

"Out. Stay here. Theon will watch over you. I need to run some errands." It was ironic how blatantly he was lying to me.

"You know, just because I don't have your power doesn't mean I can't see that you're lying."

"Stay here." Was all he said, and then he was gone.

"Ugh. . . he's so frustrating!" I grumbled, as the front door slammed shut. Theon set a bowl of some breakfast hash in front of me and I shoveled bits of what looked to be potato and egg into my mouth angrily.

"I'm sorry, little lady, but if it makes you feel any better that's how he is with everyone."

"How do you two know each other anyway?"

"Shar and I worked together a long time ago." Theon didn't elaborate further.

"I heard you guys talking earlier. Something about the Envoy, what is that?"

"You're a curious one aren't you? I'm sorry to disappoint you, but I don't think Shar would like it very much if I told you." It was obvious that Shar had some sort of past with Theon that made him wary of telling me anything he wasn't supposed to. *How did Shar have friends in the Sethen Courts?*

"Fine. I guess I'll just go follow him and find out myself." I stood from the stool, and started for the door. Theon quickly chased after me and stepped in front of the door, holding out his long metal arm and hindering any chance of escape.

"Woah, not so fast."

I put my hands on my hips and glared up at him, determined to get answers.

"I don't know what Shar has over you, but let's get one thing straight. That arrogant, grouchy, ill-tempered man is not going to dictate what I do and do not know. He can't just go ordering me around all the time. I've had enough of that in my life already." I was fuming, and Theon's eyes widened slightly as if he didn't quite know how to react.

"Okay."

"Okay?" I was confused, not expecting his reply.

"Yes, okay. I'll tell you what the Envoy is, but can we at least sit back down?" His words were soft and slow, as if trying not to provoke me further. I nodded, feeling slightly ashamed at my outburst. This man didn't even know me, he was just following orders the best he could, and I wasn't being very fair.

Theon took a seat on the couch in the front room and gestured for me to take a seat. "The Envoy is a guild. A group of trained fighters. Their training grounds are on the very edge of the Sethen Courts. Several of my friends live there and he's going to talk to them about the Galloway."

"What is the Galloway?"

"The Galloway is an arena. It's for entertainment here in the Courts. Stone-Hearted contend against one another in combat, and the winner is allotted a prize. Sometimes it's money, or a large supply of resources. Other times it's livestock or freedom from the prisons. It's every man or woman's dream to win a Galloway fight."

"Do they fight to the death?" My eyes widened in shock, not believing something could be so barbarous.

"No, it's not like that. They go until someone resigns from the fight. At any moment they can forfeit. But that's not to say people don't get seriously injured."

"What does Shar want with the Galloway?" I was confused now, uncertain how it all tied together.

Theon hesitated, before reluctantly continuing. "He wants to take the winning Stone-Hearted with him to find the tokens."

"And he's using the Galloway as a test? What sort of plan is that?"

"The people he plans to send to fight in the Galloway aren't just your average civilian. They are trained fighters, powerful Stone-Hearted, and absolutely lethal. Shar needs the best fighters he can get to go with him."

"Why couldn't he just take soldiers from the Ethydon Royal Guard?"

Theon laughed at my response as if I'd made a hilarious joke. "I'm sorry to laugh. It's just a funny suggestion." Theon forced himself to quiet his chuckles, and he became suddenly serious again.

"Why is that funny?"

"You see, soldiers from any of the kingdom's could never measure up to the type of fighters in the Envoy. The guild doesn't just take any person into their society. These types of fighters are meticulously created."

"Created?" The word sent chills down my spine.

"Does that answer your questions?" Theon asked, a small smile on his lips as if he was pleased by my reaction.

"Just one more thing. How does Shar know about the Envoy?"

Theon looked at me very seriously as he said his next words. “Because he was once a part of it.”

FIVE

I had so many questions, and Theon quickly figured out sating my curiosity was going to be quite demanding. After a while, he decided to take me out to the Drego with him where I could see the city for myself.

Theon led us down the roadway from his home, leading to the city. We passed a cluster of lonely looking flat's similar to Theon's, and then eventually more tall buildings emerged. The farther we walked, the more crowded the streets became.

"Are you going to tell me how Shar is involved with the Envoy?" I asked, still shocked about what Theon had told me back at the flat. I didn't know much about Shar, but a fighter clan was definitely not something I imagined he'd have once been a part of.

"I better let him tell you the story. He can be touchy about it," Theon said, smiling to himself.

I wanted to press but forced myself not to. I needed to be

tactful with my questions. I'd just have to ask Shar later about his involvement.

"This was the last thing I expected the Sethen Courts to be like," I commented, unable to tear my eyes away from the unfamiliar scene. The people that walked by all wore light-weight flowing clothes that made the heat easier to bear. It was untraditional and rather radical compared to the style back in Aveladon.

Most people were too busy to glance in our direction. They were moving so quickly there wasn't time to notice new faces. I perused the crowd, insistent on discovering all the Drego had to offer.

"Did you imagine dark dungeons and cages? Prison guards torturing the disobedient?" Theon joked, smirking.

The stacked metal high rise buildings situated close together and the tarnished glaze that covered everything were fascinating, and I couldn't help but admire the outlandish architecture. We walked on a thin road, passing food shops and clothing stores. Several places bartered weapons, and I even saw a store that was selling small pets. We brushed shoulders with other civilians, the road too cramped not to slightly touch.

"Actually, yes," I admitted. I thought back to the Commission, where I *had* been kept in a dark cage. The Commission seemed to be the actual location of threat. The people down here, in the Drego, appeared harmless, yet, I couldn't exactly understand why it existed at all. The mystery of the Sethen Courts and its title of "Prison" instituted a plethora of unanswered questions I had yet to figure out.

"I could understand why. Gossip in the kingdoms can be very misleading." Theon looked over at me curiously for a moment, and I could see the probing look in his eyes. But he didn't ask me, and it made me feel guilty. It was only fair to share something with him after everything he'd told me.

"I'm from Aveladon," I stated, hoping it wasn't too much information to give.

"I see. It must be really different here for you then," he assumed.

I grimaced and shook my head a little. "Everyone has a prison, Theon. Yours is the Sethen Courts; mine is Aveladon."

He didn't say anything to that, and I assumed he just didn't know how to reply.

"Why is everything made of metal?" I asked, realizing it was a recurring theme in all the buildings. There was so much of it, and I wondered if it was just a style or a necessity.

"The only building resources we receive from the kingdoms are the scraps. Each kingdom is required to give the Courts a portion of supplies. So we end up with the leftovers from the forges."

"Why not just build with the trees here in the Courts?"

"We try to preserve our natural resources as much as possible, and with the rain, the metal is better for keeping things dry," he explained.

It was a sad realization that the kingdoms were so cruel to the people in the Courts. But all things considered, they were managing quite well with the leftover resources they'd been given.

"Where is the Galloway?" I asked looking around at all the buildings bustling with life.

"Straight ahead you can see the walls of the arena." Theon pointed through the crowds of Stone-Hearted, and sure enough, I could see the rim of a large colosseum in the distance. It looked intimidating with its tall walls made of thick glistening metal panels. Speculations of what must've gone on inside filled my head.

"Do people really fight in there?" I whispered, almost afraid of the thought.

"Yes, they really do."

We turned down another street, and Theon led us into a new alleyway. It was less busy, and it smelled awfully like something was burning. It wasn't until I saw the tiny shop that it began to make sense.

A man in the safety of a small metal alcove was sitting at a cluttered workbench, amalgamating something. He seemed to be welding the metal together with his. . . eyes. It was shocking to see the hot light coming from his irises. It was a bright orange, and hard to look at directly. The heated light hit the metal with perfect precision and then sparks went flying every which direction. I was a little startled at the display.

"Hope you don't mind, I have to stop by for an adjustment." Theon led me into the small shop, and the man working on the metal lifted a pair of thick goggles from his eyes with a heavy-gloved hand. I expected to see something gruesome, two burning eyeballs maybe. But instead a pair of green eyes met mine, unscathed, and not at all seemingly affected by the heat they'd just ignited. A red rim imprint outlined his face, and I noticed he had a couple wrinkles, looking to be an older Stone-Hearted. His white hair was dusty with black grease marks. He smiled at Theon as we came walking inside.

"Theon, come for a couple new screws, eh?" the man asked, his voice louder and heartier than even Theon's.

"Hey, Finn, mind giving me a quick tuneup?" Theon asked, and the man instantly stopped what he was doing. He gestured for us to take a seat at a cluttered table with several chairs resting beside his workstation.

"Not at all. Now who's this darling you've got with ya?"

Theon brushed off the man's teasing tone. "Just a friend, Finn. Her name is Ehren, and I'm showing her around," Theon explained.

"Welcome to the Drego, Ehren." He didn't sound the least bit pitiful. It was almost like he actually considered this place a welcoming destination.

"Thank you," I stated lamely, taking a seat awkwardly beside Theon.

The man went rummaging through his shop and came back over to Theon a couple moments later with several screws in his hands. He knelt down with a little metal tool and began tinkering at Theon's metal arm. Though I knew it was impolite, it was hard not to stare. I had never seen anything like Theon's metal arm before.

"Got my forearm cut off in battle," Theon said, catching me staring.

"Still can't believe you were stupid enough to walk into that raging mess," Finn mumbled beneath his breath. Theon rolled his eyes and grinned, his brown eyes sparkling with the memory.

"It was a dangerous situation, and I threw myself into it without thinking. I was reckless as a kid. But the arm is pretty cool. I don't regret it." A smile played on his lips the entire time he spoke of his daring past endeavor. I cringed. The thought of my arm being cut off immediately made me queasy.

"There you have it. All set, lad." Finn stood from his crouched position and proceeded to admire his handiwork.

Theon moved his metal plated fingers slowly as if he was

testing out the mechanics. "Perfect. Thanks Finn!" Theon stood up and tossed Finn several coins before taking me back out into the alleyway. Finn put his goggles back on and soon the smell of melding metals filled the air again. Slowly the thick smell dissipated as we left the alley and returned to the main streets of the Drego.

"So is everyone in the Sethen Courts part of the Envoy?" I asked, noticing that some civilians didn't have the intricate tattoos like Shar and Theon. I wondered if it was just a fashion choice, or if the ink was a sign of being part of the guild.

"No, not everyone is a part of the Envoy. The Envorydians are a small population among the Courts."

I vaguely recalled hearing the man at the Commission calling Shar by that title.

"Are all Envorydians criminals?"

"That depends on your definition of criminal," Theon said darkly, and I realized then I'd stepped into unspoken territory, something not exactly light for conversation.

"What does that mean?" I dared to press. Theon looked over at me and seemed to hesitate for a second. Then finally sighed and gave in.

"Let me tell you a little story." Theon's voice lowered, his tone more earnest and secretive now. I instantly listened in, eager to hear more. "Thousands of years ago, Aveladon was broken apart into several kingdoms. There were five kings known anciently for their contentions. Do you know of them?" Instantly I knew he was speaking of the kings in the Ethirical.

"Yes, I know of the stories."

Theon looked pleased and continued on. "So as you may know, there lived a war king named Wesoltinece. He was the greatest war fighter in those times. To help him fight against the other kings when wars were breaking across the lands, he created a special force of fighters."

"The Envorydians," I answered quickly, realizing where he was headed. I had never been taught anything about the Envorydians and never read anything about them in the Ethirical, but maybe I had missed something in my study. *Or they kept it from you,* my mind retorted. It was likely a subject my father didn't want me to know.

Theon nodded, smiling at my guess.

"Yes, the Envorydians. Over time the kingdom warred against each other and eventually almost everything became extinct including the Envorydian race Wesoltinece had created. Luckily, after the final war, when Aveladon became one kingdom again, a couple of the Envorydians survived, and the Envoy continued on. For many years after the contention of the lands, the Envorydians became protectors over Aveladon."

"Protectors?"

"The kingdom had its Royal Guard, but the Envorydians were a separate entity stronger than they could ignore. They simply stopped whatever nefarious forces the Royal Guard couldn't handle, and it worked for a long time. Together between the Royal Guard and the Envoy, peace filled Aveladon."

"So they became the good guys then?" I clarified and Theon nodded.

"The Envorydians' famous saying is, 'Peace through the heart.'"

"Then what happened?"

"King Tilan came into power about a hundred years ago." The name instantly rang a bell and a shiver ran down my spine.

Tilan was the name of my grandfather. The king who reigned over Aveladon before my father.

"He didn't like that the Envorydians were so called 'uncontrollable' and he hated that he couldn't order them the way he saw fit. So he decreed them a strictly vigilante race, deemed them criminal in their efforts, and any Envorydian not willing to side underneath his direct command was to be placed in the Sethen Courts."

I gasped, stopping in the middle of the street, appalled at the history I had no knowledge of.

"What did the Envorydians do?"

"Most chose not to be under his reign and submitted themselves to the Courts honorably. Some chose to stay and bear his demands. But eventually the kingdom's began to get contentious, and kingdoms began to split. When King Tilan died, his son Casimir came into reign and Obscurum was created and then Severesi. It was all too tempting for Envorydian's to abandon the Aveladon crown and search for a different king to work for." Theon sighed and urged me to keep walking. Putting his hand to his head, he rubbed his temple and seemed almost pained to continue on with the story.

"Eventually Envorydians became a sort of weapon for each kingdom. Bounty hunters for the kingdoms' secret threats. Personal assassins they could use at will. They were put against one another, and soon Envorydians were killing Envorydians, each kingdom using their special fighters as weapons. More Envorydians were captured because of this and put into the Sethen Courts. Eventually Envorydians didn't want to fight anymore. Most of us went into hiding or came to the Sethen Courts so as not to be bothered. The Envoy is now something people in the kingdom's only whisper about.

"The Sethen Courts is a place where we can practice our skills, learn the art of the Envoy techniques without being made special pets for the kingdoms and so as not to go against what we believe. Peace."

"Are there Envorydians that don't believe in peace?" I asked.

"Most Envorydians were trained with a sense of loyalty. With our Envoy ideals still ingrained in them. But yes, some are content to stay killers. Some have chosen not to change. We don't consider them part of the guild." I watched Theon's jaw clench.

"So the rest of the people living in the Courts. . ." I trailed off, not knowing exactly how to phrase my next question. But Theon seemed to already know what I was asking.

"The Commission keeps all threatening criminals in the Commission headquarters. Everyone else is not really a threat. Most people you see either didn't want to live in the kingdoms anymore, were unfairly treated, or simply were misjudged over something they didn't actually do."

My mind wandered back to the dirty prison cell I'd come from. Memories of the other prisoners' wails and cries were hard to forget. I shivered.

"It's all so unfair," I said, frowning. We had been walking for a while and had ended up back at the flat. I looked up, surprised to see the scrappy metal building.

"It's okay, really." Theon smiled but I could see the pain behind his eyes. "Most of us are happy here. And one day the curse will end and we will hopefully be able to return to protect Aveladon as we were always meant to." It was impossible to miss the hope in his voice.

And it was then that I could finally see, and understand, after seeing the city and talking with Theon, that the Sethen Courts wasn't a prison at all, but rather a kingdom of outcasts, an empire of misfits.

And suddenly it seemed like exactly the place I needed to be.

SIX

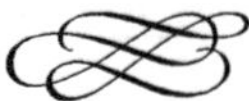

Shar didn't return that night, or the next day. Theon said he was probably fine, likely busy and that I shouldn't be concerned. I tried to not to think about whether he was okay or where he could be. He pretty much hated me, so it didn't seem logical to care about his well-being. But it was hard. I knew how much he meant to Mid. And he was the only thing tying me back to home. No matter how much he got under my skin.

With my isolation at the flat and lack of distractions, it was hard not to think about all the conflicts going on inside my head. Especially Mid. I missed him, and couldn't help but wonder about him even more now that he and Jasper's betrothal was off. *What would things be like when I returned?*

I shook my head as if that would somehow help me stop thinking about him. Then I forced myself to busy myself at the flat. I talked more with Theon. He was kind to me. Despite being put on sentry duty, he was being well-natured about the whole thing. He was a great cook too and seemed to constantly be in the kitchen cooking. I got to sample everything he made, and I began to quickly relax into the little alloy abode. Talking to Theon was a good distraction from all the other things that threatened to consume my mind.

Shar returned the following day. A torrid storm was whipping outside, rain beating against the metal roof. I was on the couch, almost slipping into sleep from the repetitive pattering of the rain, when I was startled from my faint slumbering.

"Shar?" I asked groggily. A gust of misty wet air blew through the door, and then he quickly shut the door behind him. He was soaking wet, his long blonde locks dripping at the tips. He shook off at the door, water spraying everywhere. "Where have you been?" I accused. The fog of sleep was evaporating, being replaced by the usual trepidation I held for him.

Just then Theon came down the stairs, and he looked almost surprised to see Shar standing in the doorway.

"It took me longer than I expected to talk with the Commission," Shar explained, suddenly rummaging around Theon's kitchen.

"And the Envoy?" Theon asked quietly.

"Didn't get to that quite yet. I'm going to the Academy tonight to talk to the others."

"You're leaving again?" I asked, standing from the couch.

"Sorry to disappoint. I know being in each other's company is definitely something the both of us were looking forward to." He smirked sarcastically. "But I'm just grabbing a couple things then heading out again."

Theon looked at Shar, a concerned look in his eye. Shar appeared exhausted, like he hadn't slept the last two days. Whatever had happened at the Commission had definitely taken a toll on him. He roamed the kitchen, grabbing a couple pieces of fruit and stuffing them into his pack.

"You okay to keep an eye on Ehren a little longer?" Shar asked, already heading for the door again. He slipped on a new jacket, drier than the other one he'd soaked and looked at Theon expectantly.

"Yeah, sure," Theon finally said, snapping from the thoughtful trance he was in.

"Thanks, Theo." The nickname left Shar's lips and then the door was closing behind him again. I turned to look at Theon, confusion written all over my features.

"Where is he going?" I demanded.

"The Envoy." Theon sighed and then took a seat on the couch and buried his head in his hands. He was obviously starting to get worried about the situation.

"I want to follow him," I stated forcibly and started for my boots by the door

"He wouldn't like that," his head lifted, his eyes flashing with panic.

"Theon, he's being illusive and too secretive for my taste. I need to know what's going on."

Theon stood then and came over with an exhausted look in his eye. "You're going to go even if I tell you no, aren't you?"

I stopped lacing up my boots to look into his dark brown eyes seriously. "Yes, I am." I stated simply.

He nodded as if realizing he didn't have another choice and then started to put on a rain jacket. "All right, then I'm coming with you. Don't want you getting lost in the woods."

Theon led the way out into the stormy night. The rain wasn't cold. It was hot, and the precipitation made my neck and face feel sticky. The path he began down was in the opposite direction of the Drego. We slipped into the darkness of the thick jungle trees, and it was an eerie scenery. The buzz of insects and the rustling of creatures hidden amongst the foliage was hard to ignore. I had a feeling that the creatures that lived deep within these trees weren't as friendly as the ones back in Aveladon. Palm leaves brushed up against my arms and legs while my boots squished noisily in the mud the rain had created. I couldn't help but jump a little every time a wet vine brushed up against my face or hair.

Nothing was said between us as we walked, and I worried I may have upset Theon. I hated being pushy, but I knew that without force Shar would never fill me in on his plans.

Soon the trees thinned slightly, and through the sheet of rain, I could see a house in the distance. It was four stories high and fashioned out of wood. I remembered Shar's words, and how he'd said he was going to the Academy. It looked a little run down for an academy. The wood was deteriorating from constant weather, unmanaged greenery snaked up the molded exterior, and some of the shutters were missing from the windows. But then again, I didn't know much about the educational systems outside of my personal tutoring in Aveladon. Maybe this was what all academies looked like.

Theon led me up to the front door, as we neared, I couldn't help but peer in at the windows. Warm yellow light illuminated within, and I could hear voices. Theon didn't bother knocking and simply opened the door, gesturing for me to follow after him.

The door opened to a small meager foyer. A little bench sat pressed against the wall, a houseplant shrouding one corner, leaving the other corners pitifully scant. I had just gotten a brief glance at the entrance when Theon began leading me down a hallway. I heard voices and the buzz got louder as we journeyed down the skinny corridor. The rickety wooden floor creaked beneath our wet boots as we walked. The timeworn walls and floor were old and decaying from the moist heat. I could taste the old jungle wood on my tongue as it mingled with the humidity and the smell of food. How could anyone focus on just one thing with such elevated Stone-Hearted senses?

Minutes later we were met with another door. I held my breath as I watched Theon wrap his fingers around the onyx knob and push open the door.

The room was dingy, the candles in the room and the glow of the hearth barely illuminating the small cramped space. Bodies filled chairs and full-brimmed steins, sloshing with Lush Fire, cluttered tables amongst laughter and intimate chatter. I could immediately feel that these people were different.

It was a sort of dining hall, verging on the feeling of a tattered pub. A room designated for nighttime intoxication and mingling. The decor was gaunt and shabby. Ancient alloy paneling was nailed into the ceiling to keep out leaks that may have threatened to trickle in. Everything was illuminated by dim firelight, causing shadows to cloak the room.

"Are all these people part of the Envoy?" I asked Theon, as he led me through the crowded dining hall. I immediately took notice of the common display of tattoos. In fact, every person in the room had black swirling ink somewhere on their body.

"Yes," Theon replied.

I searched for Shar among the crowd and happened to spot his blonde ponytail. He was sitting at a table in the far corner of the room, conversing with a group of three other individuals.

Theon led me to the bar and ordered us both glasses of Lush

Fire. Out of curiosity, I continued to watch Shar and his three companions. I sipped my drink, intensely analyzing the table.

"Are those the Envorydians he wants to fight in the Galloway?" I asked curiously.

"Something like that," Theon said distractedly. He was also watching the meeting.

"I'm going over there," I said determinedly.

Theon laid his hand on my arm, stopping me before I could stand up. "I don't know if that's such a good idea."

"I have to know what they are talking about."

"He's going to be upset," Theon warned.

I snorted unattractively. "When is he not upset." I shook off Theons's cool metal hand and made my way over to them.

Shar noticed me almost immediately as I approached the table. It didn't take long to get across the small room, and I almost lost my courage at the last second. But he had already spotted me, and I knew it was too late to back down. Ignoring his piercing, disapproving gaze, I focused on the single empty chair at the table. With determination I allowed the legs to scrape across the floor noisily and sat in the chair with carelessness. I tried to not be affected by the ceasing of conversation and the intimidating looks from the other individuals at the table.

"You weren't going to leave me out of the conversation were you?" I smirked at Shar and could feel the heat coming from his dagger-like expression. His jaw clenched and unclenched.

There were three others at the table. A woman with long silvery hair and a matching silver heart. She was dainty, wearing a tight jumpsuit that was tailored perfectly to her thin form. She was so petite her bones jutted out from beneath her ebony skin. Her cheekbones were sharp, her nose perfectly pointed. A beautiful twirly tattoo that breached across her cheeks; it looked like a pair of wings. She assessed me curiously with her red eyes.

Sitting beside her was a young Stone-Hearted boy with spiky blond hair and hazel brown eyes. He had a glowing blue light pulsing beneath his fighting suit. His arms were covered in tattoos and bulging with muscle. He had a cocky half grin on his face, his teeth perfectly straight. He was very handsome and could make any girl swoon a little.

"I told you to stay at the house," Shar hissed beside me.

"You must be the prisoner who burned down the Spirit Tree." The voice came from the third individual at the table. I was barely able to make out his features. He sat in the farthest corner, nearly completely shrouded in the shadows.

Surprised, I couldn't find a single line of black ink on his face or arms. He was intimidating enough without them. He had sooty black locks that were pointedly straight, barely kissing the edges of his shoulders. He looked strong but not noticeably built like the other Envorydians I'd seen in the room that night. His cerulean eyes looked at me with an intensity that rattled me. I couldn't see the color of his heart. His thick weapons vest crossed his body. His face remained set in a hard, emotionless expression, and I couldn't stop the chill that went down my spine.

"Dusane, please not right now," Shar growled.

"That was gutsy. I'm impressed," the girl piped up, her voice musically sweet.

"It's only impressive if you don't get caught," the blue-eyed man replied coolly.

"Aren't you going to introduce us?" the pretty blond-haired boy whined.

"Conland, Rouix, Dusane, meet Ehren." The only one that greeted me was the blond one.

"It's nice to finally meet you, Ehren. I'm Conland." He gave me a flirtatious smile, his eyes all too inviting and filled with a non-committal foreboding that reeked of aphrodisia.

"Can we get back to the matter at hand?" Shar barked roughly, causing the attention to return to him. "I want only the best warriors with me. I've made an agreement with the Commission to take the top five winners at the next Galloway tournament."

"What if we don't win?" Rouix asked bluntly.

"Well, we'll just have to make sure you do," Shar said simply. I watched glances pass between the three of them.

"What about her?" Dusane interjected, gesturing to me. I didn't like the scrutiny lurking behind his eyes. It was all too cold and calculating.

Shar sighed. "She's not coming."

"What do you mean I'm not coming?" I asked hotly, but he just ignored me.

"Meet me at the Foundations Field in the morning, and we'll form a plan," Shar continued, then reached over to pull me up from the chair. "Come on, Ehren, let's go."

"Shar, wait . . ." I protested as he tugged me away from the table.

His hold was vice-like, and I couldn't tear myself from his grasp. He lugged me all the way across the room and outside to the front of the Academy. My protests hit deaf ears. He released me only when we made it into a secluded part of the forest. No one was around, and the atmosphere was quiet except for the silent pelting of rain against the trees. It was the perfect place to start a fight.

"Why are you part of the Envoy and why haven't you included me in your plan to stop the curse?" I asked accusingly.

"You're not in Aveladon anymore, princess. And I don't know if you realize this, but I don't answer to you." He reached out and clutched my chin in his hand, forcing me to look at him. "You need to learn your place. You're a prisoner now, and as long as you're in the Sethen Courts, you follow my rules. I don't care who you were before, or if Midennen loves you. No more questions. No more stunts like the one you just pulled. Last thing I need is you getting yourself killed."

Midennen. . . the name shot an agonizing pain straight through my heart, and I almost reached up to clutch my chest. Memories I didn't want to recall unwillingly filled my head. I gritted my teeth, holding back tears. I couldn't think about him.

I didn't reply, too hurt to say anything. When he could see I wasn't going to answer he released me and began pacing.

"I've sent word to your family back home. I've told them you're alive and that they must send someone to retrieve you. You'll be back home soon enough. So please just stay out of my way and stop questioning me."

"I can help you Shar," I pleaded frantically, not wanting him to dismiss me.

"No, *Ehren.* You can't." He spat the name as if it was poisonous to speak the lie I'd identified myself with. It made me wonder what would've happened back in the Commission if I had told them the truth. Would Vayel have let me go if he'd known who I really was? The question was something I didn't need to debate though because I knew that I had wanted to be someone else so badly in that moment, almost needed to be. And despite how reckless it may have looked, it was as if I'd started down some destined path I'd always known I would take. And because of that pre-ordained feeling coursing through me now, the Courts were not a prison but a beginning to something I was scared to admit was sort of exciting. . . addicting even.

"Just because you are Stone-Hearted now doesn't mean you'll be suddenly helpful. You don't even know what your powers are." His words stung at wounds where his words had already infiltrated. It didn't hurt any less the second time around.

"So I'll figure them out," I said resolutely.

"Don't you see. I. Don't. Need. You." He spoke each word forcefully and deliberately.

"I know I'm capable of helping. If you'd just let me."

"You are just a princess, Sabeara. And that's all you'll ever be." He walked out of the tree line back toward the Academy.

I sighed, leaning against one of the trees for support. I let the tears fall down my cheeks, allowing each one of his harsh words to puncture my heart. When I finally could pull myself together again I sulked back to the Academy and found Theon waiting for me outside by the front door.

"Are you all right?" he asked, his face somber.

"I'm fine," I said, but it was a lie.

"Do you want to head back now?" He gestured with his bronze hand to the path that would lead us back to the Drego.

"Yes, please. I think I've seen enough."

SEVEN

I didn't sleep. I spent most of the night staring at the ceiling, my cheeks stained with tears. I couldn't stop thinking about what Shar said at the Envoy Academy. After telling me he'd sent word to my family, a sort of hopelessness settled like a cloud overhead. I wasn't a trained fighter. I didn't know anything about living outside of Aveladon. I was pretty much useless, even though I was Stone-Hearted. His words were quite convincing, and part of me did want to give up.

But I couldn't ignore the obligation I felt to stay. Something in me was reluctant to go back. I'd followed my mother's plea, burned the tree, and had ended up in the Sethen Courts with powers. Something I hadn't known would happen, yet the more I contemplated the outcomes, the more it felt like fate.

Despite the homesickness I felt when I thought about Oli or Jasper, or Mid, I couldn't ignore the feeling deep down inside telling me that maybe ending up here had been destiny after all.

But if I was going to attempt to stay and help Shar, one thing was for sure. . . I had to stop thinking about Mid. I could be stuck here for months, and I couldn't help but think that maybe with some distance he'd realize that he didn't love me as much as he thought. Even though it had only been two weeks since he'd told me he loved me at the wedding and I'd said it back. . . it felt like an eternity.

I decided that the best thing for me would be to pretend that nothing had changed, that they were still betrothed, and to continue after the destiny my mother had presented to me. Just the thought was enough to cause a painful twinge in my chest. Trying to suppress the sort of love that seemed etched into every fiber of my being, well, it might be impossible. But I didn't see another way. No matter how hard it would be to push Mid and the rest of those I loved from my mind, I had to try.

Shar had a plan. He was going to search for more tokens to defeat the curse. And I knew, if he would allow it, I could come with him and be more than just a princess locked away in a castle. I spent all night thinking, and still when the sun rose over the Drego, I didn't have any of it sorted out.

I rolled out of bed seeking a distraction. Theon had graciously stocked the closet and I tugged on a gray shirt and trousers and then my black combat boots and headed downstairs. The living room was empty, along with the kitchen. It seemed the entire house was desolate.

I ended up searching outside and found that the road leading to the Drego was quiet, except for the chirping of the birds in the trees nearby. I gazed up at the big buildings in the distance, then at the jungle saplings in the other direction that led to the Academy. I breathed in a deep breath of moist morning dew and was just exhaling when I heard loud crunching footsteps from behind me. Startled, I turned to find Theon coming from around the side of the house. In his bronze metal hand, he held a sack of fruit he must have just bought in the city. He had already pulled a ripe orange from the brown bundle and was beginning to peel it with his teeth.

"Good morning, Ehren," he greeted, spitting a rind into the bushes.

"Have you seen Shar?" I asked, feeling too anxious for greetings.

"He's at the Foundations Field. I was just heading there. Want to walk with me?"

I hesitated just for a moment. Looking at Theon I could see nothing out of the ordinary in his demeanor. I knew he'd heard part of my fight or maybe all of the fight with Shar last night but gratefully he hadn't pushed for details. I think he was kindly sparing me by pretending it didn't happen.

"That would be great." I decided at that moment that it didn't matter if Shar was angry. He couldn't instill fear inside of me. Despite his harsh words I was still determined to not cower away from him. I wanted Shar to know, and Theon too, that I wouldn't back down from what I believed I should be allowed to do.

I stepped into stride beside him, and we started into the woods. The rain from yesterday had made the air much more humid that morning. The sky still held the remains of misty storm clouds, and the palm leaves were dewy with leftover water droplets.

"Rumors are running wild about you in the Envoy." Theon began the conversation and I was grateful not to be in awkward silence.

"Rumors, is that so?" I could only imagine what people were saying.

"Yeah, you caused quite the commotion walking into the Academy last night. The prisoner who burned down the Spirit Tree has been all anyone can talk about."

I cringed. Theon had yet to bring up my crime. I wondered how he'd known. Shar probably told him. I thought back to the blue-eyed man last night and how he'd addressed me as 'The girl who burned down the Spirit Tree.' He had known who I was when I walked in. Maybe Shar had told them or news had trickled down from the Commission. I didn't know exactly how people were figuring it out, but it was enough to make me realize word traveled fast here.

"Well, I'm sure the gossip will die down once I'm gone," I said nonchalantly, trying not to let it bother me.

"Shar told me he sent word to take you back to Aveladon." There was a lingering question behind Theon's words.

"Yeah, he's trying to get rid of me as soon as possible."

"Why do you want to stay?" he asked curiously.

It was a good question. *Why did I?* Images of Mid flashed through my head, and a familiar longing swelled in my chest. If I was going to stay, I really needed to find a way to stop thinking about Mid.

"Have you ever felt like you were meant to do something?" I asked.

Theon looked at me thoughtfully for a second before finally nodding. "I always knew I was meant to be a fighter," he stated easily.

"Well, I think deep down I always knew I was meant to help stop the curse. At first I rejected the idea. It terrified me even. But now it feels like the right thing. And I know Shar doesn't believe I can help because I'm not part of this special guild. But I wouldn't be here right now if it wasn't my destiny." This seemed to silence his questions, and speaking aloud made me feel a little more resolute about my internal arguments.

We got farther and farther away from the Drego, the large buildings fading into the distance behind us. The trees soon enveloped us, and I was submerged into the wet-green world of the jungle once again. The Academy came into view where we'd visited the previous night, but it was dead, not a soul in sight. Theon led me past the Academy and we went down another path deeper into the trees. I watched curiously where he was taking me, admiring the bright foliage and foreign plant life. The trees thinned again, and soon we were looking at a giant open field.

There were hundreds of them it seemed. Envorydians were training in the clearing about the size of the castle pastures back in Aveladon. I watched in awe at the set up they had created. Obstacle courses, target shooting, combat circles. I'd never seen anything like it.

"Are all of them training for the Galloway fight?" I asked.

"Not all of them. Some Envorydians use the fields to keep up their skills. Though some probably are training for *a* fight. There are tournaments every week."

"Every week?" I asked in surprise.

Theon nodded. "Shar wants to put the people you met last night in a special fight called the Regal. That's the fight he's taking the winners from. It's much harder than the other fights. It happens once a year. All the contestants are put into the arena and they fight against one another. It's known for being the most entertaining." He winked and started into the field. I followed after him, slightly nervous as eyes turned toward me. It was definitely intimidating, all the rugged, tattoo-covered Envorydians, addressing me with their judgmental expressions.

I blushed and quickened my pace, trying to ignore the penetrating stares.

I could easily pick out Shar's undeniable blond ponytail and stocky frame among the others. Theon went to stand beside him, clapping him on the back.

"How's the training coming?" Theon asked. His bellowing voice caused heads to turn in our direction.

Shar's expression turned cold the minute he noticed me. "What part of keeping her at the house do you not understand?" Shar hissed through gritted teeth.

"We both know she would have followed me anyway." Theon was catching on quickly. I avoided Shar's gaze, still wounded from the things he'd said the night before.

"All right, she can stay. Now make yourself useful and go help Rouix with archery," Shar ordered. Theon nodded and gave me a reassuring smile before heading in the direction of the target ranges.

"As for you, stay off to the side, and please try to stay out of trouble," Shar said, giving me a dismissive glance.

I glared at his back as he walked away from me. Turning on my heel, I started for the tree line again. It was discouraging to only be permitted to watch the training, but it would be better than staying at the flat.

As I walked back toward the trees, I caught a shimmer of movement from the corner of my eye. I turned, but not quickly enough to avoid the body that came crashing into mine. I was pushed to the ground roughly, my back slamming into the dirt and grass. The air was knocked from my lungs, leaving me breathless for several moments.

"Are you all right?" The reply held little in the way of

concern. I swear I could hear a hint of annoyance lingering behind the words and the question somehow sounded. . . rude.

I groaned in pain and slowly opened my eyes. I was greeted with a familiar face I'd met the night before. It was the man with the dark hair and cold blue eyes, If I remembered right, his name was Dusane.

"I'm fine," I managed to choke out. I sat up and began wiping dirt and grass off my arms.

In the daylight he looked much younger. He appeared to be in his early twenties. His chest was defined, his muscles lean and fit. I hadn't seen the purple light burning beneath his chest the night before. He wore a loose pair of brown breeches, and his skin was tan from the constant heat and sun. His slightly shaggy black hair was ruffled, barely falling across his sweat-beaded forehead in a gentle arc. With lips parted, he panted.

"You really shouldn't be wandering around these fields," He admonished matter-of- factly, while reaching his hand down to help me up. His blue eyes were just as intense as I remembered.

"I think I just figured that out, thank you," I grumbled. When he helped pull me up from the ground, we came face to face, and I noticed we were the same height.

"You're bleeding." His eyes zeroed in on my arm where a rock or stick had successfully penetrated my skin. I looked down, still disoriented from being knocked over, and found, to my utter disbelief, that my arm was healing. Magically the blood had vanished, and the skin was pulling together again like nothing had happened.

I looked up, and our gazes locked. I could clearly see the mix of confusion and curiosity in his eyes.

"Looks like someone got hit in the crossfire!" Conland, the blond boy I'd also met the night before, came running over to us.

He too was shirtless, showing off his golden tan chest and his sun kissed blonde hair. As he jogged over, I realized that everyone in the arena had stopped what they were doing to stare at us. "Sometimes we can get a little out of control," Conland teased, but I wasn't paying much attention to him. I was focusing on my arm that had suddenly healed.

"How. . ." Dusane began, also ignoring his friend.

"I have to go," I mumbled, hurrying out of the training field and into the safety of the tree line. My breathing became short and rapid as I started into a run, taking shocked glances down at my arm as I went. I only stopped when I found a secluded spot in the trees where I could assess the injury further. I sat on the ground and poked and prodded at the spot where the cut should've been, completely taken aback. *How did I heal that fast?* I had a strong suspicion that it had something to do with my powers, and suddenly it all began to make sense. I survived the burning of the Spirit Tree and managed to be completely unscathed despite the crumbling tree limbs and blistering heat that should have killed me because I could heal myself.

"Hey, are you all right?" Conland came walking through the trees.

I jumped where I sat, not expecting anyone to have followed me. I pushed my arm behind me, even though it had healed, and felt the sudden need to hide any evidence of the miraculous event.

"I'm fine. Why did you follow me?"

"That was a hard hit. I wanted to make sure you were okay." He came over and held out a hand to help me from the ground. I looked at his outstretched palm for a moment then to the coy smile playing on his lips. I finally took his hand, and he quickly helped me up.

"I should probably head back to Theon's. Shar doesn't want me here anyway," I said distractedly, looking around at the trees, not certain where I was.

"The Academy isn't far from here. I could take you there while you wait for training to end for the day."

"Thank you," I said, surprised to find him to be actually helpful. He smiled another dazzling, perfect smile, and I wondered if he was always that way. It must be exhausting to be so charming and flirtatious all the time.

We began down the trail, a comfortable silence stretching between the two of us. The Academy came into view, and Conland walked me inside. All the tables in the dining hall were empty, and I realized looking around the room that without all the dim lighting and Lush Fire, it was just an ordinary dining space.

"Where do the Envorydians live?" I asked suddenly.

"Most of us live here at the Academy. There are rooms on the second and third floors. But some are scattered throughout the Drego."

I took a seat at one of the chairs, and Conland went behind into the kitchen and brought back a large jug.

"Oh, I'm not really in the mood . . ." I began to protest.

"It's just water," he stated with a smile. He passed the jug to me, and I took a long sip before passing it back to him.

"So are you training to fight in the Galloway?" I asked. When he wasn't making any sudden moves to leave, I figured I would ask him some questions.

"Actually, I usually don't fight much in the Galloway. But since Shar showed up and said he wanted me to fight in the Regal, I didn't think I could pass up the opportunity. "

"How long have you known Shar?"

"I actually never knew him before. None of us did, except for Theon of course. But we have all heard things about him. And honestly, I think everyone was a little shocked to see him show up." He paused looking at me with curiosity in his eyes. "Especially with you."

"I've noticed everyone sort of—"

"Worships him," Conland finished, grinning.

I laughed and nodded my head. "Yeah, I guess that's the word I was looking for."

"It's because he's an Envoy legend," he said conspiratorially. He turned one of the chairs around and folded his arms across the back.

"Really?"

"Yeah, he was an amazing Envorydian once upon a time. Until he got his job working for the Ethydon Royal Guard."

"Theon told me about the Envorydians' history. How stopping the curse may be the guild's only chance at being united again."

"Yeah, it's sort of a big deal here. The Envoy has always been rooted in the prophecies of the Ethirical, and we all knew it was just a matter of time." He tapped his glowing blue heart, the color dimmer than it should have been, like the other hearts I'd seen."Now that the curse is here and Shar's seeking the best Envorydians to help him defeat it, well, let's just say there hasn't been this much excitement in the guild in a while." It was weird to hear them all speak of the curse so lightly. It was something these people had always believed in. It was simple for them, like knowing the sky was blue.

"You don't happen to have one around do you? The Ethirical?"

He stood from the chair and went over to a bookshelf by a

wall covered in glistening silver swords and shields. He pulled a volume from the shelf and handed it to me.

"Let me know if you need any help with that," he winked, and I couldn't help but blush a little.

"Thanks," I said, flipping through the pages. Maybe I couldn't help Shar like I wanted too, but I could study here, at least until someone from Aveladon came for me.

"Can I ask you something?" he asked suddenly.

"Go ahead," I said looking up from the pages.

"Why'd you do it?" I knew what he was referring to even without him saying it. And that's when I realized that I was a mystery to them. The prisoner who'd burned down the greatest landmark in the realm and started the curse, spiraling the entire Stone-Hearted race into more chaos.

"You wouldn't believe me if I told you," I said, slightly embarrassed at his interest.

"One day you'll have to tell me," he said with obvious intrigue. He started for the door. "I'm heading back to the Foundations Field but make yourself at home until training is over." He stepped outside then, shutting the door behind him. I was left alone, the room utterly quiet. I looked down at the Ethirical, started at the top of the page, and began reading.

~

That evening back in Theons's scrap flat, I stood in front of the mirror. After what happened in the field with the cut on my arm, I had been waiting to come home and experiment more.

I had grabbed a knife from the kitchen after dinner and was trying to build up the courage to cut my finger.

It's just a small little cut, Sabeara. Stop being a pansy. I told myself. Quickly, before I could talk myself out of it, I pricked my finger. I gasped a little at the sharp sting and I looked down to see a small dot of blood pool onto my pointer finger. As quickly as the blood came, it began to disappear. The open skin on both sides moved quickly toward each other and soon the small cut was gone. It had sealed back up, returning completely to normal. I wondered if it worked on bigger wounds but was too scared to injure myself more than a small prick on the finger. I had no idea how the curse would affect my abilities, but from what I'd heard, the curse was supposed to make Stone-Hearted powers weaker over time, until eventually they faded away completely. I didn't want to risk pushing myself too far. I put the knife down on the nightstand and crawled into bed. I would have to wait until I could seek a Reminant to figure out the extent of my powers.

EIGHT

The next two weeks were a repetitive loop of events. The weather was consistently intermittent. It would storm some days then be blistering humid hot the next. Theon would make me breakfast, then I'd travel with him to the Academy and the Foundations Field. The Academy was my sanctuary as they trained, and most of the time, I was alone. Sometimes Conland would come inside and chat with me after training. He was getting easier to talk to, his flirtatious behavior making me blush less as I realized it was simply his state of being. I quickly concluded he was harmless.

Sometimes when Conland made conversation with me, Theon would join in, and a couple times even the girl named Rouix would put in a few words. I found her quiet mysterious demeanor, to be fascinating—yet quite intimidating at the same time.

One afternoon Rouix came in and sat directly beside me, looking more tired than I usually saw her.

"If Shar makes me pick up that bow one more time, I'm going to shoot him with it," she said bluntly. And the threat sounded odd when spoken in her high twinkling voice. Conland and Theon were also at the table and chuckled at her comment, though it didn't sound like she was joking.

"He's just trying to make you better at your weaknesses," Theon said positively. Rouix glared at him with her crimson eyes, obviously not appreciating the enthusiasm.

"You're good enough without it, but he's just being safe," Conland added for good measure.

"Still, I hate it." She crossed her arms over her chest and pouted a little. And for the first time, I saw a normal girl beneath the intimidating facade she so easily portrayed. She seemed to be quite young, maybe only a couple years older than me. And from the many times I'd been at the house, I had yet to see another girl. We seemed to be the only two females on the premises.

"Can I have some of that?" It took me a second to realize she was talking to me. She was looking at my stein on the table filled with water. I nodded, not knowing exactly what else to say. She quickly grabbed the cup and took a couple big gulps, letting some of the water trickle onto her chin. "Thanks," she said, setting it back on the table with a gasping breath.

It was moments like these, after they came in from a long day of training, that built my vague affiliation to the group. Dusane was the only other person I knew to be part of their little entourage, and he hadn't approached me since running into me at the Foundations Field. And I was honestly relieved. Whenever I recalled the encounter we'd had, memories of his cold blue eyes would fill my head, and I couldn't help but shiver. Something about his appearance and the blatant, almost rude way he spoke was off-putting.

The Ethirical became a familiar constant. I ended up making a map out of a blank piece of canvas Conland had supplied me with and scribbled a map of Aveladon onto it. I then pinpointed all the places I thought the tokens could be.

I would find myself reaching up to stroke the smooth ruby of my amulet as I studied, only to find it gone. I would have to find another object to occupy my unconscious twiddling.

I slowly narrowed down places that the tokens could possibly be, using the Ethirical and information Mid had given me. I was sure about three, but the other two I still had no inkling of where they might be located.

The compass, the hammer, and the amulet were the few I was certain existed. The compass I had marked somewhere out in the ocean, maybe on the Isles of Arradale. Linsulong was the one that traveled overseas, never getting lost. There was one paragraph that made me believe it could be on the Isles.

> *On the sea I have traveled far. Towns on the sea know of our voice, and the waves ripple with our rage. I am heading for the island. I know its beauty and have beheld it from afar. Maybe I will stay there. The voice inside of me is telling me the direction of this hidden paradise. I will follow it. I will see its magnificence.*

I theorized the island could be the Isles and marked it with a red ink dot.

After what Theon had told me about the history of the Envorydians, the next paragraph confirmed Mid's theory of Westolince's hammer, and it made me think that maybe the hammer was somewhere in the Sethen Courts or in Obscurum.

Knowing that Westolince had a history with the Envorydians made it all seem very interconnected.

The heat here makes me thirst, I would trade moments here for battles of the ice. The heat never ceases, the sand is constantly on my skin. The quaking from my weapon causes a mere ripple in the sandy seas here. I fear for my defeat amongst this desert land. My body may lie here if I fail to win this fight. I only wish to be buried as heros of the past.

I already had the amulet from Yamdolor so that was one mystery I didn't have to solve. But reading the passages for the other two, Ennsleon and Oxtwenel, was giving me headaches. Narrowing down what could be the token from their lives seemed impossible. The only passage remotely of any worth from Ennsleon read,

The stars are leading me to another land. I wonder if this time I will be led astray by the constellations. I barely survived the last battle that the moon guided me to. I fear if the land will ever see peace. Where are you my starlit princess? Will I ever find you again?

Ennsleon's starlit princess was another mystery–maybe someone he may have loved. As for a token in his life, the information was scarce.

Oxtwenel was the most frustrating of the five. He literally had one paragraph. Usually a small background was given about each of the kings, their powers, and then legends from their lives would appear with journal passages. But with Oxtwenel, there was only one line. No mention of his power, no journals.

Oxtwenel, king of Riopelle. Ruled for two hundred years. Cause of death: unknown.

Something had to be missing from the passages. The book also gave no indication on what to do with the tokens once they were retrieved. I didn't understand how anyone was supposed to defeat the curse based on the information from the Ethirical alone. I wondered if there was more information somewhere. *Why would someone hide such information, and where was it hidden?*

It was a frustrating couple weeks of study. Thankfully the days moved quickly, and after the first two weeks flew by, several more passed too. But despite all my searching, it did little to help the anxiousness I felt. I wondered at what moment my father, or Oli would walk through the door and say they were going to take me back to Aveladon. Sometimes I'd consider that I might actually be relieved, returning home to be with my family again. I missed them terribly each time they crossed my mind. But another part of me, a stronger part of me, knew deep down that I wanted to stay.

But no one ever came. After a month of being in the Sethen Courts, I began to wonder why it was taking so long. One evening when Theon came back from training with the others, he sat across from me at one of the tables where I was studying and I decided I would ask him about it.

"You've been doing a lot of studying," he observed as he took a seat.

"Yeah, it makes me feel like I'm doing something to help stop the curse, even if I'm actually not," I explained, hating that it sounded so pathetic.

Theon looked at the map I had out on the table, eyeing it

thoughtfully. "It amazes me that you have the patience to search through that book," he said almost as if the idea exhausted him.

"Not much for reading?" I asked lightly.

Theon quickly shook his head smiling sheepishly. "Actually, I can't read."

I looked up, shocked a little at his statement. "Really?" I asked, surprised.

"Yeah, I know crazy huh?" He reached up to rub his neck, seeming almost embarrassed for a second. A million questions entered my mind, but I forced myself not to ask them. "I had a pretty bad childhood. There wasn't much room for learning to read and write." I didn't know what to say, I wanted to say sorry but didn't feel it was exactly the right thing.

"You don't need to study books to help," I said determinedly.

Theon smiled. "Yeah, I'd like to believe my skills in the guild makes up for what I lack in education." There was a moment of silence between us, and I somehow found the courage to ask him what was really on my mind.

"Theon, has Shar told you anything about word reaching my family?"

He seemed to be expecting my question. He looked at me with a small bit of hesitation in his eyes, then looked around at the others in the room, making sure no one was listening before he continued on.

"Actually, yes. . ."

"And?" I pressed.

"Remember how I'm not supposed to tell you things?"

"Theon, please, aren't we past that point by now?" I gave him an exasperated look.

"No one has been able to reach your family. Whoever your

family is," he said, and I realized he must still be in the dark about my identity.

"They can't be reached?" I asked more quietly now.

"The letter Shar sent, well, it seems that the messenger has been unable to find anyone to give it to."

"That doesn't make sense."

"He assumes that your family has gone into hiding after the war."

"Hiding?" I murmured. I imagined the remains of our kingdom and its people disappearing to some unknown, hidden land. It was something I could see Oli instigating. It actually wasn't such a bad idea. Only there remained the question of how I would return.

"It's been weeks, Theon. Do you think anyone will ever come for me?"

He stayed silent for a moment. "I think it's likely you won't be going back home for a while." And I felt sort of guilty when his words made me feel relieved.

"I could fight in the Galloway, you know. You could train me. I could maybe win with the others and go with Shar to find the tokens." It came out before I could stop myself. I didn't realize how much I wanted it until I'd said it out loud. If I could learn to fight and defend myself, I could do so much more in the effort to stop the curse.

I was slightly shocked at my own desire. But if no one was coming for me and I would be stuck here anyway, why not train? I laughed nervously to myself, shocked at my sudden ambition.

Theon quickly shook his head at my excited proposal. "I can't betray Shar that way. He wouldn't ever allow it."

"Why do you follow his orders?" I asked bluntly and with a

tinge of annoyance. I folded my arms across my chest. Theon gave me an apologetic smile then a shrug of his shoulders.

"He was my trainer back in the day. And even though I'm not his apprentice anymore. . ." He trailed off as if he didn't know how to explain completely why he did everything Shar said.

Then after a couple moments of silence, he seemed to have another idea. His green eyes lit up as he spoke again. "You could ask Conland, or Rouix. Maybe they would train you."

NINE

The next day after the others returned to the house from training in the field, I decided to approach Conland and Rouix. I'd been contemplating asking them to train me as Theon had suggested, and I was building up the courage all morning. The two were laughing about something, and I had to force myself not to back down as I walked over to them and interrupted their humorous conversation.

"Hey, can I talk to you two?" I tried to keep the nervousness from creeping into my voice, but I don't think it helped much. Rouix looked at me curiously and then looked at Conland as if not knowing how to proceed.

"What's up, Ehren?" Conland asked, gesturing for me to take a seat at one of the tables. I sat down, trying not to lose my courage. They both sat across from me. I felt my stomach go queasy.

"I wanted to ask you if maybe. . . you both might train me?" I blurted it out quickly hoping it didn't sound too pathetic. "For the Regal fight."

Rouix's eyes widened, while Conland grinned as if finding my inquiry flattering.

"Train you? That's an awfully big request," Conland said.

"I know it would be a lot, but I really want to go with Shar to help find the tokens. And I know fighting in the Galloway is the only way he'll take me with him." As I explained this to them, Conland's confident expression that usually remained on his face faltered a little, and for the first time I saw uncertainty in his eyes. Rouix's eyes held a similar emotion.

"Ehren, as much as I would love for you to be part of the team, I'm not a trainer. I couldn't give you what you'd need to succeed in the Regal. It's hard enough for me to keep myself trained for a fight like that." He looked at me apologetically.

"He's right, neither of us are qualified for that sort of thing. But you could ask Dusane. He might be able to help you," Rouix said, in a way that made me think she actually felt bad she couldn't help.

"Dusane?" The name sent shivers down my spine.

"We've heard through the vine that you don't know what your powers are. Dusane is a Reminant. He might be able to help," Conland said. Then the two stood up from the table. With one last look of what I assumed was regret in their eyes, they said goodbyes and then disappeared up into the house where they slept.

That night when I returned to the flat, I wasn't very hungry, Theon asked if I was okay, but I simply told him I was tired and then left early to bed. I spent most of the night staring at the ceiling, trying to convince myself to ask Dusane to train me. For some reason, of all the Envoy members at the Academy, he made me the most nervous. I didn't particularly like his passive, intimidating demeanor. Something about him made me feel uneasy.

I looked out at the night sky through the small loft window. My mind wandered back to Aveladon for a moment, and I realized I was running out of time. It was luck the letter had not reached my family yet. But If I didn't convince Shar to let me stay with him and search for the tokens with the other Envorydians, I would be taken back to Aveladon, and soon. I didn't want to return home, and be a useless bystander while everyone else helped stop the curse. What if I could train for the Regal and prove to Shar that I deserved to go with him before someone came to retrieve me?

I sighed, and leaned back onto my pillow, determined that the next day I would do it. In my last ditch effort, I would ask one more person. I would ask Dusane to train me.

~

I approached the Foundations Field, trying to remain calm as I walked past the tree line and into the clearing. I had yet to return since the day I'd been run into. It was as big as I remembered, only without all the Envorydians training. It was startlingly empty. It looked peaceful in the setting vermillion sunlight. The equipment cast long shadows onto the damp yellow grass. Dusane was by the archery targets picking up arrows on the ground and stuffing them into a quiver.

It was a long walk. I'd gotten about halfway across the field when he noticed me. He stopped what he was doing and watched me finish the distance to where he was standing. Luckily he was wearing a shirt that day, the black short sleeves hugging his toned arms and chest. I could feel my hands getting sweaty. I was nervous.

His blue eyes watched me, not revealing any emotion as I came to a stop several feet in front of him.

"Hello. . ." I started pathetically.

His lip twitched with a slight smile at my greeting, but then his face turned serious again and I wondered if I'd imagined it.

"I came to ask you something. You see, I . . ."

"You want me to train you," he stated bluntly, interrupting my babbling. I looked at him sheepishly. His dark black hair was messy from training and fell across his forehead in tangled strands. It was then that I noticed his left ear lobe had the smallest silver piercing in it. It was so tiny, I hadn't noticed it before. The sun bounced off the delicate piece of jewelry, the light catching the corner of my eye.

"Conland told me you were a Reminant," I admitted, looking down again.

"Yes, I am," he confirmed.

"I want to fight in the Galloway. I need to figure out my powers and learn to fight so I can travel with Shar to stop the curse."

"I'll help you," he said easily. I looked up from my nervous studying of the grass and met his eyes with a slightly shocked expression. I was unsure if I'd heard him right.

"You will?" I questioned, hoping I didn't sound too enthusiastic. He nodded and set the quiver of arrows down to take a step toward me. He reached out and took my arm in his hand. His fingers were surprisingly soft as he touched the skin near my elbow, his brow furrowing. Speechless, I just watched him as he analyzed the skin that had been previously cut the day he'd run into me.

"Ever since I saw you heal yourself, I knew you were special. I'll help you. Out of fascination more than anything." He looked up at me, his blue eyes meeting mine, and I lost my breath for a moment. I couldn't read him. His emotions were completely concealed. I didn't know if he was being sarcastic, or if he was simply a passive character. His emotionlessness rattled me, scared me even. I hated not being able to know what he was feeling. "Meet me in the field tomorrow after training." He dropped my arm, and the spot felt tingly where he'd touched me.

"But it will just be us."

"That's sort of the point. You won't be able to keep up with the others. We'll have to train after hours, at your own pace." He began gathering his things again.

A feeling of excitement filled me at the idea of finally getting to do more than just study. Trying to hide a smile, I started back toward the tree line, barely holding myself back from jumping into a gleeful skip.

"Thank you," I called, my voice echoing across the field.

He looked up and met my gaze, but he didn't make any attempt at a reply. He simply watched me leave with the same cold, intense expression. There was something hidden underneath the cool passivity he so readily displayed, a concealed confidence that I could feel loomed beneath. There was a side to Dusane I had yet to discover. I was sure of it. And if I was being completely honest, I wanted to find out what that side might be.

TEN

I walked into the kitchen, expecting to see Theon at the table making breakfast like he usually did every morning, only to find Shar in his stead. He was cutting up an apple and stopped mid-chop as he saw me coming down the stairs.

It was a brief pause as we looked at eachother. Neither of us seemed to know how to react. It had been many weeks since we'd really had a conversation. Avoidance had been the antidote to our hostility for one another. And neither of us wanted to be the first to break the temporary neutrality.

"Ehren," he said in greeting, breaking the sudden silence.

"Shar," I returned. I carefully descended the rest of the stairs and started for the door to make my escape.

"I heard about your training."

I froze, fear tingling my skin at the tone in his voice. Though his words remained terrifyingly quiet, there was a barely noticeable indignation behind them.

"Yeah, Dusane offered while I'm waiting for someone from Aveladon to take me back." I kept my back turned to him, trying to act as if it wasn't a big deal.

"Just because I've allowed you to roam the Academy freely while I help train with the Envorydiains, doesn't mean you have the freedom to ask the residents inside of it for help with your plans. I told you, Ehren, you aren't meant for this sort of thing. You can't fight in that fight. I won't allow it."

I closed my eyes, taking in several deep breaths before turning to face him.

"You're letting the other Envorydians fight," I argued.

"You're not an Envorydian, Sabeara," he bit sharply, and the use of my real name actually stung a little. "The Regal is a lethal fight and only a few will emerge victorious."

"You aren't even giving me a chance!"

"I thought you didn't want this! Since when do you care about finding the tokens?"

"Since now!" I yelled, unable to explain to him the sudden escape the prisons had created for me. A new desire bloomed within me at the thought of being more than just princess Sabeara. I didn't realize this was what I wanted, what I needed. . . until now. "What have I done to make you hate me so much? It's like you despise the thought of me proving I'm good enough to search for the tokens with you."

He opened his mouth to say something else then closed it. He abandoned the kitchen counter and came over to stand in front of me by the door.

"I don't hate you," he finally said. But I could hear it in his voice, the energy he had to use to force the words off his tongue

"Well, it sure seems like it. Look, I know what I did was crazy, and reckless, and completely not part of the plan, but I never actually got to be part of the plan. Everyone else just decided for me that I was staying in Ethydon. I didn't want that." My voice broke a little, flashes of memories from my last night in Ethydon filled my head, and I had to force them out to stay composed.

Shar shook his head."If anything happened to you. . . Mid would—"

"That's what this is about?" I nearly shrieked, cutting him off mid-sentence."I know you feel obligated to keep me safe because of him. But please don't." My voice shook with rage.

"I don't think you realize how much he loves you, Sabeara," Shar growled, his green eyes piercing.

"You don't think I love him too? Shar, I can't be protected from everything. I can't just stay locked away because he and everyone else fears losing me!" I could feel myself unraveling. I'd done well to try and push away memories of Mid and the feelings that accompanied the way I felt for him. But in the heat of the moment, arguing with Shar, it was all coming back, and if I didn't stop the conversation soon, I'd be overwhelmed. I struggled with two parts of myself. One part of me wanted to help fight the curse, to complete a destiny I felt bound to accept. Another part of me wanted to return home, to see Mid and my family. I pushed the latter from my mind, forcing myself to stay composed.

"That's not all. The consequences of becoming a warrior are not something you can even conceive. And if you start down this road, soon you will find it's too late to return to the person you once were." The warning in Shar's tone was evident but I ignored it. I was too angry to really take it into consideration.

"Maybe I don't want to be the person I was. Maybe I want to be different." I knew Oli and Shar would never let me journey with them, fight battles, or go on missions if I wasn't qualified. At least if I was a trained Envorydian I'd have the means to defend myself and my kingdom. They wouldn't have an excuse to keep me back anymore.

Shar's jaw clenched at my words. "The only reason you made it out of the Commission was because I found you. This is not some destiny you should be chasing. It's sheer luck you're even alive," Shar insisted.

"I refuse to believe that! I am not going to let you convince me all of this was coincidence."

"I'm telling Theon you can't leave the house anymore," he said dismissively.

"You can't do that!" My voice rose with desperation.

"Oh yes I can. You shouldn't be running about. Especially not training with Dusane. The Commission could get suspicious."

"I heard you tell them you wanted to use me to help you find the tokens." I crossed my arms over my chest and set my jaw determinedly, daring him to deny it.

"That was a lie to get you out! I was trying to keep you from getting killed. I never meant it seriously."

"Well, as far as they know, I'm supposed to be fighting in the Galloway and coming with you. So training shouldn't be a problem."

"Everything I told them to get you free isn't going to apply anymore once Aveladon officials come for you, and they discover you're the princess." His face was now a light shade of red, and he clenched his hands at his sides.

"Theon told me the letter hasn't reached them. It could be months till they come for me! I'm not just going to sit around studying until someone shows up! I want to help and come with you on the mission you have planned. And if fighting in the

Regal will prove that I'm good enough to help, then so be it." I was grasping at anything now, hoping I would say something to get him to back off.

Shar let out a frustrated growl. I could see now, that my presence here was out of his control, and that the uncertainty of everything in the situation was nearly driving him mad.

"You want to train? Fine, go ahead. Train for all I care! But I'm not going to feel bad when you get hurt in the arena. And just so you know, it's my decision who I take with me. Whether you win or not." He stormed out the door, letting it shut with a resonating slam.

I wanted to scream, pound the door with my fists. I didn't miss his threat. It was loud and clear. The thought that maybe even if I trained, fought in the Galloway, and won, that he would still refuse to let me come with him. It was exactly something he'd do. It angered me but at the same time it strengthened my resolve. I would prove to him that I was good enough to come with him. I had to.

I stayed at the flat longer than normal to allow the anger inside me to simmer before making my way to the Academy. When I arrived, training still wasn't over, so I picked up the Ethirical and tried reading it. I reread the same paragraph a hundred times it seemed, but none of the words really stuck. Instead, all I could think about were the things Shar had said. . . *"You don't know how much he loves you, Sabeara."* That sentence was making it impossible to focus, which was exactly the reason I'd avoided conversation and thoughts about Mid in the first place. Everything about him was all consuming.

Soon the sun began to set and the Envorydians returned. I was startled from my pensive thinking as they clamored inside, sweaty and joking with one another. This was usually how things were after training. Loud rambunctious laughter and chatting. Then Theon would find me sitting in a corner reading, and we'd leave for the Drego. But I didn't leave with Theon this time. I had already explained to him yesterday I'd be training with Dusane and that I'd come home on my own after we finished up.

I pushed my way through the crowd of Envorydians now clamoring into the house. Conland said hello as I passed by, and I gave him a quick wave before slipping out the front door. I walked down the dirt path and into the trees, making my way toward the field. I walked by several Envorydians along the way and tried to ignore their penetrating stares. I wondered if they knew about my training and if the gossip about me had settled. I wondered what they were thinking . . . and what sort of things people believed about me. I shook my head, telling myself it didn't matter what they thought.

I clenched my hands together as I came upon the field, nervousness filling me. The sun was disappearing but was still beating down, hot enough to stir a sweat. I wondered if it ever got cold here, or if it was always this blistering.

I approached the field much like the day before and found Dusane in one of the combat arenas. He was just stepping out of the gate when he spotted me. I walked over to him and stopped several feet away, waiting expectantly.

"Come with me," he said simply, gesturing for me to follow him. He led me to a tall section of grass and took a seat. I followed suit, sitting cross-legged in front of him. He looked at me for a moment, his blue eyes still just as hard to read as yesterday. He was quiet for many moments. I thought I might burst if he didn't say something to break the quietness. Finally, he spoke.

"Today we will begin with your powers." He gestured for me to give him my hand. I looked out at his outstretched palm a little hesitant, unsure what to expect.

"How do you figure out one's powers anyway?" I asked, still not giving him my hand.

He paused for a moment and then sighed heavily. "I suppose we should start at the beginning." His hand retreated, and he started to pull out a small black pouch from his trouser pocket. I watched curiously as he poured onto the grass six colorful stones. I'd seen similar stones before when I'd gone to visit the Spirit Tree with Jasper and she was granted her powers. "Do you know how the Stone-Hearted got their name, Ehren?" The question was odd but simple, I thought, but as I tried to answer it, I found myself drawing a blank.

"Honestly, I'm not really sure," I admitted pathetically. He didn't seem troubled by my lack of knowledge and simply touched the stones in the grass, caressing each one gently.

"Reminants have been granting powers and understanding them for thousands of years. These stones are called Mediator stones. They are used to channel power from the Spirit Tree."

"How does a Reminant get the special Mediator stones?"

"Here we have ruby, emerald, sapphire, amethyst, moonstone, and citrine. There is nothing special about these stones. Anyone could acquire such stones, but they would just be stones. It is only when a Reminant uses them do they gather any sort of power from the tree." He carefully slid the stones back into their pouch. "As a Reminant, I can grant powers through the stones. Think of the stones as a bridge between you and the Spirit Tree. Essentially that bridge is broken until I come and connect it. These stones are why we are nicknamed the Stone-Hearted. Whichever stone the Spirit Tree decides to grant your power through will end up being the color of your heart."

"But the tree is gone. Can you still use your power?" I asked, feeling a heavy guilt weigh on me as I realized I'd been the one to take that away.

"I can't grant powers without the tree. But I can still identify them."

I remembered another detail of the curse: once the curse began, no one would be granted powers. It was a depressing reality.

"There's a lot more to being a Reminant than just Grantings," Dusane added.

"Who taught you how to be a Reminant?" I asked.

"The Reminant that helped me identify my powers was the one who trained me. It is tradition for Reminants who identify another Reminant's powers to take them under their wing, make them their apprentice," he explained.

I tried to imagine a younger Dusane following around an older Reminant. Memories of Elsmith, the Reminant I'd known from the Spirit Tree, filled my thoughts. I had to force myself not to get overwhelmed by the memories of that fateful night when I'd caused the curse to begin.

"So how do you find out what power someone has? And how does the tree decide what power to give?"

"It's hard to explain, but I can see it, and feel it. It is something only I can identify. And it's unknown how the Spirit Tree decides what power to give. It's extremely random. It's a concept we have been trying to understand for a very long time. My guess is that the tree grants powers depending on what the realm needs.

"For instance, if we need more people who can help the crops grow, then the tree will give more individuals those related abilities. If the realm needs more healers, more healers will be granted."

"Hmmm. . . that's an interesting theory."

"Every person gets the added benefits of being Stone-Hearted. More resilient to disease, added beauty, slow aging. But as for powers, they are not the same.

"Red and green are the most common colored hearts; these colors occur when you've been granted a power from the ruby stone or the emerald stone and are considered the least powerful on the spectrum. Blue and purple are the next most common colored hearts. These colors originate from being granted through the amethyst or sapphire stones. They are the next most powerful on the color spectrum.

"Lastly, we have silver and gold. The colors that come from the moonstone and citrine stone. They are the most powerful on the spectrum and individuals with these colored hearts are often appointed to higher positions in society, like councilmen, ambassadors, and royalty."

He finished speaking, and his eyes drifted to my heart for a second. I wondered if my golden heart would lead him to guess who I was. But I rationalized that they would just be guesses. He wouldn't be able to know for sure.

"Any more questions?" he suddenly asked, and I did have one.

"So if I have a gold heart and let's say I have the same power as someone with a green heart. I'm still considered more powerful? Simply because my heart is gold?"

Dusane paused for a couple seconds and for a moment I worried he wouldn't answer. "Yes that's correct," Dusane finally said. "Because citrine and moonstone are the most uncommon stones to be granted a power from, we deem their abilities rare."

"Is the process at all genetic?"

"It seems to be that you are most likely to be granted from the same stone as your mother or father, so yes. You'll most likely end up with the same color heart as one of your family members."

"And if you're not?"

"We call those rare individuals Scions"

"What does that mean?"

"Well it can either mean you'll be lifted up unexpectedly in society or lowered depending on the situation."

"So if all my family had silver and gold hearts and I ended up being granted a red heart I would've been. . . what? Kicked out of high society?"

"It's rare but it does happen."

"What? That's crazy! If every power granted is random and has nothing to do with the color heart you have, it's up to interpretation as to what power is the "most powerful". Categorizing people into a spectrum and ranking their power based on their color is wrong."

I thought about my family, and then those who had served us. I thought about the civilians I had seen in the streets when I visited Asmede. Power had no connection to color. And my whole life that's what I'd been trained to believe.

"It's just an esthetic. And that would mean those with "low power" hearts will have children with those same colored hearts. Making it nearly impossible for them to ever rise above their color class. It's an unfair advantage for those in high society. Just because someone has a gold heart—" My rant was cut short when Dusane bluntly interrupted me.

"That is just how it is in our society." His tone indicated that the point I was trying to make was moot.

"It's not fair." My jaw clenched as I tried to contain my anger.

"Life isn't always fair," he said curtly, and then he changed the subject, reaching out to take my hand again. "Let's try identifying your power, shall we?"

I wanted to continue. Angry at his factual dismissiveness. But somehow I knew it would be futile to try and argue with him. But I knew I wasn't going to just forget the things he'd told me. I decided I'd have to worry about it later and focus on the task at hand.

He closed his eyes and began to explain his Reminant abilities. "Once I identify your power, it's like solving a puzzle. I carefully seek out the color in my mind. I examine it, see its structure. And eventually, I slowly piece together what it's trying to tell me. And then it will show me the nature of your abilities." His voice was quiet and soothing as he spoke, and I couldn't help but listen closely, hanging onto every word with deep curiosity.

"So what is my power saying?" I asked in a mere whisper, not wanting to break his concentration.

He stayed quiet not answering right away. Eventually his brow furrowed and he squeezed my hands tighter. "I. . . I can't see it yet."

I waited longer, trying to be patient as he worked. It was five more minutes before I could see that something wasn't quite right. He let go of my hands at one point and then proceeded to lay his palm on my chest right where my heart was glowing beneath the black tank top I wore. I sucked in a sharp breath at the feel of his hand on my skin.

Sweat was beading on his brow with the effort he was exerting, and eventually he pulled his hand away and opened his eyes. He looked troubled, and slightly pained.

"What's the matter?" I asked, predicting from the look on his face that something was wrong.

"I don't understand," he mumbled distractedly. He was still looking at my golden heart, his forehead scrunched in confusion.

"What's wrong?" I asked more frantically this time.

"It just doesn't make sense. I can't read anything. I can't even feel any power."

"What does that mean?"

"I don't know what your powers are, Ehren. Your heart won't tell me."

ELEVEN

"Has this ever happened before?" I asked.

Dusane was still in the midst of confusion as he tried to figure out why he couldn't see my abilities. He had been pacing for quite some time now, and nothing I seemed to say calmed him down.

"Dusane, it can't be that crazy, can it?" I tried to sound positive, but I was actually panicking inside.

"It must be because of the curse. It has to be," he reasoned, more to himself than me.

"The curse?"

"My powers are weaker. Maybe the curse has weakened my ability to read others powers."

I feared to tell him about the fact that when I burned down the tree, I became Stone-Hearted despite not being of age yet and a Reminant not granting power to me. Suddenly I realized that me becoming Stone-Hearted was entirely impossible. But something *had* happened to me that day I burned the tree. Something unexplainable.

"Does it change things if I say a Reminant didn't grant me my powers?" I asked, wincing as I said the words.

Dusane looked at me, eyes widening. "How did you receive them?"

"When I burned down the tree, I sort of woke up, and then. . ." I gestured towards my heart. "This happened."

"Impossible. . ." he murmured, his eyes glued on the golden glow in my heart. He seemed to be in shock.

"Does this put an obstacle in our training?" I sobered, hating that I still felt so powerless.

Dusane continued to contemplate for many more minutes, not saying anything, and I feared he was going to say yes. That this would put an obstacle in our training, and that this entire thing was futile. I could only hope he wouldn't be deterred by this problem.

"No, it just means we'll have to figure out the extent of your power as we go. We know you can heal from small wounds. How far that goes and the potential you have, I don't know, but with time, we will figure it out. As for training, we will skip the process of identifying more of your power for now and start with something we can control."

"Which is?" I urged, feeling a great relief flood me at the news that we would still train.

"Combat."

He suddenly stopped pacing and started back toward the center of the field. I followed, feeling a little rattled from the sudden discovery we'd just made. He led me to a storage rack holding all sorts of weapons, and he began scanning for the one he wanted.

"We'll need to start you off with a weapon." His eyes passed over the archery equipment and several long-bladed swords to a lonely dagger. It was matte black and small enough that I would be able to hold it comfortably. He tugged it from its hook and then gestured for me to follow him to one of the combat arenas.

"We will begin with the dagger. Now, if the Regal is what you are aiming for, you'll have to learn to fight in a limited amount of time." He looked at me, his eyes locking on mine with fierce intensity again. "This isn't going to be easy, Ehren. I hope you know what you're getting yourself into."

"I know what I signed up for," I said determinedly, crossing my arms across my chest.

"I won't tolerate anything but absolutely everything from you. Every part of you must be invested in becoming the best, the greatest fighter you can become. Do you understand?" The seriousness of his words caused me to lose my breath for a moment. It was like he was peering into my soul as he spoke, shaking any doubts quickly from my mind.

"I understand," I said quietly, almost in a whisper.

"Then let's begin."

~

After a series of teaching me all about the dagger and how to wield the weapon, Dusane didn't even permit me to touch it. Something about learning before doing. It was disappointing but that wasn't the end of our training. When the sun had gone down, he started me on a circuit of conditioning. I exercised my arms, my stomach, and my legs. He made me run around the field for a very long time. Every moment I thought I couldn't keep going he pushed me further. Eventually, I literally couldn't continue on, and that was when he finally allowed me to stop.

There was no acclamation, no praise for my first day of training from Dusane. He simply said we would continue tomorrow and then walked back toward the Academy. He was callous, even heartless, during the training process. Any plea I directed at him during training he quickly dismissed. Any painful groan that left my lips was ignored. He was detached from feeling sympathy, anesthetized to compassion.

I lay in the grass for what felt like hours staring up at the stars in the night sky, questioning everything I had agreed to. Once I had cooled down, I wobbled back to the Academy. Theon was waiting inside, drinking with a couple other Envorydians. He looked at me sympathetically as I stepped inside, sweaty and barely standing. He didn't say anything as he stood from the table and helped me back home to his flat.

"You didn't have to wait for me," I said to Theon as we began our way back through the jungle to the Drego. It wasn't more than a fifteen minute walk, but it felt like an hour because of how exhausted I was.

"I know," he said simply, and nothing else was said. A sort of bond had formed between Theon and me, and it reminded me of the relationship I had with Oli.

Unwillingly, I felt a pang of sadness at the thought of my guardian. I wondered what he was doing, and if he missed me. Then I thought of all the trouble I caused him and reconsidered. *He was probably happy to not have to watch over me.*

Those negative thoughts stayed with me until we returned back to the flat where Theon graciously retrieved me a cup of water from the kitchen and then helped me up the stairs into the loft. Shar was nowhere to be found, which I was grateful for. The last thing I needed was hearing him say I told you so.

"Are you sure you want to do this, Ehren," Theon asked worriedly. I had successfully gotten underneath the bed sheets with my sore limbs. I looked at him wearily as I lay my head on the pillow. I was already half asleep by the time I replied.

"Don't worry about me," I assured him.

Theon gave me one last concerned expression before nodding and shutting the door behind him.

And that was the first night I dreamed of Midennen.

The sound of rushing water filled my subconscious. The pounding was a booming thrum against my eardrums. I looked around to find I was in a lush green forest. Pine trees surrounded me, and a dry air replaced the thick humid air I'd become so used to breathing. I followed the loud sound of the rushing water, nudging past underbrush until I stumbled out of the tree line onto sandy ground. A waterfall cascaded from a high mountain side and landed into a small pool. Rippling waves headed toward the shore until they lost momentum and turned into gentle little waves that barely lapped onto the sandy corners of the beach. I walked to the edge, and reached down to touch the crystal cool water.

"I've been trying to find you." His voice was like warm sunlight, heating every cell of my body and filling me with a vitality that made me realize I'd been away far too long.

I turned from the water to see Mid walking toward me. He strolled along the edge of the water, his bare feet making footprints in the sand that were quickly washed away by the small tide. His brown cloak was fastened at his neck, and his chestnut locks fell in waves to his shoulders. I felt a sense of calm I'd never felt before as our eyes met.

His eyes held their undeniable emerald-scarlet color and the mix of emotions that so easily sent my heart racing. Intense devotion, yearning adoration, and confident determination.

"I didn't know you were looking," I said simply.

Mid stopped a couple feet away from me, almost as if he couldn't come any closer.

"Where are you?" He asked, and I looked around at the beautiful paradisiacal forest. I didn't know where I was.

"I can't say," I replied in honest confusion. He became frustrated and, in desperation, reached out a hand to me, extending it like a lifeline.

"Please tell me where you are so I can find you and bring you home."

I looked at his outstretched palm, and I was just about to take it when I felt a disturbing sensation tugging at something deep within me. No, you can't tell him! A voice screamed inside my head. You have to stay!

"Mid, do you love me?" I asked, feeling suddenly saddened that the voice inside me was telling me not to reveal my location to him. Why couldn't I tell him?

"Of courses I love you, Sabeara." The words filled me with a fluttering sensation I couldn't quite describe. I almost was lost in the feeling for a moment, nearly taking his hand again, when the voice inside my head yelled at me once more.

No stop! You can't leave!

"Then you have to let me go. I need to stay here," I explained to him, not sure how to tell him of the urgent voice inside my head. It was so loud, so forceful. It seemed too urgent to ignore.

"I could never let you go," he said earnestly. He took another step

toward me and it was like the spell was broken; some line was crossed that should never have been breached. Something inside me jolted violently, and then I was slipping away from the dream. The image of him by the waterfall slowly faded, and just as I was about to call out for him, I woke up.

TWELVE

I was startled awake from the dream. Breathing heavily and sweat dripping from my forehead, I tried unsuccessfully to recover. I looked out the window to see the sun high in the sky. It had to be nearly noon. I sat up shakily in bed, and put a hand to my forehead. I took in several deep breaths, trying to regain my composure. *It was just a dream,* I told myself. Yet for some reason, it had felt entirely too real.

The dream about Mid was a sudden break from the recurring nightmare I usually had of the dark sitting room with the unrecognizable faces. I didn't know which one I preferred.

Being in the Sethen Courts had almost felt surreal, but dreaming of Mid had brought back a crushing reality. The one that I was burying so deep. Memories of him, and what could possibly be happening back in Aveladon were some of the thoughts that resurfaced. *Had he forgotten me? Had he moved on?* I shook my head back and forth, trying to shake myself from the feelings that were all consuming. Everything about Mid was overwhelming, passionate, and blazingly untamed. Memories of Mid and feelings connected to him risked ruining everything. The heartache was nearly crippling when I thought about our goodbye, and now was not the time to be crumbling. I had to remind myself that staying here was what I wanted.

I decided that I definitely preferred the nightmare to dreaming about Mid.

Everyone had gone from the house already, and I was left alone as I began getting ready for training. I expected every muscle to protest as I washed my body of the dirt and grime that had accumulated the day before, but my limbs moved normally without the slightest protest. I brushed through my tangled hair and rid it of the dirt and rocks that had sunk against my scalp. Then I changed, tugging on my shirt and trousers with ease. I reached out to touch my shoulders, my arms, my legs. Everywhere I pressed I expected a soreness to radiate from beneath. But it never came. I went over to the mirror, shocked to find that my body already looked stronger. *That's not possible,* I thought to myself.

I held my arms up and noticed that my biceps looked leaner, maybe even bigger. I dismissed it as my own imagination and headed down the stairs. I rummaged through the kitchen, searching for anything to feed my nutrient-starved body. I found an orange and a couple other pieces of fruit that I immediately peeled and stuffed into my mouth. The citrus sweet juices helped me to feel a little better.

I pulled my boots on at the door and then left for the Academy. The jungle was quiet, and the bustle of the Drego quickly faded behind me as the trees enveloped me. It had rained again during the night, and a tangy wetness penetrated the air. As I walked I wondered if I could really do another day of training. Yesterday was the hardest I'd ever exerted myself. The thought of repeating yesterday's exercises made me exhausted. But I felt stronger today. Maybe it would be easier.

When I stepped inside the Academy, the main dining hall was empty. I walked over to the kitchen counter and got myself some water. I sipped the drink from a silver stein, the only available cups to drink from at the Academy. I fell into one of the chairs and proceeded to lay my head in my hands and told myself I would start my studies with the Ethirical after resting my eyes for a minute.

I woke hours later. I had drifted asleep without intending to. The Envorydians that had been training that day shuffled into the house, and I groggily fluttered my eyes open. I saw from the view of the windows that the sun was going down and had nearly disappeared. Theon was among those coming back from training, and he came over to sit across from me at the table.

"Hard day?" he questioned.

I shook my head. "Just tired."

He gave me a skeptical smile as if he didn't quite believe me and then gestured to the door. "He's waiting in the field for you."

I nodded and stood from my chair. As I walked, I tried not to feel worried about what might be in store for me that day. When I emerged into the grassy clearing, Dusane was talking with Shar. The two were in a heated conversation, and I slowed my pace, not wanting to interrupt.

"I can't have her injured. You don't know what kind of trouble I'll be in if she gets hurt."

"She's not going to get hurt, Shar. I promise. Her powers would never allow that to happen."

"You don't even really know what all her powers entail!" Shar growled menacingly.

"I'll figure it out." Dusane was completely calm, not riled by Shar's furious stipulations.

"She can't win in that fight. I don't know what you're thinking."

"You don't know that. And until you give her the chance, you'll never know."

As I got closer they finally noticed my existence and instantly ceased their argument.

"Hello, Shar," I said loudly enough so he could hear my sarcastic civility. "Come to order me around some more?" I folded my arms across my chest and glared at him.

"I was just leaving," he stated flatly and started for the trees.

I wanted to yell after him. Scream as loud as I could that I could do this, but I knew it would fall on deaf ears. So I settled for glaring at the back of his ponytail as he disappeared amongst the jungle foliage.

"How are you feeling?" Dusane asked from behind me, all too calmly. I turned toward him, my cheeks pink with anger. He was nonchalantly walking over to the archery targets, like he hadn't just been fighting with Shar. I forced myself to take a breath and push aside the exasperated feelings beating inside my chest. I hated the way Shar so easily manipulated my mood.

"I'm fine, why?" I followed after Dusane and watched him set up several targets on bales of grass.

"You weren't at all sore this morning?"

"No. . . I mean, I slept a lot, but I was only sore for a little while after our training last night. I was fine this morning."

"Then it is just as I suspected."

I looked at him, confused. "What is just as you suspected?"

"Your power. You see last night's training would have left any beginner completely useless this morning. You would be sore, unable to get out of bed and probably would have trouble moving. But because you heal quicker, the time it takes for your muscles to heal and become stronger is rapidly decreased. We can push you twice as hard in training, and you'll become a skilled combat fighter much quicker." He looked up at me, his face completely serious. I didn't say anything for a moment, shocked he was already testing out theories on me. What I'd thought were sympathetic inquiries about my well-being were actually just calculated assessments of my abilities.

"So basically because I heal quicker, I'll become stronger quicker," I said, trying to simplify his explanation. He nodded and reached for one of the bows laying on the ground.

"Today we are going to work on archery."

"I thought you said I was going to start with the dagger."

"We'll be learning many weapons. Just in case in the arena you don't have a dagger to wield."

"Why wouldn't I have a dagger?"

"You start in the arena completely weaponless. You must obtain a weapon from what they call the Island. It's in the center of the arena. There will be a variety of weapons to choose from, but you must be fast enough to get the one you want."

"Wait a second. You're saying not only do I have to fight against other Stone-Hearted but that I have to fight for my weapon too?"

"Yes, that's exactly what I'm saying." He was once again showing no emotion. It was like nothing bothered him. "Are you ready to begin?" He gestured toward the bow.

"Is there room to hesitate on that question?" I asked, only partly teasing.

"Envorydians don't hesitate, Ehren. We are agile in our way of thinking. Cursory in our behaviors. There is no time for lengthy contemplation, only action."

~

The weeks of training flew by like a dream. Come rain or shine we trained every night. I'd come back to Theon's flat exhausted, sleep it off the next morning, and then my body would recover and we'd start over again.

At times I found myself missing the luxuries I'd once had at the castle: soft bed sheets that felt like clouds and hot baths that smelled like lavender to soak my tired muscles in. But my slight homesickness for royal comforts wasn't enough to make me rethink my decision to train.

I became strong, quickly. It was shocking to see my body in the mirror each day. Muscles I didn't even know I had began to be more prominent on my body. After the first couple of sessions of being unable to touch the weapons, Dusane finally allowed me to try using them. I learned to do the basics of hand-to-hand combat, bow and arrow, and dagger fighting in a matter of weeks. And when we weren't physically training, we were trying to figure out more about my powers. In all that time, no one came for me. Shar didn't say much of anything to me in those weeks during my early training. He was still angry at me for choosing to train for the Regal fight. But each time he gave me one of his grueling glares, it only encouraged me more.

One evening when I showed up for training, the usual

weaponry for our sessions wasn't laid out on the field. Dusane stood calmly in the grass, his hands behind his back.

"Is something going on?" I asked, looking around at the unusual cleanliness of the field.

"Follow me," he ordered.

Together we walked from the field and into the treeline. The palm leaves and vines shrouded us and when we came to a halt I could barely see the field through the trees. I was confused until Dusane pointed above our heads.

"Today we are going to practice overcoming fear."

"What does that have to do with training?" I asked nervously. Above us were a series of contraptions. A long wooden log spanned across two trees. A thin rope spread between two branches. A rope bridge with flimsy wooden steps. It was an obstacle course. Each connected one tree to the next and below each obstacle was a dangerous thirty foot drop.

"Fighting isn't always about the physical. Training the mind is just as important as training the body," Dusane explained. He guided me to one of the tree trunks and motioned to a thin ladder that ran up the moist bark.

"You want me to climb the tree?" I asked.

"I want you to go across the obstacles."

"With a safety rope? Or a net?"

Dusane just looked at me with an impassive expression, and I already knew the answer.

"If I fall, I could get seriously hurt," I said, hoping to make him see sense.

"If you fall, you'll heal."

"But it still hurts!" I argued, beginning to feel my hands shake.

"Then don't fall," he said matter of factly.

No amount of arguing was going to get me out of this. Nervously I bit my lip and settled my trembling hands on the rungs of the latter. Slowly I began climbing.

I used to climb the trees near the castle all the time, but I never climbed very high and I never tested my balance on such narrow obstacles before. It took me a solid five minutes to reach the top where the first obstacle was. The plank extended across to another tree and my stomach dropped. It was so much thinner and higher than it looked from below.

"Dusane, I don't think I can do this," I said, my voice quavering.

"First rule of overcoming your mind. Be confident. "

"What's rule number two?" I called, feeling for the branch beside me and clinging to it. I began to feel dizzy.

"Gaining control of your emotions. You must not allow fear to control you."

"How do I do that!" I nearly shrieked, fear already overtaking every cell in my body.

"Take a deep breath, Ehren, now imagine yourself doing the obstacle," Dusane's voice was methodical as he instructed. Somehow he was always so calm and composed.

I tried to picture myself walking across the plank to the other side.

"Now repeat the steps to accomplish the task. Tighten your core, keep your arms out for balance, walk swiftly but not too quickly. Keep your eyes on the end of the plank."

I began repeating the steps in my mind, over and over again until I knew exactly what I would do once I crossed to the other side.

"Then once you feel you are ready, go ahead and walk across to the other tree," he instructed.

I took a deep breath forcing myself to put the very tip of my toe out onto the wooden plank.

It took me several more seconds to move my other foot, barely edging myself away from the safety of the tree. My heart was beating so fast I feared it would jump from my chest. I could hear the pounding in my ears, along with my erratic breathing. I tried to look at the very edge of the plank, forcing myself not to look down. I dared take another step.

The wooden board creaked and out of fear my eyes flitted down to the board. It was a big mistake. I took in the thirty foot drop and my stomach clenched so tightly I nearly doubled over. I wobbled. Then my right arm flailed and the next thing I knew, I was falling.

I screamed, the sound echoing throughout the forest and scaring several birds from the jungle branches. The feeling of falling lasted only a couple seconds and then I hit the ground. Hard.

The air left me, I tried to breathe but nothing came in. I knew something in my back was broken, but I didn't have the capacity to moan in agony. Tears filled my eyes and I clenched my jaw trying to endure the pain. My body reacted fairly quickly. My spine cracked as it moved back into place, and soon the searing pain in my vertebrae was gone and the air rushed back into my body.

I heard Dusane's casual footsteps as he came to stand over me.

I was taking in gasping breaths when I looked up into his cerulean eyes, and that's when I saw not an ounce of emotion on his face.

"Again," he said.

I watched him walk away, and with what strength I had,

pushed myself up into a sitting position. I glared at his back, not believing someone could be so cold.

But he just returned to his spot of observance, waiting for me to start again. I grit my teeth and stood from the ground, dusting off my pants. I started for the ladder again and began climbing.

THIRTEEN

It was three months into our training when Dusane asked if Rouix would come and help with some knife training. It was a set of weapons I had only been briefly affiliated with. She agreed and showed up one evening just as the stars were beginning to peak out into the night sky.

"You call, I come." Rouix's tinkling voice caused both of us to turn and look as she made her way across the field.

We were working on takedowns and had stopped just before I was about to do a leg swing. Both of us were still square in a fighting stance.

"Thanks for coming," Dusane said, straightening up and wordlessly pausing our fight. "Ehren, I've decided that it would be a good idea to bring in other Envorydians to help with some of your skills. You'll gain more knowledge from someone who is an expert in a specific area than from someone who is mediocre in all of them," he explained. I nodded, trying not to let myself feel too nervous about the new training tactic. I had originally tried to get Rouix and Conland to train me. When they declined, I assumed that meant they wouldn't be helping at all with the process. I wondered what Dusane had said to make Rouix agree to help.

"You could've done this on your own," Rouix said as she began looking through a set of knives on the weapons panel. The panel held a variety of weapons the Envorydians used for training. Once she found what she was looking for, she came to stand by us.

"I'm not as good at knives as you," Dusane said matter-of-factly.

"You underestimate yourself," Rouix said easily. Dusane rolled his eyes at her, and it was more emotion than he usually showed in one day. They obviously knew each other well. The way they talked back and forth was like a careful dance. Quick, familiar, and effortless.

"Are you going to help or not?" Dusane questioned sharply. Without saying another word, Rouix came to stand across from me and assessed me with her intimidating crimson eyes. She looked small in the tall grass, dainty and nearly breakable. I worried if the wind blew too hard she might float away. I had yet to see Rouix fight though and knew that her appearance was probably misleading. Her silver heart shone brightly in the night, and I wondered what sort of power she possessed.

"Let's start with how to hold the knife." Rouix handed me a small knife with a leather crafted handle. She went through several steps on how to position my palms and fingers correctly on the hilt before beginning. Once satisfied with my attempt she stepped back and held up her knife directly in front of her face, preparing for a fight. "I assume you've had training with the dagger and sword?"

"Yes," I said mirroring her fighting stance. I took in a deep breath, preparing myself.

"Good. Now throw all that out the window because knife fighting is nothing like it," she said smoothly, like she hadn't just completely crippled me with her words. My eyes widened in surprise, and when she took the first swing, I barely moved away in time not to get swiped. "Knives are smaller and require quicker reflexes. You have to react instantly and think ahead." She took another swing, and I lifted my knife again just in time to deflect her second blow.

"You need to find your inner balance. Think of the knife as an extension of your hand." She started to swing faster, and my breathing began to get heavier as I barely remained unscathed. Each of my movements were wobbly and choppy. It was sheer luck I hadn't been cut.

She moved with a lithe grace that was impossible to imitate. Her body moved as if she were doing a routine she'd practiced a thousand times. She may have been small, but the way she wielded a knife was absolutely terrifying. I tried to hold onto my fear, the way Dusane had taught me to do during a fight. He had drilled into me that weakness was usually mental. He said if I could conquer my mind I would be a better fighter. I forced myself to focus and not shy away from the fight.

Gaining a little courage, I gripped the knife tighter and tried to push back against each of her sharp blows. She kept up easily, but took several steps back as if to change pace with me.

"You're getting the hang of it," she said easily, her breathing just as even as when we started. I was panting now, struggling to keep up. Soon my arms began to tire, and I could feel myself getting sloppy. Eventually I faltered and wasn't quick enough, and her blade sliced me. It was a clean cut right across my left cheek. I gasped aloud and stepped away reaching up to stop the gush of blood that came spilling down my face.

"Rouix, stop." Dusane intervened, stepping between the two of us. He came over to me and laid a hand on my shoulder, turning me towards him. "You must keep going, Ehren."

I nodded, already feeling the wound heal. Something began boiling deep within me and it took me a second to realize it was anger. I looked at Rouix and didn't see even a flicker of sympathy cross her features. "I can keep going." It was the line I'd been repeating often. Dusane was adamant about confidence. About control.

Dusane nodded in approval."Start again."

I pushed Dusane's hand away from my arm and headed for Rouix again, a new determination fueling my fire.

I didn't back down this time. I threw myself into the fight, allowing the knife in my hand to become a part of me as I tried to avenge the wound that I'd received. Despite it already being healed, the memory of it was still very much alive. I swung with all my might, forcing myself not to get weary. We went back and forth for a long while, and at moments I thought for sure she'd get the upper hand, but I pressed on, determined not to be beaten. At one point in the fight, she switched hands to take another swing. The brief pause allowed me the tiniest window to retaliate. I turned swiftly, grasping onto combat training I'd had ingrained in my head over the last several weeks. Seeing she was in a weak position and knowing I could get the upper hand, I came up behind her and raised the knife to her neck. Everything stopped and the fight came to a sudden standstill.

"How was that?" I asked her, I couldn't help the tiniest bit of pride from shining through my tone. Rouix didn't reply and I released her, wondering if I'd wounded her dignity. She turned to face me then, and at first I couldn't read her emotions. Then the tattooed wings spreading from the bridge of her nose slowly wrinkled and she smiled. It was the first time Rouix had ever smiled at me. It was as if our fight had broken some invisible wall and I was suddenly approved through my efforts.

"That was actually pretty good. I'm impressed," she said simply.

I was taken aback by her sudden acceptance.

She reached out and patted my shoulder. "I think my work is done here." She looked at Dusane, a wordless conversation passing between the two of them, and then she turned to leave the field.

~

The entire week following I continued to train with Rouix on knives. Once Dusane was satisfied with my knife skills, he brought in Theon to help with the bow and arrow.

"Glad to see you could join us," Dusane greeted as Theon entered the fields. I immediately felt at ease when Theon arrived.

Theon came to stand by me and gently clapped me on the shoulder. "It would be a shame to not let the lady be trained correctly on bow and arrow," he said pridefully, his tone teasing.

"All right, let's start with the close range targets," Dusane ordered.

As we approached the archery targets, I felt something I'd never felt before during training–excitement. I'd trained a little already with the bow and arrow. But I was curious to see what Theon would be able to add to what I'd learned. Dusane stepped aside and watched from the edge of the field as Theon began teaching me more about the bow.

"Go ahead and pick up the bow, Ehren," he instructed. I did as he said and lifted the weapon as Dusane had taught me, notching the arrow against my knuckle. Theon critiqued my positioning a little and very carefully fixed the way I was pinching the edge of the arrow with my fingers.

"There, perfect. Now go ahead and aim for the target. Take in a deep breath and keep your posture steady. When you release, make sure to maintain position so you don't alter the direction of your arrow. Steadiness is the key to aim." The way Theon taught was straightforward, and calm.

When I released the arrow, a quiet swoosh sounded, but to my disappointment the arrow sailed right past the target. It landed pathetically in the tall grass, and I winced.

"That's alright, let's try again," Theon encouraged and I took a deep breath trying not to let my failed attempt rattle me.

I got into position and Theon helped me hold the arrow correctly again.

"Very steady now, Ehren. Breathe in slowly."

I released the second arrow but it once again landed in the grass and my heart sank. I waited to hear a disappointed remark from Theon. But he simply had me start again, his encouragement not failing.

It took me ten more tries, but eventually I released an arrow and the grass bale shook slightly as the very tip met with the red center target. I smiled to myself, pleased with where my arrow had landed.

"I did it," I said excitedly.

"Great shot, Ehren. Let's do a couple more," Theon said, smiling widely.

It was nice to have a brief reprieve from Dusane's passive, cold instruction. Motivation was hard to come by when it came to Dusane and with Theon it came naturally.

That week I trained more with Theon on the bow, and it was a breath of fresh air. When the next week arrived, I had a feeling another person was going to be joining us. My inkling proved correct when Conland showed up to the fields. I immediately wondered what knowledge he'd be imparting.

It was a rainy day when he came to train, and his blond hair was already dripping when he arrived. I had been out in the drizzle for some time and was already soaked to the bone. But Dusane didn't care. He didn't see the rain as anything but a helpful training tool.

"Ehren, lovely to see you this morning," Conland drawled, winking at me.

"Hello, Conland," I said, not bothering to hide my disgusted expression.

I could've sworn I heard Dusane sigh as he came over to greet his friend. "You're here to help her learn sword technique. Not flirt," Dusane reminded him. Conland shrugged his shoulders and went to grab a sword from the weapons panel.

"Don't see why I can't do both," he commented. Dusane didn't reply, I assumed it was because if he answered he'd only urge Conland on.

Conland handed me a silver longsword and then took a battle stance across from me. Dusane, as usual, stood off to the side, assessing.

"Lift your sword to ready position, Ehren." I did as instructed, trying to blink away rain droplets that were dripping into my eyes.

"A powerful overhead slash, or a nice round lash is the way to go when it comes to sword fighting. If you master those, you'll be in good shape," Conland explained.

He quickly demonstrated and I met his sword with a resounding ring. He grinned seeing that I was paying attention. I clenched my jaw and met each one of his sweeping strokes with fervor.

"Good, now don't forget that a good thrust can be just as powerful." He quickly jabbed his sword directly at me. I jumped to the side, caught off guard by the unexpected maneuver.

"My best move is the thrust," Conland commented, sending another quick jab directly at me. "And I'm not just talking about sword technique," he winked again, and Dusane groaned audibly from the sideline.

Silencing his provocative joke, I thrust swiftly back at him, making him jump to the side so my sword wouldn't slice a whole through his stomach.

"You're such a prick," I muttered under my breath, but he only laughed.

"That was very good," he purred, and we went on like this until I could barely lift my sword anymore.

"That's enough," Dusane said, coming over to halt our fighting. The rain had stopped, and the rain clouds had dispersed to reveal the stars twinkling in the night sky.

"It was good doing training with you," Conland said, taking my hand and pressing a kiss to the tops of my knuckles.

"Goodbye, Conland," I said tugging my hand away sharply and giving him an eye roll. I was hoping it would damper the cocky expression on his face. It didn't.

FOURTEEN

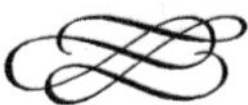

Power training was completely different from my Envoy training. Instead of all day being compiled with relentless physical activity, it was a day of concentration, a day for me to search inside myself. Search for my powers.

Dusane still didn't know what more my healing abilities entailed. So days spent trying to figure out more about my powers were incredibly boring. Dusane would sit me down in the field and he would do different exercises to see if we could figure out what I could do with my healing abilities.

One day he grabbed a knife from the weapons panel, and he sliced his arm open. I gasped, watching blood ooze down his forearm onto his fingers.

"Dusane!" I reached out to grasp his arm, my eyes wide. "What do you think you're doing?" I scolded.

He gently tugged his arm away, not the least bit fazed. "It's time to see if you can heal other people," he said, then he pulled his shirt over his head and used it to wipe off the excess blood. I had a very hard time averting my eyes from his impressively built chest and abdomen. I forced myself to focus on his arm where he'd just cut himself.

Eventually, the wound clotted and he pulled his shirt away from the wound. I could see that it wasn't as deep as I imagined. But it was still a long cut, and I could see the red fleshy center of the wound, and I felt a pit build in my stomach.

"What if I can't heal you?" I asked worriedly.

"Just try, Ehren," he pressed.

I sighed while placing my hand on top of his arm. I concentrated deeply, trying my hardest to heal him.

"Focus on what you feel, locate the power inside of you, and then use it," Dusane instructed. I desperately searched in my mind and body for what he was referring to but I came up completely empty. After ten minutes of gripping his arm and clenching my eyes closed, trying to find the power. Finally, I sighed and released him.

"I can't feel anything," I said with frustration. My eyes popped open, and when I looked at Dusane, his expression was unreadable. I felt a tremendous amount of guilt knowing I'd failed him.

"We will try again another day," he said. His dismissive demand didn't help my inner self defeat. If anything it only made me feel worse.

Wrapping his shirt around his arm again, he stood and ended training for the day.

A couple weeks later, I was on Theon's couch, lazily leaning against the pillows while he made breakfast. Some wonderful smelling aroma was coming from a pot over the fire, and I couldn't wait to taste what he was making.

"Theon, why don't you live at the Academy?" I asked. My eyes were closed. I was listening to all the little shuffling noises as he worked in the kitchen, and the background sounds relaxed me.

"The Academy is mostly for Envorydians who train a lot. It's a good way to bond with the other Envorydians for those just starting out."

"Aren't you training?"

"No, I'm a trainer. I've just been helping Shar prepare the others for the Regal fight at the Galloway. I don't really do fighting anymore."

I sat up on the couch now, opening my eyes to look at him.

"You're not going to fight in the Regal?" I asked.

He shook his head. "As much as I would love to go with Shar again on a dangerous adventure, I've already had my fair share of close calls."

"Couldn't you just tag along?"

Theon quickly shook his head. "I can't just leave. There's only two ways you get out of the Sethen Courts: Death, or winning a Galloway fight. The Regal fight is different from the others in that whoever wins is allowed freedom from the Courts. That's why it only happens once a year. Shar worked a special deal out with the Commission this time so that not just one person gets freedom, but the top five who win that night."

"So it's to please the Commission," I concluded.

"There is always a price to pay with the Commission, and

they've just gotten more blood thirsty over the years," he affirmed sadly.

Knowing that the only way out of the prisons was either by death or by winning a Regal fight only made me want to fight in it more. I didn't want to get the easy way out, I didn't want to be granted a special release because of my name and title. I wanted to earn my way out. Just like everybody else.

"He's sure going to a lot of trouble to get a couple of Envorydians to go with him," I murmured, more to myself than Theon.

"Shar always has more to his plans than meets the eye."

"Do you know something I don't?" I asked quickly.

Theon laughed at my accusing tone. "No, I just know Shar. And something I've learned not to do is assume that you know what he's thinking."

I sat quietly for a moment, pondering what Theon had said about the Galloway and the Regal fight. Then another question popped into my head.

"Theon, what is your power?" I'd seen the green light in his chest a couple times now but hadn't had the time to pester him about it yet. I remembered Dusane telling me the color green came from the emerald stone.

"It's nothing special," he said factually, not sounding disappointed in the least. "I have a greater ability to feel empathy. I can notice when people are sad, and I sympathize with their pain." It wasn't a physical power really, but it made me realize why it was so easy to be around him.

"That's kinda beautiful," I said and Theon merely chuckled.

"It wasn't the greatest thing to have as a warrior. I hated it in the beginning, feeling everything my opponent felt. But then eventually it helped me become a better Envorydian."

It was silent between us for many minutes after that. I closed my eyes again and leaned my head back against the couch cushions. I wasn't expecting Theon to make more conversation so when he spoke again, I jumped a little.

"So are you coming to the bonfire tonight? I heard Dusane gave you the day off," he said. Dusane had told me to take a break from training, and that there was going to be a bonfire at the Academy if I wanted to go. We'd been nonstop training for four months now, and a break sounded heavenly. But what made me hesitant was that all the Envorydians were going to be at the bonfire.

"I don't know if I'm going. Aren't those get-togethers supposed to be for Envorydians?" I asked. I'd heard talk of the party and knew it would be time they spent together drinking and talking. It seemed to be a more formal event than the usual chatter that went on every night at the Academy. I didn't know if it was something I could intrude on.

"You are basically one of us now. You definitely should come."

~

When we arrived at the Academy that night, I was expecting the other Envorydians to be inside. But the house was empty, and Theon escorted me past the house and toward the fields where training usually took place. I knew I spent pretty much every day at the Academy, and training in the fields, but for some reason, I felt like an intruder showing up for the party that night. I could hear the hum of conversation echo through the trees as we approached. When we stepped past the tree line into the open, I saw that a bonfire had been fashioned in the middle of the Foundation Fields. The Envorydians were sitting around it, talking amongst each other, drinking and laughing.

I spotted those I knew huddled in a group by the fire. Theon and I made our way over to them. Shar was there too, nursing a large stein of Lush Fire. He barely looked up when I took a seat beside the others on one of the thick wooden logs that had been put as seats around the fire.

"Well, look who decided to show up," Conland teased. He gave me a playful wink, and I rolled my eyes at him good-naturedly.

"Pass me one of those?" I asked, referring to the Lush Fire that was being distributed. In response, Rouix handed me a cup of the bubbling drink. I took a sip and immediately felt myself relax.

"So what did we miss?" Theon asked, leaning his elbows on his knees casually. Readying himself for a long conversation it seemed.

"Not much. Shar is drinking himself to death. Dusane is refusing to take a sip and loosen up. Conland needs someone to shed some energy off of him, and I'm just here to watch for fun." Rouix giggled and all three men beside her glared.

Theon was the only one who laughed and nodded in agreement. "Sounds about right."

"I'm not drinking myself to death," Shar said forcibly.

Rouix gave him a disbelieving look. "Yeah and my heart isn't silver."

"What's going on?" I asked, and Theon looked to already know what was going on without even having been there.

"There are a couple Envorydians that have heard about the Regal and want to fight for their freedom in a couple weeks," Theon explained.

"I told you Shar, it's their decision," Conland said, smirking. "If they want to get beaten up, it's their choice."

"I didn't think anyone from the guild would want to participate," Shar admitted, a painful expression in his eyes.

I had already deduced early on that Shar wanted the people currently sitting next to me to win the fight. It sounded as if he only intended them to get involved. He had gone to them first, and he was focused on their victory. But with the way gossip spread around the Envoy it didn't surprise me that other Envorydians were trying to participate in the Regal. I knew Theon said a lot of them were complacent being in the Sethen Courts, but I didn't find it hard to believe that some of them would want freedom.

"Freedom makes people irrational," Theon said sympathetically.

Shar nodded but still looked unconvinced. "The last thing I want to happen is brother to be put against brother," he said darkly.

"If the other Envorydians here aren't fighting in the Regal, who is there to fight against?" I asked.

"Anyone living inside the courts can participate in the Regal," Theon explained. "It's not just Envorydians that fight in the Galloway."

"And there are other fighting guilds that live in the Courts," Rouix said. I could sense a tension in the circle.

"Other guilds? Like the Envoy?" I asked, my eyes widening.

"The Envoy used to be the only fighting guild in the Courts, but the Envoy is selective on who they accept. Those who couldn't agree to live by our standards decided to create their own fighting guilds," Theon explained.

I remembered Theon telling me when I first arrived that

some Envorydians that were sent to the courts chose not to accept the mantra of peace.

I looked around the fire at the other Envorydians and felt a sudden sense of melancholy as I realized what would happen if more Envorydians here tried to fight in the Regal. Only five could emerge victorious and *if* it was me, Conland, Rouix, and Dusane that left only one other person that could win. If there were any more than five, it could potentially end up resulting in a fight between guild members. Someone could get hurt, and from what I knew about the Envoy, fighting against one another was something they were trying to get away from.

"You guys have to stick together, help each other win," Shar suddenly blurted out.

"What else did you think we were gonna do? Rouix may be obnoxious but that doesn't mean I want her to get hurt," Conland said smirking at Rouix. She stuck her tongue out at him but it was given jokingly.

"Hopefully we won't have to hurt any of our own. If we play our cards right, someone or something in the arena will make them forfeit." Dusane spoke for the first time, and I looked over at him. His eyes appeared almost black, and the fire did little to illuminate his features. His dark, impassive demeanor looked even more intimidating in the shadows. It reminded me of the first night I'd met him.

"The Beast isn't going to allow his team to lose. Don't worry." Conland grinned and reached his arm across the back of the wooden log where I was sitting. It seemed he was associating me with his "team."

"Who's the Beast?" I asked, and this suddenly brightened the conversation.

"It's Conland's nickname," Theon explained, a smile tugging at the corners of his mouth.

"Why do they call you the Beast?" I asked curiously.

"Well, other than my incredible good looks, I have a special power that emerges when I get riled up," he smoldered arrogantly but didn't elaborate.

"He means angry. And not typical angry, like furious kill-mode. It's unhealthy," Rouix reprimanded.

"It's just part of who I am," Conland pushed back. Obviously Rouix had hit a soft spot.

"Well, I hope to never see the Beast directed at me," I said, and teasingly elbowed Conland beside me.

"Just come live at the house for a week. You'll see it emerge," Rouix vowed.

"Yeah, why don't you come live at the house E? We could always use more company." Conland's suggestion sort of shocked me along with the sudden nickname he'd used.

"Live at the Academy?" I asked meekly. I could see Shar and Theon exchange a glance, and then they looked at Dusane. Everyone went sort of quiet for a moment as several unsaid conversations passed between the group.

"Oh I don't know. Shar probably wouldn't want me to. . ."

"I think it's time you start training with the others in the mornings. And living at the Academy will be more accommodating." All eyes turned to Dusane as he made the unexpected interjection.

"You want me to train with the others?" I asked him, my eyes widening. "Do you think I'm ready?"

"I wouldn't exactly say ready. . ." he retracted.

Something inside me flared at his lack of acclamation.

"You just don't want me to get it into my head that I'm actually doing pretty well," I said, not expecting the comeback to leave my lips. A flicker of his eyebrow revealed he wasn't amused by my over confidence. "Come on, Dusane! Can't you just admit that I've progressed a lot these last couple months?"

"Your hand in swords is sloppy at best, your dagger posture still needs work, and you may be able to get yourself through a hand-to-hand combat fight, but your skills are hardly polished," he said and with a hint of annoyance. Everyone looked a little amused, and maybe even surprised, at our little squabble. "But despite all of that, I do think working with the others will help your performance," he finished in a clipped tone.

I smirked at him, but he just looked over at me calmly, his eyes revealing no emotion. This had been a new constant in our relationship. At first it was intimidating—his quiet subdued personality. But over the last several weeks, I found myself talking a lot in the quietness during our training sessions, and it balanced out his silence rather perfectly. I could now differentiate between his serious stares. There was a slight twitch of his left brow when he wasn't amused by something I'd said and a slight twitch of his lips when he thought something was funny.

"What do you say, Shar?" Theon suddenly interrupted. All eyes turned to Shar.

"Why are you looking at me? Do you really think she'll listen to me anyway?" He reached for his Lush Fire taking a long sip.

Rouix giggled and Conland gave a loud whooping cheer. "Welcome to the Envoy, E!"

FIFTEEN

Later that evening after everyone was humming with the effects of the Lush Fire, and conversations had somewhat dwindled, I was sure the party would soon be coming to an end. But then one of the Envorydians approached the fire.

"Everyone please gather around!" The other Envorydians who had wandered off a far distance in the fields all started back toward the bonfire.

"What's going on?" I asked Conland, who was sitting on the other side of me.

"They're going to tell us about the legends of the Envoy," he explained. I waited with curiosity as everyone settled in. The man who had called the other Envorydians together turned and faced towards Shar.

"Would you like to do the honors?" The Envorydian asked, and Shar looked about to protest then sighed and nodded.

"I only know a few stories," Shar warned, but the other

Envorydian didn't seem to be worried and sat down, showing that he and everyone else were ready to listen.

All the talking had ceased, and all eyes were suddenly on Shar. I felt a suspenseful twitter in my stomach waiting for him to begin.

"I'm going to tell my favorite legend. It's about an Envorydian by the name of Telsiver. Long ago when contentions in Greater Aveladon began, and the realm started to divide, Wesoltinece the war king desired a warrior that could help guard him. Telsiver was a very powerful Stone-Hearted, and was known for his ability to fight. He never lost. His power required him to access a type of fighting that was unknown to other Stone-Hearted. He named this style of fighting the Envoy. His ability was uncanny. It helped protect Wesoltinece and he quickly became a well-known warrior among the realms. Over time, contentions grew hotter and more chaotic. Wesoltinece needed more than just his one warrior. And so Telsiver agreed to train others to fight using the Envoy technique that his power had graced him with. Over time this technique became an exclusive weapon for Wesoltinece, and he named his guild of fighters the Envorydians.

"What was so different about this technique some may ask? How was the Envoy fighting different from normal battle techniques being taught for thousands of years? It was their concentration, discipline, and having absolute control over their own minds. It was more mental than it was physical, and it was something that only the Envorydians had mastered.

"This technique made them absolutely lethal in comparison to other fighters who had the tendency to lose control and allow their emotions to get away from them. It was a simple difference that made momentous changes in the war between the kings.

"As we all know, the story of the five kings does not have a graceful end. It was a bloody time in history, a mark on the Stone-Hearted race that will never be forgotten. But the Envorydian race was not yet done. There was one remaining survivor in the final battle, Telsiver's daughter, Raiel. . ."

A chill went down my spine at the mention of a woman Envorydian being the last one standing.

"Raiel had come to the conclusion through her training that the Envorydians could be a great benefit to Aveladon when used for good. She longed for a better future, a greater cause than just killing for power. For several peaceful years, Raiel built the Envorydians again, and they helped keep the peace in Greater Aveladon. As we know, that peace didn't last forever, but the Envoy philosophy is still rooted deep within the guild, and one day when the curse is defeated, the Envorydians will do everything they can to return and help keep peace among the Stone-Hearted people.

"You must stay true to your most powerful purpose. 'Peace through the heart.' Do not give up hope that one day you will be free. Captivity is better than being a weapon for an unfaithful cause."

A hush fell over the group of Envorydians, and I could feel the reverence in the circle as Shar finished telling the story.

I felt the sensation of someone's gaze on my face and turned to catch Dusane looking at me. Our eyes met, and I couldn't read the emotion in his expression. Rouix was sitting next to him, and she whispered something to him. He turned to her, breaking our gaze. I felt my cheeks heat slightly, feeling suddenly embarrassed for some reason.

I wondered what they were talking about. Maybe they were talking about me, questioning my ability as an Envorydian. *Did*

Dusane think I could live up to the title? Now that I would be living in the Academy, I would be even more immersed in the Envoy. And the more that I spent time with the Envorydians, the more I began to feel as if I belonged. But I'd only just begun my training. I felt I was getting the hang of it, but it would be months. . . maybe years before I began to feel qualified for a fight like the Regal. I felt discouraged again, thinking about the fighters around me who had been part of the guild for much longer, and were still perfecting their skills. If it weren't for my powers I don't think I'd be progressing at all.

Something inside me burned with an eagerness, to be accepted by these fighters. To become one of them. I vowed then and there, looking around the circle of Stone-Hearted Envordyians, that I would do my best to win in the Regal. That even if it was impossible and I failed, I'd continue in the fight for peace.

~

The party gradually dispersed a couple hours later, and despite how late it was, I didn't even feel tired. My mind was reeling with the stories Shar had told, and I felt enlightened with an excited fire.

Conland stood from beside me and began following Shar and Theon back toward the Academy. Rouix and Dusane also stood from the fire and Rouix strode after the others. I was just about to follow but noticed that Dusane was making no move to accompany her. His hands were pressed into his pockets, his dark hair falling across his forehead in a smooth arc. We looked at each other for a moment, and I found myself frozen where I stood.

"Want to take a walk with me?" he suddenly asked. The others were almost halfway across the fields now. I was about to protest, feeling some invisible obligation to stay with the group, but then I realized nothing was stopping me.

I found myself nodding. "Sure," I said.

He started in the opposite direction of the Academy and I followed several steps behind him into the trees.

"That was an interesting history about the Envoy," I said, breaking the silence between us. It wasn't silent—exactly. The wind was rustling the leaves in the trees, sticks crunched beneath our shoes and I could hear the rustling of animals in the jungle foliage. But he was always so passive, and his demeanor made the quiet atmosphere deafening. I nervously talked to fill the void.

"I'd heard a little bit of the story from Theon, but never in such detail," I added.

We'd fallen into stride beside each other, but he still didn't reply. He simply looked on ahead, his cerulean eyes not giving anything away.

"Why did you want to take a walk?" I pressed, wondering if I'd have to have this entire conversation with myself.

"It's a nice night," was all he said in reply. I nodded, and tried to stay quiet, seeing if he'd continue but he never did.

"How do you become part of the Envoy?" I asked, hoping the question would spur more than a one sentence answer from him.

"My father was an Envorydian for the Obscurum Kingdom. He raised me from a young age in his beliefs, and from that point on, I knew I didn't want to be anything else."

I was about to ask him how he ended up in the Courts, but then he unexpectedly spoke again.

"Ehren, can I ask you something?" The sudden inquiry caught me off guard.

"Yeah, sure," I replied quickly, almost worried he'd change his mind.

"Do you think I'm a good trainer?" he asked. It wasn't exactly the question I was expecting, and it took me a moment to answer.

"Yeah, you're a great trainer, Dusane. I mean you've taught me so much in such a short amount of time; that should be a testament to your abilities."

"Do you think I'm too hard on you?"

"Well, that's debatable. . ." I smirked at him, hoping he'd see I was joking, but the side of his mouth barely quirked up in a smile, and then his face was serious again. *Why is it so difficult for him to show emotion?*

"I'm kidding, Dusane. You push me just enough," I explained sincerely. He was a difficult trainer to please, but it made me work harder.

"Good," was all he said.

I smiled to myself thinking that even if it was the smallest of insecurities, it showed that he really wasn't as emotionless as he seemed.

"Am I a good student?" I asked. I nudged his side a little to show him I was being playful. It took him a moment but eventually his lip twitched a little.

"That is private information for the trainer, that I'm going to politely withhold," he said and I laughed, seeing that he was blatantly deflecting the question.

"I'm more difficult than you planned aren't I?" I pressed, and he let out a soft chuckle, which immediately surprised me. It was a husky, throaty sound, that made something inside me flutter a little when I heard it.

"Far more difficult than I planned," he confessed.

I pretended to appear offended. "What's that supposed to mean?"

"I've never trained anyone like you. You're stubborn, refuse to listen to me sometimes, and you talk too much," he said easily.

I couldn't help but be amused by his blatant honesty.

"You talk too little," I said. "Maybe if you talked more, I wouldn't have to fill the silence," I accused. "And as for my stubbornness, I think I've got just the right amount," I said standing a little straighter.

"My point exactly," he rolled his eyes, and my laugh echoed through the branches of the jungle trees.

"Dusane, I know I probably won't be an expert fighter like the others for years to come. That my powers are the only reason I've even gotten this far but. . . I know I can do this."

"Well, good news is I think you have just enough iron will and determination to do it," Dusane admitted and I smiled.

"Do you mind if I ask you something else?" I asked, and the tone of the conversation turned suddenly serious again. I'd had another question to ask him, something that had been on the back of my mind for some time now.

He merely nodded for me to continue.

"You and Rouix. . . is there something between you two?" I felt my cheeks heat a little when the question left my lips. *Why was I prying?* I scolded myself for being so curious all the time.

But Dusane didn't seem the least bit affected by the question.

"There is not a romantic relationship between us, if that's what you are asking," he said simply. I nodded, but couldn't help but remember the way Rouix acted around him. As if he could tell I was still thinking about it, he spoke again.

"We've known one another a long while. Both of us were sent to the Courts at the same time. We're comfortable around each other, because time has a way of doing that. But nothing more than friendship extends between us.``

For some reason, his explanation made me relieved.

We talked for a little while longer, walking side by side, until Dusane decided we better turn around and start heading back to the Academy. When we returned, Dusane gave me a simple goodbye and slipped into the house where he slept. Soon I'd be at the Academy too, and I could feel a flicker of nervousness at the thought.

I made the short walk back home to Theon's flat, and as I lay in bed to sleep that night, replaying the conversation we'd had in my head, for once I didn't have any bad dreams.

SIXTEEN

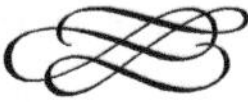

There wasn't much to move out of the flat. I didn't really have any belongings other than a couple pairs of clothes and my boots. So the next morning when I showed up to the Academy as usual, it was a quick transition.

"You'll be upstairs in a room with me," Rouix said, leading me up the stairs to a part of the house I'd never seen before. There was a long hallway and multiple doors. She led me down to the very end and opened the door to a pleasantly quaint room. There were two small beds and a blue tassel rug on the floor. Pretty crystal prisms hung from the window casting rainbows onto the beige walls. A book shelf with volumes nearly spilling from its shelves was beside the bed that had a blue and white comforter. For some reason it was the last thing I'd expected. Rouix didn't have typical girlish qualities. Her bedroom was the most feminine side of her I'd ever witnessed. I guess unconsciously I had been expecting black painted walls and knives to be everywhere.

The other bed in the room had a basic grey sheet on top and a lonely white pillow. It was not nearly as decorated as her side, and I assumed it was where I would be sleeping.

"That's your bed over there." She pointed to the plain bed, and I carefully set my meager belongings onto the gray sheet. Rouix then gestured back towards the door. "I heard you're training with us today. Want to walk with me?" she offered. I nodded, eager not to be alone traveling to the field that morning.

I had been particularly nervous thinking about training with the other Envorydians. I had barely slept and felt queasy. I knew it would be different from training at night with Dusane. I could mess up when it was just the two of us. I didn't mind making mistakes because no one else was around to watch me make them. I didn't know how training with the Envorydians would be, but I could only imagine it would be different, and different made me nervous.

When we came upon the field, the sun was just barely coming up into the sky. Another thing I was going to have to get used to—training in the sun. There were about forty other Envorydians there that day. Rouix led me over to a group where Theon, Conland, and Dusane were talking amongst each other. Conland let out a conventional loud cheer when he saw me with Rouix, catching the attention of those around us.

"Look who it is, if it isn't the fledgling coming up in the ranks." He was grinning ear to ear. I blushed slightly at his comment, not really wanting to be acknowledged.

"What do you think, Tyro? Do you think you can keep up?" Theon challenged good naturedly.

"Fledgling? Tyro?" I asked sheepishly. "Should I know what those words mean?"

"It means young soldier or beginner," Rouix explained. "Stop pestering her, you two. Or I won't hesitate to shut you up. She's one of us now." Rouix glared at each of them with her scarlet eyes, and they immediately stopped their teasing. I was grateful someone was sticking up for me. Honestly, in the beginning, I didn't know if Rouix and I would be friends. I guess being the only two girls in the entire Envoy made it a little hard not to be.

"I'd be careful with your words, boys." Dusane suddenly came over to stand by me. He slung an arm over my shoulder casually, and I tried to hide my surprise at the lighthearted gesture. He had been silent so far in all of their joking. "I'm putting her against you today in the arena, and you might just lose."

"Ha, lose? That word is not in my vocabulary." Conland smirked, challenging me with his smoldering gaze. I was about to say another sarcastic comment in return but was interrupted by someone shouting from the middle of the field.

"Attention everyone. Please come to the combat circles. We're starting with faceoffs today." Shar was standing in the middle of the field instructing everyone to head to a section reserved for hand-to-hand combat fighting. I followed the others, confused as to what was happening.

"Faceoffs? I thought we were training." I spoke quietly to Dusane as he walked beside me.

"It is training. Shar thought it would be a good idea to take a break from conditioning and have us practice fighting against some of the other Envorydians."

"I'm not ready to go against someone in hand-to-hand," I said nervously.

"You go against me all the time," he pointed out.

"Yeah but that's different, and you know it," I hissed, hating how calm he was being.

"Do I hear hesitation in your voice?"

"Yes! Indeed that is hesitation in my voice! I thought we'd be doing archery circuits, or sword practice. Not actual hand-to-hand combat in front of everyone!" Our whisperings stopped when we came upon the four combat circles, each one already filled with paired Envorydians.

"You know the rules. Once someone taps out, you stop. Otherwise, anything goes." Shar explained the rules, which happened to be only one, and then stepped off to the side to watch. The first fight began, and I couldn't help but watch, completely fascinated.

Rouix was first in the ring facing off to an intimidating bald man with tattoos literally covering every square inch of him. He was tall and probably three times her size in body weight. Rouix just grinned and pranced around the ring like she was some sort of slinky fox.

"Come at me, Ren. I'm waiting," she taunted in her singsong voice. The man growled and lunged for her like a barreling animal. In an instant, she was gone, like literally gone. She disappeared for a moment then suddenly reappeared again on the opposite side of the ring. I gasped, shocked and confused as to how she did it. Over and over again he would take a swing and miss because she would turn invisible again. I'd yet to witness her power, and it was mesmerizing to watch.

Eventually, the other Envorydian did get a hit on her, and her invisible form glimmered like he'd shaken whatever magic was cloaking her. But she came back with a vengeance, regaining the upper hand after their game of cat and mouse and pinned him to the ground. He tapped out, and then Theon went into the ring.

I had learned Theon's power the day before and knew he didn't have any physical abilities. But he was good in a fight. He was still remarkably strong and somehow almost as quick as Rouix. His metal hand was another helpful factor, and he quickly hindered his opponent with a solid metal punch to the gut. The fight lasted a total of three minutes.

After a couple more fights, Conland jumped into the ring, and Shar called out to the crowd, searching for another opponent.

"Who's next?" Shar yelled, but no one made a sound. Conland grinned, as if thrilled by the lack of willing participants.

"I think it's Ehren's turn." As Conland nominated me, all eyes in the field turned toward me. I saw a mix of emotions on the Envorydians' faces. Some looked fearful as they eyed me, others disgusted. I literally froze in place. I realized most all of them probably knew me from the wild gossip as the girl who burned down the Spirit Tree. And now I was training with some of their guild members, and most probably viewed me as an intruder. They displayed their preconceived notions on their faces.

"I don't know. . ." I began but I was quickly cut off.

"Scared Fledgling?" Conland taunted. He bounced up and down in the ring, his beautiful bronze chest glistening in the hot sun and the bright blue hue of his heart pulsing. I couldn't handle his cocky, self-assured demeanor. No matter how justified he was in his vanity.

I could see Dusane watching me carefully to see what I would do. Then my eyes flickered to Shar. He revealed no emotions. He was off to the side, arms folded across his chest. I realized then this was my time to prove myself. Not only to Shar and the other Envorydians, but to myself.

I jumped over the fence and landed on the other side indicating that I was going to fight. A couple of taunting chuckles were heard from several of the men watching. Others were simply observing quietly with judgmental eyes.

"All right, now let's calm down," Shar called, the hum of the crowd settled, and I took a combat stance across from Conland.

He was several feet taller than me. His muscles bulged in ways that intimidated me immensely. I could feel something switch on inside my brain, turning on the fighter inside of me. Dusane had taught me how to collect myself before a fight, how to center my mind and remain calm. As I was repeating the steps in my head, Shar shouted for us to begin. At that moment, everyone around us disappeared. My mind, my body, my soul was trained on Conland. I didn't have time for distractions. It was easier to tune everything else out.

He was the first to take a swing. His right arm came out in a perfect right hook, and I quickly dodged it, ducking to the side. He grinned widely at me.

"Beginners luck," he purred smoothly. He started after me again, only quicker this time. He kicked his leg out to sweep my feet out from beneath me, but I'd been trained to see it. I was already two steps ahead of him. The muscles in my body somehow remembered exactly what they needed to do, and I quickly jumped out of the way. Taking the opportunity, I hit him with an offensive jab to his side. He didn't even flinch, like my jab had been a mere love tap.

He didn't waste any time then and headed for a takedown. He came barreling toward me, tackling me by the waist and sending both of us to the grass. He was on top of me for a moment, but it only took me a couple seconds to remember what Dusane had told me to do in this situation. I held up my fists in a defense pose, knowing he would probably strike. But the blow never came . . .

"Do you want to tap out? I know it's your first time. We can just call it a round."

I pulled my hands down away from my face to see Conland smirking down at me. The look on his face was so certain that I couldn't handle this, that I couldn't take him.

"Scared to hit a girl?" I taunted, and it was the first time I'd ever provoked a contender, and it worked better than I meant it to. When his fist met my side, I had to force myself not to scream. I could feel my rib dislocate where his first met my side, and I felt all the air in my lungs leave me. It was a half a second of blinding pain and then the adrenaline took over.

My world suddenly sharpened, and I became absolutely cognizant of the strength in me. I gathered a deep breath and delivered the most forceful right hook I could to his perfect cheek. I split the precious skin just above his cheekbone, and his head fell to the side. A spray of blood flecked the grass beside us, glistening bright scarlet in the sunlight.

His hold loosened, and I quickly rolled out from beneath him and took up my fighting stance again. I could feel my ribs healing as I stood, waiting for him to get up. My rib moving back into place beneath my skin was an uncomfortable sensation.

"You're going to pay for that," Conland said as he got to his feet, and when he faced toward me again, the grin was gone from his face. The blood dripped from his cheek and onto his lips. The crimson staining only made him look more vicious. I recalled the others joking at the bonfire about Conland and how he turned into the Beast. I now understood in that moment what they meant. He was no longer the cocky, lighthearted guy I'd come to know over the past couple weeks. He was a lethal, dangerous fighter.

His eyes darkened menacingly, and with an angry huff, he raised his hands toward me again, and then before I could even begin to realize what was happening, fire shot from his hands.

The hot flames came straight for me, and I tried to jump out of the way, but I wasn't fast enough. A hot stinging sensation erupted across my left shoulder, and I groaned aloud, unable to hide the fact that he'd hurt me. I fell against the flimsy wooden fence, clutching the rail with one hand and my shoulder with the other.

"Ehren!" I heard someone yell, but it was a muffled cry in the background. I wasn't paying attention to the others surrounding the circle. They all could have been screaming and I wouldn't have taken notice. My heartbeat pounded in my eardrums as I peered at the wound, finding the skin on my shoulder to be burned, black, and blistering. The tail of my braid was singed. The scorched ends still held several hot sparkling embers. Tears pricked the corners of my eyes as I felt the full force of the blinding pain the burn was already eliciting. I looked over at Conland with wide shocked eyes. He had power over fire, and he had literally just spewed it from his hands.

He was angry. His chest heaved as he looked at me from across the circle. After several seconds, the anger dissipated from his face, and he seemed to realize what he had done.

"Ehren, I'm so. . ." he began. Others had entered the arena at that point. Dusane and Shar came over to me, putting themselves between me and Conland.

"Ehren, are you okay?" I didn't register who said it. I was too far away in my mind to care.

It was a matter of seconds that this entire incident occurred, but soon my shoulder started to heal, and the Envorydians gasped round the arena. All eyes were on me as they watched the burn heal and fresh pale skin replaced the blackened wound. I pushed Shar and Dusane aside. I wasn't paying attention to them. My eyes were still locked on Conland across the ring. A raw anger had started burning inside me, causing red to appear in the corners of my vision and the blood in my veins to boil. Conland was looking at me, his expression one of pure disbelief now.

"How did you. . ." Those were the last words he said before I hit him again, this time so hard he fell to the ground, clutching his nose in pain. I felt my hand break, the fingers displacing with my vexed effort. I grunted but knew that I would heal.

"Ehren!" I heard someone call from behind me again, but I didn't turn around. I jumped over the fence, out of the combat circle and pushed through the buzzing group of Envorydians back toward the Academy.

SEVENTEEN

"Are you sure you can do this?" I asked Rouix wearily. When I went running off from the fight in the fields, the group had followed me to make sure I was all right. After insisting I was fine nearly a thousand times, Rouix had made me sit in one of the chairs in the pub and proceeded to try and fix my hair.

The fire had singed off a good portion of it. Apparently my healing abilities didn't involve restoring my hair.

"I've got this. Now be quiet so I can concentrate," Rouix scolded, holding a knife in her hand with chilling expertise.

At first I'd been so angry about what happened. It took Shar, Dusane, and Theon to coax me to tell them if I was all right. It was more humiliating than anything. My first fight and I had failed miserably. On top of that, I was extremely upset that everyone had neglected to warn me about Conland's power and furious at Conland most of all for what he'd done. He had followed me back to the Envoy house as well, but I was ignoring him. He'd taken up perch on the bar and would apologize every five minutes, but I was determined to give him the cold shoulder until I felt I could forgive him.

"I'm really sorry, Ehren. I didn't mean to get out of control," Conland said for the hundredth time.

"Shut up, Conland," Theon said, obviously also irritated with the repetitive apologies.

"Everyone is mad at me! What can I do to fix it? I told you, I didn't intend to let it hit her! And I mean she healed in like five seconds, so I don't really see what harm was done." I had realized Conland was incapable of realizing his faults, just when I thought he'd actually deliver a heartfelt apology his arrogance would eradicate everything he'd previously said.

"She hit me too you know. I mean it's not like I didn't pay for it," His nose and cheek had stopped bleeding a little while earlier. He seemed to be in near perfect condition after the punches I'd delivered. The only evidence that I'd even managed to hit him was the little cut on his cheek bone.

Dusane glared at Conland."You didn't know she could heal, which means you're just a lucky bastard and a real big—"

"Okay, let's stop before another fight breaks out, shall we?" Shar scolded Dusane. My trainer closed his mouth, his blue eyes brooding. After the fight, he hadn't said much, but I could tell he was mad.

"I think I'll cut off a couple inches," Rouix said thinking out loud to herself. Her sleek crimson eyes were narrowed, concentrating on the locks of my hair she had between her fingers.

Dusane stood from his chair and walked toward the bar to get himself a drink

"Don't cut it too short," he suddenly muttered to Rouix as he passed by. It had been said quietly, but not quiet enough that I couldn't hear.

Puzzled by the comment, I looked up at Rouix. She just rolled her eyes and blew out a long breath.

"Men," she retorted, like that was all the explanation needed. I looked over at Dusane as he got his drink, confused by the sudden demand he'd delivered. It was odd, a little possessive if I did say so myself. I wondered why he'd said something. Did my hair length have something to do with my training? I knew the answer before I even finished asking myself the question. My hair had *nothing* to do with my training.

"Ehren, I'm sorry, I really am. Please, please for. . ." I'd had enough at that point and quickly went to cut off his apology.

"Okay, Conland, I get it. I forgive you. Now will you please stop apologizing." I finally gave in, my grudge not worth the torture he was inflicting on me. Conland sighed as if the weight of the world was lifted off his shoulders.

"Thank you. That was getting exhausting," he said desperately. He jumped down from the bar and came over to where Rouix was now slicing off pieces of my hair. Chunks of black were falling to the floor, and I had to make myself focus on something else.

"I promise nothing like that will happen again," Conland vowed then leaned in to press a kiss to my cheek. I feigned a look of disgust and wiped away the kiss with my arm.

"Ew, stop it," I said, but something in me knew that deep down I couldn't hate Conland. Yes he'd hurt me, but I'd healed, and he hadn't broken any rules technically.

"We need to get out of here for a while, release some tension," Theon suddenly piped up.

"What exactly do you have in mind?"Dusane asked.

"We should go to a Galloway fight tonight. Ehren hasn't seen one yet, and it could be fun," Theon suggested.

"Absolutely not," Shar suddenly said, standing from his chair. His face contorted into its usual mask of indignation. "Last thing we need is more fuel on the fire." He looked pointedly at me, and I glared at him.

"Oh come on, Shar. It will be fun. There's a great fight going down tonight, and it will be good for her to see what it's gonna be like. Considering our training got cut short today, think of it as a way to make up for lost time," Theon coaxed.

"I think we've had enough excitement for one day," Shar fired back, looking at Conland now. Conland smiled sheepishly.

"I would like to go," Rouix said sweetly behind me adding her point to the argument.

"I don't think it's such a bad idea either," Dusane interjected.

Shar looked pointedly at Dusane, but then finally seemed to see he was outnumbered and sighed heavily. "Okay fine, we'll go. But I'm coming, to make sure no one gets into trouble." I knew Shar was referring to me, but I didn't care to acknowledge that point. I was just glad to be doing something other than training. And going to the Galloway would get my mind off things for a while.

Conland clapped his hands together then rubbed them excitedly while grinning at me. "The Fledgling's first Galloway fight. This should be fun."

~

I had yet to see the Drego since Theon had taken me with him a couple months back. It was just as I remembered it. The streets were teeming with people. Everyone moved in different directions. The peculiar clothing style and absence of cloaks didn't unsettle me like they had the first time I'd been in the city. It was getting dark, and the streets were bright with lamp light. I walked beside Rouix, taking in the misshapen glittering beauty of the metal city once again, while the boys walked behind us.

The Galloway was hard to miss with its tall dark architecture protruding from the center of the city. When we neared the structure, I finally got a good look at its framework. It was much taller up close than it had looked from a distance. It was made of fragmented pieces of metals painted black and had a large front gate with a line of people waiting out in front of it. I could hear the noise from inside. Screaming and shouting vibrated through the alloy walls.

Excitement and fear prickled my skin.

"How do we get in?" I asked Rouix beside me.

"How you get into anything these days," she said, gesturing to the coin pouch at her waist. Shar had provided everything for me while I was in the Courts and I felt a pang of nervousness when I realized I had no money of my own.

I began to panic wondering how I was going to tell the others I couldn't pay. But when we got to the gate, my fears were quickly assuaged. Shar and Theon in front of us paid for the group and then we were all allowed access inside.

The noise was amplified, and the loud screaming and yelling stung my ears. The Galloway was essentially a giant oval theatre without a roof. Seats lined the circular walls, and in the very center was an arena. It was a large ring, with a sand foundation. People were already inside the arena fighting. As we proceeded to take our seats, I caught myself slowing to see the fight that was taking place.

Two people were facing off; one held a sword and the other had no weapon at all. It seemed the weaponless contestant was losing, and the man with the sword was about to win the match. Before I could see what happened next, I felt someone tug on my arm.

"Come on, Ehren. You gotta keep up," Rouix said to me, and I hurried to follow after her up a lengthy strip of stairs to some vacant seats. Rouix took a seat beside Conland. Then Theon and Shar sat beside one another, and that left one empty spot beside Dusane.

"What do you think?" Dusane asked suddenly as I took a seat beside him.

"I can't believe they fight for entertainment," I admitted.

"This is where the Regal fight is going to take place."

I looked away from the arena for a moment and noticed a secluded section of seats on a balcony up in the stands. A couple of lone spectators were sitting on the balcony watching the fight.

"Is that the Commission?" I asked, pointing to the isolated figures across the arena.

"Yes, sometimes a few of them will come and watch," Dusane explained, his expression hard.

"When we fight in the Regal, you said there would be an island where people can choose a weapon," I said to him. Dusane pointed toward the arena and I had to squint to see what he was pointing to.

In the middle of the sandy arena, there was a thick gray structure almost like a stage. A granite figure clutching the handle of a weapon sunk deep into the stone kneeled in the center of the stage.

"Who's that a statue of?" I asked Dusane, while still squinting at the island.

"That's Wesoltinece, the war king. The statue was made in his honor by the Envorydains."

"I thought the Galloway wasn't exclusive to Envorydians," I said, suddenly confused again.

"It's not, but the Galloway was created by them a long time ago. At first it was a training ground, a place for the Envorydians to spar and keep up their skills. Once the Commission got word of the little practice, they made the structure even grander, and it evolved into a game that others could participate in as well," Dusane explained.

I stopped asking questions then, and turned my attention back to the fight. The man with the sword had successfully cut the weaponless contestant across the shoulder, and the man had crashed to the ground, crimson blood oozed onto the sandy floor. Someone in the stands raised a red flag, and the fighting suddenly stopped. The crowd cheered as the winner was displayed, and then they were moving on to another fight, carrying the wounded man away. Fear struck me as they disappeared, and I could only hope the man would be all right.

The next round was much different from the previous fight. The arena was empty for a long time, and I watched impatiently from my seat as a large gate on one side of the arena finally opened. The sharp onyx gate receded, and from a pitch black tunnel, a thunderous growl erupted.

"What is that?" I whispered in shock. Before Dusane could answer, a creature emerged from the den and came barreling into the arena. The crowd went wild, cheering vehemently. The sight of the dangerous beast seemed to electrify the bystanders watching. They fed off danger it seemed, too caught up in the game to recognize the barbarity of their frenzy.

The creature was a lion. Well, part lion. It had a lion's head, but it had a pair of jagged white wings protruding from its shoulder blades. The beast had large feet that were fitted with bird claws, and its tail, much like a snakes, tapered off to a sharp glistening point that looked undoubtedly lethal.

I had never seen anything like it before.

"That is a Lichabra, a hybrid creature," Dusane explained. "They are usually created by accident. A mistake while breeding."

I gazed in pure amazement as the beautiful, yet distorted creature, pawed the ground and let out a hearty roar. Another gate screeched open and a lone individual came walking out of the dark tunnel.

"That person is going to fight the animal?" I asked, appalled. Dusane looked over at me, a small smile coming to his lips. He seemed slightly amused by my disbelief.

"Why else would he be walking out into an arena with a wild Lichabra? Of course he's going to fight it." He smirked and I didn't know what I was more shocked over—the creature running at the man in the arena, or the fact that Dusane had just smirked and said something playful.

The man ran for the island in the center of the arena, and was lucky enough to get his hands on a bow and arrow before the creature got a whiff of his scent. The creature whipped around, suddenly realizing it wasn't alone, and instantly started for the man.

I was unable to tear my eyes away. Somehow the man held his ground. He raced inhumanly fast around the arena to avoid the large creature while bombarding its fur with arrows. The creature flew around the arena, howling in rage every time one of the arrows pierced it. Over and over again, the creature tried diving for the man, but he could never quite touch him. The whole display made me extremely anxious, and I had to close my eyes at times. I gasped aloud at one point when the man was barely swiped by one of the creature's claws and Dusane chuckled at my reaction.

Eventually the creature tired out, falling with a loud thud to the sandy arena floor. The cheers were deafening as the man took the creature down. Seven men emerged from the tunnels, operating together to drag the nearly lifeless body of the creature out of the arena. The crowd cheered as the man was claimed the winner, but I couldn't help but feel sorry for the creature.

"Scared yet?" Dusane suddenly asked, breaking the spell the fight had me under. I turned to face him, and his blue eyes searched mine carefully.

"A little," I admitted.

"It's not too late to back out," Dusane reminded me, and I could've sworn I saw a flash of hope cross his expression.

"I'm not backing out. I want to go with Shar to search for the tokens. And this is the only way to convince him to let me come." I clenched my jaw determinedly, but I couldn't lie. The fighting I'd seen in the arena had affected me. I think I'd tried to imagine it in my head, but it made it more real seeing it for myself.

I wouldn't back down from the fight because of what I'd seen. But I would train harder. The Regal wasn't going to be easy, and these battles were proof of that. But I had to believe I could do it. A new resolve settled in as I watched the remaining fights that night. I *would* fight in the Galloway, and I *would* be one of the last five standing. I had to be.

EIGHTEEN

After the Galloway fight ended the others didn't want to go back to the Academy just yet. Conland convinced the group that he was hungry, and so we wandered the crowded streets of the Drego to get something to eat. The city was flooded with people. It was impossible to walk through the crowds without squeezing through hordes of Stone-Hearted civilians. I was just beginning to feel claustrophobic when we finally escaped into the safety of a tall metal building. The noise was immediately quieted.

The room we stepped into was small and had a smokey air to it like someone had been smoking a cigar. A tall blonde-haired woman stood behind a table ready to greet us, and Theon proceeded to speak with her. After a moment she motioned for us to follow after her, and together we started up a flight of stairs.

It was a lengthy climb that eventually led us onto the roof. The place was spacious, and covered with tables where people were seated eating and making conversation. Light from the bright starry sky dimly illuminated the scene. Over the edge of the roof was a view of the Drego. I could see clearly the metal buildings pressed closely together with their odd architecture and misshapen uniqueness, and I was struck with awe once again by the city's foreign beauty.

The woman led us to an empty table, and we all sat down together. Moments later another woman came to our table and handed each of us large glasses of Lush Fire.

I listened quietly as the group chatted, sipping my drink. Conland started making jokes and shamelessly flirted with the waitress at one point. He didn't bother to hide his motive to take her home with him at the end of the night.

"It looks like you need a break from working, darling. I'd be happy to help you relax," Conland purred as she came over with more rounds of Lush Fire. The woman rolled her eyes at him but couldn't hold back the giggle that escaped her lips. She was a beautiful Stone-Hearted with auburn red hair and wide green eyes that matched the beautiful emerald color of her heart.

"I'm sure you would," she retorted then flicked her hair over her shoulder before sashaying back to the kitchen, leaving Conland to stare wistfully after her.

"You've got a little drool," I teased, pointing to the side of his mouth. The others at the table laughed, which only made Conland grin wider.

I slipped easily into their lighthearted conversation, surprised by how much fun I was having. Shar even seemed to be enjoying himself a little, which was out of the ordinary. The waitress brought out endless plates of food, and I tasted dozens of unknown exotic dishes.

I was glad to be able to get my mind off other things for a

while. And it also felt good to feel included in the group. I realized while sitting there and talking with them that I could now call them my friends. Even after the incident with Conland, I was grateful for the unexpected group of individuals I'd become acquainted with.

After a while of conversation and sampling unknown foods I'd never before tasted, I noticed Dusane excuse himself from the table. I curiously watched him walk away and disappear through an archway leading to an unknown section of the roof. Worried something might be wrong, I excused myself and followed after him. I passed through the archway and was surprised to see it was a secluded terrace with another beautiful outlook of the city. No one was around, and it was peaceful and quiet. Palm leafed plants lined the edges of the hideaway, and I could see Dusane dimly illuminated in the moonlight leaning against the metal railing. He seemed to be deep in thought when I approached. As my footsteps alerted him of my presence, he turned to see who was walking toward him.

"Ehren," he said in greeting.

"Dusane," I replied, leaning against the railing beside him. "What are you doing?"

"Thinking," he said, while refixing his gaze on the city below. It was the response I'd expect from Dusane. Simple, and vague.

"About what?" I pressed. I wished I could see into his mind, understand the way he thought. The earring in his ear caught a small sliver of light from one of the lanterns near us and I'd almost forgotten it was there.

"You," he suddenly said. I was caught off guard by the reply.

"What about me?" I asked, trying to calm my now rapidly beating heart.

"I keep asking myself why you did what you did. But I can't

figure it out." His voice held a hint of puzzlement, and he turned his gaze on me suddenly, his blue eyes honestly questioning.

"Would you believe me if I said I burned down the tree because I was trying to help?" I asked, knowing it sounded crazy.

"Maybe," he admitted, looking down again.

I suddenly felt the need to explain myself.

"I went to visit my mother," I began, hoping I wasn't giving too much away. "She died a while back and I wanted to see her in spirit. To get answers about the curse. When I went, she appeared. She told me to burn down the tree. I had to let the tree experience the flames so that Aveladon could live again." As I said the words, I was filled with a fearful uncertainty. *What would he think of me? Would it sound like insanity to him?* The memory was so vivid in my mind then, and I could instantly recall the smell of burning tree roots. If I concentrated hard enough, I could remember the way it felt as the ashes burned my fragile skin.

"Who are you?" The unexpected question took me off guard. He was looking at me again, and I met his gaze with wide eyes. The deep blue color held mine with earnestness, gently urging me to tell him the truth. But I couldn't.

"You know I can't tell you that," I whispered.

"I know," he sighed and then gave me the smallest of smiles. "But it was worth a try." He was very handsome when he smiled. It was a rarity, and every time he did show the unexpected expression, I felt something burn inside of me. But I couldn't quite identify it. It sort of felt like when Mid would smile at me, but not exactly the same.

"Dusane, why don't you have any tattoos?" I suddenly asked, changing the subject.

"I have a tattoo," he said simply.

I raised an eyebrow, urging him to explain. He saw my expression, sighed softly, then gently brushed back the locks of hair that reached past his ears. He pushed the hair to the side and leaned slightly away from me so I could see it.

Just behind his pierced ear, a very small symbol was etched into his skin. It was too hard to see without leaning in closely.

"What is it?" I asked quietly.

"It's the symbol of the Envoy," Dusane explained. It was then that I realized I'd seen the symbol before. I'd seen it mixed in with elaborate tattoos, and as a lone sketch on someone's arm or shoulder. I'd even seen it within Rouix's wing tattoo.

The tattoo was a small semi-circle adjacent to a phasing moon. Sun-like spikes jutted out from these symbols, while thin dripping lines that appeared to be falling stars cascaded down from beneath the sun. Then three crescent moons turned sideways ascended upwards into his hairline.

"What does it all mean?" I asked him curiously.

"The semi-circle represents peace. The phasing moon symbolizes purity of the heart. The small shooting stars represent attaining your higher self. Then the three crescent moons represent controlling fate. And the half sun represents strength as a guild. Basically we believe that we can create peace throughout the land as long as we are pure in heart and have discipline over our soul and mind. We also believe that as a guild we are stronger and with an Envorydian mindset, we control our own fate, not the other way around."

"Peace through the heart," I said gently, recalling the words Shar had said at the bonfire. "Why don't you have more tattoos like the others?" I realized he stood apart from the rest of the guild with only the one. The other Envorydians seemed to wear their markings with pride, as if they wanted to show them off.

"I guess I just haven't had a reason to get another." Dusane let down his hair and turned back toward me. I had yet to move, so when he twisted around, our faces came mere inches apart.

I was suddenly frozen. With him so close to me, my mind went blank. He didn't pull away, he stayed completely still, calmly looking back at me. Our breaths mingled together in the small space between us, and I felt the world suddenly stop.

Before I could even think about what I was doing, I felt myself leaning in.

I prepared myself for the feeling of his lips against mine, and the twinkling sensation that would erupt inside my stomach when it happened. But just when I thought our mouths would meet, he turned away.

"I think we should head back to our table," Dusane suddenly said.

The spell was broken, and the reality of what I almost did crashed down on me, and I became utterly and completely mortified.

"I. . . I'm sorry," I said, turning away from him. My cheeks turned red with embarrassment and my entire body felt hot with shame.

"The others are probably waiting." Dusane didn't seem phased, his expression unreadable. I hurried underneath the archway and back to the part of the balcony that was filled with people. I could feel myself shaking. I was confused and most of all upset at myself.

When we reached the table, the others were getting up to leave. I fell into stride beside Rouix, and she seemed to immediately sense something was wrong.

"Everything okay, Ehren?" she asked suddenly.

"Yeah, just tired," I stated simply. Luckily she didn't push the subject further, and I hoped that meant she couldn't see how red my cheeks were.

I allowed myself a glance at Dusane as we all started for the stairs that would lead us back to the streets of the Drego. And to my frustration he looked completely at ease. It was as if nothing had even happened. And for some reason, that made it all so much worse.

NINTEEN

The next morning I lay awake in my bed, having not slept a lick. I'd been up all night, tossing and turning, mentally replaying what happened with Dusane over and over again. I was beating myself up, berating myself for being stupid enough to try and kiss him.

I don't know why I did it, but I had to deem that it was because I was going a little insane. And despite the decision I'd made to push Mid from my mind, I couldn't help but feel sort of guilty. But I had to remind myself: I had nothing to feel guilty for. Mid and I weren't in a relationship and nothing had even happened between Dusane and I . . .

Rouix had already left the room thirty minutes earlier, and I was now alone in the room, staring up at the ceiling. Light showered in from the only window in the room, and I could feel the need to get out of bed. I put a hand to my forehead, dreading having to face Dusane in the fields during training.

I finally forced myself to get up and change my clothes. I was just walking out the bedroom door when I ran into someone. I could feel warm, bare skin, as our bodies collided, and I recoiled quickly.

"I'm so sorry," I said, jumping back, only to see Conland shirtless and grinning.

"Well, good morning," he said lewdly, winking at me.

"Conland," I glared, while trying to push past him, but he quickly stepped in front of me, hindering my escape.

"Hey, just so you know, my door's always open," he looked down at me with pure flirtation in his eyes.

"In your dreams," I said, rolling my eyes at him.

"Conland, let her go." The voice came unexpectedly from down the hallway, and I saw Dusane walking out of his room. He hadn't left yet for the Foundations Field. I wanted to crumble in embarrassment. I didn't want to see him yet. I wasn't prepared to face the shame I felt.

"I was just kidding, Dusane. No need to get all protective." Conland stepped aside, and I gratefully slid past him.

"Ehren." I was almost to the stairs when Dusane had said my name. I froze in my tracks, fear rippling through me. It took all my will power to turn around and face him.

"Yes?" I said, unable to fully meet his eyes.

"Don't go to the field. Meet me downstairs. We're doing something else for training today."

I quickly nodded and hurried down the stairs, eager to be free of the awkwardness now looming in the hallway.

As I appeared in the dining hall, other Envorydians were huddled around getting ready to leave for training. I found Rouix sitting at a table eating her morning apple.

"Hey, Rouix," I said, while sliding into the seat next to her.

"Hey, training starts in five minutes, want to walk with me?"

"Apparently Dusane is taking me somewhere else today. A training exercise," I explained. Rouix nodded in understanding, but I could have sworn I saw jealousy flicker in her eyes. *Did she know about what happened last night?* I quickly shook away that thought. *No, he wouldn't have told her. Plus, he hadn't even wanted to kiss me. Nothing happened.*

"Well, I'll see you after then." Rouix stood from the table and headed out the door. Most all the others followed after her, and soon the house was completely empty. I waited impatiently in my seat for Dusane, panicking a little at having to go somewhere and train alone with him.

When he came down from the stairs, I jumped a little. He went to the bar and grabbed himself a cup of water. He sipped it slowly then calmly walked over to where I was sitting.

"You ready?" he asked, his cold cerulean eyes assessing me. He seemed to be acting just as he always did.

"Where are we going?" I asked.

"The stables," he said.

~

I had yet to visit the stables. I didn't even know there was an Envoy stable and was shocked when we came through the trees and it came into view. It was about another five-minute walk from the main training field and just as big in size. A vast barn came into view, three times the size of the Academy. It was structured from scrap metal like everything else in the Courts. It must've been large enough to house dozens of animals. Open pastures surrounded the large barn with an assortment of fenced off pens that housed many animals. Some of them were ones I knew, others were species I had never seen before. I noted several Envorydians wandering about, working or training with the animals.

"What are we doing here?"

"After watching the fight last night, I realized we had yet to do any training with animals. I figured we could come to the stables today, and you could pick out one to use for your training "

"I haven't seen any animals in the Envoy before," I stated, still confused by the stable's existence. *What need did they have for animals like these?*

"That's because most of us live at the house and are within walking distance of the Drego. But we all have animals. We use them in Galloway fights sometimes, and we have them as an Envoy custom."

"What custom?"

"Every Envorydian has an animal." It sounded so simple when Dusane said it. I followed after him, curious to learn more.

We entered the large barn and inside were rows and rows of stalls. We passed by several before stopping at one. I peered through the bars only to find a lion sleeping lazily on its side in a bed of straw. It was a female lion with glistening tan fur. As Dusane unlatched the stall door, the lion fluttered open her eyes and when she saw who had come, shook out her fur and loped over to Dusane.

"Ehren, this is Elesame." The lion let out a throaty huff and brushed lovingly up against Dusane's side. He greeted her just as warmly, petting her as she nudged him.

"She's beautiful," I murmured, a little awe struck by the creature.

"Dusane! What a pleasant surprise to see you here!" The voice echoed off the barn's tall ceilings, and we both turned to see a man walking toward us. He was of shorter stature with dirty blonde hair and dark brown eyes. A faint red pulsing glowed beneath his chest. He had tattoos running up his arms and I noticed one among them to be the Envorydian symbol. He had hooked to his shoulder a little brown monkey. The creature clung to the man, eyeing Dusane and I curiously.

"Lisle, I'm glad to see you here." Dusane stepped away from Elesame and walked over to greet the man.

"Who might this be?" The man turned toward me, eyeing me skeptically with his brown eyes.

"This is Ehren. Ehren meet Lisle." Dusane gestured between us, and Lisle gave me a small smile in return.

"What brings you to the stables?"

I watched in curiosity as the monkey jumped from one shoulder to the other, his tail wrapping around his owner's neck affectionately.

"Ehren here has just joined the guild. We are looking to find an animal to train with for the Regal," Dusane said easily. I was a little startled when Dusane said I'd joined the guild, but maybe it was just easier than explaining my complicated entanglement with the Envorydians.

"Lovely, well I have some new animals out in the fields we can go take a look if you'd like," Lisle offered, gesturing toward the fenced off field behind him.

"That would be great," Dusane said. After saying goodbye to Elesame, Dusane and I followed after Lisle. My eyes wandered around curiously, taking in all the beautiful animals as we walked. I saw jungle cats, Crykon horses, large wolves, and more. The animals ranged from common to extremely rare and exotic, and they were all incredibly beautiful.

Soon we arrived at a gated off section of land surrounded by a wall of thick jungle trees. Inside the fenced area were several animals grazing peacefully.

Dusane walked up to the edge and rested his elbows on the railing. I took up the same position and watched Lisle's disposition change as he easily slipped into a more business-like character, pointing to several animals in the fields.

"I've got several that might work for the girl. I have a very gentle Crykon, a well behaved wolf that is eager for a companion, and a beautiful white tiger that might be to your liking. All are very well natured and would make great companions."

As Lisle droned on about which animals he had, I found myself getting distracted by a loud noise coming from farther down the field. The commotion caught my eye, and my focus was quickly altered.

It was a lonely round pen, with a black creature inside. The animal was leaping into the air, again and again. It took me a couple minutes to see that it was attempting to escape. The black creature had wings, and would leap into the air, flapping its wings erratically and then reach a peak almost as if it was hitting an invisible barrier, and then come back down to the ground moments later.

"What is that?" I asked, not realizing I'd said it aloud until the two men turned toward me.

"What are you looking at?" Lisle asked. When I pointed to the pen in the distance he chuckled darkly to himself. "That is a new residence we just received. Particularly wild and uncooperative. You don't want him for a companion."

"What is it?" the creature was a blurry mass as it recklessly flapped around the pen. Making a raucous that was impossible to ignore.

"A pegasi," Lisle said easily, then he resumed talking to Dusane again.

I watched the black animal fly into the air again, neighing in frustration. I'd seen only a couple of winged horses in the Drego, but compared to the ones I'd seen, this one was utterly magnificent. A set of chains wrapped around the horse's neck and legs, the force that was keeping it from flying away. But despite the chains preventing the Pegasi from escaping, the poor creature continued to hurt itself against the confines of the black unyielding chains. I immediately felt sorry for the animal and wished I could set it free.

Dusane urged my focus back over to him, and I had to tear my eyes away from the pegasi. They both decided to start with the wolf, and together we walked into the gated area where it was being kept.

The wolf trotted over to us, and I noticed it was a beautiful gray-brown color, and had bright red eyes.

"This is Mera," Lisle said, gesturing to the wolf. The monkey on Lisle's shoulder made a squeaking noise as if scared of the animal.

I stared at the wolf, a little afraid as well. Something about wolves was off-putting to me. The creature whined and came over to sniff my hands and feet. I froze in place, unsure what to do. Soon the wolf's tail began to wag, and it let out a loud howl.

"I think she likes you," Lisle said, appraising the canine with a wide smile.

"She does?" I asked warily. I couldn't get past the sharp teeth, and the way she pushed her head against my hand to pet her.

"Ehren, are you scared of wolves?" Dusane suddenly asked, obviously noticing the way I was reacting to the animal.

I looked over at Dusane with wide eyes. "A little, I think," I admitted.

"Let's try another one then, shall we." Lisle quickly amended the situation and started for the next creature. He showed us the tiger, but I wasn't any less uneasy around the tiger than the wolf, and it didn't really take a liking toward me. Then we observed the Crykon, and it was decided that that was probably the best fit. The Crykon was named Faella, and had a more purplish scaly hue than other Crykon horses I'd seen. She had scales on her entire hindquarters and beautiful swirling fins shooting from her mane. Crykon were enchanting creatures. They could swim in the water without any problems but could also be on land. They mostly lived in more humid parts of the realm and liked being near water.

As gentle and beautiful as the creature was though, I couldn't help but think about Tassadar. I'd had nightmares of the Crykon horses he and his comrades had ridden in an attempt to kidnap me. I shivered at the memory.

"You can come visit her whenever you need. She's yours now," Lisle said as we began walking back toward the barn. The sun was high in the sky now. It was probably late afternoon. Choosing an animal had taken longer than I'd expected.

The little monkey was now asleep on Lisle's shoulder.

"We'll be back tomorrow to do animal combat training. She'll need to learn how to defend an attacker that is riding and also defend from in the saddle," Dusane explained.

"I'll see you tomorrow then." Lisle waved to us as we walked away, and the stables faded into the distance behind us.

TWENTY

The next morning we returned to the stables and the almost kiss seemed to be completely forgotten, which I was grateful for. Dusane didn't treat me any differently, and things had already turned back to normal.

Dusane took Elesame from her stall, and Lisle helped me retrieve Faella. Lisle showed us to an open field where Dusane could train me.

"Are people allowed animals in the Regal?" I asked Dusane, as I mounted the Crykon. The beautiful creature was stable, steady, and didn't seem bothered at all when I mounted her back.

"We won't know the rules until the day of. You could potentially be allowed an animal, other times it's prohibited. It all depends on the mood they're in," he explained. "We need to be prepared for anything, because it's all unknown, and we don't want you to be caught by surprise."

I nodded, realizing more and more that the Regal was going

to be difficult. I didn't know what to expect and. It was like the Commission wanted it that way.

"We'll practice fighting with the height difference, and the new variable of having Faella." Dusane launched into a whole lesson on fighting while on horseback. We practiced with a variety of weapons. Sometimes he even charged at me while on Elesame to make a realistic situation. Over and over again, we played out possible scenarios. I had to learn to maneuver my weapons with completely different dynamics, and I became exhausted, using muscles I'd never used before.

Dusane went on to teach me how to fight a big creature, one like the Lichabra. And I tried not to think about the possibility of fighting such a vicious creature. I listened closely to Dusane's words, trying to make sure I retained as much information as possible.

A couple hours passed by and the sun began to go down. Dusane allowed me to take a break, seeing that I was dripping with sweat. I gratefully walked over to a shady spot by the barn and sat down with exhaustion. I lifted my canteen to my lips and sipped eagerly. I couldn't wait to fall asleep, have my muscles heal from the training efforts, and then convert what I learned to muscle memory. I always felt stronger waking up the day after a hard day of training.

I was abruptly pulled from my thoughts when I heard a sudden chorus of yelling. I turned to see a group of Envorydians passing by the barn. They were each holding a chain firmly in their hands tugging at the creature they had constrained. It was the black pegasi.

He was in obvious distress. Thick iron chains clamped his wings down. The Envorydains struggled as the creature kicked and thrashed against their confines. They yelled to one another to pull tighter, desperate to not let go.

The poor thing was neighing and thrashing against the chains. His majestic black feathered feet stomped the ground with incredible force. It was the most beautiful creature I had ever seen.

I dropped my canteen and ran over to them.

"Hey, stop! You're hurting him!" I yelled, but my voice was barely heard among the arguing and loud neighing from the creature. "Stop, please!" Without thinking, I stepped directly in front of the pegasi. What happened next occurred so quickly I didn't have time to process that I was in danger.

He reared up on his hind legs, and stretched his wings out several feet in each direction.

I should be running, I thought. *I need to move out of the way.* But I stared up in awe at the wild horse, not worried about myself, just needing his distress to be eased. His front hooves slammed back down to the ground, landing maybe a couple inches from where I stood.

"Get out of the way! You'll get yourself killed!" The other Envorydians screamed at me, but their voices faded to background noise when I locked eyes with the creature.

His eyes were black as midnight and filled with a wild fire that resonated with my soul. The pegasi had stilled, his attempt at escaping suddenly halted.

"Easy," I said, not really knowing if it would be possible to calm him, but I needed to try. Sweat gleamed in wet streaks down his neck and I reached out a shaking hand to gently stroke his warm nose. He was burning up, his black fur absorbing all the afternoon's heat.

"Shhh, it's okay," I whispered, gently stroking his nose.

Though he stood suddenly still, every muscle remained taut with rigidness. When I turned to look at the other Envorydians, the shock was evident on all their faces. Some had dropped their chains, stunned by what they saw.

I took one of the chains from one of the Envorydians standing next to me. "Why don't you come with me," I urged the creature. I very carefully unhooked all the other iron confines from his wings. He twitched with unease while I worked to get the chains off of him, but he didn't try and run. Then with as much courage as I could muster, I gently tugged for him to follow me.

Surprisingly the creature stepped forward. I could feel he was a little wary, jumping slightly as he stepped on a large rock in the grass. But he didn't try to fly away, didn't try to fight against me. He simply followed, and I was grateful he had decided to cooperate.

When I came up to the gate where Dusane was waiting, Lisle was suddenly there beside him. They both appeared to have seen what happened.

Absolute shock was written on Lisle's features, and Dusane had a smug smile on his lip.

"Well Lisle, I guess we won't be needing Faella after all."

TWENTY-ONE

The connection I felt with the black pegasi was something I'd never experienced before. After calming down the horse, he didn't seem to want to leave my side.

"He's chosen you," Dusane explained. We were in the field now. The pegasi stood easily beside me. He seemed to have calmed down, the anxiety gone from his eyes.

"What does that mean?" I asked, reaching out to stroke his soft nose again. He huffed, and nudged my hand as if wanting more.

"I don't have much more explanation other than that he chose you, and you chose him. Some animals can just sense the person they want to follow, and once they find that person they are loyal unconditionally. It's nature."

"So he's my companion now?" I asked for clarification.

"According to our Envorydian guild, yes, he is your animal

companion," Dusane shook his head a little like he still couldn't believe his eyes.

"So can I ride him?" I asked suddenly, looking to the spot behind the pegasi's wings. A thrill of excitement threaded through me at the idea of being able to fly on such a magnificent animal.

"I'm unsure if he's been ridden before, but we can try." Dusane came to stand by the large wings expanding from the horses back. "You want to?" He was sincerely asking me if I wanted to risk it. This pegasi could be dangerous if I tried to mount him. He could easily throw me, but something in me trusted him.

I nodded firmly. "Yes, I want to try."

Dusane nodded and offered me a helping hand as I swung up onto the creature. I fit snugly on top of him, his soft black fur a comfortable cushion. I could feel him breathing beneath me, powerful and strong. I waited for him to take off running and try to throw me, but nothing happened. He remained completely still, his ears merely flickering back and forth as I became situated on his back. I gripped his mane in my hands and held on tightly to the dark ebony strands. Then Dusane jumped up behind me and reached around to also hold some of the pegasi's mane in his hands.

"He should be an intelligent creature, guided easily if he's being cooperative. Gently tug on the mane in the direction you wish to go. If you want to fly, simply kick his sides and pull upwards on his mane," Dusane explained easily.

"Have you done this before?" I asked hesitantly, wondering how he knew so much.

"Once or twice," he said, and I could hear faint amusement in his tone, as if there was a story I had yet to hear.

Taking in a deep breath, I gathered my courage and gently squeezed the pegasi's sides, and pulled upwards on his mane. Without any delay, he recognized the signal and leaped into the air.

The wind quickly rushed past my face and initiated a loud howling in my ears. Strands of my hair began whipping in the wind, dancing around my face erratically. I stared wide eyed, not believing the sights surrounding me as the pegasi's wings quickly lifted us several hundred feet off the ground in a matter of seconds. Soon the stable was just a speck, and I could see above the entire jungle.

I let out a little panicked squeak as we continued to soar, clutching tightly to the pegasi's mane.

"You're okay, relax," Dusane shouted over the noise of the wind and the beating thrum of the pegasi's wings. He gently squeezed my shoulder in reassurance. I relaxed a little, but not entirely, trying to calm my racing heartbeat.

I spotted the Drego in the distance, and the Commission headquarters up on the hill. The walls that surrounded the entire length of the Courts were utterly magnificent in size, and I stared in awe at the scenery.

"What's keeping us from flying away from here?" I yelled. We were climbing higher and higher into the sky. With ease, we could have slipped over the circular barricade around the prison.

"A shield above the Courts keeps anything from leaving. It's made from Stone-Hearted magic so you can't see it, but it keeps the prisons enclosed, so stay relatively close to this height. You won't want to go too high," Dusane cautioned. I looked up but I could see nothing preventing an escape. A magnificent purple sky with patches of pumpkin-hued flecks stretched endlessly above us. I shivered, not wanting to know what could happen if we accidently ran into the invisible barrier Dusane spoke of.

I shifted my focus back down at the Courts below and butterflies filled my stomach. Now that the initial shock had settled, I didn't feel so afraid. Up so high, looking down at everything, I felt peaceful, free even. The hot wind continued to blow through my hair, and I closed my eyes for a moment, basking in the exhilarating, energizing feeling that was rippling through my veins. Dusane had wrapped one of his arms around my waist, making sure when the pegasi veered left or right that we stayed securely in place. I was relaxed with his strong arms around me, certain that I wasn't in any danger. The Pegasi slowed its wings, and soon we were riding the wind, drifting through the tropical air.

"Are you going to tell me that story now?" At a slower pace the wind was less wild, and conversation was easier.

"What story?" He asked.

"You know, the one about how you learned to ride a pegasi?" I pressed, barely containing a smile.

Dusane chuckled. "Oh that one. Well, it was when I first arrived here. As you may know, in the kingdoms rare creatures aren't really allowed. I'd always wanted to know what it was like to fly and so I sort of borrowed one. . ."

"Borrowed?"

"They are hard creatures to come by in the Courts and none of the other Envorydians owned one. So I decided one night after a Galloway fight, that I'd just borrow one."

"You stole someone's pegasi?" My mouth fell open.

"Just for a night," he tried to reason.

I shook my head. "I can't believe that." My utter shock gradually dissipated into laughter.

"What can't you believe?"

"That you'd be the type of person to steal from someone!"

"Well, there are alot of things you don't know about me."

It was true. I didn't know much about Dusane. There were still so many things I needed to discover. But every little tiny piece of the puzzle I put together only made me want to know more about who he was.

"Can I ask you something else?" I asked.

"Sure."

I bit my lip, debating if I should ask him.

"Theon told me once about the Envorydians and how some chose to come to the Courts rather than be under royal reign. Did you choose to come here?"

There was a long stretch of silence from Dusane, the gentle flap of the pegasi's wings the only noise for a moment.

"No, I didn't choose to come here. I used to be an Envorydian for the Obscurum Royal Guard." I remembered Dusane telling me about his father who had once worked for Obscurum, and how he'd been the one to train him in the Envorydian techniques.

"How did you end up here?"

Dusane chuckled darkly behind me. "It's a long story," he said, not expounding.

"I've got time," I whispered. Even though I thought for sure the breeze drowned out my reply, he suddenly sighed and continued on.

"Well, I did something to make the king very angry with me."

"What did you do?"

"There was a servant girl that lived at the castle in Obscurum. Her name was Amara. I saw her often because each Envorydian was required to take watch over the king for at least two days during the week and she was always waiting on him. One night when it was my shift to guard the king, he began taunting Amara. He said many suggestive, profane things to her. She was helpless to deflect the comments. If she even considered defending herself she would have been imprisoned or worse, killed. And let's just say, I didn't let him get very far with his redolent comments," Dusane growled.

"You were put in prison for that?" I asked, completely appalled. He had merely been defending a helpless girl.

"The Stone-Hearted that are considered less powerful in our society aren't treated very fairly. In other kingdoms it's not so bad, but in Obscurum or Severesi, the color spectrum can mean life or death for some. Her heart was red, and when I defended her, I was defending her lowly position. And the king didn't like that," Dusane said darkly.

I thought back to when he'd taught me about the colors and how each one determined a Stone-Hearted's level of power. It was unfair to only look at the color of someone's heart and decide their worth. I'd heard him say once, "That's just how it is in our society." But I didn't want to believe that.

"I'm sorry. . ." I didn't know what else to say. I had no power to go back in time and fix the wrong doings that he or that girl had endured.

"It's all right. I'm content. My people are here in the Courts, and that's all I can ask for," he said softly, the anger evaporating from his tone.

"Dusane, I want to thank you. For training me," I blurted out suddenly.

"No need to thank me. It's been good for me to observe such a unique Stone-Hearted individual."

"So I'm just an experiment then?" I asked, laughing slightly. But I was only partly teasing.

"No, you're not just an experiment. . ." Dusane trailed off, almost as if he couldn't find any more words. I thought for sure he wasn't going to continue, but then suddenly he spoke again. "You're different, Ehren, and I hope one day I get to know more about why."

He seemed to be troubled over my secret identity. I wondered if he'd be disappointed when he found out I was the princess of Aveladon. It sort of scared me actually that I'd be viewed as less of a fighter because of my past. I wanted Dusane to see that I was a capable warrior, and I couldn't help but think my title as Princess Sabeara would somehow taint that cognomen.

"I hate to diminish your hopes, but who I was before all of this was really not that interesting," I snorted.

"For some reason I doubt that," he said thoughtfully.

The sun was almost completely gone, and I realized our ride would soon need to come to an end.

"We should head back," I said, feeling reluctant to conclude our little flying adventure.

"Land back in the fields, by the barn," Dusane directed.

We flew back down on the wind, quickly eating up the distance to the stables. It was a swift landing as the pegasi expertly loped to a standstill. Dusane helped me down off of the Pegasi's back, and I felt a little wobbly when my feet hit the ground. I gathered my bearings and then carefully led the creature to an uninhabited stall in the barn. He seemed reluctant to see me leave and let out a sad whinney when I closed the stall door behind me.

"I'll be back soon, I promise," I told him, while gently petting the long fetlock that fell into his midnight black eyes.

"What are you going to name him?" Dusane suddenly asked beside me. I thought about his question for a moment, eyeing the creature carefully.

And then it suddenly came to me. A name that fit the wild pegasi and his untamed spirit.

"I think I'll name him . . . Diablo."

TWENTY-TWO

Loud yelling and sudden hooting shouts jolted me from my dreams. The door to the bedroom slammed open, causing the walls to shake. I sat up in my bed, not quite registering what was happening.

Several people filled my bedroom. It was dark, nearly pitch black, and fear pumped through my veins at the sight of them. Their faces were painted, and I couldn't make out anyone in the darkness.

"It's time for Ehren's initiation!" A voice yelled above the others. "Are you ready to join the guild little E?" I recognized the voice, and the nickname was impossible to miss. Conland.

I was so perplexed, and a little terrified. My mind was still reeling with the sudden intrusion. I was barely awake. But I didn't get to reply, didn't get to call out to Rouix who was in the room with me, before one of the face painted Envorydians reached and picked me up out of my bed and slung me over his shoulder. I squealed in surprise, and soon I was being carried from the room. The riled group moved together, taking me down the stairs and out into the tropical night air.

"Let me down!" I protested, trying and failing to escape from the grasp of the person now carrying me.

"Hold still, E, or I'm gonna drop you if you keep wiggling like that." Conland was obviously the one carrying me, and realizing I was not going to be able fight him, I stilled in defeat. I watched the dirt forest floor from my upside down position over Conland's shoulder, trying not to be afraid of where they were taking me.

The group continued to shout excitedly, aflame with some sort of rash, rowdy energy.

"Please, Conland," I tried to say, but my pleas were quickly muted by all the shouting. I was going to have to suffer through whatever initiation ceremony they had in store for me. I groaned aloud.

Soon Conland stopped, and then I was suddenly right-side up again. The floor met my feet, and I swayed unsteadily at the unexpected landing.

"Form the circle!" Conland commanded. The symbol painted on their faces made it almost impossible to pick out anyone I knew in the deep black of the night. So far I had only recognized Conland, his voice easily distinctive.

The Envorydians formed a circle surrounding me, and I looked around, trying to figure out where we were. We weren't in the trees now. We had stepped out into a clearing that was unfamiliar to me. It wasn't the fields. There was no grass beneath my feet. Instead, I felt tiny pebbles pushing through the spaces in my toes. Frantically, I looked behind me and spotted through the wall of individuals a reflected shimmer of water in the distance. We were at a lake, and I could only imagine what fate awaited me.

"All right, everyone, quiet down. Let the captain speak." Suddenly all the murmuring from the group was silenced. I could hear the quiet lapping of the lake's waves hitting the shore, and the clicking hum of the insects in the trees. My breathing was short and rapid amidst my nervous thoughts. I was dressed in nothing but a scant tank top and shorts. I wrapped my arms around myself, feeling all too exposed even though the darkness mostly shadowed me.

Someone else stepped forward, breaking the perfect circle they'd created. I watched hesitantly as the individual walked toward me. And it wasn't until he was a couple feet in front of me that I recognized who it was.

Cerulean eyes, deep and intense, locked on mine. I could see the faint glow of his amethyst heart, and I instantly knew it was Dusane. The Envorydian symbol was painted across his face and the color of his eyes was a striking contrast.

"As tradition when entering the guild, we must appoint you as an Envorydian. If you accept the invitation, please repeat after me."

It was deathly silent as the others waited for me to answer. Frozen and a little stunned, I merely nodded in understanding. Dusane continued on.

"Say—I Ehren, promise to be a sister to all my Envoy family. Protect them and protect the realm."

I quickly repeated the words, stumbling a little.

"Say—I will stay true to the techniques and values of the guild. No matter the situation. And lastly I will maintain peace. 'Peace through the heart.'"

After I finished echoing the theme to them, the silence of the circle erupted into loud cheers and an uneasiness filled me. Somehow I just knew it wasn't over yet.

"You must now be cleansed," Dusane said, and I realized with horror that he was going to throw me into the lake. I looked into his fierce blue eyes, seeing they were completely serious. Our nearly identical heights made it easy to equally assess one another.

My eyes narrowed.

"You wouldn't," I said, my voice almost a whisper. Despite all the boisterousness coming from those in the circle around us, it felt suddenly as if it was just us two. Our quiet conversation was isolated amongst the outside commotion. He didn't say anything for a moment, then his lips pulled up into a smirk.

"Oh yes I would," he challenged. I'd never seen Dusane smirk like that. It was taunting and flirtatiously provoking.

My eyes widened, and before I could protest, he had me over his shoulder.

"Dusane! No, no, no!" The circle parted, and suddenly he was striding toward the water with me in tow. I could hear the immediate change when we left the softness of the sand and started onto a dock. His boots tapped rhythmically across the wood and I watched with anxiety from over his shoulder at the weathered slats as we neared the water.

"Please, don't do this!" I shrieked, not wanting to be submerged into the inky blackness. I could smell damp lake grass and the pungent smell of fish. And I couldn't help but fear dangerous creatures that might be lingering beneath the dark waters.

We came to the end of the dock, and swiftly, with an unexpected gracefulness, Dusane lifted me from his shoulder and into his arms. He was suddenly cradling me, easily holding me against him.

The taunting yells from the other Envorydians were still a loud chorus on the beach.

I looked up into his eyes, and for a moment we just stared at each other. I knew I should keep struggling, but I was frozen by his enigmatic expression.

He leaned down, pressing his lips to my ear. "Take a deep breath," he whispered.

And then I was falling. The drop made my stomach do flips, and suddenly the water was surrounding me. It encased me in it's warm embrace, and I was grateful to find the water wasn't cold. I sunk down and felt for the bottom. When my feet met the rocky floor of the lake, I quickly pushed off it and swam up to the surface. As my head broke the water, I looked over to the dock to see the group of Envorydians standing together. They cheered some more, and then others began jumping in too.

Realizing that the worst was over, I found myself laughing. I swam back to shore and stepped from the water just as the sun began breaking over the horizon.

I layed on the sand and allowed my heartbeat to regulate. Slowly the sky turned from black, to dark blue to a light pink.

"You survived," Rouix's sweet, musical voice came from beside me, and I sat up to see her take a seat next to me. I should've known she'd be a part of it too. She was wet from jumping into the lake, and the water had washed the paint from her face.

"I wasn't expecting that," I admitted.

She laughed, and the sound was musically sweet."I'm glad to have another girl in the Envoy. I was getting tired of only having boys around," she joked, gesturing to the playful fighting that was going on in the water.

"Thanks, Rouix," I said sincerely. I was glad to see she approved and that she didn't seem to be harboring any resentment toward me. I must've imagined that look of jealousy in her eyes the other day.

"I'll see you back at the house?" she asked, standing from the sand. I nodded and then watched her disappear into the trees.

Eventually the others left the water too. Envorydians passed by me on their way back to the Academy, congratulating me on my acceptance into the guild. Conland and Dusane were the last to exit the water. I didn't see Theon or Shar yet and expected that they hadn't been invited. I could just imagine Shar's moodiness being an obstacle to an event like this, and Theon being too loyal to leave him behind.

"Sorry I had to kidnap you, E," Conland teased as he came walking up the beach. He didn't sound remotely apologetic.

"I would say I would get back at you, but somehow I don't think I'll be able to do that," I admitted.

"I'd let you kidnap me any time," he winked and I rolled my eyes at his innuendo.

"Get out of here," I said jokingly. He chuckled then disappeared into the trees after the others.

It was quiet then, and a sudden awkwardness filled the air. Dusane was the last one on the beach, and he carefully took a seat next to me. His hair was wet and slicked back away from his forehead. The paint was gone from his face, and his eyelashes dripped with water droplets. He looked over at me, and there was a brightness in his eyes that didn't usually exist.

"Are you mad?" he asked suddenly and I watched his lips twitch with the hint of a smile.

"A little," I admitted.

"So how does it feel to be one of us now?" he asked.

"Honestly, great. But there's just one thing missing still," I said, and Dusane's expression turned puzzled.

"What?"

"I don't have the tattoo," I said, gesturing to the little ink symbol behind his ear. He chuckled aloud, the same deep husky chuckle I'd heard only a couple times before, and the sound made my heart flutter.

"Another day, how about that?" he said, and it was one of the rare times I'd seen him so lighthearted. The emotionless, neutral facade he usually maintained had slipped away. And for a moment, I could see underneath it all. Witnessing what was hidden beneath made me realize I craved this side of him. It was unpredictable and incredibly attractive. I wondered why he hid behind the hard, emotionless personality he so readily displayed.

"You never told me you were the captain of the guild," I suddenly blurted. I'd heard Conland say the title during the initiation.

"Captain Nevrair at your service," He said mockingly. "I've told them many times I don't want to be the captain. But Conland can be annoyingly persistent."

"I can tell they look up to you," I said, remembering the way Conland and Rouix had both told me to ask Dusane to train me instead of themselves. It seemed they held him to a higher standard.

"The guild isn't really supposed to have a captain. We all are equal to one another," Dusane said.

I thought about all the times I had seen Dusane with the Envorydians. He wasn't a flashy character and wasn't flaunting the position he held. Honestly, if Conland hadn't said anything, I wouldn't have known. But maybe that was what made him a good leader. His modest and humble nature.

"So what are we doing for training today, Captain Nevrair," I teased, a thrill going through me at using his last name. He ignored the comment and simply continued on like he usually did when I made teasing remarks.

"The Regal fight is next week. We need to finish polishing some of your skills," he said. The news hit me harder than I expected it to. A week wasn't far away. *Had another three months passed so quickly?*

"Is it really so close?" I whispered and Dusane nodded reluctantly.

"Are you sure you want to do this?" he asked suddenly.

I turned to look out at the lake, thinking quietly to myself for a moment. "I know what I want Dusane." My words were confident and certain. I prepared for some sort of pushback, but he didn't question it further.

"Then I'll see you in the fields in an hour. Go clean up. You smell like fish," he stood up, and I watched his nose wrinkle in disgust. I stood up beside him, and dusted off the sand from my sleep shorts.

"Hey, you smell like fish too," I accused, eyeing his soaked shirt and trousers.

He smiled a little at my rebounded allegation."Then I guess we should both go get cleaned up."

We walked quietly back toward the house until the lake faded behind us, becoming a twinkling speck in the distance.

TWENTY-THREE

I was suddenly cold. Something I wasn't used to since being in the Courts. It wasn't the hot humid atmosphere I usually endured. Snow surrounded me, and I was in an alabaster blanketed meadow. Not a tree in sight. The sky stretched on endlessly overhead, nothing but whiteness. Not a single tree or bird greeted me. I took several steps into the freshly fallen powder and laid three delicate footprints in the pale perfectness.

"Little Bear," the voice called. I whipped around, the sudden echo of my nickname causing goosebumps to erupt down my spine and not from the cold.

I spotted him suddenly in the distance, his dark brown cloak a stark contrast with the snow.

"Mid?" I called back, uncertain if it was really him. The hood was up, shrouding the face beneath the cloak. He came closer until he was finally within recognizable distance. I already knew it was him as he began lifting the hood from his head.

His emerald-scarlet eyes met mine, and I felt something in my chest wrench painfully. A surge of unfamiliar, bruised feelings, pierced me and I gasped for breath. It had been so long, like an eternity it seemed.

"It's me, Sabeara," he said gently, taking another step toward me. A gentle breeze picked up, and I could smell his pine scent just as distinctly as if he was really with me.

But then just like when he'd been with me at that waterfall, an invisible line seemed to be stretched between us. One he was unable to cross. He didn't come any closer. He seemed frustrated that he couldn't.

"Mid, what are you doing here?" I asked. Seeing him reminded me once again just how much I missed him. I needed to regain control. . . control. That was the center of an Envorydian. And with Mid every single lesson of discipline was quickly consumed in a wave of unstoppable feelings.

"You can't win this fight Sabeara, let me save you," he said gently, coaxing me, urging me.

"I can do this Mid. You have to trust me," I pleaded with him, hoping he would understand.

"Sabeara you're aren't strong enough. . ." Already the dream began to slip away. I felt an urgency to fight against the dream, to stay with him. But I knew I couldn't.

"I'm strong enough, Mid. I'm strong enough!" I called to him just as the white, snowy landscape disappeared completely, and I woke from the dream.

I had gotten used to the nightmares. But dreams of Mid. . . they were so much harder to shake. I woke with a start, much like the time I'd had the first dream about Mid. It took me several minutes to calm down.

Every night the same nightmare would occur. The dark sitting room and the blank faces. I had gotten used to it by now. It was no longer scary, more like a nuisance. I hadn't dreamed of Mid since that one night several months ago, and I assumed I was getting better at suppressing my feelings. But it seemed I wasn't doing so well after all. As much as I hated the consistent, confusing nightmare with no faces, I was less afraid of it then dreams about Mid. Maybe my subconsciousness was trying to warn me about tomorrow.

It was the day before the Regal, and as dawn broke the sky, I left my room. The dream I'd had had set me on edge, and I needed to burn off some steam.

When I entered the fields, the other Envorydians hadn't arrived yet. I wasn't surprised to see Dusane already setting up. He always got up before everyone else.

"Ehren, it's a little early. . ."

"I know. But I wanna do a couple exercises before the others come," I interrupted, not in the mood to explain. He paused from setting up an archery target and seemed to finally understand that something was wrong.

He nodded and then gestured toward the equipment around us. "Where do you want to start?"

"Hand-to-hand combat," I said, jumping into the ring, already bouncing up and down to warm my muscles.

He carefully slipped through the fence rungs and eyed me suspiciously. "Ehren, are you all right?"

"Yes, I"m fine," I stated, but images of Mid in that snowy landscape still hadn't left my head. And to make things worse, I couldn't stop thinking about the Regal and what awaited me tomorrow.

"It might be a good idea to take a break before the fight."

"I don't need a break, Dusane. Now, can you please just get in here so I can practice?"

His eyes narrowed slightly, not liking my tone. But at that moment, I didn't care that I was mouthing off to him. I hoped he'd push his frustration into the fight. I really needed to hit something at that moment.

He didn't say another word as he took up a combat stance across from me, readying himself.

I didn't hesitate. I took an instant jab to his face. He deflected it easily, his movements smooth and calculated. Dusane's skill was uncanny. I wouldn't want anyone else in the ring with me. He challenged me, but he was also teaching me with every movement. He didn't want to just end the fight and prove his dominance. He deflected, jabbed, and side stepped, in ways that allowed me to use the skills I had. And each one of his movements taught me something so that I would be better. It was from him that I learned that being a great fighter didn't mean just having the ability to beat someone up.

I moved harder and faster than I ever had before, my mind occupied by dark thoughts that morning. The thoughts of the fight were taking over. Images of Mid right alongside them, only added fuel to the fire.

I faltered a step and it was a step that I wouldn't have usually missed. Dusane wasn't even expecting it and his fist nailed my side, taking my breath away for a moment.

"Focus, Ehren," he ordered, not slowing his speed even a little. I grit my teeth together, throwing my fists faster, trying to shove the distractions from my mind. My breathing became ragged, the internal battle inside of me as difficult as the physical one I was currently participating in.

What if Mid was right, what if I wasn't strong enough? What if I fail the others during the fight? What if I lose? I needed to be completely focused. This fight was my chance, to show Shar I could help him with the curse, and to earn my freedom. I knew someone would come for me if I didn't end up winning, but that would be worse than losing. . .

I stumbled again, my combat stance faltering and allowing Dusane to land another jab on me.

Dusane stopped our fight, his hands reaching out to suddenly clasp my wrists, halting my rash movements. I was breathing heavily, my chest aching with emotion.

"Ehren, stop, look at me."

I could barely focus on Dusane, my vision was blurry with—tears. I blinked them rapidly away, looking away from him ashamed that I'd just used him as a physical punching bag to figure out my emotional problems.

"I said, look at me, Envorydian," his fingers pressed on my chin, firm, yet gentle. And I reluctantly looked back at my trainer. The deep blue of his eyes held me, grounding me.

"I'm sorry," I managed to choke out. His jaw remained set in a firm position.

"You can't allow yourself to lose control like that. You'll make mistakes. And too many mistakes will get you hurt."

"I know," I mumbled, hating that I was breaking right before the fight. This was why I had refused to think of him.

"You're getting in your head."

"I don't know if I can do this—" I started to say, and just like that his hand released my chin and he sighed.

"Come with me," he said.

"What?"

"I said come with me," he repeated, more demanding this time. "Obviously fighting isn't helping."

I followed after him. He first stopped at the Academy, ordered me to stay outside so he could grab something, and then returned with a small brown sack. He didn't say a word as he began leading me away from the house and back into the jungle. We passed the field and kept journeying into the trees similar to the same place we'd walked together after the bonfire. Only we went much farther this time. Eventually, the trees dispersed, and the lake came into view, the one where my initiation had occurred only a week before. He walked up to the edge of the glassy water and settled into the sand. I sat beside him, unsure what we were doing.

He didn't say anything as he dumped out the contents of his bag and then grabbed my left arm with one of his calloused hands. I looked curiously at the small brown bottle halfway submerged in the sand, alongside what looked to be some sort of quill. Dusane grabbed the bottle, unloosened the cap, and then dipped the long black quill into it. When he pulled it out, glistening black ink covered the fine point.

"Wait, what are you doing?" I asked, suddenly panicked as I began to assume what he was about to do.

"I'm giving you a tattoo," he said simply, and before I could pull my arm away the cool sensation of the ink met my skin and I froze. I remained very still then, too afraid I'd bump him and cause a permanent smear to be etched onto my forearm.

"But—"

"Weren't you the one that said you wanted one?"

"I was sort of joking," I said tightly, letting off a nervous laugh. I was staring at his hand as he etched the delicate symbol onto my arm. I thought it would be painful, but it wasn't. It felt just like he was painting, and it tickled more than anything.

"Well, you are one of us now. So you get one whether you like it or not," he said simply.

"What if I didn't want it there," I said, narrowing my eyes at him. But honestly I didn't care where it was. Deep down I knew I just wanted to be accepted by them, and I would've taken the tattoo anywhere. The soft skin of my inner forearm, a couple inches above my wrist, seemed like a good enough place as any.

He didn't respond, and I assumed it was because he was concentrating. After ten minutes he finally let my arm go and put the ink and quill back into his brown pouch. I looked at the stark black symbol now on my arm and was struck with awe admiring the intricate symbol.

"How does it not get rubbed off?"

"The ink has magic properties that make it permanent."

"Who makes the ink?" I asked, fascinated by the way the ink had already dried against my skin.

"Stone-Hearted of course," he said.

"Hmmm. . . the power to make permanent ink, it seems—"

"Unnecessary?" Dusane interjected, and he gave me a soft smile. "Each one of us has a purpose, Ehren. Some powers may seem insignificant in comparison to others. But each one works to help society in some way."

"And you have a purpose too. I can see that you have been trying to prove yourself. And I don't know what was going on in your head back there. But I need you to know—" He paused, and I felt my breath leave me for a moment. He never usually talked this long.

"You are a great Envorydian, and a powerful Stone-Hearted. And even if we don't win that fight tomorrow, you'll still be all of those things."

"But—" I started to protest, but then his hand reached out

and he touched the symbol on my arm again. I suddenly forgot what I was going to say.

"Ehren, trust yourself. Believe in yourself. Because the only person that can ever make you feel worthy is you." His blue eyes remained locked on mine as he gently brushed the symbol with his fingers, and I felt my heart skip a couple times in my chest.

I could do this. I could win tomorrow and prove to Shar that I was strong enough to come with him. I would be free from the Courts and I wouldn't be just a princess anymore, sitting on the sidelines.

He dropped his gaze, and then released my arm. He stood from the ground. I was still recovering from the moment between us when he reached down to help lift me from the sand.

"Thank you," I said, a little breathlessly.

He merely nodded and gestured toward the trees. "Let's go back to the fields, and you can show me a real combat fight."

~

The next morning I traveled to the stables and visited Diablo. No one usually came to the stables at this hour, and the pastures were quiet, the animals barely rousing, or still sleeping.

I sat on the edge of the fence, and Diablo put his nose in my lap. I gently stroked his forehead and looked down at his beautiful black nose. He let out a soft whinny, and I smiled weakly.

"Today is the day," I said to him. Diablo gently fanned out his wings in response, and shook himself a little.

"I know, I'm not ready either," I whispered to him. He wandered away from me, taking up grazing on a patch of grass.

"Dusane said I'd find you out here." The voice startled me

from my pensive thinking. I turned around and saw Theon walking my way.

"Theon," I greeted. His presence was a pleasant surprise.

He took a seat beside me on the fence rail.

"I wanted to wish you luck," he said gently. I sighed and felt my shoulder sag a little. The sun was barely coming over the horizon, its warm yellow light blanketing the jungle trees.

"I don't know if I'm ready, Theon."

"Are you worried that you won't win? And you'll have to stay here?"

"I know that if I don't win alongside the others, my family will come for me." I thought about Oli, my father, and even Jasper. I had no doubt they *would* come for me, eventually. "I'm not afraid of that. I'm more afraid I won't get to prove that I can get out myself." I didn't mention the other fear, that if they came for me, I'd most likely be shoved back into royal life, useless once again.

"Well, if it helps, I think you are ready for this," he said assuredly.

"Are you coming to watch the fight?" I asked hesitantly.

"I couldn't bear to watch my friends fight like that. I'm sorry," he said, disheartened.

"I understand."

"Ehren, I just wanted to say it's been a pleasure watching you become an Envorydian."

I looked over at him, and I couldn't quite read the emotion in his eyes. I wondered if he worried I'd fail, or that I'd get hurt. It sounded almost like he was saying goodbye.

"Thanks for being such a great friend to me, Theon," I said, and then he reached over to hug me gently. His metal arm was cool against my skin, and I felt more emotional than usual at his farewell.

Suddenly it was all too real. The goodbye that awaited me. This place had become a sort of home for me over the last several months, and if all went well, I'd be leaving it behind, hopefully to go on a journey with Shar to find the tokens. It was sad to think I'd probably never see it again.

Theon walked me back to the house a little while later. All the Envorydians were still asleep when we returned. Theon wished me one last goodbye before heading back to his flat, and then I went upstairs to change. Rouix's bed was already made, and she was nowhere to be found. I wondered if she was also out thinking alone before the fight. She was always so sure of herself. It seemed unlikely.

I put on my clothes slowly, taking longer to tie my boots than usual, then braided my short hair tightly against my head the best I could.

The fighting clothes Rouix had supplied me with for the Regal were similar to the ones she wore. Black and sleek. The jumpsuit fit tightly against my body, like a second skin. I thought it might be stifling against the humidity, but the material was surprisingly lightweight and was made of a mesh fabric that offered plenty of ventilation. The combat boots I wore laced up clear to my mid-calf but were pleasantly snug. I gazed at the golden glow in my chest and gently pressed my hand to my heart with a sigh.

Knowing I couldn't stall any longer, I went back downstairs, only to find the kitchen still empty. A little confused, I walked outside, and to my surprise found the others already waiting for me.

Diablo was patiently resting outside in the same place I'd left him, underneath a palm tree. Dusane was beside his lion, Elesame. Rouix was next to Dusane, her beautiful Crykon grazing beside her. Conland was nearly jumping up and down, the most excited in the group, with his companion animal also with him. He had a beautiful tri-colored wolf the size of Diablo with features more fox-like than canine. I'd only seen the creature a couple of times, but it was terrifying enough to make me shiver every time I saw it. Shar was standing a little ways off in the shade. His rather ordinary chestnut gelding grazed beside him.

No one said anything as I descended the steps and mounted Diablo. A silent understanding seemed to pass between all of us and the others followed suit. Then we turned to Shar. He sighed, his piercing green eyes meeting each of our gazes, then he gently nodded his head.

"Let's go."

~

The fight was scheduled for noon. When we arrived at the Galloway it was one hour until the fight. We halted our group near the contestants' entrance of the tall colosseum, and the guards at the door instructed us on where to go. We all dismounted, and I led Diablo along with the others.

The Galloway had a tunnel where the fighters could wait to enter the actual arena. When we entered the tunnel, it was bursting with people preparing for the Regal. I caught sight of many other creatures and Stone-Hearted. We got several wide-eyed glances from people walking by, and I could only assume it was because of the Envorydian symbols on all my comrades.

I forced myself to remain calm as Shar led us to the section we'd been directed to wait. There was a trap door, and behind the bars, light filtered into the tunnel from the arena. I could see through the ebony lattice, civilians filtering into the stands to watch the fight.

Rouix and Conland sat on the dirt floor of the tunnel. It would be a while still before the fight would begin.

"I'm going to see what the rules are for the fight, I'll be back," Shar said suddenly, and then he disappeared down the tunnel again. I sighed and leaned against the cool stone wall of the passageway. Dusane walked over to me, and took up a similar position beside me. Nothing was said for a moment, and I tried to calm my racing heartbeat. In an attempt to relax, I looked at the cracks in the tunnel wall and found there to be little drawings etched into the stone. My interest was piqued, and I stared intently at the little symbols.

"It's the story of Wesoltinece," Dusane suddenly said. He was watching me eye the characters.

"Why is it on the wall?"

"When the Galloway was created, the Envorydians etched their history into it. These symbols are Envorydian symbols, they all mean different things. We have the universal guild symbol, which we all get when we join the guild." He gestured towards my arm. "But there are many ancient Envoy symbols that, as you've probably seen, Envorydians will tattoo on their bodies."

I remembered him telling me once that the Galloway had been created by Envorydians, and that the Commission had been the ones to turn it into a place for entertainment. Looking at the symbols I realized that they looked so familiar. The other tattoos I'd seen on the Envorydians looked much like the symbols etched on the walls. I didn't know any of the other symbols' meanings besides the guild symbol, and I could only imagine what stories they told.

"Is it the same story Shar told us at the bonfire?" I asked.

"Yes. The legend of Wesoltinece, the greatest war king, and Telsiver the first Envorydian," he explained, letting one of his fingers trace the outline of one letter. "But there are many more."

"Dusane," I said, my mind suddenly far from Envoy legends and Westolince the war king.

"Yes?" he answered.

I turned toward him, and our eyes locked on each other. "Do you think we'll win?" I asked, and my voice was barely a whisper now. I could only hope it was us four in the end. That we all remained standing and gained our freedom to leave. For a moment, Dusane didn't answer, and the sound of people and animals moving about through the tunnel echoed off the walls, filling the silence between us.

"I think so," he said quietly. He ran a hand through his dark hair, and I caught sight of his Envorydian tattoo for a brief moment.

"I'm glad to be a part of your team," I admitted, smiling a little. I was trying to remain light-hearted and failing.

"You're a valuable asset to the group," he said seriously.

"This fight will definitely determine that statement," I said.

Dusane laid a hand on my arm, and I looked up, not expecting his gentle touch. "No, Ehren, this fight doesn't prove you are a worthy warrior. You need to remember that."

I was about to respond when Shar suddenly returned. We all looked expectantly at him as he came through the throngs of people. He seemed suddenly frazzled.

"What happened?" Conland asked, standing from the floor.

"They aren't allowing animals into the arena," he said. And we all looked at eachother. Yes, it would have been nice to have our creatures in the arena, but it wasn't a complete setback. We'd prepared for this.

"Is that all?" Rouix pressed.

Shar looked at all of us wearily. "There are other rules they've created." We all waited for him to continue. "They are only providing a dozen weapons on the island." I watched Dusane's jaw clench beside me.

"What does that mean?" I asked, obviously not understanding the problem.

"There are forty fighters going into the arena, and if only twelve weapons are available. . ." Conland trailed off.

"So twenty eight of us will not have weapons," I stated, feeling the weight of the realization wash over me. "Have they ever limited weapon numbers before?" I asked, feeling my heartbeat quickening.

"They have in the past, but not this much," Dusane explained.

"I don't need a weapon," Conland said confidently.

"You don't, but I can't stay camouflaged for that long. And what about Dusane and Ehren? They can't just hide behind you," Rouix spat with obvious frustration.

"You all will have to do your best to get to the island and get a weapon. Otherwise this fight is going to be very, very short," Shar said, his green eyes darkening.

I leaned against the wall, letting the cold stone cool my flushed skin. Suddenly the tunnel was getting very hot, and it was almost hard to breath against the humid heat.

"It's okay, Ehren. We'll be alright," Dusane said beside me. It did little to comfort me. My combat skills were good, but that was during a fair fight. And although I knew I couldn't be critically injured, I could definitely still feel pain.

A voice coming through the tunnels suddenly shouted over the hum of commotion.

"Prepare to enter the arena!" The messenger continued to herald the announcement, making sure everyone heard it.

"It's time," Shar said suddenly. "I'll be here, waiting in the tunnel."

The screeching sound of the gates opening suddenly echoed throughout the tunnel, and fighters began entering the arena. Dusane met my eyes one last time before following after Rouix and Conland.

I turned to Diablo and gently stroked his mane, trying to calm myself.

"I'm sorry you can't come. It would've been nice to have you in there with me," I whispered to him. He whinnied softly, and then I reluctantly left his side to go follow after the others.

Just as I was about to pass through the gate, I felt a hand on my wrist and I was being abruptly tugged to a stop. I turned to see Shar, the one who'd halted me.

"Ehren, wait," he said. He pulled me away from the entrance into the arena and back into the safety of the tunnel shadows.

"What is it?" I asked, worriedly glancing at the open gate, afraid it might suddenly close again.

"You're going to need this," he said suddenly. In his hand was my mother's amulet. He placed it around my neck, and I touched the familiar ruby tentatively.

"Thank you," I said, looking up at him.

"Please don't get hurt," he said abruptly. And I didn't know if he was saying it because he actually cared about me, or because he felt a duty to protect me because of Mid.

"I'll try," I said gently. Then he nodded curtly and gestured toward the open gate again.

I took a deep breath, stopping just at the mouth of the entrance. Then with as much courage as I could procure, I stepped out of the shadows of the tunnel and entered into the arena.

TWENTY-FOUR

My boots sunk into the yellow sand as I walked. From all sides of the tunnel, contestants emerged for the fight. It was surreal, looking up and seeing all the people cheering and yelling from their seats. The walls of the Galloway were so much bigger from this perspective, and I felt so small in comparison. I could see the balcony where members of the Commission were watching. They were sitting in large seats, much like the thrones I'd seen them lounge in the first time I'd met them. They were watching the fighters below, observing with critical eyes.

A circle was forming, and one of the arbitrators of the fight motioned for me to stand on a red line colored in the sand. I started to protest, wanting to be with my team, but they insisted I stand in a certain spot. I hesitantly walked up to the line and stood beside two complete strangers. Both were men, and nearly double my size. One of them looked over at me. His head was bald, his biceps protruding unnaturally with thick corded muscle. He snarled at me, and I felt fear threaten to seize me. But then Dusane's words echoed through my head. *"This fight doesn't prove you are a worthy warrior."*

I had nothing to prove. I already knew what kind of fighter I was.

I was an Envorydian. I was strong, skilled, and powerful.

I forced myself to take a deep breath and looked across the arena to see Rouix. We locked eyes, and then I scanned the rest of the circle forming, searching for Dusane and Conland.

During my search, my eyes caught sight of the island that was in the middle of the ring of fighters forming. It was several hundred feet away, and I could see that twelve weapons were spaced equally apart on the platform. The statue of Wesoltinece, with his weapon dug into the stone, was in the very middle. The large statue cast shadows onto the assortment of weapons, and I could make out a set of daggers and a bow and arrow.

I could hear my heart beating inside my ears. I could feel the anticipation. It pierced every nerve in my body. I waited, barely breathing, as the circle was completed and one of the arbitrators came into the middle of the circle. He stood on the platform. He wore a bright red tunic and held a red flag in his hand.

He began explaining the rules, but I wasn't listening. I had gone into an intense focus, analyzing the people around me, the island, and how I was going to get a weapon. Once the rules were explained, I could see him raise the flag high above his head.

Time stopped for a moment. The crowds reverberating thrum became muted, fading into the background. I heard the barely audible intake of my breath as my eyes locked on the set of daggers on the slate platform. Then the flag dropped down and I was running.

The sand made me feel like I was moving in a nightmare, no matter how hard I ran the sand resisted. I gritted my teeth, determined to reach the destination in the distance. Adrenaline enlivened every cell in my body, and I pushed harder against the sand, pumping my legs faster than I ever had before.

It felt like an eternity crossing the circle. But ever so slowly the distance to the island diminished, and I could almost taste victory on the tip of my tongue as I came within a few feet of the stone platform. I wasn't paying attention to the chaos erupting around me, all my focus on the weapons. When I finally got to the island, I immediately went for the set of daggers. They were glistening silver with decorative twisted handles. Relief flooded through my body and I reached for them.

And then I was hit, an unexpected impact to my side quickly impeding me.

I crashed into the sand. A body suddenly on top of mine knocked the air from my lungs. Sand fell into my eyes, and I blinked rapidly trying to restore my vision. I grunted in frustration, and finally, when my perception cleared, I caught sight of the person who'd attacked me. It was a woman. She was about my size with auburn hair and dark menacing brown eyes. She had a red heart glowing a beautiful ruby shade beneath her shirt. She sneered at me and lifted her fist to take a hit.

Quickly, I blocked the blow and proceeded to wrap my hands around her fist as it plunged toward my face. I twisted her arm, and tugged her off of me with as much strength as I could muster. We went sprawling across the sand, rolling atop one another, both of us trying to get the upper hand. I was so close to pinning her when she suddenly got her arms around my neck. I don't know how she'd slipped through my defenses, but her combat training was immaculate. *I was going to lose,* I suddenly thought to myself. *My first fight in the arena and I was going to lose. How pathetic,* I thought. *What was I thinking going into this with so little experience?* The dread quickly flooded through my body. I could see dark speckles beginning to cloud my vision. I wouldn't die, but she'd successfully knock me out. And that would easily be considered a surrender. They'd take me from the arena the minute I lost consciousness.

Then her tight grip around my neck was abruptly gone, and she was falling to the ground beside me, cradling her cheek where she'd looked to have been hit. I turned around frantically to see Dusane, the one who had saved me.

The woman groaned from her position in the sand, and I waited for her to get up, but she didn't. She raised her arm as if to say she was giving up. An arbitrator came over to her from the side lines, quickly taking her from the arena. It was a matter of ten seconds that they took her, and then we were back in the fighting.

"Thanks," I said breathlessly, turning to Dusane beside me. His blue eyes were bright with a wild energy, and he smiled, then gestured toward two more people suddenly coming toward us.

"It's not over yet," Dusane said, taking a fighting stance beside me. In his right hand he had a long bladed sword. He'd made it to the island.

"I don't have a weapon," I stated, watching anxiously as two other combatants came charging at us.

"Trust yourself, Ehren," he encouraged, but took an extra step forward so he was partly in front of me.

They were on us moments later, the one heading for Dusane had a dagger in one hand and the man that came for me was the bulky bald man I'd been standing next to in the beginning circle. I took a deep breath and readied myself into a combat stance.

Dusane swung his sword into a wide arch and met the dagger of his opponent. I could hear the ring of their weapons colliding as I carefully backed away from the man coming for me.

The bald man did not appear to have a weapon but he was threatening enough without one.

"You're a pretty thing aren't you? What are you doing in a fight like this?" he asked sardonically. His eyes flickered down to my gold heart and I could see the curiosity in his eyes. I glared at him and took a couple more steps back. I was stalling, trying to give myself a little more time to think through how I was going to fight him.

"I've come to win," I stated confidently. He laughed aloud, his head thrown back with sheer amusement. Then, I lunged for him.

I landed a punch to his cheek, and his head fell to the side. Blood spattered the yellow sand. I could feel one of my knuckles pop painfully, probably breaking it, but the pain was quickly erased moments later as my body balanced the blow. The man had a similar reaction as Conland the day I'd hit him. He touched his cheek where my fist had landed. His eyes darkened. And then he surged toward me again, growling like an animal. His brawny arm pulled back and swung straight for me, but I dodged his hit. He was big, and incredibly strong, but it made him slow. I was small enough and quick enough that I could elude him. Carefully, I danced around him, landing a couple good punches to his side. I was doing well, but when I heard Dusane cry out from beside me, I faltered.

The man with the dagger had landed a sizable cut on

Dusane's arm, and Dusane was clutching the wound. My moment of distraction was the perfect opening for my opponent and the bald man quickly sent me flying across the sand.

I went skidding along the arena floor, the gravely particles digging into my skin. The momentum of my body sent me several feet and then I was halted by sand. I felt the pain radiate from my gut where he'd precisely landed his fist. I lay balled up on the arena floor, clutching my stomach. I waited for the pain to abate and slowly I felt myself start to heal. I groaned and opened my eyes to see the bald man walking toward me again.

I'm not surrendering. I told myself. *I'm not surrendering.*

And then abruptly his knees buckled, and he collapsed to the sandy ground. Crying out in pain.

I watched in wide eyed astonishment as the bald man clutched his head, screaming in agony. And then he raised his hand, calling for a forfeit. An arbitrator took my opponent to the sidelines and when I found my strength, I carefully stood from the ground. I was suddenly confused. I hadn't done anything to the man, and I'd only ever seen someone cry out in pain like that a couple times before. It was so sudden, so unexpected. It seemed to be a hallucination. . . an illusion.

I looked around the arena, and the fighting was a mass of chaos. Dusane was still sustaining a fight against the man with the dagger and I could see Conland and Rouix across the arena. Conland's flames were lighting up one section of the sand in vermillion fire. Rouix glimmered as she disappeared and reappeared beside Conland in a combat fight.

The numbers had diminished, and only half of the Stone-Hearted fighters remained in the arena. I scanned the enthusiastic crowd, trying not to panic. It was noisy, and I was just noticing how loud the congregation was. I could feel my apprehension increase, constricting my muscles as I continued to scan the citizens in the stands.

It can't be, I told myself. *It's not possible.*

And then I looked to the balcony where the Commission was watching the fight, and I felt my heart stop in my chest. There were more people on the balcony now, about ten more individuals that had not been sitting with the Commission before. I felt my breath leave me as realization dawned, and I caught sight of one man in a dark brown cloak.

And then suddenly, I was looking into a pair of emerald-scarlet eyes.

TWENTY-FIVE

Everything stood still as I looked up at him.

He was on the balcony with the Commission, and the others that had joined him looked to be part of the Ethydon Royal Guard. It took all of a couple seconds for me to realize what was happening.

He had come for me.

I felt so many emotions, all in a matter of seconds. I'd gotten it in my head that it would be Oli or my father that would come retrieve me from the Courts. But never did I expect it to be Mid.

He looked the same, his tall, tan figure dressed in his signature brown cloak. It was the same Mid that had been in my dreams. His face remained passive, but his eyes were dark with emotion.

Someone began calling my name, and that's when the spell broke.

"Ehren!" Dusane called beside me, snapping me from the trance I was in. He was running over to me, still clutching his forearm where he had been cut. I couldn't see the man that had been fighting him, and assumed he'd forfeited.

"Are you all right?" Dusane asked as he got to my side, I looked at him. A million questions were swirling around inside of my mind, and I felt detached from reality. He ripped some of his shirt and wrapped it around the wound.

"Yeah, are you?" I asked, distractedly.

He nodded curtly. "I'll be fine." He handed me the dagger he'd salvaged from the man he'd just defeated. "Here take this, and let's go to Rouix and Conland." I could see the pain on his face. He was hurting, but he was still in the fight and that was all that mattered. I took the dagger numbly, not really registering that it was in my hand.

Dusane took off across the arena toward the others. I looked back, locking eyes with Mid on the balcony one more time. I feared he would disappear and that maybe I was seeing things. But he remained on the balcony, his eyes still watching me with a fierce intensity. I felt my heart skip a beat in my chest.

I finally turned my attention back to the fight and started running after Dusane.

The adrenaline now coursing through my veins was partly due to the fight, and partly from seeing *him* on the balcony.

I couldn't even begin to explain the way I felt seeing him there. It was a mix of happiness, nervousness, heartache, and fear. I couldn't go home, not now that I was so close. But seeing him was almost enough to break me into emotional pieces.

When we got to Conland and Rouix the numbers in the arena had decreased yet again. There were only twelve people left.

I gripped the dagger tightly in my hand, and took up position between Conland and Dusane.

"Good to see you, E," Conland greeted, grinning. He let out a sweeping wave of fire from his palms, stopping a woman with a bright green heart from coming near us. I could feel the heat of the flame wash over me and warm my skin. My skin was already sweaty, the hot noonday sun beating against me. It felt like a furnace with Conland's flames encasing us, and I didn't know how he handled it for so long.

"Conland, let me touch you," I said urgently. Conland turned to me, eyes wide for a second and then a smirk grew across his features.

"If you want to, E. I mean, it's not really the best time but I'm not going to object."

I rolled my eyes and reached out to touch his skin. "Not at all what I meant," I growled through gritted teeth. I focused intently on trying to pull the power from his body and into the amulet. Once the amulet began to glow the bright blue like in Conland's chest, I stepped away. Rouix was staring at the amulet, eyes wide. Dusane also looked at me, as did Conland, a similar expression on their faces.

"I'll explain later," I said hurriedly. And no one was going to argue because several people were heading straight for us.

Four individuals, side by side, came walking across the sand. Somehow in a matter of minutes there were only eight of us left in the arena. At first my apprehension was minimal. I was eager to finish this. But then I noticed the dark symbols on three of them, and realization dawned, causing icy cold fear to spread through my veins.

Envorydians.

Of course it would come down to this. *Who were they? Had I seen them at the Academy?* But none of their faces registered in my memory. I'd been so caught up in my own training, I'd barely had time to memorize names and faces. Shar had said that some of the Envorydians wanted freedom, and despite him telling them not to fight in this battle he worried some might still try.

"Are they all together?" I asked Dusane.

He nodded his head, jaw clenched. "It would appear to be that way."

"Do you know them?" I asked, and his silence was all that I needed. Yes, he did.

There were three men and one woman.

"Do we fight them?" I heard Rouix ask, hesitation in her voice.

Dusane's eyes narrowed. "They've brought this on themselves."

"A little competition is always fun," Conland smirked.

"I'll take the girl," I suddenly said. She was tall, almost as tall as the men she was with. Her long blonde hair reached clear to her waist, pulled back into a tight ponytail. Her heart was a shiny silver and my determination thickened.

"I'll take the one on the left," Conland said.

"I got the one on the right," Dusane said.

"I guess I'll take the middle," Rouix said, her jaw clenching.

The space between the other group quickly diminished as I ran, barreling forward to attack. With the dagger in my hand, I felt much more confident. I swung the dagger gracefully through the air, and the woman quickly deflected my blow with a pair of knives she was wielding. We went back and forth for a while. She was fast and reminded me a lot of Rouix and her skill with knives. They'd had similar training. This woman was a part of the Envoy. I forced myself not to think of the symbol on her right arm and focus on the fight. I kept up with her, determined.

I was doing well, warding her off when suddenly the voices started.

It was an urgent slithering sound, swirling into the corners of my mind. I couldn't make out any words that the voice was saying. It got louder and louder in volume, and suddenly pain filled my head.

The woman grinned at me, and I realized she was using some sort of mind power. I didn't know what it was, mind control or something. But the voices got louder, harsher, rushing like a frantic river and disorienting my mind. I dropped my weapon and fell to my knees, the voices physically hindering me.

I looked up at the balcony where Mid was standing. He still watched me, the look on his face a mix of torture and rage. Fighting against the woman's power, I forced my head to shake back and forth. It was difficult against the voices that were disabling me, but I didn't want him to intervene.

This was my fight.

I struggled against the voices and then shakily reached my hand out toward the Envorydian. My hand shook with tremors, fighting against the paralyzing voice in my head. And flames exploded from my hand.

The woman jumped back, and instantly the voices ceased. She screamed as the fire caught her skin, burning her hand. I gasped in relief as the voices disappeared, and I could see through the wall of flames the woman clutching her wound. She took off toward the sidelines, surrendering. The arbitrators quickly took her away.

I struggled to stand, gathering my bearings. And as I slowly recovered, my breathing haggard, I turned to see Dusane who was still fighting one of the other Envorydians. Dusane's opponent was about the same size as Dusane but unnaturally fast. He moved with abnormal speed, and sometimes his body blurred because he was moving so quickly.

I was about to run and help him when I spotted Rouix. She looked to have defeated the other Envorydian and was running to assist Dusane. Seeing he was being helped, I shifted my gaze to Conland.

Conland was up against the last comrade, and I didn't know if this one was an Envorydian. I couldn't see a symbol on him anywhere. It didn't even appear that he had any physical powers. He was wielding a beautiful gold sword, but against Conland's power, I didn't think he stood a chance. I thought for sure that Conland would have quickly defeated him with his flames by then. And that's when I saw it. The gold on his skin. Conland desperately threw fire at the man, but the man's skin would quickly appear glistening gold and reflect the heat. I hadn't noticed it before because if I wasn't focusing, it just looked like the sunlight was bouncing off his skin. It was a shield, a protective layer that he seemed to be able to produce at will. It appeared that Conland's flames were useless against him.

I ran over to Conland, and quickly raised my dagger to land a blow on the man unexpectedly from behind. But just as the dagger fell on the man's shoulder, the metal on his skin appeared and my dagger bounced off the gold material with a high pitched zing, nearly sending me into the sand again. I gritted my teeth, stumbling back. The man turned on me, his eyes wild with amusement.

"Well, look who decided to join the party," he purred. I lifted my dagger, readying myself for another blow.

His features were beautiful. He had full red lips and high cheekbones. Honey blond hair covered his head in short tousled waves, and his eyes were a deep topaz. His heart shone gold like the protective covering he produced on his skin, and then that's when I saw it. The symbol on his arm. It sparkled, the tattoo the same golden color as his mystical shield. It was barely noticeable with the bright sun beating down, making it shimmer almost too brightly to make out. But I wasn't mistaken. It was the Envorydian symbol.

The man didn't seem to notice my gawking. He laughed, obviously not viewing me as a real threat and turned back to Conland. Conland looked drained. His large chest was heaving, his blond hair drenched in sweat. He looked about ready to fall over. It didn't ever occur to me that Conland had a limit, but it seemed he may have reached it.

"You've gotten stronger, Conland. I'm impressed?" The man snickered, and walked over to Conland, suddenly ignoring me. They knew each other, and I didn't know how. I would've definitely remembered someone like him walking around the Envoy.

"But it would appear that you may not be as strong as you hoped. Time to give up, brother?" he taunted. Just as he was about to take another swing at Conland, I lunged for him.

I tried to hit a portion of his flesh not protected by the gold shield, but then he turned around, his hand reaching out to grab my wrist in a vice like grip, twisting my arm painfully. The dagger fell from my hand, and I gasped as an unusual sensation threaded through my palm. I ripped my hand from his grasp and stared at my hand. A veiny, spiderweb progression of gold crawled across my skin until it abruptly stopped halfway up my forearm. And suddenly half my arm was solid gold.

TWENTY-SIX

"You really shouldn't have done that," the man smirked. "That stuff is permanent." He lifted his sword, and I quickly took several steps back, knowing he was going to try and swing at me again, or worse turn other parts of me gold. I grabbed my dagger from where it laid buried halfway in the sand and raised it in front of me. And that's when my hand began to heal.

I waited, standing in a battle stance ready to take him. But his arm lowered slowly, and he stared at my hand in awe. I looked down to where his perplexed expression was directed on my hand and found the gold disappearing. Slowly my arm returned to normal.

"That's not possible," he whispered, and with that small distraction, Conland lunged for the golden Envorydian once again.

"No, Conland, don't!" I screamed.

Conland ignored me and continued to barrel toward the

Envorydian at an uncanny speed. In a desperate effort to stop him from coming into contact with the golden power. I gritted my teeth, preparing myself for what I was about to do next and then I threw myself between them.

The Envorydian threw his fist, his intention to hit Conland but instead the blow landed heavy in the center of my chest. The force of the punch sent both Conland and I flying into each other. We went tumbling backwards several feet across the sand. As we skidded to a stop, everything went suddenly still. I felt a thick painful feeling radiate from my chest. I pushed myself up onto my side and looked down to see the place he'd hit me was turning gold as my hand did, and I suddenly couldn't breathe.

"Now that's really impressive," the man said, beginning to walk toward us again. Conland quickly stood from the ground, shaking the sand from his skin. But I remained on the ground, gasping for air. Like a fish on dry land, I couldn't seem to obtain any oxygen amidst the golden paralysis.

I could see Dusane and Rouix still trying to defeat the other Envorydian across the arena now. I couldn't depend on them to come save us. I would have to take care of Conland and me. There were only six of us left, and only five could win. All I had to do was take out this golden Envorydian and the fighting would end.

We were by the island now. My weapon had been knocked from my hand and was too far for me to reach from where I was. The pain in my chest slowly faded as I began to heal and soon I could breathe again. Taking several deep gulps of air, I finally stood from the ground and started backing up toward the island.

"A healer. The ability to recover from any wound. I would dare say you are an immortal. I don't believe my eyes," The golden Envorydian continued to taunt me, his topaz eyes sparkling.

I could see his skin was back to normal now, and tried to think of a way to injure him before he could turn it to the golden shield.

I frantically looked around the arena in search for something to aid me.

Conland raised his fists again and put himself between me and our opponent. Conland was powerless against him, yet he didn't back down, determined to finish the fight.

"Leave her alone, Rosen. This is between you and me," Conland growled.

I made it onto the slate gray island, searching for anything that I could use to end this. And that's when I saw it.

The statue of Wesoltinece was a couple feet away, in the very center of the island. The Wesoltinece statue had his hands wrapped around his weapon, half buried in the ground. It appeared to be made of stone, and completely immovable. Then the pieces connected, and it came to me in an aggressive whirlwind.

"When he traveled into battle he took a war hammer. It was said to be able to break up the earth, split it into two."

The words that Mid had told me of Wesoltinece so long ago suddenly returned, and I knew exactly what to do. The statue looked immovable, the hammer submerged into the rock. I don't think anyone would've even thought to try and tug it from its resting place before.

I reached for the hammer, and with as much strength as I could muster, pulled on the handle. I willed it to release from the stone, needing it to be real. Needing it to make sense.

At first it resisted. But I continued to pull, a loud war cry leaving my lips as I tugged with all my might. Then all of a sudden the ground shook and the entire arena floor quivered. The stone cracked deafeningly, and I pulled the hammer from the stone platform.

I stumbled back with the momentum of the weapon's release, and hurriedly tried to steady myself on the now fractured island. I lifted the hammer up in front of my face, and was filled with awe, not believing my eyes.

It was large, and looked more like a pickaxe than a hammer. My hand barely wrapped around the thick handle. Then a golden veining spread across the hammer, covering the twisted handle and then the long narrow head. After several seconds, the entire thing was made of gold. I looked down at my amulet, seeing the golden light that it had harnessed slowly fading from the ruby.

A hush had fallen over the crowd and I could feel the eyes of every person in the arena centered on me.

TWENTY-SEVEN

It took me several moments to figure out what I should do next. But soon instinct took over, and I swung the hammer above my head, and smacked the very tip of its head into the sand. I didn't know what to expect, but I definitely wasn't prepared for the rippling force that shook the entire Galloway. A giant sand wave went soaring across the arena, tall enough to swallow anyone in its wake. I'd sent the force of the weapon in Rosen's direction, hoping it would hinder him and end this once and for all.

But the wave never swallowed him. The earthquake didn't do much of anything to him other than make him stumble a little. His hands met the wave of sand and instantly turned the entire thing into gold. It quickly became a wall of frozen gold metal. He stepped cockily away from the gold wave now protruding from the sand in an impressive sweeping arc. I gaped at how he'd managed to remain unscathed, and those watching seemed just as amazed.

The crowd that was silent moments before suddenly erupted into cheers, and I frantically looked for Conland, only to find him pulling himself from the sand where he'd been buried beneath the wave I'd induced. I had done more damage to my teammate than to the person I'd intended to be my target. I gritted my teeth about ready to try again when the fight suddenly ended.

It took me a moment to realize why everyone was cheering.

A loud horn blew throughout the arena, waking me from the intense focus I'd been swept into during the fight. I looked around to see what was going on. And then I saw Dusane and Rouix, now suddenly alone. The Envorydian they had been fighting was being carried from the arena, a large wound in his side.

The fight was over. . . and we'd won.

But not just us, the golden Envorydian also.

I didn't get to finish the fight, didn't get to wipe the smirk off of Rosen's face before the arbitrator announced the fight was over and the winners who had won their freedom.

I came back to reality, my eyes flickering to the Commission balcony only to find it vacant. The fight was over, and they had come for me.

Conland and several arbitrators were suddenly at my side, taking us from the island and back into the tunnels where Shar was waiting. Rouix and Dusane were right behind us, and my mind was racing with so many thoughts. *We'd won. I was free . . .* Those thoughts were accompanied by w*hy was Mid suddenly here to rescue me? Where would Mid and his guards take me now?*

When I emerged into the tunnel, it was a mass of chaos. Shar was there to greet us, and I could feel myself slip into a state of mild shock, trying to understand all that had just happened.

"You bastard!" I heard someone yell. I turned to see Dusane shove Rosen against the tunnel wall. The arbitrators quickly went to pull them apart, and Shar and Conland rushed to help.

"Dusane, stop!" Shar demanded.

"How dare you call yourselves Envorydians. You're just filthy rouges! You shouldn't have shown up here today!" Dusane continued to angrily shove Rosen, the man I'd just fought in the arena. Shar with Conland were pushing the two apart, trying to keep them from tearing each other to pieces.

"Shar," I said, and I hadn't realized I was shaking. Rouix was at my side suddenly grasping my arm.

"Ehren, are you okay?" she asked, worry scrunching the wing-like tattoos on the bridge of her nose. I didn't answer her.

"Shar," I called again, louder this time.

Shar finally heard my plea, and turned from Dusane and Rosen's fight, leaving Conland to break the two apart. He came over to me, his jaw visibly clenched. And I knew from the look on his face that he'd seen them on the balcony too.

"They're here," I said, my stomach twisting with nausea. I leaned against the wall for support. Shar reached out to grip my shoulders, keeping me steady so I wouldn't double over and vomit.

"Give me the hammer," was all he said, and I gratefully handed him the weapon. He hooked the hammer at his side and bent down slightly so he could be level with me. His green eyes blazed with a frantic fire.

"They are going to take me back. . . they are going to take me back. . ." I mumbled in a daze. I could just see it now, the group of them probably already making their way down to the tunnels to seize me.

"Listen to me, Sabeara." The use of my real name was barely

enough to pull me from my shock. "I didn't know they would show up like this. But it was never my plan—" He trailed off, looking almost pained to have to rush the explanation he was giving me. He growled and continued on. "This was not how this was supposed to go. Dusane was supposed to grab the hammer, and I was going to leave after the fight–"

"Wait, Dusane knew the hammer was in the arena?" I shrieked, suddenly my mind sharpening to acute awareness with the news. Rouix squeezed my arm, probably to try and be reassuring, but it did little to calm me.

"I was going to take the hammer and rescue Embrosine. I lied to you. In the beginning this was about the tokens. I came here to get the Envorydians, retrieve the hammer, and then take them with me on a journey to find more of the tokens. But then when they took her... I have to save her..."

"Save Embrosine?" Suddenly everything made sense. What was once a jumbled puzzle began fitting into a perfect picture. He wasn't planning on taking us on a journey to find the tokens, that may have been his plan in the beginning. But now that Embrosine was kidnapped he'd been trying to save her all along. I recalled the moment back in Aveladon, when Embrosine had fought in the tea room. The shattered glass, the black cloaks swarming us. Then when we were rescued I'd seen Shar cup her face...

I gasped, realizing there was something going on between them, but I didn't have time to ask him about it because he continued to explain. He seemed desperate not to waste time. They'd be arriving in a matter of minutes.

"If Midennen finds you down here, he will take you back with him. And if he finds out that I'm not actually going to find tokens he'll forbid me to leave. He knows a mission to save

Embrosine is reckless and dangerous. He'll want to spend weeks calculating the mission. I don't have weeks. I need to rescue her now. And as his guardian, if he asks something of me—"

"You have to do it." I finished the sentence for him, knowing from experience the power a royal had over their soldiers. I had never inflicted a royal command on Oli, I wasn't able to. He reported to my father. But that didn't mean I didn't understand what was required. Absolute obedience. I'd seen it in the way my father ordered Oli around. Shar would have to follow Mid. He'd made a royal oath to obey. But if Mid never had the chance to ask him to stay. . .

"We have to get out of here," I said. And Shar looked to visibly relax, realizing I'd caught on.

"I'm not going to ask you to come with me though. This is a dangerous mission."

I glared at him with as much force as I could muster with my exhaustion. "Don't you dare tell me what to do, Shar. I'm coming with you."

I expected him to fight back, but he simply smiled. "I was hoping you'd say that."

And with those words I knew I'd done it. He finally trusted me. Believed in me. It was enough at that moment, and suddenly we were rushing to leave.

With my heart pumping wildly in my chest, I mounted Diablo. Conland had successfully broken up the fight between Rosen and Dusane, and he addressed the two with impatience.

"Dusane, we gotta go. It's not worth it," Conland said, shooting a disapproving glare at Rosen. The golden Envorydian only smirked knowingly at Dusane who was still fuming.

"We have to go," Conland said again, pressing a little harder on Dusane's chest. "Come on, Captain."

"Dusane," Rouix pleaded from atop her Crykon. We were seriously running out of time. Dusane finally huffed and went to mount Elesame. Shar and Conland followed suit and just as we were about to take off into the tunnel, Rosen stepped in front of Shar's horse.

"Let me come with you," he said.

"Move out of the way, Rosen," Shar commanded. I didn't know how they all knew each other, but it was clear that a past existed between all of them. I had so many questions, but they would have to wait.

Shar tried to move his horse around Rosen, but Rosen just sidestepped and blocked him again.

"Come on, Shar, I know you need my help. Plus I'm free now. Why not take me with you?"

I could not believe the audacity that this Envorydian had. His cocky self-assurance, his pretty face. He reminded me of Conland, only much worse. There was a darkness behind his expression that I didn't like—something unruly and seriously untamed.

"I said move aside, Rosen," Shar growled impatiently.

"I can see you are in a hurry, which means this must be a very important matter. Let me help you. I'd be a valuable asset to the team," Rosen smirked again, standing his ground in front of Shar. I looked back down the tunnel where arbitrators and other contestants that fought were still lingering in groups. At any moment they would be coming through. I considered trampling Rosen but then forced myself to abandon the thought.

"Fine. You can ride with Rouix," Shar snapped, and without further argument kicked his horse into a run, forcing Rosen to have to jump out of the way to avoid being hit. Dusane and

Conland were immediately on Shar's tail. My mouth fell open, and I watched Rouix mirror my appalled expression.

"No way in hell. . ." Rouix began to say, but before she could even finish her sentence, Rosen hopped up behind her with the ease of a trained Envorydian. He grabbed the reigns in his hands and kicked the Crykon firmly in the sides. They took off down the tunnel together. I didn't have time to contemplate what had just happened. I urged Diablo into a full on gallop down the tunnel, following after the others.

Adrenaline still burned hot in my veins as I contemplated how we were going to get away. People jumped frantically to the sides of the tunnel, shouting and grumbling their protests as we came barreling through. The exit appeared soon enough, and without any hesitation, we slipped out into the Drego. The sun was setting, but the city was far from winding down. Our group pushed through the crowds with just as much fervor as in the tunnels, and I watched several people dive and swerve out of the way. I flew with Diablo above the crowds, avoiding the masses.

I knew exactly where we were headed as I watched Shar leading the group through the metallic polis below. I could see it on the hill in the distance. The Commission headquarters. That would be where we finally escaped.

TWENTY-EIGHT

When the Commission headquarters came into view, the tall gray compound, with its spiked walls and tall spires, was exactly as I remembered. I pushed down the feelings of nervousness as we neared. Memories of the dark cell and the damp stench that accompanied it were enough to make me shiver.

When we approached the front gates, we came to a stop. Shar dismounted to greet the guards.

I listened carefully as Shar conversed with them.

"I need to speak with Vayel. Tell him I have the Galloway winners with me," Shar ordered. One of the guards nodded then disappeared into the gates. It was several minutes later that they opened again. One of the guards motioned for us to follow him inside.

When we entered, we were greeted with more Commission sentries, and they ordered us to keep our animals on the outside of the compound in the courtyard. I reluctantly dismounted and handed Diablo to one of them.

"I'll be right back," I told him, petting him on the nose quickly before following after the others. The silvery spider web material that covered the outside of the prison along with its pointed silver spires was intimidating, and I had to remind myself that as much as I didn't want to go inside, it was the only way out. When we stepped into the doors of the compound, the blank sleek interior caused my stomach to twist into knots. I was near Dusane, and I edged closer to him, feeling extremely uncomfortable in the place I'd once been kept prisoner. No one said a word, and the only sound was the quiet echo of our footfalls as we walked.

When we came upon the throne room that I'd once been interrogated in, the sun shined brightly down from the skylight and illuminated the panel of thrones and the Commission. Vayel was already standing to greet us.

"What a surprise," Vayel said, but I could tell that it wasn't. He seemed to be expecting us. His same regal black clothes graced his body, along with the tattoos that decorated his face.

"I'm here to cache in on the bargain we made," Shar didn't bother with the theatrics.

Vayel's jaw clenched and unclenched, but it was such a quick movement I wondered if I'd imagined it. "Your friends arrived earlier today. I was expecting you would be leaving together," Vayel said, keeping his tone light.

I realized then that he must not have been at the Regal fight. I didn't know how many Commission members had witnessed the fight, but it must not have been all of them.

"Plans have changed," Shar insisted.

"Pity. Well, I'm guessing you are here to leave on your journey." I could see Vayel shift his gaze to me, and a new expression crossed his features. "It seems she didn't betray you, after all," Vayel said, and I could see then the tattoos on his face had the symbol of the Envorydian etched into one of the designs. The realization that Vayel was part of the Commission and an Envorydian was not something I had expected.

"She has proved to be a valuable asset to the team," Shar said curtly.

"Yes indeed. And it seems she has even helped you retrieve an item from the Galloway." Vayel's eyes shifted from me to the hammer at Shar's side. "Might I ask what it is?"

"This hammer will be used to stop the curse. It is my duty to protect it, and report back to the kingdoms with it," Shar said with a slight edge in his tone.

Vayel's eyebrows rose. "Is that so? Last time I checked, the kingdoms didn't own the Galloway."

"Are you going to stand in the way of a kingdom official doing his duty, Vayel?" Shar challenged.

"Not at all. I just wanted to make sure I knew where your loyalties lay," Vayel replied darkly. I didn't miss the insinuation behind his tone. The tension between the two of them was palpable.

"Are we done here?" Shar pressed, becoming impatient.

Vayel smirked at Shar's question. "I will admit, finding out she was the princess made all of this more interesting."

My body froze as the words left his lips. All eyes turned on me, and I forced myself to stay facing forward, not daring to look any of my friends in the eye. I knew it would come to this at some point. I couldn't keep the secret forever. But I was really not looking forward to explaining everything when the time came.

"You seem to have a habit of rescuing lost princesses," Vayel mocked.

I could see Shar tense beside me, and I immediately wondered what Vayel meant.

"Are you forgetting the other half of the bargain?" was all Shar replied.

"Oh yes, I almost forgot. You need provisions for your upcoming journey. And I wouldn't want to be rude by not helping a *kingdom official* fulfill his duty." The poison behind Vayel's words was evident. "The supplies are waiting for you outside," he concluded, and his eyes flitted to me one last time. I tried not to squirm underneath his penetrating expression.

Then without further explanation, the guards escorted us out of the throne room and back into the hallway. Soon we arrived at another door and then we were outside again, only on the other side of the compound. On the backside of the Commission was another silver gate, but it wasn't part of the Commission walls, but the massive barricade that surrounded the entire Courts. I could see beyond its twisted bars the jungle trees in the distance. This was the way out. Our escape.

Our animals were waiting for us, along with another horse that the Commission provided for Rosen. Then to my surprise, I saw that our saddles had been equipped with traveling supplies. Food, water, and tents now filled the saddlebags. It was a generous supply, and I immediately became curious about the bargain Shar had made with Vayel.

We all mounted our animals, and I could feel the tension as we neared the exit to the Courts. I held my breath as Shar nodded to the guards and one of them began to open the gate.

A slight breeze came through as they opened it, ruffling my hair, and it felt wonderful against the sticky heat. Shar led the way through, and I thought for sure at any moment someone was going to stop us. But when we passed over the threshold and became encased in the jungle trees once again, I heard the gate close behind us and knew it wasn't just wishful thinking.

We had escaped the Sethen Courts.

~

I don't know how long we ran. It must have been hours. I feared at any moment I would hear hoof-beats behind us, indicating that Mid and his soldiers had caught up to our group. But the sound never came. I could only hope we had gotten far enough away.

When the sun began to set Shar finally slowed to a walk, and I gently patted Diablo's sweat-slicked shoulder. Shar motioned for us to stop in the midst of a small clearing of trees, and then he dismounted his steed.

It took all of one minute for the accusations to begin.

"Does someone want to explain what's going on?" Dusane asked, jumping off Elesame and looking at me and Shar with a pointed expression.

When my feet hit the ground, my legs shook. Despite my body's ability to heal, I was still exhausted after the fight and all the riding we'd done. I closed my eyes for a moment, gathering my bearings before what I knew was going to be an equally exhausting conversation.

When I faced Dusane, I could see that his arm was still wrapped in it's makeshift bandage, soaked with blood. His eyes were on me, and I dared a glance at the others in the group. Rouix, Conland, and Rosen were looking at me with equally confused expressions.

"Before everyone starts interrogating me, I would like to know why all of you were in on this plan to rescue Embrosine and get the hammer and I was not," I said hotly. "And while we are at it, Shar, do you want to explain why you let *him* come along," I pointed to Rosen.

It was an old habit, deflecting when I was being accused. But I couldn't help it.

Shar sighed and pinched the bridge of his nose. "I was planning on telling you after Dusane got the hammer and we won the fight. And I wasn't going to rescue Embrosine for several more days. But plans changed when they showed up," Shar explained.

"Shar and I are old friends, and I think that's all that needs to be said about that," Rosen answered, his haughtiness made me want to punch him.

"Don't deflect the question, Ehren. I'm talking about how the Commission leader called you princess. . ." Dusane pressed.

Rouix's red eyes remained steadily on me, obviously more interested in Dusane's inquiry as well.

"And who were those people on the balcony with the Commission?" Conland interjected, only adding more fuel to the fire.

"I'll answer the questions when you answer mine," I fired back. "How do you all know each other?" I asked, gesturing to everyone in the circle. "You act like you all were old friends once." I knew it was unfair. But I wasn't ready to say the words yet.

"We met a long time ago, when Rosen was traveling in Severesi. We happened to cross paths and we became acquainted with one another," Shar said, obviously reluctant to elaborate.

"I was taken to the Sethen Courts a couple years later and I joined the Envoy," Rosen said.

"He didn't join the Envoy," Dusane spat.

"You didn't let me," Rosen accused pointedly.

"Because you're a rouge," Dusane growled.

"What does a rogue mean?" I asked, my voice rising with exasperation.

"An Envorydian that doesn't mind killing other Envorydians," Conland interjected. "He hangs out with the other rogues in the court. How did you guys get word we were fighting in the regal anyway?" Conland asked accusingly, his attention now on Rosen.

I remembered Theon telling me about Envorydians that refused to accept the mantra of peace. Suddenly it made sense why I'd never seen Rosen, or any of the other Envorydians we'd fought in the arena, at the academy before.

"We heard some of your guild members talking about it at a pub in the Drego. We thought we'd join the fun," Rosen said, and it was impossible to miss the hint of mockery in his voice.

"All right, enough about Rosen. Why did he call you princess?" Rouix finally cornered me again, and I knew I couldn't ignore the question any longer.

"And who were those people on the balcony?" Conland added.

"Okay, okay. . ." I looked at Shar, and he gave me a curt nod. It was now or never. "The people on the balcony were from Ethydon. They came to retrieve me from the Courts." I briefly glanced at Dusane, then quickly looked away again, unable to look him in the eyes as I said my next words. "Because my name isn't actually Ehren . . . It's Sabeara Aigoviel. I'm the princess of Aveladon."

TWENTY-NINE

I explained everything. I told them where I'd come from and why I ended up in the Courts. I explained how the amulet worked and more. The only thing I left out was my relationship with Mid. I told them that soldiers from Aveladon and Ethydon had come to take me home, but I avoided detail.

When I finished, everyone in the group was silent for many minutes.

"We need to get on the move again. We'll stop in a couple hours and set up camp," Shar said, breaking the silence.

I was watching everyone's reactions to my words but most of all Dusane's. He wouldn't look at me as he headed toward Elesame and mounted her back. I tried not to get offended and reminded myself that it was a lot to take in.

Rouix walked over to me and laid a hand on my shoulder. Her red eyes were piercing as she spoke. "No more secrets, okay? You can trust us," she said softly and I had to try very hard not to let tears fill my eyes.

I bent my head in gratitude. "Thank you, Rouix. That means a lot."

"Well, should I call you Your Highness from now on?" Conland smirked.

I rolled my eyes. "Absolutely not. I'm still the same person I was before. There is no need to treat me differently." There was a hint of pleading in my voice.

Rosen gave me a long glance and looked about to say something too then thought better of it and mounted his horse.

We started into the jungle again, and I felt a pit build in my stomach the longer we journeyed. Dusane still hadn't looked at me. *Was he angry?* It was definitely a possibility. *Did he think less of me now?* I would've been upset if he'd kept a secret like that from me. But I also expected him to try to understand why I'd done it and at least attempt to forgive me. *Maybe he just needed time,* I told myself. *You at least owe him that,* I insisted.

I sighed and forced myself to stay focused on the path ahead.

The sun eventually disappeared, and the jungle got eerily dark. Insects and creatures fluttered amongst the vines and every once in a while I would catch a pair of yellow eyes in the foliage as we ran. I shivered, preferring to stay in ignorance of what sort of creatures lingered in these parts of the realm.

When we finally stopped the animals were spent. I could feel Diablo shaking beneath me, and I felt immediately guilty for pushing him so hard. I jumped down and helped give him some water from a canteen at my side. Then I let him freely munch on the jungle greenery as I went to set up camp with the others.

Conland made a fire while Rouix and I set up a tent that we intended to share. The rest of the men simply set up makeshift beds by the fire. Food was passed around, and I tried desperately as we ate dinner to catch Dusane's eye again. He didn't eat. Instead he worked on dressing the wound he'd received in the arena. I waited for him to finish so I could confront him, but the second he completed wrapping his arm he crawled underneath his blanket and turned his back to the fire, indicating he was not in the mood to talk.

But I knew at least one of the others, if not Dusane, was bound to have more questions and I was right. Conland and Rouix unleashed their curious inquiries on me not long after. They were civil enough. They asked me about my life back at the castle and what it was like to be a princess and coming to the Courts. Rosen sat listening intently from the shadows as I answered each of their questions. Shar merely watched my reactions, looking ready to step in at any moment if needed.

Rest was essential and Shar reminded us of that a couple hours later after they had interrogated me for some time. One by one the others in the group crawled into their beds and soon I was the only one awake.

The camp was eerily quiet with everyone asleep. The night air was just as thick and moist as the Courts. I stared into the flames of the fire, watching the wood reduce to nothing but hot glowing orbs beneath the peppery ashes.

I tugged the small blanket around my shoulders despite the heat. It was comforting. I had too much on my mind to find relief in unconsciousness. So much chaos had transpired over the last day. It was weird to be in utter quietness now. Even the sound of insects had rescinded, and it was just the lonely crackling of the fire against the quiet jungle.

A gentle rustling interrupted the silence, and from one of the makeshift beds across the tree circle I saw someone stand and walk over to the fire. His shadow moved quietly until finally the light of the fire illuminated his features.

"You should really sleep," Shar said, taking a seat beside me. I sighed, my expression returning to the fire with irritation.

"I'm fine, Shar," I stated flatly. He seemed to tell I was not in the greatest mood. He settled in on the damp jungle floor and gazed into the flame with his dark green eyes. The intensity that usually dwelled within them had faded, and some unknown emotion lingered.

"You're brave, you know?" he acknowledged quietly. I looked up a little shocked to hear the compliment.

"For doing what?"

"Walking away," he stated simply. "I know what it feels like. To walk away from the one you love, for a greater cause."

"Well, it was more of a selfish decision than anything, so I wouldn't say I'm brave by any means." I didn't deny the word love when Shar said it. Because I did love Mid. But I was afraid to face him. . . because I wasn't ready. To see him, to feel my heart ache when I saw him, and to potentially hear him say he didn't want me anymore . . .

I'd also started to care about defeating the curse—more than I ever imagined I could. In the beginning, it was to keep from going home and also to fulfill my destiny. Now I felt it was more than that. I wanted to protect, to save, to conquer Obscurum. Saving Embrosine was a big part of that purpose I felt I needed to claim. I also wasn't about to surrender who I'd become to go back to Aveladon and be absolutely useless. I was made to do this, made to fight and defeat Obscurum.

"Well, I want you to know that I'm sorry for the way I've treated you," he said quietly.

The apology was so shocking, my mouth fell open slightly.

"Did I just hear you apologize, Shar?" I asked, my tone a little teasing.

He rolled his eyes. "Truce or not, Ehren?" he asked irritably.

I smiled and nodded. "I'll forgive you for underestimating me. On one condition."

"What is it?" he asked, his gaze hardening.

"Tell me what's going on with you and Embrosine."

A million different emotions passed across his face, and then he looked away from the fire abruptly so I couldn't see his reaction. When he returned back to me, his expression was back under control, hard as stone again.

"I don't know what you're talking about," he said gruffly.

"Oh, so going on a forbidden mission to save Embrosine has nothing to do with your feelings for her?" I asked mockingly.

He glared at me then and he looked about ready to fight me, then he suddenly sighed. Defeated. "You can't tell Midennen," he said suddenly.

"I won't," I stated firmly. And I knew it was true. Now that I was an Envorydian, I felt a loyalty to my guild, and as much as it irritated me, Shar was a part of it.

"No, I don't think you understand. You really can't say anything, Ehren. He'd kill me for lying to him all these years. And trust me, it's better if no one really knows what happened," Shar said, speaking more urgently now. I noticed for the first time ever that he had recognizable fear in his eyes. I nodded and tried to show with my expression how serious I was.

"Shar, you can trust me." I reached over to him and laid my hand on his arm.

It was weird. It seemed that after he asked me to come with him, something changed. The emotions between us were less hostile, more trusting. It must have been because of everything that had happened over the last several months.

He sighed and started into his story. "It began eighteen years ago, when I was an Envorydian. I was working in Severesi, as the king's personal guardian. It was a peak time in history when the Envoy was spread out across the kingdom's. Envorydians being put against each other. Ethydon was a newly established kingdom. It was a very controversial time. Another kingdom dissenting from Aveladon created some worry throughout the realm. The king of Severesi, King Niuadi, had already begun forming his plans to weaken them.

"He wanted to kidnap Embrosine and bring her to Severesi. He wanted to get information from her to see what he could figure out about Ethydon. He was afraid that the other kingdoms would become more powerful than his. At this point in history the kingdoms weren't really allied, but they weren't enemies either. And despite everyone's apparent peace, it was only a matter of time before things became contentious.

"I was ordered to capture her. And for a very good amount of money. More than I'd ever been presented with. So of course I took the job."

I tried to imagine Shar kneeling before the Severesi king, then hunting down a young Embrosine. A shiver ran through my spine.

"I took a group of Envorydians with me, and we immediately started on our journey to kidnap her. We created a plan. One of us would capture her, and the other would pretend to save her. We'd gain her trust and claim we were taking her home. Then instead of returning her to Ethydon, we would take her to King Niuadi.

"It worked better than we planned. Ethydon didn't have the

Royal Guard it needed to protect itself very well at this stage and penetrating their line of defense was almost effortless. She quickly trusted me as I pretended to be her savior during the raid we'd created, but I was really there to betray her."

Shar paused and continued to glare into the fire. His jaw clenched as if remembering what he'd done. It seemed to pain him.

"The plan didn't work as we intended. Something unexpected happened and the plan failed."

"What happened?" I whispered, completely engrossed in his story.

"I fell in love with her," he said gently. And my breath left me. To think of Shar being in love, to even think about him being able to show affection, was extremely hard to imagine.

"I took her back to Ethydon instead of going through with the plan. Embrosine didn't know at the time that originally I was going to betray her. She didn't find out until later.

"The queen was so grateful she offered me a position on the Ethydon Royal Guard. And in a moment of weakness I took it. I knew I had betrayed my oath as Envorydian. That King Niuadi would never forgive me. I would have been cast into the Sethen Courts for not fulfilling his command. It was a merciful escape to join Ethydon. Even when King Niuadi died and another king took his place, I never risked returning.

"So I became part of the Royal Guard. And eventually became Midennen's personal guardian."

"What happened to you and Embrosine?" I asked frantically, my voice rising with desperation. I was far too invested in the story now.

"In order for Ethydon to function against the larger kingdom's around it, they needed more soldiers. They sought help from the Isles of Arradale. Then they married Embrosine to Ashelor, the prince of the Isles. And that is the end of the story. . . " he trailed off, his expression hard as he continued to gaze into the burning ashes.

"But you still love her," I stated quietly. It wasn't a question.

"With everything inside of me," he said so quietly, it was barely audible.

"Shar, I'm so—"

"I really don't need you to pity me," he laughed darkly.

"And Mid doesn't know?" I asked. Tears filled the corners of my eyes.

"What's there to know? Embrosine is with Ashelor, and they have a daughter. Any type of future for us is absolutely impossible. And I will never do anything to make that marriage unfaithful." His jaw clenched. Now all the things Embrosine said about love and how it was a weak contender when fighting against actuality made sense.

We sat in silence for a moment as Shar's story sunk in. A melancholy cloud surrounded us, and everything was suddenly somber.

"We'll save her, Shar," I said quietly. "I promise." I worried if she would still be alive when we arrived, but I couldn't think that way. I had to hope that she would be okay, that we would succeed. It was the only way I wouldn't crumble.

He nodded, his eyes lost in thought. "Yes, we will," he stated firmly.

As the silence enveloped us again another question popped into my mind.

"Shar, what did you offer Vayel, to get all those favors?"

Shar pursed his lips."I told him I would try and speak to the king about lifting his sentence."

"Vayel is a prisoner?"

"Not exactly. He used to be a royal official. But was reassigned to the Courts because he upset the king." Shar said.

I thought back to the massive throne room, and the elegant black clothes the Commission members wore. It didn't seem like Vayel was suffering.

"Why does he want to leave?"

"You know as well as I do that when someone is in a place where they didn't choose to be, the need for escape is incurable. No matter how pretty the cage is."

I remembered my time at the castle. I had everything, and yet I still wanted to escape.

Shar stood from the fire, and looked down at me. "We have an early morning. Get some rest, and that's an order," he said, but the threat in his voice was minimal.

I nodded sullenly and watched him walk away. His feet crunched against the jungle floor, and suddenly he disappeared into the inky shadows, and I was alone once again.

THIRTY

The fire was deadened ashes when I awoke. The sound of rustling movement and whispering conversation was what brought me from my dreaming. I'd fallen asleep awkwardly beside the fire, leaning up against a tree stump. The others were already packing up, and I rubbed my aching neck as I stood up to start gathering my things.

Diablo was beside Rouix's Crykon when I went to load up my saddle bag, and he was eyeing the other creature warily.

"She's a friend," I said to him, petting his long black mane. He huffed in response. For a horse he was awfully moody. "I mean it. Be nice," I said forcibly. He settled but still looked as if he were leaning away from the Crykon and all the other creatures in the camp for that matter. The wolf was still unsettling, but luckily it slept beside Conland on the other side of the camp. And Elesame though tame and puppy-like in nature was still a very intimidating animal.

"We need to depart. They'll catch up if we stay here any

longer," Shar said to everyone in the group. "We're about two days from Obscurum. Be thinking of a plan to raid the castle."

We all mounted our animals and followed after Shar who didn't hesitate to start running through the trees again. Soon the only sounds were the rhythmic beating of hooves and an occasional song from a bird in the jungle branches.

When Diablo would tire of running he would fly instead. He breezed silently through the foliage and somehow wove gracefully through the obstacle of trees and vines. It was a thrilling feeling, one I hadn't quite gotten used to.

Around midday, Shar ordered everyone to slow down. The animals needed resting, and it was immediately quieter as we all came to an easy walk. I was beside Dusane, and I looked over at him, expecting him to look over at me too, but he stayed looking forward. A little wounded that he didn't seem up for conversation, I led Diablo to the rear of the caravan.

Ever since the news that I was princess of Aveladon, Dusane had been acting weird. Every time I tried to catch his eye, he avoided it. He didn't approach me unless he had to. And as quiet as Dusane was, I couldn't help but feel that this was different. He was definitely upset. And for some reason that bothered me. I felt a fiery sensation build in my chest. After all, he'd been the one that wanted to know who I was. And now that he knew, it seemed almost like he didn't want anything to do with me. *Well sorry it wasn't what you wanted,* I spat in my head.

I was grumbling angry comebacks in my mind when Rosen pulled up beside me. I immediately stiffened. After the fight and the argument at the camp, he was the last person I wanted to talk to. He grinned over at me, his expression one of pure arrogance. It reminded me of the way Conland always smiled. But it wasn't quite so innocent. Something more devilish, more malicious, was lurking behind his deep topaz eyes. I shivered.

"Good morning, princess," he mocked, winking at me.

"It's, Ehren," I snapped. I never thought I'd retort so easily, but it seemed that name had officially become my identity. Being called princess was almost an insult now.

"Well, Ehren, I think we've gotten off on the wrong foot. Or should I say, hand. . ." he looked over at my hand that he had once turned to gold. I rolled my eyes at him and decided it was easier to look away from his pretty face when talking.

"I really don't like you. And I do not approve of Shar allowing you to come along," I stated. I heard Conland chuckle in front of me, and I shot a glare at the back of his head.

"Shar and I have a past, and because of our past, he knows I can be of help." Rosen grinned widely again.

"Whatever," I grumbled. I had successfully become deeply grumpy. And every time I spotted Dusane at the front of the line conversing with Shar, my bad mood worsened.

"You know, I've never seen anyone heal like that before. It really was quite impressive."

I didn't respond. But he didn't seem put off.

"If I had to guess, I bet your heart was granted from the same stone that my shield is made from." This pulled me from my pensive thoughts and I turned to regard him, barely holding back my disdain.

"What?" I asked, suddenly all thoughts of Dusane had disappeared.

"Oh nothing," he said, dropping the subject suddenly. It didn't take me long to figure out he was baiting me.

"You can't just say stuff like that and not explain," I growled angrily.

"You don't like me," he said sardonically.

"Just tell me," I barked, hating the games he was playing.

"It's a long story. Are you sure you want to hear it?" He turned to give me another dashingly handsome smile. His topaz eyes gleamed with amusement.

"Spit it out," I said, with just as much irritation.

He laughed and finally continued to explain. "When I first gained my powers I had no idea what the golden shielding was. But it wasn't true gold. I figured that out quickly enough. If it had been gold, it would have been easily bendable. For years I wondered what I was made from, agonized over it actually.

"I had my theories. Maybe it was some sort of metal I didn't know about. Maybe it was citrine, the stone that grants people the golden color in their hearts. Then one day, I decided to go figure out for myself what the Spirit Tree had granted me. I went on a long journey seeking out a well-known Reminant that I thought would have the answers. When I found him. he told me about amberidium."

"Amberidium? What's amberidium?" I asked, unable to contain my curiosity.

"It's the seventh stone," he said easily.

"Seventh stone? There are only six."

"That's what everyone thinks," he said knowingly.

"You're saying there's a seventh stone you can be granted from? And it's the color of gold too, and it's called amberidium?" It sounded completely ridiculous when I said it aloud.

"But you see, it's not quite the color of the citrine stone. Amberidium is deeper in color. And its golden color can be mistaken for the citrine stone."

"You think the color in your heart and the material of your shield is from amberidium?"

He shrugged his shoulders. "It's just a guess."

"What other nonsense did this Reminant tell you?" I asked, trying not to show that I was seriously considering his theory.

"The Reminant told me that I was granted an amberidium heart so that I could help defeat the curse. He called me a Chosen."

My mouth fell open slightly, unsure how to take in all of the things he was saying.

"Then he told me more about the curse and said that the Ethirical was incomplete. And that if I wanted to find out the truth about the curse, I needed to find a place called Pendilore."

"And did you find it?" I asked skeptically.

I noticed then, that the entire group had gone quiet. Everyone was listening to Rosen's story.

"I searched for five years. But I never found it." He looked over at me, his eyes sparkling with the secrets of his story.

"So you assume my heart is gold from being granted through the amberidum stone?" I pointed to the gold in my chest, and the sparkle in his eye didn't fade.

"If I had to bet my life, I'd say your heart was granted from amberidum stone, not citrine."

"Why?" I pressed urgently.

"Because your power is unlike anything I've ever seen. It would just make sense."

I scoffed, suddenly realizing how crazy it all sounded. Dusane had told me that powers weren't connected to color. If that was true, then he wouldn't possibly be able to assume a connection to my power and the color of my heart.

It was crazy. An unknown stone we'd never heard of. Chosen Stone-Hearted, and a place called Pendilore that had more information about the curse. But I couldn't help but consider that Rosen wasn't lying despite his arrogance. The thought disturbed me a little more than I liked.

"It's impossible," I whispered to myself.

"Say what you want, but it could be true," Rosen smiled dauntlessly, like he'd won some invisible battle.

Unfortunately his words only complicated the current situation. Already I felt so many things about the curse were unknown. *What if these were the answers? What if Pendilore existed? But if it did exist where was it located?* I shook my head forcing myself not to get too invested in Rosen's story. *On what grounds could I even trust him?* He was a rouge, as Dusane had called him. And until Rosen proved himself, I wasn't going to believe anything about amberidium, the Chosen ones, or this place called Pendilore.

~

We didn't stop when the night fell. Shar insisted we keep traveling into the following morning. I was barely keeping myself from falling off Diablo when we finally decided to set up camp again.

Wearily, I climbed down to the ground, and a soreness radiated from my inner thighs from being on horseback for so long. I groaned and looked with annoyance at the sun flirting through the jungle canopy. It was morning and we were just resting.

"We'll stop for a couple hours, and then get on the road again," Shar ordered.

Rouix jumped down from beside me and gave me an impish smile. She too looked utterly exhausted.

"He's trying to kill us," she said seriously.

I chuckled weakly. "Sometimes it seems that way," I admitted as I hobbled over to where Dusane and Rosen were laying out their makeshift beds. I laid out my bed by the fire Conland was lighting and started to climb into the covers, my eyelids heavy.

"You look awful, E," Conland commented across the circle. I glared at him, too tired to handle his teasing.

"You should see yourself," I jabbed back and stuck out my tongue at him before turning my back to him and trying to find a comfortable place on the hard ground. Once again, I found myself wishing for a comfortable mattress, and silk sheets.

It was the briefest of sleeps. It felt as if I'd only closed my eyes for a couple seconds before I was being shaken awake again.

"Ehren, time to go," someone whispered, shaking my shoulder. I fluttered my tired eyes open to see Shar above me. He didn't look the least bit disheveled. His ponytail was still perfectly positioned at the nape of his neck, his eyes bright with awareness. There wasn't even a trace of a sleeping imprint on his cheek. I wondered if he'd slept at all.

"One more hour?" I moaned, feeling my limbs protest as I tried to sit up.

"Unless you want to confront Midennen, I suggest you get moving."

"I'm up," I said abruptly, suddenly standing. For some reason the thought of seeing Mid again caused a rapid fluttering to erupt in my stomach. It verged on being nausea, excitement, and dread. I didn't really know how to decipher it. But like I had done for so many months, I did my best to suppress the feeling and forced myself to focus on the task at hand.

After doing the best I could to tame my short hair into a braid, I mounted Diablo and waited for the others to depart. Rosen and Shar took the lead while Conland and Dusane talked together in the middle. Then I was in the back with Rouix. I didn't bother to hide the scowl I was throwing at the back of Dusane's head. He'd still had yet to even acknowledge my existence since learning about my identity. It was bothersome how easily he pretended I didn't exist.

"You okay, Ehren?" Rouix asked from beside me on her Crykon. I turned to her, startled from my pensive thinking.

"Yeah, I'm fine," I said hurriedly. But she didn't look convinced.

"Want some bread?" She offered, reaching into her saddle bag and ripping off a small piece from the loaf she'd been carrying. I took it and gratefully bit into the soft white grain while we rode. It soothed my hunger, and I washed it down with a swig of water from my canteen.

"Thank you," I said.

Her crimson eyes assessed me skeptically, but she wasn't one to pry and she focused on the path ahead, not asking me if I was all right again.

I was still brooding when a noise came through the trees. I turned, watching to see if something would move in the underbrush. But I could see nothing out of the ordinary. The skin on my arms stood up and a shiver coursed through me.

I was just about to turn away when suddenly the noise came through the trees again, and then a large dark object lunged out from the thick vines beside us.

THIRTY-ONE

The creature was pitch black and sleek with speed. Diablo immediately reared at the sight of the animal.

"Diablo! Easy!" I yelled, but it was too late. The force of the unexpected movement sent me tumbling off his back to the ground. It took me all of a couple seconds to stand and unsheathe the dagger from my side. Diablo flapped his wings recklessly at the creature.

The animal let out a loud roar, shaking the forest with a vicious cry.

It wasn't just any animal, but a cat. A big, vicious, black panther.

Diablo gave a high pitched neigh, and stomped the ground, trying to attack the panther. This set off the other animals. I watched Dusane lean down into the neck of Elesame and the lion let out a deep throaty growl, preparing to pounce at the black cat.

Then six dark cloaked figures emerged from the trees, suddenly surrounding us. It was instant recognition.

The others had already dismounted and pulled their weapons. It didn't take long to realize this was an ambush. The long dark haired individual with the dark black eyes was impossible not to recognize, and I felt a surge of adrenaline and fear flood my body.

Obsidian walked leisurely over to the black panther. The animal was growling,; it's fur bristled. He gestured for the animal to relax.

"It's good to see you again." Obsidian stated cooly, his eyes meeting mine.

Everyone in the group went still, waiting for just the right moment to begin the fight.

I could see the confusion on my friends faces. They had no idea who these people were. They didn't know about Obsidian or what he was capable of. Except for maybe Dusane who had once worked for Obscurum.

I could see the gold glowing in Obsidian's chest, and couldn't stop the terror that coursed through me. I wasn't mortal anymore. I was Stone-Hearted, and he could hurt me.

"I heard you're headed to Obscurum. Need an escort?" Obsidian grinned and turned his gaze to Shar. Shar gave nothing away, he simply held Wesoltinece's hammer in his hand, ready for a fight. Obsidian didn't even seem to notice the weapon, or if he did, he wasn't fazed.

I don't know how he'd found us or how he knew about our plans, but I didn't get time to consider the possibilities because Conland gave a battle cry, and sent his wolf lunging for two of the Obscurum guards.

Chaos instantly filled the tree circle.

Rouix and I began fighting side by side against two of the black cloaks. We worked quickly. I got a decent slice on one of the soldiers arms and the other didn't even have time to react before Rouix landed two knives into his chest. They were down in minutes.

Then the earth shook as Shar sent the hammer into the ground. I barely kept my balance as a crack in the jungle floor erupted across the tree ring. A nearby tree split in two with the momentum, and Rouix and I had to jump quickly away so we weren't impaled by the falling limbs.

I turned around panting and was appalled to see what was unfolding. Dusane was with Shar both attacking Obsidian, while Rosen and Conland were fighting off the remaining Obscurum soldiers.

Rosen had turned his opponent's leg solid, and Conland had already burned the other man pretty severely. The wolf went to finishing off the two black cloaks, sinking its teeth into them for good measure. But I wasn't worried about Rosen and Conland. Obsidian was facing off against Shar and Dusane, and despite the tremble Shar had sent into the earth with the hammer Obsidian was already back up on his feet and ready to attack again.

The panther was in a cat fight with Elesame. The two animals rolling across the tree ring in a flurried mass. Their ear splitting roars shook the trees around us. I began running toward Dusane and Shar. When I was just about to reach them, Dusane's yell echoed through the tree ring.

The panther had escaped the clutches of Elesame and effortlessly in one fell swoop raked its paw across Dusane's chest. Dusane fell to the ground, his face contorting into pain. I could see the flash of crimson begin oozing from his chest, and fresh droplets spattered across the jungle floor.

"Dusane!" I screamed. Rouix who had been right behind me, pulled the bow she had strapped at her back and sent two arrows straight into the creature's side. The animal faltered and let out a vicious screech. The cat snapped at the embedded arrows in its side, but it was useless. The animal soon fell in defeat beside Dusane, no longer breathing. Elesame let out another mighty roar and gripped the neck of the panther in her teeth before dragging its carcass into the trees.

Rouix and I immediately knelt beside Dusane, assessing the damage. I wanted to stop everything, wanted to make sure he was okay, but I knew the fight was far from over.

"Rouix, help him," I ordered before I reluctantly stood and started toward Shar who was still fighting Obsidian. I felt my heart constrict as I watched Shar's entire body freeze as if suddenly being controlled by some invisible force. The hammer fell from his hand, thumping against the jungle floor. Obsidian's face was one of pure concentration, and I knew instantly that he was killing Shar. I ran toward them, desperation consuming me.

"Stop!" I yelled. Shar fell to the ground, now seeming unable to breath. I remembered watching Obsidian nearly crush the heart of one of his comrades in Severesi. I could see Shar slipping away. At any moment he would be gone.

"Please Obsidian, don't do this! We're family!" I begged, falling to the ground beside Shar where he lay contorting in agony. My voice was on the edge of hysteria. Obsidian stopped using his power and I finally heard Shar gasp for breath. Obsidian turned his gaze to me.

"What did you just say?" His attention snapped back to me, and I continued to plead.

"If you truly are my cousin, Obsidian, why are you doing this?" Tears filled my eyes unexpectedly as I thought back on the faint memories I had in my mind. Me running through the woods as a child, Obsidian beside me. Blurry images of his father also accompanied the muddied memories and I could barely recall this uncle of mine. *What had happened?*

"You know exactly why! Don't pretend you don't know what your mother did!" I had triggered something in him. His eyes were wide and accusing, but no longer did his expression reek of mockery, or devilish power. But pain. Deep, agonizing pain.

I realized then that it was a facade. The powerful captain of the Obscurum Guard. The wicked laugh and devilish smile. It was a mask.

"I don't know what you mean, please Obsidian. Let's talk this out. It doesn't have to be this way!" I begged.

Obsidian shook his head, his dark eyes somehow childlike now as he looked at me. I could see a sliver of vulnerability, and a softness in his expression that clearly showed he'd been wounded.

Eyes that were usually hard and cold like obsidian stone I now knew had the potential to be... warm.

"No, it can *never* be the same after what she took from us!" I noticed then the slightest resemblances in his face. He had almond shaped eyes like my mother's. Faint pink lips like Jasper's, and a straight nose like mine. I'd never noticed before, but the likeness was uncanny.

He gripped me by the front of my jumpsuit, then pulled me from Shar's side and shoved me up against the trunk of one of the jungle trees. I groaned as the bark dug into my spine and tore at my skin.

Rosen and Conland had finished taking down the rest of the

black cloaks, the wolf beside them. Elesame had emerged from the trees and was now laying beside Rouix who was on the ground holding Dusane. Shar was coughing on the jungle floor next to them still trying to gather his bearings. I was pressed against the tree, at Obsidian's mercy. It wasn't looking so good. I could see Conland's eyes harden with determination and his wolf growled menacingly beside him.

"Conland, no, don't. He'll kill you," I said, my voice surprisingly calm. Luckily they listened and neither Conland nor Rosen moved.

"And the worst part is, you knew all along." Obsidian whispered, and the anguish in his coal black eyes suddenly vanished. Anger took over his expression and his other hand reached up, holding a knife to my throat. I forced myself to remain calm and told myself it would be okay. Better me than my friends.

"What are you waiting for?" I asked, not backing down. I knew that I was finally facing the nightmare that had been haunting me for so very long.

"Ehren, don't do this," I heard Shar gasp. He was still trying to stand but was failing miserably. Rosen and Conland took several careful steps forward, but I glared at the both of them to stay put.

"I'm fine, Shar."

I watched the depths of Obsidian's eyes harden into glittering obsidian orbs and become fueled with a sadistic excitement that was exclusive to a devilish mind.

"This is going to hurt a little," he said happily.

And then the pain hit.

He could've sliced my throat. Ended it quickly. But he wanted me to suffer.

I could feel the pressure on my chest, like it was being

suddenly crushed. I gasped for breath, losing all ability to inhale. It was an agonizing couple of seconds. Obsidian's laugh echoed throughout the trees. And then my body responded and pushed back against his power with a vicious force. The crushing pain ceased, and I could breathe again.

The confusion on his features was unmistakable. "What?" he muttered suddenly. His gaze hardened as if he was trying to deliver his power harder. I grinned now, grateful my heart hadn't failed me.

"Sorry to ruin your fun," I said sarcastically.

This angered him. Seeing that his power was useless against me and I took my chance while he was semi-distracted to knock the knife away from my throat. The blade disappeared, getting lost in the thick jungle shrubbery.

In a swift movement he growled menacingly and yanked me away from the tree. He slammed me into the ground and my head smacked against the dirt roughly in a similar fashion as my body. He repeated the motion for good measure and just as I was about to fight back the weight of him was lifted off me.

Conland's wolf let out an angry howl as the canine tackled Obsidian to the ground. The creature opened its mouth, its large teeth glistening as he went straight for Obsidian's head. I watched wide eyed waiting for the fight to come to an abrupt end, when I suddenly heard the wolf whelp and let out a heart-breaking whimper. Obsidian shoved its limp form away from him, and I could see a large knife embedded in the wolf's thick furry chest, directly into its heart. The wolf whimpered as it fell onto its side. One last wheezing breath escaped the creature and then it died.

I heard Conland let out a raging battle cry, and in an angry frenzy, he attacked Obsidian. What happened next seemed to go in slow motion. The two collided, and I could hear a punch that Conland landed onto Obsidian's cheek. I started toward them, the panic rising inside of me as I watched Conland reach out his palms, about ready to release the inferno. And then clutched his chest. I reached out to him, but it was too late.

It felt as if time stopped. Obsidian looked over at me, his eyes vacant of feeling. Then the blue light drained from Conland's chest like sand in an hourglass, and then he slumped to the ground.

"No!" I screamed. I ran to Conland's side. Dropping beside his lifeless body. I grasped his shoulders, shaking him desperately. His eyes were open, staring blankly at the sky.

"Conland! Wake up!" Tears spilled down my face and the fear and terror that pierced every nerve in my body was the most awful feeling I'd ever felt. I'd watched my mother die. Seen her life slowly slip away from the sickness that had plagued her. But I'd begun to heal with time, however difficult it had been. And now the crushing pain that only death could bring returned full force, and it's awful clutches were just as agonizing as it had been the first time I'd had to endure it.

"This is a reminder, Sabeara, from the king. That if you cross us, there will be consequences," Obsidian threatened, while wiping off a streak of splattered blood from his cheek. His dark eyes were still cold and emotionless. Not an ounce of regret in their sidious expression despite the life he'd just taken.

I looked at him, hatred in every fiber of my soul. I couldn't find the words to respond, I was too angry and too devastated to speak. I didn't even try to fight him as he disappeared into the trees.

Rosen started to follow after him, but Shar immediately called for him to stop.

"No, Rosen. Let him go," Shar ordered. Rosen cursed under his breath but didn't chase after Obsidian.

Shar was beside me then, and he pushed my hands off Conland's chest where I was gripping his shirt in my hands. "Go help, Dusane," he said gently. I barely heard the words, my mind numb. "Ehren, now."

I stumbled to my feet and barely got myself across the tree circle to kneel beside Rouix who was trying her best to keep pressure on Dusane's wounds.

I slowly slipped into a state of shock, barely registering what was happening. But there was one thing I was sure of—and that was that I wouldn't be able to handle it if Dusane died today too and I instantly pushed the possibility out of my mind, not wanting to lose precious focus. I continued to let the adrenaline fuel me, hoping it would remain in my veins long enough to get me through what I was about to do next.

"Let me try something," I said, not knowing if it would work but needing to try anyway.

He was sweating heavily, his breathing short and shallow. The jungle heat only added to the beads of perspiration on his brow. All irritated feelings I'd had toward him the last couple of days vanished, and a desperation consumed me. I looked into his pained cerulean eyes and willed them to remain open.

"It's going to be okay," I said to him. Wishing my words had more faith. I had done these exercises with him many times, but none of them had been successful. I didn't know if I could do it, didn't know if it was possible.

I watched several tears leak onto Rouix's cheeks as she helped me cut off Dusane's bloodied shirt to expose the wound. Dusane moaned at the movement, and I could see his jaw clench in agony.

Angry red claw marks were fresh across his chest, and they continued to trickle with blood. Even though our kind was more resilient, a wound like this would be fatal without a healer. I forced myself to focus, and not to think of the other body laying only several feet away from me.

I stretched my hand out and laid my fingers on the deep gashes on his chest. My fingers were instantly drenched in thick scarlet blood, and I tried not to get queasy. I could only hope I was capable of what I was about to attempt. That somehow, it would work.

I closed my eyes and focused as hard as I could.

THIRTY-TWO

The entire group went silent as I worked. The only sound for many moments was Dusane's ragged breaths and the quiet whistling of the breeze against the leaves of the trees. I focused as hard I could, pushing out thoughts of Conland that threatened to overtake my focus.

I cleared my mind, imagining my power leaving my chest in the same way I'd imagined with the amulet. I didn't know if my power reacted in the same way, but I had to try. Soon I could feel something, and it wasn't what I'd expected. A burning sensation spread throughout my body. I ignored the unusual feeling suddenly covering my body and continued to try and allow my power to heal Dusane.

I knew it was beginning to work when I heard Rouix gasp. I forced myself to keep my train of thought, and pushed through the burning sensation.

I peeked open one eye and saw that the claw wound on his

chest was almost completely healed. I pushed a little harder, starting to feel exhausted with the effort.

When I checked again, the wound was gone. Curiously I undid the bandage on his forearm and found the cut he'd acquired back in the arena was gone too. I sat back on my heels, and took in several deep breaths and met Dusane's wide blue eyes.

"You did it," he murmured, looking at me from beneath hooded lids. All I wanted to do was lie down and cry, but I forced myself to hold it together.

"We almost lost you too," Rouix said, her voice breaking with emotion.

"I'm here," Dusane said and I watched him reach out and clasp her small hand. She clung to it like a lifeline, and my chest ached at the display.

"I didn't know if I was going to be able to do it," I admitted, still in a state of shock.

"Thank you, for saving me." Dusane's cerulean eyes met mine.

We stared at each other for a moment, and then I turned my attention back to Rosen and Shar. I could see them kneeling over Conland, his wolf beside him, and I couldn't hold back the nausea anymore. I ran to the bushes and vomited. Once everything inside of me had been heaved from my stomach, I sat back onto the ground, my head in my hands.

"We need to bury them," I heard Shar whisper.

"Let's take them back to the Courts. Bury them where they belong," Rosen insisted.

"We aren't going back," Shar said, no room for argument in his tone.

"Stop this nonsense Shar. We are never going to get into the castle now that they know we're coming."

"We are not giving up."

And we didn't.

Dusane slowly regained his energy. It seemed my healing had done the trick. The rest of the night was spent burning the bodies of the fallen Obscurum soldiers and digging a burial ground for Conland and his wolf.

Just before setting his body into the ground, I reached out to lay my hand on his chest, tears filling my eyes. "I'm so sorry, Conland," I whispered, tasting the salt of my tears. And then in a last ditch effort to save him, I pressed all my power into him. I knew it was probably futile that my powers could extend to bringing someone back to life. But I had to try. The burning sensation flooded my body, tingling my every nerve.

But he never reopened his eyes.

And I knew it was useless.

It was a solemn moment when together we covered them with dirt and vines. No words were said, the pain too fresh to express it in words. But we stood together in unified silence for a time, and I knew what we all were thinking.

We'd never get to hear him tease or joke again, that his flirtatious smile would no longer be directed at anyone of us. I had only known him for a short time but I had considered him my friend. And he was one of the many casualties in the war we were fighting.

It was then I understood why Shar refused to return.

We couldn't let them win.

After everything that had happened, we owed it to Conland to finish the rescue mission that we started.

THIRTY-THREE

Three more days passed on our journey. We stopped only when we had to and rarely rested. On the third night when the stars started peeking out from the sky and the animals were too tired to keep going, Shar finally called us to a halt.

"We need to stop," Shar said, and we all slowed to a walk.

"Let's find a safe place to set up camp," Rouix said. Together we looked around for an area that would be inconspicuous.

"I think I saw a cave a couple minutes ago. It was east a little ways," Rosen interjected, and we all turned to Shar for approval.

Shar sighed and nodded. "Lead the way," he consented.

We followed Rosen through the trees, and about a half a mile later, we came upon the cave he'd seen. It was pressed against a little knoll in the ground. Jungle trees nearly consumed it. It wasn't big enough for everyone, but it would still help shield the group more than just the trees.

We laid out our belongings without much conversation.

Rouix and I started a fire, while Dusane and Shar began talking about the distance to Obscurum.

"We are close. And the rescue could be staged tomorrow if we are efficient," I heard Dusane say to Shar. They were positioned over a map they had laid out on the ground. A lantern illuminated the ancient markings on the paper.

"If we don't move quickly, they'll catch up. We don't have another choice. Tomorrow is our only chance," Shar confirmed.

I felt a thread of fear realizing we'd be trying to sneak into the Obscurum castle tomorrow. It couldn't be easy, and I didn't know how we'd get past their defenses. I forced myself not to consider that it may be a suicide mission and went to sit by Rouix. She had out some fruit and bread, and I began picking at some of the provisions beside her.

"Who was that man, that attacked us?" Rouix whispered beside me, her crimson eyes staring blankly into the fire. She'd barely said two words over the past three days, and I knew she must've been replaying all that had happened with Obsidian and his men. It was impossible not to replay the horrific scene of Conland's death. And each time it did, it made the ache in my chest deepen.

"His name is Obsidian. He's the captain of the Obscurum Guard," I explained to her. My every word was emotionless, numb.

"What did he do to. . .?" she trailed off. She didn't need to say his name. I already knew who she was referring to.

"He can crush Stone-Hearted hearts," I stated flatly. She didn't ask any more questions after that, for which I was grateful. The others ate some food as well, and then we were all set up for bed. Rouix and I took up shelter in the cave while the boys slept outside with the fire in the middle of them.

When the stars came out and the night successfully took over the sky, I still couldn't sleep. Rouix turned over beside me, and I noticed her red eyes were wide open staring at me in the darkness.

"You need to go to sleep, Ehren," she said. I remained looking up at the cave ceiling trying to grasp onto reality.

"He killed Conland," I blurted. And saying the words aloud made it all the more real.

Rouix sat up from her makeshift bed. "I know," she whispered.

I thought back on what Obsidian had said so long ago in the music room, that I'd pay for my mother's sins. His ramblings about my family were still unknown to me. I couldn't help but wonder what had happened all those years ago. *What had caused such hatred between our families?*

"Obsidian may be powerful, but I'm going to find his weakness. And when I do, I'm going to kill him the way he killed Conland." The words came out harsh and cold, and Rouix squeezed my arm.

"You are not a murderer, Ehren. . ." she started to say but I shook her off.

"No, but I'm an Envorydian. I keep peace. And the only way our realm is ever going to have peace again is if Obsidian and the king of Obscurum die."

I scolded myself for believing for a single second that there was something else in his expression that day. I'd thought maybe I'd seen pain in his eyes—a vulnerability. But I was wrong. He was a monster. Whatever I'd witnessed must've just been my own hopeful imaginations.

Rouix didn't say anything more, didn't try to convince me

not to be vengeful. She simply nodded and turned back to lie on her side.

At some point I must have drifted off to sleep because soon the sun came up, and in the dim light of the early morning, my eyes fluttered open.

I saw someone stand from one of the beds by the dead fire and carefully leave into the trees. When I couldn't see who it was, I inevitably followed.

THIRTY-FOUR

I stood and tiptoed out of the cave. I walked through the camp, and past the others still sleeping and wondered if it was Shar, who never seemed to sleep.

I came around a bend of shadows in the trees and found Dusane leaning against a large palm tree, looking up at the pale pink sky. Speckles of sunlight filtered through the leaves, illuminating his perfect Stone-Hearted features.

"What are you doing out here?" I asked him, walking closer to him so I could speak quieter, as not to wake the others.

"I just couldn't sleep any longer," he explained, and our eyes met for the briefest of seconds before he quickly averted his gaze.

"How are you feeling? You had a pretty bad hit during the fight, " I said, trying to ignore his lack of eye contact.

"I'm fine. And it could've been worse," was all he said, his tone darkening. And he was right. He easily could have lost his life. Like Conland, but instead he had lived. I wondered if he was harboring some sort of survivor's guilt. I knew I was. I'd thought many times over the last several days about Conland and what would have happened if I'd been the one to die instead. *Would Obsidian's hatred have been sated? Would he have left everyone else alone?* The possibilities were too excruciating to entertain.

"I'm glad you're all right," I commented, trying to evoke some sort of response from him.

"Thank you, for healing me," he said quietly, almost a whisper and then he turned to walk deeper into the trees.

"Where are you going?"

"I need to take a walk." He didn't even turn around as he said this.

"Are you ignoring me?" I asked suddenly, and he stopped in his tracks. He didn't turn around. "Ever since I told you I was princess of Aveladon, you've been acting strange." I wanted so badly to be able to talk to him about what had happened to Conland and the pain I felt. I wanted to talk about my family ties to Obsidian and the complicated puzzle that was our past. I wanted to tell him how much I missed my family. . . I wanted to lay my head on his shoulder and cry . . yet, I didn't know why I sought his comfort. It was stupid really. He would never tolerate such weakness from me.

Dusane finally faced me, and his blue eyes were lighter than usual in the morning sun.

"It's not because you're the princess," he stated simply.

I crossed my arms over my chest. "So you're ignoring me?" I deduced from his lack of answering the first question.

"Does it matter if I am?" he asked, and it wasn't at all bitter. It was emotionless, detached, like he always seemed to be.

"Yes, it does actually," I snapped.

He sighed, then turned around and walked deeper into the

trees. I followed after him, determined to demand an explanation. I had done nothing to deserve his cold shoulder.

"Stop following me, Ehren. Go back to sleep," he ordered in his trainer voice.

I caught up to him and reached out to grip his arm, forcing him to stop and look at me.

"What's your problem?!" I said louder than I intended. The frustration and anger from everything that happened the last couple days had reached its peak now. And I wasn't backing down.

He didn't answer, simply shook my hand from his arm. He glared at me, and I was glad to see a small ounce of emotion.

"If it's not about me being the princess, then what is it?" Memories unwillingly resurfaced of that night in the Drego when I'd tried to kiss him. It was a long time ago, but I couldn't help but wonder if maybe he'd been holding a grudge all this time without me knowing. "Is it because I tried to kiss you a couple months ago?" I hissed, my eyes narrowing in realization. "Look, if you don't like me that way, Dusane, I understand. It was a mistake, a stupid mistake and I'm—" something happened, as I continued to ramble. His eyes got darker and darker with emotion, and I didn't realize what I'd done until it was too late.

Like a dam, harboring passionate blue waves, he broke. And the current rushed out, creating a rapid unlike any I'd ever witnessed. More emotion than I'd ever seen suddenly flared in his eyes. He ran a hand angrily through his hair, causing the sunlight to reflect off his silver ear piercing.

"No, Ehren, you've got it all wrong," Dusane growled, and the reverberation from the snarl instantly silenced me. I looked at him, wide eyed with shock at his reaction.

"Of course I wanted to kiss you that day," he said suddenly, his eyes locking on mine with an intensity I didn't even know he was capable of emanating. "But now that I know everything—I can't just demand your affections. I can't storm into the situation and declare my feelings."

I hadn't expected the conversation to take such a turn.

"I can't touch you." He reached for me then and because we were exactly the same height, I looked directly into his eyes as he pulled me to him. My arms remained limp at my sides as one of his hands gripped my waist and the other reached up to cup my cheek.

"I can't hold you like this." He leaned in, and our lips came a mere breath apart. "I can't kiss you. . ." he trailed off, and I watched his eyes shift down to my lips for the briefest of seconds, as if he were considering it.

"Why not?" I whispered weakly. There was a long pause before he answered.

"Because"—his jaw clenched—"can you honestly say you aren't thinking about *him* right now?"

It took me a moment to register what he'd said. Then the memory of emerald-scarlet eyes unwilling came rushing back to me.

"Did you really think I wouldn't find out?" he asked skeptically.

I struggled for an explanation. "Who—who told you?" I stuttered.

He released me suddenly, taking several steps back. "No one had to. I've suspected for some time that there was someone else, which is why I didn't kiss you in the Drego. I've kept my distance, hoping that faraway look in your eyes would fade. But it never did. And then I saw you panic at the fight when those men showed up. And it wasn't hard to put the pieces together once you told me who you were. Whoever he is, you still have feelings for him. And that's why I'm acting differently. I can't get close to you. I'd be a fool to get involved with whatever royal drama you're caught up in." He looked saddened, maybe even pained for a second, and then abruptly all the emotion was gone. It was like an instant change when he went back to being hard and impassive again.

"Dusane. . ." I started to say, but he just shook his head.

"You don't have to explain yourself, Ehren." He turned around and started to walk away again, and this time I didn't chase after him.

THIRTY-FIVE

When I returned to the camp, the sun had risen completely, illuminating the baby blue hue of the sky. I thought I was the only one awake in the camp, but to my surprise, I spotted Rosen and Shar leaning over a map. The two talked quietly together as they examined it.

I went to sit by them on the ground and listened as they planned. I tried desperately to distract myself from thinking about the conversation Dusane and I had only moments before, but it was a lost cause.

Had it really been that obvious that I was thinking of someone else? I thought I'd been doing a good job at suppressing my feelings back in the Courts. But Dusane was more observant than I'd realized . . .

I wanted to argue more with him, but part of me knew he was right. It wouldn't be fair to pursue my feelings for him when I was thinking of Mid. But the feelings I'd had when Dusane had touched me. . . those had been real. And I definitely wasn't thinking about Mid when he'd been inches away from kissing me.

"We can't get into the main entrance. They'll have too many guards, even at the weak hour we're trying to exploit. It will be impossible," Shar said, and I could hear the aggravation in his voice.

"But the other doors will be securely locked. It could take some time to pick the locks, and the chances of us being seen by someone is incredibly high," Rosen countered.

"What seems to be the problem?" I pushed thoughts of Dusane and Mid away and forced myself to focus on the matter at hand. The map in front of them I could see now wasn't a map at all but a blueprint of the Obscurum castle.

"They can't figure out how to get in," a voice said behind me. I turned around to see Dusane. He returned from his "walk" in the woods, and I quickly looked away from him.

Dusane nonchalantly came over to the map and began pointing to several of the black shaded markings.

"We know how to get into the dungeon and how we'd rescue Embrosine. But actually getting in and out of the castle without being seen is our biggest issue," Dusane said.

"Why are you trying to break into the doors? Why not just have someone open them for you?" I asked, suddenly looking at the map and realizing quickly that the map was of the interior. It showed little tick marks for the doors, but it lacked showing the physical exterior of the building.

"What do you mean?" Shar asked seriously, his gaze turning to me.

"Why don't we enter from the roof and then one of us can open the doors, no breaking in necessary," I suggested and there was a moment of silence from the men as they all looked at me. I felt my cheeks redden at their shocked expressions. I watched Rosen's lips spread into a grin.

"And how do you suppose we get on the roof?" he asked, almost sarcastically, as if it was a good idea, but not easily executed.

"I can fly Diablo onto the roof, and once I get inside, I'll open one of the doors for you guys so you don't have to break in. Then we can all go together down to the dungeons."

"Is there an entrance on the roof?" Shar turned to Dusane for approval.

Dusane responded with a curt nod. "There is, over the north quarters," he said. I remembered that Dusane used to work at the castle. The blueprint must have been solely from his memory.

"Okay, and suppose that it does work, how do we leave?" Shar asked, the question directed openly to the group.

"I'll leave with Diablo from off the roof, and you all will leave out the dungeon doors. If you need to, you can knock out the guards, take their uniforms, and escape." All of them went silent again as if not really believing I'd actually come up with a good plan.

"I told you I could be of help," I said pointedly to Shar.

"We need to leave as soon as the sun goes down," Shar said, ignoring my comment."We'll travel as close to the Obscurum border as we can, set up a camp on the edge, and then journey into the city."

I could feel the excited motivation radiate from the circle as the plan fell into place.

"It's settled then," Rosen said, rubbing his hands together eagerly.

"Wake Rouix. We need to get on the move," Shar ordered.

I returned to the cave and shook Rouix till she woke. As a trained soldier, it didn't take much to get her up and moving. We cleaned up camp quickly. After doing it a couple times now, it had become easier.

I mounted Diablo and gently stroked the soft wavy locks of his ebony mane.

"You ready, boy?" I whispered to him. He gave me a gentle snort. Despite the looming danger that seemed always present with Obscurum, I felt oddly peaceful. It was different going to the castle on my own free will rather than as a captive prisoner. I remembered nearly a year ago when I'd been taken to the Severesi camp and almost been delivered to King Elysian. I was willingly walking into the mouth of the dragon this time, only I was free of chains and a trained Envorydian. I felt a feverish determination seep into my blood, and it vitalized my resolve.

THIRTY-SIX

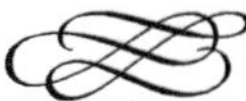

The jungle seemed to be endless from the Courts to Obscurum. But eventually Shar called us to a halt. I was grateful to finally slow to a standstill. Shar dismounted his horse and I watched him disappear into the trees.

"We've made it," Shar called moments later from somewhere in the foliage.

I jumped off Diablo and followed after him.

I pushed past thick branches and vines until abruptly the trees dispersed and then they disappeared completely, and suddenly I was looking out at a vast sea of yellow sand.

Glittering golden grains stretched endlessly out before us, meeting with the horizon in the distance. Not a single piece of architecture interrupted the landscape. A heat, different from the jungle humidity, radiated from the top of the sand, and I could nearly see the heat waves coming off the surface.

"Whoa," I said more to myself than the group. The others had also come through the trees to see the border. They gazed with wide eyes at the sea of sand. Dusane seemed to be the only one unaffected by the scene. Instead, a darkness filled his blue eyes I'd never seen before. Memories of his past life must have been running through his mind. And I suddenly wished I could know what he was thinking.

"We need to set up camp and then start journeying. It will take us several more hours to get to the castle," Dusane said, and then he turned back toward the trees.

We set up camp in the shade and passed around some provisions to prepare for the rescue.

"At this point, the others won't be far behind us," Shar said, sounding worried.

"That's if they journeyed all day," Rouix pointed out.

Shar met my gaze. An unsaid conversation passed between us.

"Okay, so let's say for argument's sake they aren't far behind. Do you think they'll follow us into the castle?" Rosen pressed.

"Maybe," Shar said, obviously not certain of Mid's motives.

"Let's just get on the move. The sooner we leave, the better," I said, a little too eagerly.

We grabbed our things, clad our weapons, and left our camp set up to return to later—*if we made it out alive from Obscurum,* I thought to myself.

I mounted Diablo and followed after the others.

His hooves sunk into the sand, and I could immediately feel the way the landscape changed. I looked at the ground and gasped at what I saw. As Diablo's hoofs scraped through the sand, the top layer was displaced showing beneath it another layer of dark black. But oddly enough seconds after the displacement, it would settle and return to its original yellow color. I watched, fascinated at the black sand beneath, and admired over and over again the way it would appear stark ebony and then blend back to yellow.

"It's incredible," I said quietly to myself.

"I think one of us should go ahead and search the area," Rosen suddenly announced beside me. I watched everyone's eyes turn to Shar.

"It's not a bad idea," Shar finally admitted after a couple minutes of deafening silence.

"Split up? Are you sure?" Rouix asked, obviously not liking the idea.

"It will allow us to be less conspicuous, and we can scan the area for possible trouble," Shar added, seeming to like the idea the more he reasoned through it.

"I'll go with you," I stated suddenly. "We can travel faster on Diablo and can go ahead to scout out the area."

Shar nodded and suddenly brought his horse to a halt. He handed the reins to Rouix and then came to mount Diablo behind me.

"We'll stop when the city's in sight. Meet us at the edge of the water," Shar said to Dusane

I started Diablo into a run and then allowed him to hover above the sand. When he flapped his wings it would send ripples across the black and gold surface. It was much quicker flying, and it cut the journey in half. Suddenly the yellow horizon transformed, and it was no longer just sand. The distinct glistening of water came into sight.

When we came to the edge, I brought Diablo to a halt and could see the kingdom of Obscurum in the distance.

Following the shoreline to the north several miles, black city walls encased the city. The kingdom and its city gates loomed over the flat sand and sea.

"We wait here then?" I asked, and Shar nodded, jumping off behind me to walk up to the edge of the water. He looked down the shore and put a hand up to shield his eyes from the setting sun.

"We can't get any closer without risk of scouts seeing us. We'll want the sun to be completely down before we attempt entering the gates. You'll be able to fly over and straight in, but we'll have to sneak inside the walls pretending to be Obscurum civilians. Then when we get to the castle we will wait for you to grant us access to the side door." He reached into his pack and handed the map to me. "Start studying the layout so you know where to go."

I sat on the sand and opened the map on my lap. I stared out at the seashore, admiring the glistening water for a moment before taking in the lines and squares Dusane had drawn on the piece of paper.

Shar paced up and down the sand as I studied, and the sun got lower and lower in the sky as we waited for the others. He seemed to be in deep thought. I looked up after about a half hour, realizing he was driving himself insane.

"Shar, we're going to get her out," I said softly. He stopped suddenly in his tracks and nodded, sighing a little.

"I can only hope she's alive," he said, and I realized suddenly with great fear that maybe there wasn't anyone to rescue. *What if they had killed her?* I shook my head, determined not to think the worst.

"Do you think there will be any tokens in Obscurum?" I asked suddenly, hoping to offer him a distraction.

"It's possible." I watched him reach for the hammer at his waist. He hadn't let go of it since the day I'd handed it to him after the Regal fight. Instantly my hand went up to my amulet. I clutched the ruby in my hand, and noticed it was glowing the shade of violet in Dusane's chest. I must have accumulated it during one of the moments we'd interacted. Unconsciously, when I had intense emotions, it seemed I somehow pulled power from others. The last time we'd talked, I'd definitely been fired up.

"I tried studying about some of the tokens when I wasn't training, but there are still two that have me struggling to understand," I said.

"I doubt we're the only ones with tokens. But I can't imagine they are leaving them unprotected if they do have them."

"But what if they aren't hidden? What if we could find a token in Obscurum and save Embrosine?" I asked, suddenly hopeful.

Shar looked at me and smiled a little. "You're over ambitious, Ehren," he said suddenly.

"Do you know anything about the other two tokens?" I pressed.

Shar sighed and came to sit beside me on the sand. The sun was now dipping beneath the ocean, and the stars were beginning to show faintly behind the dark purple sky. I noticed the flickering of scales in the water and admired a herd of wild Crykon swimming in the waves.

"As you know, Midennen thinks Linsulong has a compass, we have the amulet, and then the hammer was from Wesoltinece. As for Ennsleon and Oxtwenel, I have only small theories that are very unreliable. There is not much information on the two of them."

"Do you think Rosen was telling the truth? That there's more information about the Ethirical in that place called Pendilore?"

"It would help if it was true. We could go and find out what we've been missing," he admitted.

"And the Amberidum?"

Shar pursed his lips. "It's a strange theory, but I suppose it could also be true."

"But can Rosen be trusted?" I asked, not bothering to hide the skepticism in my voice.

"Rosen has a tendency to be on the side that benefits him the most. He's not bad, but he's not always good. So it doesn't necessarily mean he isn't telling the truth. We just have to make sure he stays on our side." Shar's words did little to help me in the way of trusting Rosen.

"Do you think any of the tokens are in Obscurum?"

"Ennsleon's," he stated assuredly.

"What do you think his token is?"

"The Ethirical speaks of his love for the stars and how he could read the constellations. They helped him know his enemies motives, changes in the weather, and even future events that were going to transpire. The stars guided him. So I think it has something to do with that," Shar explained.

"The stars. . ." I trailed off, thinking of all the possibilities.

"Maybe it is a device that helped him gaze into the universe," Shar said. It wasn't a bad theory.

"And Oxtwenel?" I added hopefully.

Shar shook his head. "A complete mystery. It has actually been a source of real frustration for me over the years—why so little information was given about him."

The fifth king had a very small excerpt in the Ethirical, and I agreed that it was the most vague. I wondered how we'd ever find the token connected to him.

"Well, maybe we'll find something to do with Ennsleon on this rescue mission," I said hopefully.

"My only worry is Embrosine. And as selfish as that may seem, Ehren, that's the only thing I'm focusing on at the moment."

"I understand, Shar. And we're going to find her." I reached out for his hand, and oddly enough it didn't feel weird at all as I gave his hand a reassuring squeeze. It was a friendly gesture, something I would've done for Oli or Jasper. Another question came to my mind. "Can I ask you one more thing?"

"Sure," he said.

"What would happen if the tokens got into the wrong hands?"

"No one has told you?" Shar asked, surprised. I shook my head, realizing I'd heard of the consequences of the curse. If we didn't defeat it, we'd lose our powers as a people over time, and no one would be granted powers anymore. But I'd never asked about the enemy, and what would happen if King Elysian won.

"If King Elysian gets the tokens, he can use them to become the most powerful Stone-Hearted in the realm."

My eyes widened. "What? How?"

"The tokens can either be used to defeat the curse, or they can be used to become the most powerful Stone-Hearted that has ever existed. How, I don't know exactly. I only know it's possible, and if King Elysian gets his hands on them. . ."

I suddenly remembered the words of Sydidel when Mid and I had visited him so long ago. He'd said something about a demon running the land. The image was easy enough to conjure. King Elysian would be an all-powerful ruler if he gained access to the tokens. And we would all suffer under his rule.

"I won't let it happen," I said determinedly.

"And that's why the kingdom needs a warrior like you, Ehren," Shar suddenly said.

I shook my head. "I don't know about that," I blushed, turning my face to the side to hide my embarrassed face.

"You've defied all odds. I honestly didn't think you could win in that fight. But you did. And I have immense respect for you because of that," he said seriously.

I looked up at him, meeting his intense green eyes, and gave him a sheepish smile. "So, you aren't mad at me anymore for disobeying you?"

He chuckled despite the stress obviously strung through his body. "Something tells me I'm just going to have to get used to that," he said.

~

The others arrived just as the sun was disappearing, and soon all that filled the night sky were twinkling stars and the light of the pale moon.

As the others came trudging through the sand, they halted at the edge of the beach and they climbed off their animals so we could collaborate.

"It's time to head toward the city. Ehren is going to fly over the walls and onto the castle. We'll have to sneak through the gates," Shar explained.

I handed him the map so he could point to areas he needed for visuals.

"Couldn't I just come back down and fly you all up with me?" I asked. "You could avoid having to sneak into the city gates altogether."

"It's already going to be risky enough having you fly in without being seen. You'd have to fly two or three times to get us all and the chances of castle archers seeing you are more likely."

"Are you sure you can sneak in?" I asked nervously.

"Oh trust me, we can," Rouix said, and I suddenly remembered her power. I didn't press the subject further.

Shar continued to explain the plan again, and the longer he talked, the more anxious I became. It was no longer just a plan. We were actually going to raid the Obscurum castle and save Embrosine. I felt the adrenaline begin to pump in my veins.

When Shar was done explaining, everyone turned to look at me.

"Someone should go with her," Dusane said suddenly.

"I don't know—" Shar began to protest. Dusane and I met each other's gaze. The cerulean intensity from his eyes felt like it might be able to physically burn me.

"It will be easier for you to sneak in with one less person, plus we'd be riding together. The risk would be the same," Dusane pressed.

Shar pursed his lips, obviously not liking the sudden plan change. "Okay, you go with Ehren. The rest of us will meet you at the door," Shar relented.

I didn't know why Dusane was offering to come along exactly. I'd expected he'd want to stay as far away from me as possible during the mission. I walked over to where Diablo was waiting for me, and Dusane followed. The black ocean waves were crashing onto the shore, and a saltiness filled the air that I could taste on my tongue every time I breathed.

I mounted first, and Dusane settled in behind me. It reminded me of the first time we'd ridden together. The memory caused nervous butterflies to erupt in my stomach.

I took one last glance at the others getting ready to leave on the shore. I locked eyes with Shar for a brief moment. Then we were off into the sky.

THIRTY-SEVEN

The air was a warm current and the whir of the wind a gentle whistling in my ears. I was pressed against Dusane, trying to concentrate on anything but the feel of his hard chest pressed against my back. It didn't help that a dozen questions swirled around inside my head. *Why had he wanted to come with me? Was it really for the sake of the mission? Or was it to be alone with me?*

I pushed out those thoughts and feelings and tried to just enjoy being up so high in the sky as we passed quickly over the sandy terrain. Diablo blended nicely with the night and it wasn't long before we came upon the city.

Black flags and sharp spikes lined the very tips of the ebony walls. As we flew directly over the perimeter, I felt myself shiver. I could only hope the others would get inside safely.

The city was now beneath us, and it was filled with tall dark buildings. Dim lanterns lit the empty streets, but we were up so high, I could barely make out any detail. I could see that sand filled every corner and crevice of the kingdom and that it didn't appear to have much in terms of foliage. Only every once in a while I would see a bush or a tree. My first impression was that it was eerily dark and barren.

"What's it like in Obscurum?" I asked, too curious not to inquire.

"King Elysian rules with an iron fist. Be grateful you didn't grow up in Obscurum." I was surprised when Dusane responded. "Half the people are starving, and let's just say it's not easy to escape if you want to leave."

A knot formed in my stomach as I tried to imagine the awful reality of his words.

The castle came into view not long after, and it was placed in the very center of the city. It was a very terrifying piece of architecture. It too was made of the same ebony stone as the city walls, and the windows were dark. It appeared to be a solid confine—obscure, and inviolable.

I guided Diablo toward the tops of the castle, my focus sharpening as the situation got more dangerous.

"Did you study the map?" Dusane suddenly asked from behind me. His soft breath tickled my neck and I shivered, while trying to hide it with a nod.

"Yes,"

"Land as gently as you can on the north side," Dusane instructed.

I guided Diablo as carefully as I could to the north quarters. Every muscle in my body strained as we approached the onyx gables of the castle roof. There was a small flat stretch between two tall spires and it would be the only safe place to land. I directed Diablo to the flat surface, and he easily descended until his hooves landed with the quietest of clicks on top of the black stone. When he settled, we came to a perfect standstill. I let out a huge sigh of relief.

Dusane didn't seem as anxious as I was, and he quickly jumped into action. He slid off of Diablo and quickly helped me down from his back. He showed no emotion other than intense concentration. His brow was furrowed, his cerulean eyes alert.

"We'll need to cross over this section of roof to the other side where the latch door is located." Dusane gestured to a triangular section of roof, where the shingles were sleek and black like the castle stone.

Before following him, I ordered Diablo to wait for us. I gently patted his neck.

"Stay here, I'll be back soon. Try and be quiet, okay?" I asked him, and he seemed to understand. He snorted and I leaned over to press a gentle kiss to his midnight nose.

I started after Dusane then, and he was already halfway over the gable. As I approached the section I had to climb over, I looked at it skeptically. Despite the fact that Dusane and I were the same height, I immediately wondered how he'd gotten over. It was about a foot higher than me and didn't look like it had any good holding points. I forced determination into my body and tried to climb over.

The shingles were slippery, and I almost lost my hold as my fingers gripped the sleek stony crevices, but Dusane grasped my hand from the other side and helped me over before the panic could really settle in.

I landed on the other side of the gable where another stretch of flat roof greeted us.

"Thank you," I said to him. He just nodded, quickly averting his gaze from mine and continued across the roof.

The latch door blended seamlessly into the black stone. The

only distinction that it was a trap door was the silvery circle handle that stuck out from the top of it.

"What is going to be on the other side?" I asked while staring curiously at the door.

"Underneath here is a sitting room. And if I'm correct, it should be empty at this hour." Dusane sounded pretty certain of himself, but I remained skeptical.

"How long has it been since you've been back here?" I asked him, not bothering to hide my hesitation.

"Five years," Dusane said, and then he looked at me for a moment, giving me a narrow eyed expression. "Do you doubt me?" he asked, suddenly understanding why I'd asked.

"I don't doubt you. I'm just double-checking," I retorted, glad to be able to bite back. I needed a fight. Fighting was a much better outlet for my feelings.

"I thought you'd learned to trust me by now, Envorydian," he bit back, speaking to me as if he was my trainer again.

"I'm not your student anymore, Dusane," I snapped. "As your equal in the guild now, I think I'm *allowed* to verify your plans."

His eyes narrowed into deeper slits, and then he grumbled something under his breath and opened the latch on the door.

"Be quiet and follow me," he ordered. And then he was gone, jumping down through the square hole in the roof. I peered down over the edge and saw nothing but total darkness.

"Dusane!" I whispered into the empty abyss.

"Jump down, Ehren. I'll catch you," his whisper echoed from the void.

"You're joking, right?" I asked, feeling fear grip me at the idea of blindly jumping through the hatch.

"The others are going to be here soon. Jump," he ordered.

I swung my legs over the edge of the hatch and felt the stone snag the fabric of my pants. I forced myself to take in several deep breaths and then closed my eyes and pushed myself off the side.

I clamped my lips and eyes shut so I wouldn't scream, and then suddenly I felt my body drop into his arms and chest. I thought for sure the impact would send him wavering, but he remained immovable, not faltering even an inch as he caught me. He cradled me tightly in his arms with ease, and I realized this wasn't the first time I'd ended up in his arms like this.

I could see now that the room wasn't as dark as it appeared to be from up above. Faint light shone through the windows, and I hoped Dusane couldn't see my blush. When I felt his eyes on me, I looked up and met his bright blue depths in the darkness.

We gazed at each other for several long seconds, his expression hard and completely unreadable. Our faces were mere inches apart, and I felt the same tug in my body when I'd been with him on the roof in the Drego. Just when I thought I couldn't take any more of his piercing expression, he cleared his throat and let me down.

"That wasn't so bad was it?" he asked flatly, his tone not really light enough to be sarcasm.

"Don't expect me to do that again," I stated firmly.

Dusane didn't reply, and peered around the sitting room. The room had several long chaise lounges and a decorative table in the center. The curtains on the tall floor to ceiling windows were dark blood red, and the rug was made of plush black fur. Dusane walked over to the door that I assumed let into the hallway, and he gently pushed on the handle. He peeked through the crack, letting in a small sliver of yellow light, before quickly closing the door again.

"We have to get down to the main floor," he stated, and I walked over to where he was, feeling fear grip me.

"How are we going to do that?" I asked.

"We're going to walk there," he deadpanned.

I glared at him, realizing now that he was just being rude. "You're really not being very pleasant," I stated.

He turned to me, mirroring my glare with his piercing blue eyes. A ripple of some unrecognizable feeling passed through my body. I wasn't used to this side of him.

"Well, neither are you," he fired back.

"Can we just get to the main floor?" I snapped.

"Gladly," he hissed, and then he opened the door.

We slipped into the hallway. It was lit by several candles, and appeared to be completely empty. I followed after Dusane, my heart pumping wildly in my chest. We turned another corner and luckily it too was empty. I worried at any moment an Obscurum guard was going to come out from around one of the bends, but somehow we remained unnoticed all the way across the corridor and down two flights of stairs.

We began to hear voices as we got to the main floor. Dusane hurried and pulled me into the safety of one of the large door frames. He pressed me against the door and shielded me with his body. I got a whiff of his scent with him pressed so close to me. I smelled a distinct jungle musk that made my head spin a little. He smelled wonderful.

"Okay, let's keep going," he whispered when the voices passed and it was quiet again. We ventured back out into the hallway and walked until Dusane came upon a door that I assumed led to the outside.

"If all went well, they should be on the other side of this

door," Dusane said. He looked at the handle for a moment and then back down the hallway we'd just come from.

"What are you waiting for? Open the door," I said hurriedly, knowing every second we were out in the open we were risking our lives. I reached for the handle when I realized he wasn't attempting to open it, but he quickly stopped me. His hand clamped down over mine, and I looked at him with a bewildered expression.

"Wait," he said.

"There isn't time to wait. We need to get them in here!" I hissed angrily. But his hand remained firmly on mine, refusing to let me turn the handle.

"I have to do something first," he said. And I saw a little part of the Dusane I'd seen in the forest the other day when he'd admitted he'd wanted to kiss me, but couldn't. His cerulean eyes locked on mine and they seemed to be beg me to understand what they were trying to convey. They held no entreaty. His eyes weren't asking me for permission. They were filled with an unapologetic desire and he seemed to have already made some decision I was unaware of. And I didn't realize what was happening until he was suddenly kissing me.

THIRTY-EIGHT

I stood, shocked. It was the last thing I'd expected. He cupped my face in his hands and kissed me hastily. His lips were soft and warm as they moved against mine, and then it was suddenly over and he was pulling away. I didn't get to say anything before he opened the door and the others were revealed on the opposite side.

"Hurry, get in," Dusane ordered. His face went back to it's controlled, serious expression.

I was stunned, and the only thing that snapped me from my reverie was Shar's hand on my shoulder.

"You okay, Ehren?" Shar whispered. I nodded numbly. The door was still open where they'd come in, and I could see the unconscious bodies of several guards laying on the other side.

"Yeah, I think so," I said.

He didn't look convinced but pushed me along after the others. "We've got to go," he pressed.

I suddenly returned to reality. Embrosine and the mission to rescue her brought me back, and I hurried and followed after them.

We went down several hallways positioned close together, mere inches apart, in the line we'd formed. I followed directly behind Shar, trying to even out my breathing.

Dusane was in the lead, taking us to the place he knew that Embrosine was being held. We journeyed down a set of stairs, and then a couple more hallways. When there were guards, we quickly jumped into the closest room or doorway. It was relatively smooth getting down to the dungeon. It wasn't until we met with the dungeon guards that we ran into trouble.

There were two guards at the main entrance to the dungeon. Dusane motioned for us all to stay still. I was pressed to the side of the corridor, and just around the corner was the prison door. Dusane then jumped from behind the safety of the wall and attacked the two guards. Rouix joined him and together the two of them brought the guards down with ease. I stepped over one of the bodies that lay unconscious on the floor and spotted an Envorydian symbol on one of the man's wrists. I forced myself to look away and pay attention as Dusane took the key from the guard's cloak pocket and turned it into the keyhole. Soon we were all inside.

It reminded me of the prison back in the Commission. Black cages housed Stone-Hearted captives and a rotten aroma permeated the air. The dungeon was hot and dark, and except for the faint glow in some of the prisoner's chests, it was nearly pitch black.

"Embrosine!" Shar called. He seemed to no longer care to keep himself hidden. He frantically began searching the cells, and we all followed, going to each one and calling out Embrosine's name. The other prisoners began to get riled up at our presence. They yelled and shrieked at us. Some reached through the bars of their cages. I felt some of their fingers brush my arms and legs, and I shied away from them, feeling an icy wave of fear thread through me at the desperation in their eyes—and the insanity that seemed to linger behind their expressions.

My blood pumped wildly in my veins, and a gut-wrenching desperation twisted my stomach hoping we'd find her. I peered into a dozen cells and found no evidence of her existence. It was a couple precious minutes later that Shar ordered everyone to be quiet. We all stopped talking, but the sound of the other captives in the dungeon continued to rage all around us.

"What is it?" I asked. When I finally got to the front of the group, I found Shar standing in front of a cell. The door was open, the inside was barren. All that remained inside was muddied, soiled straw.

"Shar. . ." I began but immediately trailed off as I realized that our worst fear had been realized. She was nowhere in the dungeon.

"She's not here," a voice penetrated above the shrieking voices of the prisoners. It echoed off the walls and caused ice cold fear to spread through my body at its familiarity.

I turned around and could see past Dusane's shoulder the distinct black shadow of a figure standing between the dark cages.

"Where is she?" I demanded. Anger flooded my body. Hearing his voice instantly brought back images of that day in the tree ring and Conland's lifeless body.

I pushed past the others and came face to face with Obsidian. We had ignored his warnings and walked right into his trap. We were caught, and I couldn't help but think our fates were the same as the others in the cells around us, or worse.

Several guards stood behind him, waiting for his command.

"Oh don't worry, she's still alive," he sneered. The look in his expression made me question if he was telling the truth.

I felt Shar come up beside me, and the tense feelings rolling off him were nearly visible in the darkness.

"What do you want?" Shar suddenly demanded.

Obsidian laughed cynically. All the prisoners had suddenly gone quiet. He stepped closer to us, and I could clearly see his dark eyes then, and the golden glow in his chest beneath his cloak. His long black hair fell around his face, and he reached up to tuck a lone strand behind his ear. I searched for signs of his injury. But he must've been healed because I couldn't see any bruising from the hit Conland had landed on his cheek.

"The king wants to meet with you, and negotiate a compromise," Obsidian explained.

I was shocked to hear his words. I had been preparing for a fight. I could feel the others around me tense with readiness to jump into a brawl. But the unexpected inquiry for a negotiation was the last thing I had thought he'd broach.

"A compromise?" I asked in disbelief.

"We both are in need of something, and the king is willing to work something out," Obsidian said. The darkness in his eyes was fierce. Once again I wondered how I thought I'd seen a flicker of humanity in him.

"Take us to the king," Shar suddenly relented. I heard a noise of protest come from behind me, maybe Rouix, or Dusane.

"Shar!" I hissed, not wanting to give into Obsidian's demands.

Shar shook his head at me. "It's our only chance, Ehren," his eyes pleaded for me to try. After a couple moments of battling internally with myself, I finally nodded, forcing myself to not attack those in front of us—yet—and avoiding an instant bloodbath.

"Excellent!" Obsidian clapped his hands together seeing he'd won and motioned for his guards to surround us. The other guards herded our group from the dungeon and back into the halls of the castle. Dusane ended up on my left and Shar on my right. I could feel the rigidness in their bodies, matching the tensity in mine.

We were led back through the halls and ended up at two large double doors, reaching clear to the ceiling. The big timbered pieces of wood created a masterpiece with their twirling designs on the exterior and large black handles made of cold steel. Obsidian pushed open the doors and stepped into the room. We were shoved inside after him.

What awaited us on the other side was a massive throne room. It had dark black marble floors and intricate ebony chandeliers hanging from the ceilings, dripping like icicles. Guards lined the gray walls, all standing in the same position, holding long spears firmly in front of them.

At the very end of the room were three chairs, the middle much bigger than the others. It was a throne, also dark and insidious like the rest of the castle's design. A dark red velvet cushion lined the armrests and seat. Sitting in the chair was a man. One I had only heard of.

King Elysian.

I wasn't expecting what happened next. My vision went fuzzy, and abruptly I was back in the nightmare I'd had so many times before.

I was shrouded in the shadows of the dark sitting room. Jasper had refused to come with me. I'd been the one who had wanted to sneak into the room.

My father and his guard were standing near the hearth, their faces no longer blurred. They were looking at the two other individuals across the room: Obsidian and his father. Obsidian was just a boy. Yet he had a small dagger hung at his waist, and he glared menacingly. My memory sharpened, seeing Obsidian's father beside him. And everything made sense. The blue eyes and the dark hair. The unmistakable similarities in his face.

My mother's brother. Elysian.

"How could you do this?" My father asked, and I watched Elysian chuckle darkly as he walked across the sitting room floor.

"It was the only way," Elysian said.

My mother was dead. My mother was gone. And I knew why. I looked at my uncle, no doubt in my mind that he was the one that had done it. He had been the one to poison her.

"You aren't going to get away with this," my father spat, and he gestured for his guards to attack. The entire room erupted into chaos, and I ran to hide behind the sofa as the ringing of swords clashed and the grunts of men fighting filled the sitting room. Someone grabbed me and I tried desperately to flee the scene, but instead I was spun around, coming face to face with dark black eyes. Obsidian. My cousin, my close friend. We had played together, laughed together, and even shared secrets. As a child I didn't understand as he lifted me by the front of my dress and shoved me to the floor. My head smacked against the marble floor.

The memory returned in a matter of moments, sharpening with perfect clarity and shocking me to the very core. Where the memory had come from and why it had suddenly resurfaced were unknown to me. Gradually the throne room came back into view, and I was looking at King Elysian again.

What just happened? I thought.

The king stood from his chair, and I could see he was tall and dressed in nice sleek clothes and a cloak. It wasn't black though. It was a dark blue. I could clearly see the green glow of his heart because he left the collar of his shirt open, the ties on the tunic left to dangle loosely down his muscled chest as if on purpose. He had dark unruly styled hair swept back from his face. A few strands fell around his nicely angled cheeks and chin. His nose was gently pointed, and his eyes were framed with thick lashes. His eyes were a striking blue that strongly resembled my mother's, and it was uncanny to see someone so beautiful have such an ugly soul.

I'd remembered a small piece of the puzzle. He was my mother's brother, and he'd been the one to kill her. But that was only the first piece because I still didn't know the reason why.

"What a pleasant surprise!" King Elysian greeted us from where he stood on the stairs leading up to his throne, making him several feet taller. He acted as if it wasn't just the physical distance that separated us. A superiority graced him that was unmistakable.

The guards pushed us closer to the throne, and I could begin to make out more detail. His cloak wasn't just blue. It had intricate designs sewn into the fabric, lines and dots—stars maybe. They looked like constellations. I didn't have time to dwell on the cloak because another guard entered the room.

The guard came through a side door holding captive an individual. And that's when I realized it was Embrosine.

She was dressed in a ragged day dress, her hair mangled and matted. She appeared to be starved, her skin sunken and bruised. She didn't even register the sight of us. She merely flickered her dead eyes to where we stood and then looked away again. She appeared emotionally broken and completely hopeless.

Beside me Shar started for her, but the guards quickly hindered him, and a menacing growl reverberated from his throat.

"Shar. . ." I cautioned. It was a fragile situation. I could feel the tangible tension in the room. If we were going to get out of here alive, we'd need to be tactful, and not let our feelings get in the way.

The guard that had held her threw her to King Elysian's feet. He didn't even acknowledge her existence as she fell to the black marble. She didn't fight. A set of chains remained around her hands, and she simply kneeled submissively before the king.

Shar stopped trying to fight to get to her, but the tormented expression remained on his face.

"Thank you for coming!" King Elysian greeted joyously, seeming completely at ease with the situation.

"When I heard you were headed for the castle, my son wanted to get rid of you. But I figured that would be irrational, considering we could be of use to each other. " The conversation was one sided. No one answered him, but he didn't seem to be bothered by the silence.

"I also couldn't refuse the chance to say hello to family."

My eyes flickered to Obsidian who was now standing beside King Elysian, his hands clasped behind his back. He didn't seem very happy about what was going on, as if he would rather be ending our lives than negotiating.

I looked away from Obsidian and back to King Elysian and reluctantly met his gaze. I could see the amusement in his eyes.

Why hadn't I remembered until now?

King Elysian walked closer to us and he kept his eyes on me the entire time.

"Sabeara Aigoviel," he said, almost in awe. "How incredible. You look exactly like her," he breathed. He gestured for the guards surrounding us to disperse so he could then reach out and touch my face.

Disgusted, I shied away from the feel of his fingers on my cheek.

"What do you want?" I snapped at him, my eyes going to Embrosine on the marble floor again. An intense feeling of desperation came over me. I needed to get to her.

And then he slapped me. Hard. My head snapped to the side with the momentum, and I fell to the floor. I clutched my now bleeding, throbbing cheek and forced myself not to moan in pain. Dusane tried to reach for me, but one of the guards quickly halted him.

"I wouldn't do that if I were you," one of the guards said.

Slowly I began to heal and I remained on the marble, trying to regain my bearings.

"That is no way to talk to your uncle," King Elysian cooed. He stepped away then, and the guards resumed their barricade around our group. I felt Shar's hand at my shoulder, and he helped me stand. Luckily none of the guards stopped him, and soon I was back on my feet.

I watched with fury as King Elysian walked back up over to Embrosine and grabbed a fistful of her hair and made her stand. She whimpered, but he ignored her cry of pain and tugged her close, so her face was mere inches from his.

"Now, Embrosine, why don't you tell Sabeara what happens to women who disrespect me," King Elysian hissed.

I felt Shar tense beside me, as if he knew what was coming next. And I sucked in a frightened breath.

The king pulled out a dagger from beneath his cloak. It was unlike any weapon I'd ever seen. A beautiful shade of purple illuminated the sleek silver blade, and when he pressed it to the skin of Embrosine's cheek, she screamed. I watched in horror as smoke came off her skin where the blade touched, and I realized it was burning her.

I gripped Shar's arm, holding him back, but I could feel the mirrored agony in Shar's body as he forced himself not to try and run to her. Her screams filled the throne room, and I knew I'd never possibly be able to forget them. They would be seared into my memory forever.

I had feared Obsidian for so long. He had killed Conland and been the one to kidnap me. But watching Elysian torture Embrosine, I started to think that maybe I'd been fearing the wrong monster.

Elysian ran the length of the blade across her cheek and down her neck, leaving a bright red burn in its wake. When he finally pulled the weapon away, she fell back to the marble floor, weeping.

I could feel myself shaking with fear and most of all cold-blooded anger. Everything inside of me wished to break through the guards and end this once and for all. I imagined myself grabbing the dagger from Elysian's hands and plunging it into his heart and then doing the same to Obsidian beside him. It was a vivid image, one I wished so badly to bring to life. But I remained where I was, forcing myself to wait for the right moment.

Elysian walked back to his throne, and suddenly a tangible

feeling unlike I'd ever felt washed over me. I stumbled back a little as I felt the unusual sensation. A distinct feeling, something intensely powerful, radiated from Elysian. As quickly as the feeling came, it was gone. It was then I noticed the purple color in my amulet suddenly fade, turning back to the ruby stone. I turned to look at Dusane, the source of the sudden power, but he wasn't looking at me, he was concentrating on King Elysian sitting on his throne. The hateful stare he had directed at the king was filled with loathing.

"I want the tokens," King Elysian demanded and I felt Shar tense even more beside me.

"No," I stated firmly.

King Elysian laughed, his head thrown back with vicious amusement. "I don't think you're in a position to be uncooperative." I didn't miss the insinuation behind his tone. I glared at him. He could hurt me all he wanted. But I wasn't backing down.

I could see the hammer at Shar's side and feel the amulet on my neck, and knew that if they got into the wrong hands, it would have devastating effects on the Stone-Hearted race. He would use them for his own personal gain and become the most powerful Stone-Hearted in the entire realm.

"What do we get in return?" Shar questioned, and I felt my mouth drop open. He couldn't be considering giving up the tokens. It seemed impossible for such a thought to cross Shar's mind. His calculating, logical mind.

"I get the tokens"—he gestured toward Embrosine—"and Embrosine goes free," he bartered. I felt anger blur red in the corners of my vision. Everything about waiting for the right moment to strike suddenly left me.

"That's not a fair deal," I snarled through my teeth.

"I will also grant you safe passage from my kingdom, and you can go home free."

It was madness. We had walked right into his trap, and he'd get everything, and we wouldn't be able to bring peace back to the land.

I wasn't about to allow that to happen, and I wasn't going to go down without a fight.

I didn't think before I lifted the dagger from my side and with a war cry attacked the guard beside me.

THIRTY-NINE

The dagger sunk with ease into the shoulder of the guard, and with a grunt, he fell to his knees, clutching the wound. It didn't take long for the room to erupt into chaos.

Rouix vanished, appearing beside another one of the guards several feet away and taking him out with her knives. Rosen grabbed the man directly next to him, and the instant golden plague took over the guard's body. Dusane twisted against the black cloak holding him. When he got free, he landed a satisfying jab to the guard's cheek.

Shar pulled out the hammer from his hip and with an elegant sweeping arc slammed the tip of its sharp golden edge into the marble. Instantly the ground shook, and black marble cracked. A large line shot across the perfect floor and literally exploded the carefully crafted stairs leading up to the throne. The quake caused all of us to stumble including King Elysian and Obsidian who fell to either side of the sudden cavern created down the middle of the stairs.

Shar navigated his way across the shattered ebony floor toward Embrosine who had also been jostled by the sudden impact the hammer had created. When he reached her, he lifted her into his arms.

Elysian rose from where he'd fallen and he started toward Shar. Obsidian reclaimed his balance, but before he could follow after his father, I started for him, a murderous motive in my veins. When I approached him, I instantly thrust my dagger toward him. He hindered my efforts with a sword he pulled from his side. He knew he couldn't kill me with his power. And without his power to hinder me, it was a fair fight. Our weapons met with a loud clang. We went back and forth, deflecting one another's blows.

In the midst of our fight, the hammer hit the floor again and we stumbled back away from each other. I fell to the ground. Not expecting the sudden quake. I crashed to the hard surface of the floor. Pain radiated through the left side of my body at the unexpected rough landing. I moaned and turned to see another crack erupt across the floor. Parts of the flooring broke, creating more dangerous shards.

Through the sudden wreckage, I could see Shar and King Elysian. They stood in the center of the room on a section of marble that had been unaffected by the rippling quakes. The king had his glowing dagger in his hand. The weapon was an interesting opponent to the hammer Shar wielded. A satisfying clang echoed off the walls each time their weapons collided. It seemed the dagger had met its match.

Shar would slam the hammer into the ground and it would send King Elysian stumbling back. Then King Elysian would ram the dagger into the marble and it would slice through the stone like butter, leaving a smoking trail where the blade touched. The dagger acted as an anchor when plunged into the floor and once the waves from the hammer ceased he'd pull it out and they'd start fighting again.

All of this transpired in a matter of seconds. Then my body recovered from the fall and I ran for Obsidian again. Just as I raised my dagger to strike, I watched from the corner of my eye as King Elysian's knocked the hammer from Shar's hand. Shar fell back into the rubble. His palms crashed into the sharp marble shards and blood covered his hands as he caught himself on the mangled flooring.

"Stop!" I heard Embrosine scream. Everyone in the room turned to the unexpected shriek that pierced through the sounds of fighting.

Dusane and Rosen battling Obscurum soldiers on the other side of the room halted. In the middle of the fighting more black cloaks by the door, Rouix stopped and turned. I lowered my dagger several feet from Obsidian, who had also turned at the sound of Embrosine's sudden cry.

"Please! Don't hurt him!" Embrosine ran to Shar, her hands still bound. She didn't seem to care when her feet were cut on the sharp flooring as she raced for the one she loved. She fell at Shar's side and looked up at King Elysian who had raised his dagger again about to finish Shar. All it would take was one simple strike.

And that's when Midennen walked into the room.

FORTY

He strode inside, his brown cloak barely kissing the edge of the floor. He halted at the tormented edge of the marble. Five Ethydon guards filed in after him. Several Obscurum soldiers surrounded them, but Mid didn't seem to notice. He was looking straight ahead, a smirk on his lips, eyes locked on King Elysian.

The breath left my body, and I could only stare at him, trying to calm my racing heart. His hair was short. Something I hadn't noticed from a distance while in the arena. The wavy locks that usually fell around his face had been cut off. The new hair style sharpened the angles of his tan cheekbones and chin even more without hair falling into his face.

"King Elysian," Mid spoke. His voice washed over the throne room causing every cell in my body to hum to life. Emotions I hadn't known I'd been suppressing, were suddenly pounding against the walls of my chest. The sight of him evoked feelings of homesickness, love, regret, and so many others.

"What have we here?" King Elysian lowered his glowing dagger down to his side and moved away from his position over Shar and Embrosine.

As King Elysian stepped over the broken marble, everyone in the room watched with agonizing suspense. It was tangible static that at any moment could ignite the room into fighting once again. But everyone remained still, watching curiously as the king approached Mid.

"Certainly this can't be Midennen, the prince of Ethydon. Could you be coming to save Embrosine as well?"

Mid was the perfect candidate to entertain the sarcastic humorous insanity of the king. He easily kept his smirk, liking the games almost as much as the king it seemed. "I caught the tail end of the fight from down the hall. It would appear that you are driving a hard price for my sister's freedom," Mid replied easily. His eyes flitted to Embrosine for a second but then quickly returned to the king.

"I think it's a rather fair bargain, but your friends seem to think otherwise." King Elysian stroked the hilt of his violet dagger as he spoke. "I don't mind a fight. I quite enjoy a little entertainment. But tell me, Midennen, did you come to join the fun? Or are you smarter than the rest of your friends?" the king goaded.

Mid smiled, his eyes glittering. "I'm actually willing to make a negotiation, if you're still open." Mid gestured to the mass destruction that had overtaken the room in a matter of minutes, and as he did, I looked across the wreckage toward Dusane. He was still in his battle stance beside Rosen, the two frozen like statues. Dusane's dark blue eyes were zeroed in on Mid and King Elysian, gauging carefully the conversation. Rosen was watching them as well, his arms still wrapped around an Obscurum soldier he had in a headlock.

"You are much smarter than the others I see. But I'm afraid my negotiation is determined. The tokens, and your sister goes free," the king reiterated his demands.

Mid smiled. "If I give you the tokens, then I must demand something as well. Embrosine must be handed to me before the tokens are given to you and that all of my friends and myself be granted safe escort from the castle," he countered.

The king's eyes narrowed. "So be it," he finally agreed.

I felt everything inside me screaming at Mid to stop being so stupid. I wondered why he wasn't making the king fall asleep, why he wasn't just taking out everyone in the room with his illusions. But I didn't want to move, afraid for Embrosine's life, and also too stunned by Mid's presence to cause another blood bath to erupt. Obviously fighting was out of the question. The king with his dagger was too powerful, and Obsidian's power inflicted on anyone else would be fatal. A negotiation was our only way out, even if it meant giving him everything.

At least I tried to fight, I told myself.

"Will you tell your guards to stay back while I retrieve the tokens then?" Mid gestured towards the Obscurum soldiers surrounding him and his group of Ethydon guards. King Elysian motioned for his guards to stand down.

Mid remained all too confident and calm as he walked over to Shar. Shar was harboring Embrosine safely in his arms when Mid approached them. The two looked at each other intently, and I could see the conflict in Shar's expression. Shar had managed to retrieve the fallen hammer, but he handed Mid the weapon from his side. I watched as Mid pulled the token from his friends bloody hands with only mild resistance. Then he started for me.

My heart stopped completely as he walked across the room to where I lay on the marble. His emerald-scarlet eyes met mine, and everything I'd ever felt the day I'd left him came rushing back to me. I couldn't read his expression, couldn't decipher what he might be feeling. His mask of perfect collectiveness was hard to penetrate in that moment.

He stopped a couple inches in front of me and reached a hand down to where I was still sprawled on the floor. I laid my shaky hand in his and allowed him to help me stand. He was a foot taller than me, and as he looked down at me with his emerald-scarlet eyes, I felt weak and not because of the fighting.

"May I?" he asked gently, gesturing toward the amulet around my neck. I wanted to fight, pull away from him, and demand that we don't give the king everything. But I was too stunned, too spell bound by his presence to do anything. He reached for the amulet, and I felt the gentle brush of his fingers on the back of my neck as he lifted the chain over my head. Then he turned around and strode back toward the king.

He waited patiently in front of King Elysian, holding the tokens.

"Embrosine, and then I'll give you the tokens," Mid reminded him. The king nodded.

Shar immediately helped Embrosine away from the rubble and went to stand beside Mid. It was like an invisible line was between them. I reluctantly followed them, and stood beside Shar. The others seemed to understand as well, and soon we all stood together, across from King Elysian, Obsidian, and their group of black-cloaked soldiers.

Mid carefully handed King Elysian the hammer and the

amulet. King Elysian smiled as he passed them to a servant who quickly took them and left the room. Suddenly everything we'd ever worked for was gone.

"I am grateful this negotiation went smoothly. Despite the condition of my throne room, I have to say, it's been a pleasure doing business with you," King Elysian smirked. Obsidian beside him met my eyes. It was a menacing glare that he gave me, and I returned it. We hadn't gotten to finish our fight, and I was surprised at the equal amount of rage that seemed to be present between us. Like some silent agreement, that we both wanted to finish this. There was an unsaid promise that one day we would fight again, and next time, I'd win.

"Escort them from the castle. Do not harm them," King Elysian ordered.

The defeat settled in as King Elysian's men pushed us out of the throne room and down the hallway again.

"Do visit again soon!" The king called from the throne room.

I was waiting for something to happen—for him to take back his word and for more fighting to break out, but he simply let us go. With the tokens, he was suddenly sated, and I realized with despair that everything we'd accomplished had been ruined in a matter of moments.

I walked between Rouix and Dusane, and ahead of us was Embrosine between Shar and Mid. They both had a protective arm firmly wrapped around her weak, limp body. With each step they took, bloody footprints from Embrosine's feet were imprinted on the marble. My gut clenched at the sight.

Rosen and the other Ethydon guards were in the back of the group. A circle of black cloaks surrounding all of us as they escorted us from the castle.

When we arrived at the front gates, I instantly recognized

Elesame standing next to Rouix's Crykon. Beside them Shar and Rosen's steeds stood waiting. There were other horses as well, that appeared to belong to the Ethydon guards, and then there was Diablo. Someone must have found him, and he was certainly not happy about it. His wings beat furiously, kicking up sand that had fallen between the crevices of the cobblestone. Four Obscurum guards tried to constrain him with long ropes. I pushed through the group and ran to him.

"Hey! Careful with him!" I screamed. My nerves were already frayed. I was too tired and too emotional to remain composed. I reached Diablo and instantly yanked the ropes from the men's hands. They gladly stepped away from Diablo, and I quickly reached up to stroke his neck, trying to soothe him. After several angry whinnies and snorts, he began to calm down.

The remaining Obscurum guards stepped away and allowed us to mount our animals. I turned to Shar, instantly realizing there wouldn't be enough horses for everyone. Shar and Mid still held up Embrosine. She looked exhausted, starved, and in really bad shape.

"I'll take Embrosine," Mid said, already trying to take her from their joint hold. Shar reluctantly held her tighter to him, and I heard Embrosine whimper.

"No, I will," Shar stated roughly, and I saw a mix of anger and confusion cross Mid's features.

"Neither of you are taking her," I said sternly, stepping between the two of them. "With her condition, it will be best if I take her on Diablo, I can get her back to camp quicker." I looked at Shar, and I could see the reluctance in his eyes. But he knew it was the most logical thing. I could heal her. I would be the best person to handle her.

"Do you think your hands will be okay until you get back to

camp?" I asked, glancing at the cuts on his hands, the blood was beginning to dry, but the wounds badly needed to be dressed.

"I'll be fine," Shar grunted.

I looked back at Mid and met his gaze. Something inside me ached to—*what? Yell at him? Hug him? Kiss him?* I didn't exactly know what I was feeling, but the urge was incredibly strong. But now was not the time to let my emotions get the best of me. There would be plenty of time to unravel what happened in the throne room when we arrived back at camp.

I turned back to Shar before my composure could wane.

"Shar, please trust me," I said quietly, my voice softening. After a moment, he finally sighed, then nodded and helped me move Embrosine onto Dibalo's back the best he could with his injured hands. I ended up clutching Embrosine's small form in my arms as she leaned limply against me. Her breaths were shallow, her dark brown eyes vacant again. I looked down at Shar from atop Diablo's back.

"I'll meet you back at the camp," I stated. I ignored both Dusane and Mid's expression's as I pushed Diablo into flight. I honestly didn't know what was going to happen when we met up again. I would have to face them both. And the thought terrified me more than anything else I'd done that night.

FORTY-ONE

It didn't take long to cross the sandy sea, and return to the camp we'd established on the border. Once Diablo landed safely in the shadow of the jungle trees, I helped Embrosine down and toward one of the tents. I situated her on several blankets and grabbed some food rations. I ripped up some small pieces of bread, hoping to introduce the food slowly to her. Her eyes were half drooped, and her skin was so pale it shone in the darkness. I shakily helped her eat some pieces of bread and a small cup of water. She shivered as the jungle cooled slightly after the sun went down. I quickly went to start a fire. It took me longer than it would have if Conland was around, and the thought made my heart ache. Somehow I managed to start a small spark and nurse the flame to life.

I went back into the tent and found that Embrosine's brown eyes slightly more awake.

"Sabeara," she mumbled, while trying unsuccessfully to sit up.

"I'm here," I said, rushing to her side and helping her sit up so she could lean against me.

"Where's Shar?" she asked, disoriented. "What happened?" I shushed her and stroked back her long auburn hair to try and calm her. Her feet were cut and dried with blood from the sharp marble floors she'd run across, and the angry red burn running from her cheek down to her neck looked to only have worsened. My heart lurched at the sight of it.

"You've been hurt. Lie still. I'm going to help heal you," I said. Embrosine didn't protest, just closed her eyes again sleepily, and I began trying to use my powers. I focused as intently as I could, laying my hands on her arms and imagining my healing ability covering her, reaching for her. Visualizing my power expanding seemed to do the trick, and soon the unusual burning sensation started to flood my body again, and the wounds on her body began healing. The cuts on her feet disappeared and the red burn on her cheek turned back to pale white, and some healthy color returned to her face. I pulled my hands away after several moments, and I watched her smile softly, her eyes still closed

"That feels wonderful," she said.

I felt a little out of breath from the small exertion but it was worth every effort to know she was okay.

"Just sleep now. You need your rest," I whispered, and I gently helped her lie back onto the blankets again before I exited the tent. I felt less anxious knowing Embrosine was healed, but a new anxiety was overwhelming me that had nothing to do with Embrosine's condition.

Mid.

They would be returning to the camp soon, and I racked my brain for what I might say.

Why did you give the tokens away? What were you thinking showing up to the Courts at a time like that? Do you still love me?

I pushed all those thoughts out immediately as they began to get severely irrational.

But then there remained one other thing that was pestering my thoughts—the kiss with Dusane back at the castle. I had feelings for Dusane too. I couldn't deny that, and I'd wanted him to kiss me, but he made it clear that he didn't want me thinking about another person. *So why had he kissed me?* I growled aloud, hating how complicated everything had suddenly turned out to be.

I paced the forest floor while the rapid flickering of the fire paralleled the furious emotions inside me. I stilled instantly in my tracks when I heard the sound of hoofbeats, and I felt every muscle in my body freeze with apprehension.

The group emerged through the jungle foliage into the camp. The Ethydon guards came first followed by Rosen, Rouix, and Shar. My eyes moved past them, looking for the two my heart was actually seeking, and then they both finally emerged.

Dusane came first, riding on Elesame. Mid was beside him atop a chestnut steed, his emerald-scarlet eyes assessing our camp. They both came to a standstill and dismounted. That was when Mid's eyes found mine.

After all the questioning I'd done and all the thoughts in my mind I'd battled with, I suddenly came to a conclusion. I knew exactly what I wanted to say, and it was impossible to hold it back.

The unexpected feeling of intense anger came so roughly it shoved me forward. I stalked across the camp. It was instinctive to reach up and shove his beautiful, hard chest. He barely stepped back, probably more by surprise than being unbalanced.

As my hands shoved against his pulsing silver heart, the words I'd been holding in came out in a mad flurry.

"What were you thinking! You gave him everything!" I growled, and everyone in the camp turned to stare at us, obviously stunned at my sudden outburst.

"Ehren," I heard Shar caution beside me. I ignored him, and pushed against Mid's chest one more time. It felt satisfying to match the action to my anger. His eyes danced with amusement, obviously not reacting the way I wanted him to at my harassment.

"Do you know how hard it's going to be to get those back! You arrogant, stupid. . ." His hands reached out and clasped my wrists easily between his hands. I fought against his restraints, glaring at him as I struggled to free myself but couldn't.

"Careful, Little Bear," he chuckled, and the nickname caused an electric shock to shoot through my body. He was very close now, and I could smell his pine scent, and it immediately unleashed painful memories as it surrounded me.

"Let go of me!" I said through gritted teeth. He instantly released me and I stumbled back. I glared at him menacingly as I put several feet between us.

"Ehren, hear him out," Shar demanded.

My breathing came in and out in sharp, ragged breaths now, but I remained silent, too angry to speak. Mid took the opportunity to explain.

"I didn't give him the real tokens," Mid said easily. The confusion, and realization washed over me all at once. "I tricked them into thinking I was giving them the real tokens."

"How did you know?" I accused, looking at Shar. I'd been just as convinced as the king.

"I've known Mid a very long time," was all Shar said. The two exchanged a glance.

"So you didn't give him the tokens?" I asked, turning back to Mid, still trying to grasp onto the news.

Mid grinned, and shook his head. "No, I've got them right here." He pulled the hammer from the belt beneath his cloak and then lifted the amulet out from beneath his shirt. "They'll figure out soon that the others were just illusions. So we'll have to pack up this camp and leave quickly. But it was sufficient to help us escape."

I felt suddenly humiliated at my outburst. I looked away from him, my cheeks flushing.

"I'm sorry," I mumbled, and I could hear the smile in his voice when he replied.

"You're forgiven," he answered. My outburst had seemed to amuse him.

I huffed under my breath and turned on my heel to stomp away.

"Not so fast," Mid said. And it was all too familiar, the heat, the indignation, the violent wave of feelings that somehow only he unleashed. He was my personal catalyst. And the effects of the reaction we created were detrimental.

I reluctantly turned back around and glared at him.

"What?" I snapped impatiently.

"Can I talk to you, somewhere private?"

I looked around at the others still watching us. I met Dusane's eyes. I couldn't read the emotion in them. I assumed he'd already put the pieces together. It probably didn't take him long. I worried what it would mean if I followed Mid, what would happen in the dark shadows alone. But something in me knew I couldn't ignore the conversation forever.

"Fine," I relented and stormed off into the saftey of the trees. I could hear him follow behind me, his footsteps steady, not at all hurried. Once I thought we'd gotten far enough, I turned on him again.

"Mid—" I didn't even get the sentence out before he crushed me to his chest, hugging me tightly against him. It was so unexpected I couldn't move for many moments. A couple seconds later, all the anger evaporated and my arms wrapped around his neck. I felt tears spring to my eyes, and I allowed myself to hug him back for a moment. Once he released me, I had to rapidly blink the tears away.

"That was how I should've greeted you the first time," he whispered, leaning his head against mine.

"Mid—" But I didn't get to finish again. He gently closed the gap between us and reverently brushed his lips against mine. All the questions and logical reasoning in my mind exploded into tiny pieces. His lips were so soft, so familiar. *This can't be real,* I told myself. But then he reached up to gently tug on the end of my braid and I knew it was absolutely real. Feelings of longing and intense desire burst forth. And a sense of belonging that I'd forgotten existed greeted me, and it suddenly felt like I was home. When he released me, our ragged breaths mingled together.

"You don't know how I've longed to see your face again," he murmured while reaching out to touch my cheek and then proceeded to finger the end of my braid between his thumb and pointer finger. "You cut your hair," he said suddenly, eyeing the short locks of black hair suspiciously.

"That's the first thing you notice?" I asked, astonished. I was about to mention how I wasn't the only one to change my haircut, unable to help admiring once again how handsome he looked with short hair, but then his husky chuckle distracted me. He looked down at the glow in my chest and his expression turned suddenly serious again. "You're so beautiful," he murmured. All coherent thoughts and retorts left my mind as his hand reached across the black fabric of my jumpsuit to caress the golden light, then he slowly moved upwards to gently trace the curve of my neck, and then my cheek. . .

It took everything in me, every ounce of willpower and practiced control, to put my hands on his chest and push him away. I managed a single inch. That was all my willpower was capable of.

"Mid, a lot has happened since I last saw you. And there are things we need to talk about. . ." I trailed off, not knowing where to begin. He blinked a couple times, shaking his head as if he suddenly realized something.

"I'm sorry for not thinking about how overwhelming this must all be." He slowly released me from his grasp.

Overwhelming was an understatement.

"I'm sorry for snapping at you back there. I think I might need—"

"Some space?" he flashed me a gorgeous lopsided smile, and I very nearly swayed into the tree next to me.

I nodded, laughing weakly. "Yeah, maybe just a little—" I knew he probably didn't understand the extent of my reasoning —that there was another person, that even with all the overwhelming feelings and emotions he'd evoked with his presence, that I was thinking about someone else too at that moment. How ironic that whenever I was with one, I was thinking of the other.

"When we get back home, we will talk," he concluded, reaching up to trace his finger down my cheek.

"Where exactly is home?" I asked.

"After the war we found a safe haven that our people can dwell. It's in the Upper Territory, hidden in the mountains."

So that was why the letter hadn't reached them. They had disappeared to a place where Obscurum wouldn't be able to find them.

I nodded, feeling my breath leave me again. "All right. We will talk when we get back home then." That would give me some time, a couple days to sort through my feelings.

It was silent for many moments as we looked at each other, and then he pulled his hand away from my cheek and sighed. "You'll have to tell me how you ended up in that arena," he said, trying to make his tone sound light, but failing. I could see the questions in his eyes, and a mix of some kind of pain. The tormented expression on his face I'd seen when I looked up at him in the arena came flashing back into my memory.

"And you'll have to tell me how your wedding got raided," I stated, only partly teasing.

He smiled a rather sad smile and then chuckled weakly. "We'll have plenty of time for explanations," he said assuredly. Then as if suddenly remembering, Mid reached up and unhooked the amulet from around his neck. "I think this belongs to you," he said.

I bent my head a little so he could place it on me. When the ruby fell against my chest, I realized I didn't feel totally complete without it.

"Thank you," I said.

He nodded and gestured back toward the camp. "We should go check on Embrosine," he said, and I followed him back through the trees.

The first thing I noticed upon returning was Dusane talking

with Shar next to the tent where Embrosine slept. Everyone else was packing up.

I walked over to them and could see the blatant worry in Shar's creased forehead. I briefly met Dusane's eyes and could see the smallest flicker of questions there.

"How's she doing?" Mid asked Shar.

"She's doing fine now, thanks to Ehren." Shar gave me a grateful look, and I could see the confusion in Mid's eyes as he saw the exchange between us.

"I can heal people," I explained quickly. "Which reminds me, Shar give me your hands."

Shar stretched out his palms to me and luckily they were no longer bleeding. But dirt and sand had made its way into the wounds and needed to be cleaned. I proceeded to grab a canister from my pack to wash out the debris.

Shar made a small grunting noise as the water hit the open cuts.

"Sorry," I said. Once his hands were clean I concentrated on my power and felt a warmth flood my body. After several minutes the cuts were gone, his hands like new.

"Thank you," Shar said.

Mid was looking at Shar's hands, his eyes wide.

I ignored Mid's surprised expression and lifted the tent flap to peek inside at Embrosine. Her small form slept soundly in the blankets.

"We will have to get on the move again soon. Do you think she will be strong enough?" Mid asked.

"She'll have to be," Shar said, not sounding sure of himself. We all stood silently by the tent door for many moments.

"Shar?" The sound of Embrosine's small, weak voice came from inside the tent and Shar immediately went to her. I looked over at Mid, realizing that I knew something about Shar that he didn't. I wondered if they'd talked about running away from the Sethen Courts to save her on the way back from Obscurum. *Didn't Mid find his abrupt actions to save his sister—out of the ordinary?*

"I'm going to go help the others pack up," Dusane suddenly said beside me, and I was pulled from my thoughts. He'd been so quiet I'd forgotten he was even there. I turned to look at him, and met his deep blue eyes. I could see a mix of emotions in his expression. I suddenly could vividly remember the way he'd kissed me back at the Obscurum castle, and my pulse increased.

Between the two of them, my heart was going to get tired from beating so frantically. I forced myself to remain calm as I looked back at him.

"Dusane, can we talk?" I whispered to him quickly. He looked at me, his jaw tightening and then his eyes shifted to Mid who was standing behind me.

"I don't think that will be necessary," he said gruffly and then turned around to leave. Panic threaded through my veins, and I quickly reached out to stop him from walking away.

"Dusane, please," I begged.

He turned to look at the hand I had clasped around his forearm. "Part of being an Envorydian, Ehren, is knowing which battles to fight." his eyes shifted behind me again to Mid still standing by the tent. "And this isn't one of them." He tugged his arm away and left me frozen in shock as he walked away.

I turned around slowly, feeling like Dusane had slapped me. The night couldn't have gotten any worse. But I was wrong. The minute I looked back at Mid, it wasn't hard to see that he'd put all the pieces together. His arms were crossed over his chest, and his eyes narrowed.

"So *he's* the reason why you need space," he bit sharply.

"Mid. . ." I started to say. And I tried to finish the sentence, but nothing else followed. I even reached out toward him, but no more words came. He shook his head and took several more steps away from me. My hand dropped lamley back to my side, and I closed my mouth.

"You don't have to give me an explanation. I understand perfectly now," he suddenly said, abruptly turning and walking off into the trees.

When it was just me left in the camp, standing there alone I could feel the crushing reality of everything that happened weigh heavily on my heart. Tears pricked the corners of my eyes, and I hated how everything had gone so wrong, so quickly.

It seemed that Mid's feelings hadn't at all lessened with the time we'd been apart. And he imagined we would be picking up right where we left off. But despite the feelings that still existed between us, and the love that remained, there was still something. . . someone holding me back.

Dusane had conflicted my emotions, making it hard to really know what I wanted. And I couldn't just erase the way I was feeling toward him.

But now they were both angry with me. I didn't know how things were going to work themselves out. I growled under my breath, hating the emotional drama that had suddenly encompassed my life. I tried the best I could to push the romantic issues from my mind and focus on more important matters.

It was only fifteen minutes later when Rosen yelled to the group that we needed to get on the move again. We couldn't stay. An entire Obscurum army could be headed for us after they realized the tokens weren't real.

Shar exited the tent with Embrosine. She looked slightly

better than when she'd arrived. Shar helped her mount his steed and he climbed up behind her. I walked over to Diablo, and just when I'd swung up onto his back, I caught sight of Dusane. He walked over to Elesame, and tied a couple of his belongings to the saddle bag. He didn't look at me, and I could feel that he was back to ignoring me.

I caught another movement from the corner of my eye and turned to see Mid also saddling his horse. He must've left Ghost back home. I hadn't caught sight of the big polar bear anywhere.

As the camp was cleaned up and we prepared to leave I could feel the tension beginning to swell, permeating the air. It reeked of disdain, and calculated aversion. I sighed and gathered a fist full of Diablo's mane in my hands before facing forward.

This is going to be a long ride.

FORTY-TWO

Mid and his guards led us back to the hidden kingdom. They knew where the remaining survivors had ended up. I stayed in the back beside Rouix, trying to remain a safe distance from any further confrontation with Dusane or Mid.

Dusane had taken up riding with Rosen near the middle of the caravan. Considering they hated one another, it made me realize just how much Dusane was attempting to avoid me.

I tried to keep myself from overthinking as we journeyed. But it was difficult. My thoughts kept wandering from my recent discovery about King Elysian being my uncle then to what happened back at the camp and how bad everything had turned.

The sky was beginning to turn blue, revealing it was almost morning. Rouix turned to me just as the first bits of the sun came poking over the horizon. I was biting my lip, thinking deeply when she abruptly pulled me from my thoughts.

"You're going to bite your lip off if you keep doing that. I know you can heal and all, but still," she reprimanded. I turned to her, and noticed her bright crimson eyes judgmentally assessing me.

"Sorry," I mumbled.

"It's your lip, not mine," she concluded, then turned her attention back to the path ahead.

I sighed and forced myself to stop chewing. Needing to do something more than just think, I urged Diablo to pick up his pace, and fell into stride beside Shar who was riding with Embrosine. For the last several hours, Mid and Shar had been switching off riding with her.

"Shar," I hissed earnestly. He turned to look at me. Embrosine was asleep against Shar's chest, and I tried to whisper so as not to wake her.

"What is it?" he asked.

"Why is Mid not acting more upset about what happened?" I asked suddenly. Shar's face remained set in confusion. "Was he not mad that you ran to save Embrosine without his permission? And then took me with you?" I clarified. Shar looked back to the trail ahead, and I could tell he didn't want to talk about it.

"We spoke on the way back to the camp. He was upset with me. And he asked me why I'd do something so reckless and stupid. . ."

I remained quiet, urging him to continue.

When he could tell I was still waiting expectantly for him to finish he sighed and finally admitted, "I told him it was your idea."

My jaw dropped open. "You what?"

"I knew he'd forgive you. And I couldn't risk him finding out about—" He gestured to Embrosine in his arms.

"And protecting her so possessively isn't risking him finding out?" I asked skeptically.

"Mid is blind to what is right in front of him. Ever noticed how people tend to ignore what they don't want to believe?"

"You think his subconscious is telling him it's nothing," I deadpanned.

He winced. "I think because I've been his guardian since he was a child, he doesn't know the difference. He thinks I'm protecting her. Just like I protect him. He's known me too long to see anything other than my protectiveness as something of my nature." He didn't look certain.

"One day he's going to figure it out." I glanced down to Embrosine in his arms. "And I have a feeling if you keep this up, eventually he's going to notice," I pointed out. He glared at me, and I glared back.

"You need to tell him, Shar," I pressed. "It will be easier if you just get it over with."

"I can't," he instantly replied. I sighed knowing how stubborn he was.

"Well then enjoy the moment while it lasts because we're going to be home soon," I bit, hoping it would rattle him. It seemed to do the job, and he looked down at Embrosine in his arms wistfully. I knew it was harsh. But taking these moments with her was bound to be short lived and cause him more harm than good. Then another part of me considered I was wrongfully lashing out at him because I had no other outlet for my current frustrations.

I let Diablo fall back into place beside Rouix and began listening to Rosen and Dusane talk in front of us.

"What do you think his dagger was made out of?" Rosen asked.

Dusane shrugged his shoulders. "I don't know. I've never seen anything like it."

Memories of the purple glowing weapon filled my head, and it only added to the unanswered questions piling up. I'd never seen a weapon like the dagger King Elysian had wielded. The only other magical weapon I knew of was the hammer, and it was one of the kings' tokens.

"Do you think it could be one of the tokens?" I asked. And suddenly everything clicked into place. A magical weapon, in Obscurum, wielded by King Elysian. *Could it be Ennsleon's? Oxtwenel's?*

Rosen seemed surprised that I had jumped into the conversation.

"I guess it's possible," Rosen said and he seemed to consider the possibility.

My mind began to spin, wondering about the dagger and if it had been a token right in front of our eyes. I had felt a powerful presence in the room, probably due to Dusane's Reminant abilities being able to sense powers. Because that had been the ability currently in my amulet when I'd been in the throne room, I'd felt the weapon's power. If that were the case, then that would mean that there were only two more tokens that hadn't been found. My mind stayed on that thought for a long while, wondering which of the king's it could be and trying to remember what I'd studied.

I was pulled from my thoughts when Mid shouted from the front of the caravan.

"We've come upon Aveladon. We will pass through and then camp when the sun goes down," he said.

As we entered Aveladon's outskirts, I noticed there were smaller homes and farms dotting the area, each residence completely vacant. I could barely tear my eyes away from the desolation. The homes had been ransacked with nothing left inside it seemed. I could see shattered windows, broken roofs, and kicked in doors.

As we traveled farther, I feared what it would look like when we came upon Asmede, the grand city that I used to have a view of from the castle. I remember its grandeur and it's undeniable beauty. I could feel the uneasiness increase inside me as we traveled.

The twirling iron gates—just as I remembered them—were the first thing I noticed. Only this time the gates were wide open. Not a single soul guarded the vast entrance. Everyone grew very quiet as we approached the main gates to the city.

"Should we travel around or go through?" I heard one of the guards ask.

"Let's travel through," I suddenly said, pushing my way up toward the front. I could feel Mid's gaze hot on my face as I approached where he was. "I want to see it for myself," I insisted.

The guards looked to each other, and then at Mid who merely nodded.

We walked through the gates, and what I witnessed nearly broke me. The moment we passed through, I could see the destruction. Every lively red brick and crimson flag that used to exist was replaced by a layer of black ash. The buildings that used to fill the city had been completely consumed by fire. And if anything happened to remain, it would be a lonely burned wall or roof. It was the minimum bones of what the city used to be. I tried desperately to blink the tears that filled my eyes, but several escaped unwillingly onto my cheeks. I swiped at them quickly, forcing myself to hold it together.

"You okay, Princess?" One of the guards asked beside me. I

turned at the unexpected voice, having gotten lost inside my thoughts. I nodded to the guard and swallowed back the lump in my throat.

"I'm fine. And it's Ehren," I corrected. The guard's eyes widened, but then he quickly nodded, blushing slightly. I was too concerned with the state of the city to even feel guilty for correcting the guard.

I urged Diablo farther forward. As we walked through the remains of Asmede, I took in every black piece of rubble and felt my soul sink deeper the more broken homes and ash piles I witnessed.

There was a solemn cloud over the caravan as we took in the horrific scene. I was stunned speechless, and when we emerged on the opposite side of the city an hour later, my gaze shifted up onto the mountain side.

I knew it was going to be difficult to see, and that I'd have to face the reality at some point. When my eyes found the castle, it was in a similar state as the city. Only two walls stood and what remained was stained ebony from soot. The rest was just crumbled remains of the walls and glass that used to be the place I called home.

"Once we get up the mountainside, we can camp in the forest and start up again in the morning," I heard Mid say a couple feet away from me. I turned to glance at him, and my face must have shown the shock I was feeling because when he looked back at me, there was a softness in his eyes that hadn't been there before.

"Up toward the castle then," Shar ordered. We started on the pathway that led up to the remains of the castle. I couldn't look too closely or I was surely to notice where the gardens used to be, where the stables used to exist. And that would've been too much.

I looked on even farther up the mountain where the Spirit Tree should have been shining and found its usual glowing presence gone. Everything that made Aveladon the powerful, beautiful kingdom it was had been completely destroyed.

Some of the forest behind the castle and on the mountainside had been burned, but overall, the damage had been minimal. When we were enveloped in the trees once again, leaving the castle and Asmede behind us, I knew they were the same trees where so much of my life had taken place. The beautiful yellow aspens mixed with the oaks and pines felt more like home than anything else. But I knew this wasn't the end of our path, not even close. Mid had said they were hiding in the Upper Territory. And if that was really where they'd taken the remaining people, it was going to be another several days, maybe more before we reached where the people were hiding. I don't know what existed in the Upper Territory, but part of me was nervous to find out.

When Shar finally decided to stop and make camp, the sun was gone. Together in almost complete silence, except for a couple murmured conversations, we all set up our tents and started a fire. We shared supplies, and with a little bit of food inside me, I took up a spot by the fire.

A numbness settled in. Seeing Asmede had pushed out all other thoughts in my head, spreading a blank, empty feeling through my body. I didn't know if my soul would ever awaken. It was more devastating than I imagined it would be. I don't know why I'd insisted on going through the city. It was cruel to put myself through that kind of pain. But pain was the only reminder that it had happened.

For so long it had felt like a dream. Waking up in Ethydon and seeing the smoke when Obscurum had begun the war. It was hard to believe then when I couldn't see it for myself. I had awoken in another place, not seeing the effects. Now I was wide awake, and I could see exactly what had happened. I had witnessed the aftermath, and it was confounding to accept.

"You okay?" Rouix came to sit beside me, and I was startled once again from my pensive thinking. I hadn't even noticed that five others had joined the fire. Rouix, Rosen, Dusane, Shar, and Embrosine. Mid and the Ethydon guards had stayed by one of the tents, talking amongst each other a little farther away.

I dared glance at Dusane, and I when I met his blue-eyed gaze I expected to feel something. But the numbness radiated so intently I could feel nothing as we looked at each other. His eyes were trying to tell me something, but I wasn't in the mood to translate the expression. At that moment, my other problems seemed so insignificant.

"I'm fine," I finally answered.

Rouix pursed her lips, and I could see Shar next to her giving me a similar disbelieving look.

"I have something that will cheer you up," Rosen suddenly interjected. I was surprised at the sudden invitation. Rosen grinned and scooted closer to the fire until he was only a couple inches away from the flame.

"Watch this," he said cockily. I watched without much interest as he held his hands out to the fire. All of a sudden he touched the tip of one of the flames and right before my eyes turned it into a chunk of solid gold. It clinked to the side of the fire, rolling on the ground. I reached out to touch the now solid flame and held it up in my hands. It was hot, and definitely made of gold, or amberidium as he claimed.

He did it again, touching a couple of sparks that floated casually into the air like bright yellow stars. As he tapped each one, they clinked to the ground as little gold flakes.

"Impressive," I heard someone say from the side of the fire. Everyone turned to see Mid joining the group. He took a seat beside his sister, and she smiled at him weakly. He reached his arm around her while eyeing Rosen suspiciously.

"I've heard that you assume there is a seventh stone, and a place called Pendilore that has records about the curse," Mid said to Rosen.

Rosen grinned and then chuckled. "Don't believe me?"

Mid shook his head, his face serious. "I think it's an interesting theory. I'm just wondering how you know it exists if you've never been there."

"I haven't been there, but I know others who have," Rosen replied easily.

"Who?" Rouix jutted in.

Rosen turned toward her and addressed her narrowed crimson eyes with ease. "The Reminant I spoke to. He knew of its existence, and said he's once gone himself."

"Yes, but you don't actually know if this Reminant was telling you the truth," Mid pointed out.

"Why don't you keep your accusations to yourself, *Your Highness*," Rosen smirked and Mid's jaw clenched.

"Let's talk about something else, shall we?" Dusane suggested, his eyes flitting between Rosen and Mid who were suddenly glaring at each other.

Could no one get along? I inwardly sighed.

"Have you found the other tokens, Mid?" The soft voice spoke so gently it was barely audible. All eyes turned to Embrosine. Mid's expression softened as he looked down at his sister sitting between him and Shar. She'd been barely audible since we'd rescued her. She'd been sleeping most of the journey and seemed to be still numb with shock. Hearing her speak for the first time sent goosebumps across my arms.

"We think we've located the compass," Mid said. Everyone went silent as he continued. "We traveled a ways across the ocean from the Ethydon port in the direction of the Isles. From our studies, we knew that Linsulong was a sea captain. We met with some villagers before we'd left and heard rumors of a sunken ship. We followed the directions one man gave us. It was a whim really. And then we found it, sunken deep within the water. We just have to find out how to get down to the ship and how to last that long without air."

"But you've located the ship, and you're pretty sure it's there?" I asked. The numbness was suddenly beginning to fade with talk about the tokens.

Mid turned towards me, and met my gaze briefly. "Yes, I'm fairly certain."

It was quiet in the camp then, and I could feel myself getting sleepy. I was just about to get up and go to my tent when Embrosine said my name.

"Sabeara, would you mind helping me get ready for bed?" Everyone in the group turned to look at me. The use of my real name made me grit my teeth together. But Embrosine meant no harm, and I knew I was being irrational with the name thing, so I let it go.

"Of course," I consented.

Shar helped lift her from the ground, and then I took her arm. Together the two of us walked back to her tent. When we entered, I helped her change into a new nightgown and then she crawled into the small makeshift bed.

"We haven't gotten to talk much," Embrosine said. Her dark eyes, suddenly wide awake, were soft and probing.

"I can't imagine what you've been through. I haven't gotten to apologize for what happened back in Ethydon," I said, feeling a lump form in my throat.

Embrosine laid her hand on my arm, stopping me from continuing. She smiled softly at me. "Sabeara, you saved my daughter. You have nothing to apologize for. She is my life. What you did means more to me than anything."

I felt my chest tighten at her words.

"I wish I could've saved you too," I whispered.

"I'm here now. That's all that matters." She smiled at me, but I could barely return it with a weak smile.

"Embrosine, may I ask what happened to you?" I asked softly, hesitantly. Images of King Elysian's dagger on her cheek and the way she'd screamed made me inwardly shudder.

"I was lucky. They mostly kept me down in that cell. I will admit, they didn't feed me very often, but I was lucky enough that they mostly left me alone. I think they were counting on someone coming to rescue me. I was leverage, and they weren't about to risk killing me. So it was just several long months of darkness, and hunger. . ." She shuddered. "It took me a while to grasp I was finally free. I honestly thought I was dreaming," she chuckled to herself.

"I'm so sorry, Embrosine," I said, shocked at how well she was taking everything.

She looked down at my arm where her hand was still grasped. The Envorydian tattoo was visible and I watched a variety of emotions cross her face. I pulled my hand away, tucking it behind my back self-consciously.

"Sabeara—" she started to say, but I just shook my head.

"A lot has happened, Embrosine." I could see the wheels turning in her head, and knew she must know about the Envoy. With Shar being part of her past I didn't doubt she had knowledge of the guild.

"I guess I'm not that shocked," she admitted, but her eyes were still a little wide. "As long as this is what you want."

"It is," I said seriously.

She nodded and sighed. "You and Mid still don't seem to be getting along," Embrosine changed the subject.

It was my turn to sigh. "It's complicated," I said.

"I think I've heard that one before," she said teasingly.

I laughed weakly. "I've changed. And what happened between me and Mid a year ago. . ." I trailed off.

"You are worried things won't be the same? Can't trust your feelings? Are unsure if your heart belongs to someone else?"

My mouth dropped open at the accuracy of her guesses.

"Sabeara, let me tell you something," she grew suddenly serious again and reached out to grip my other hand this time.

"Sometimes the constellations align, and create an unstoppable force between two people. And no matter how many times you try and tell yourself that it's impossible, you put yourself up against the universe. You'll never win if you try and fight something that was written in the stars."

"But what if there are two?" I whispered.

"Two what?"

"What if the universe gives you two stars?" I didn't know if she'd get the analogy I was trying to make, but she seemed to finally understand.

"It's simple Sabeara. Which one is the sun?" she whispered.

My heart twisted in my chest painfully as I tried to process her words. It was all too complicated. I had feelings for both of them, and that made it so much harder. Was it horrible that I didn't know which one was the sun in my universe? I inwardly sighed. It seemed I was on a completely different planet at the moment. I put my head in my hands and felt Embrosine's gentle hand stroke my hair.

"It's going to be okay," she said.

"I shouldn't be the one being comforted right now," I said between my hands, and she chuckled.

"I'm all right, Sabeara, honestly." Her fingers continued to stroke my hair.

"You should get more sleep," I said after a moment, lifting my head from my hands.

"I've slept so much. I think it's you who needs some sleep," she admonished. I nodded and stood from the tent floor.

"I'll see you in the morning?"

"Sleep well, Sabeara," she said, just as I slipped out of the tent flap.

FORTY-THREE

The next two days we continued on farther into the mountains. And the things Embrosine said to me, despite my desperate attempt to push her words from my mind, haunted me the whole journey.

Dusane and Mid continued to ignore me, and I wondered if they were both so angry with me that they had given up. *That would make everything much easier,* I thought. *if they both decided they didn't want me anymore I wouldn't have to choose either of them.*

We had traveled all day, and I had stayed near the back of the caravan, hoping to avoid talking with anyone. It was when the sun began to set again that I noticed where we were.

We had crossed into a different part of the forest. It was rockier, less lush than the forest we'd come from. The air was getting a tad colder, and I had gotten so used to the hot humid jungle that I shivered.

"How far are we from our next stop?" I asked, to no one in particular.

"We are close. Once we pass over this side of the mountain, we will reach a place we can set up camp," Shar said from the middle of the group.

"How much longer are we traveling?"

"Two days," Mid called from the very front of the caravan. My eyes widened at the news, and I wondered if it would be snowy in the Upper Territory or if it would be hot like the Sethen Courts.

Just as I was contemplating the new destination of the hidden kingdom, I heard a loud snorting sound echo through the trees.

I dismissed it at first, wondering if it was Elesame who had made the noise. But when the trees rattled to the right of me, I realized it wasn't any of the animals in our group.

By the time I knew what was happening, it was too late to get out of the way.

A large Twal boar came barreling out of the bushes. At the tail end of the group, I was a prime target. A loud growling squeal came from the animal, and I watched in shock as the brown, hairy creature with long ivory tusks and a wet snout headed straight for me.

Diablo reared and flapped his wings at the creature. I clung to his mane, hoping not to fall, but when Diablo darted to the left, it was too fast a motion for me to remain steady. I fell to the ground with a grunt, and Diablo flew into the air, desperate to get away from the creature. I didn't have time to reprimand him and quickly stood to face the creature.

I was going to have to have a talk with Diablo about his reaction to other animals.

I pulled a dagger from my belt and readied to face the boar.

When the boar slammed into me, I sunk the dagger into its

shoulder. The impact sent me straight into the ground, and I slid across the dirt and rocks of the forest floor just as one of the boar's tusks pierced my left arm. I yelped in pain at the same time the boar screeched in response to the dagger I'd stuck into its shoulder. The creature pulled away from the unexpected blow, and I took the opportunity to get to my feet. The boar spun around again and charged at me once more, seemingly unaffected by the stab wound I'd inflicted. I readied myself for another hit.

"Ehren!"

The group responded immediately as they realized what was happening. I heard an arrow soar past my ear. The tip of it sunk into the tree behind me.

"Do not shoot me!" I screamed to the person sending arrows in my direction. In response, another arrow soared and finally landed in the boar's back just inches before it reached me again.

It faltered a little but still it kept coming. I planted my feet in the ground, trying to ignore the stinging pain and the blood now seeping from my left arm. When the impact of the boar hit me again I flew backwards and slammed into the ground again. Air left me, and I grunted as I tried desperately to get up. The boar squealed and snapped its large jaws in my direction. I covered my head with my arms in a last minute attempt to not be skewered.

The pain I thought I would feel when the boar hit me again never came. And I slowly pulled my arms away from my face to see Elesame had rammed directly into the creature. The lithe lion sunk her teeth into the boar with ease and the boar squealed. The sound died off as the creature became lifeless. The lion flung a large piece of the boar's head into the bushes and I looked away, feeling suddenly nauseous as the rest of the boar's body thumped to the ground.

"Ehren, are you all right?"

"Bear, are you okay!"

It didn't take long for the group to swarm me. Dusane was the first one next to me, examining the puncture wound that was soaking my jumpsuit with blood. But there was nothing to examine. It had already healed.

Mid came on my other side and wrapped an arm around me, holding me up in a sitting position. Embrosine and Rouix stood over me, a look of shame on Rouix's face.

"Sorry, I almost shot you. You know I'm bad at bow and arrow," Rouix said sheepishly.

Shar, Rosen, and the Ethydon guards came over too after assessing that the boar was indeed dead, and soon the entire caravan was surrounding me.

"I'm fine. Now, everyone back off!" They all took a couple steps back, except for Mid who kept a firm hold on me. Dusane looked at Mid's arm still wrapped around my waist, and I was surprised to see him blatantly glare at Mid.

"She said back off," Dusane said.

"Why don't you stay out of this," Mid bit back.

"Stop it you two! I'm fine!" I growled.

"But, your arm. . ." Mid insisted, looking at the blood staining my sleeve. Exasperated I reached and ripped the torn and bloodied part of my sleeve so that the wound underneath would be clearly visible. Where a puncture wound should have been the flesh was already healed.

Rouix handed me her canteen, and I quickly washed my arm off with some water.

"How. . ." Mid trailed off as he realized I was unharmed.

"I'm fine, see." I pushed myself up from the ground and felt my cheeks blush at the large group that was surrounding me.

"I should've known that boars would be in this area," Shar said darkly.

"It's okay. Let's just keep moving," I said, still embarrassed from the incident. I stomped off and found Diablo by a pine tree, and grabbed him by the mane.

"You've really gotta stop doing that," I said sternly to him. He snorted, and I think he had the decency to look guilty.

"Next time you fly off, try and take me with you, okay?" I said, and unable to stay angry at him, I reached out and stroked his ebony forehead. He whinnied softly and nuzzled my hand. I believed it was his way of apologizing.

"I'm fine, don't worry about me," I said to him while climbing up on his back. Everyone dispersed and soon we were moving again.

From that point on, every once in a while I would catch Dusane looking back at me, and then Mid would look back too. I ignored both of their worried expressions, still upset that they had snapped at each other. Last thing I needed was the two of them getting overprotective for no reason. The hostility did little to help my confused emotions.

"We have to travel on. I don't want to camp in these woods with the boars around. We'll keep going until we reach the hills," Shar said.

I didn't ask where the hills were. I knew that soon I would see for myself.

The sun went down a couple hours later, and the trees became an inky blackness. I watched Rouix's Crykon ahead, focusing on the bright glittering scales as they shimmered in the moonlight.

We eventually exited the forest and emerged onto a hillside. I urged Diablo forward toward the others who had stopped. When I reached the edge, I looked out at the view and gasped softly.

I'd seen a hill before. But this wasn't just one hill, it was many hills. Grassy, green hills. They rolled across the horizon like an emerald sea. The grass blades swayed in the gentle breeze while the moonlight glistened against the fresh blanket of green. The hills eventually met a tall mountain range in the distance.

"Is that where we're headed?" I asked, pointing to the tall mountains that were at the end of the rolling hills.

"Yes," I heard Mid say beside me. I turned toward the sound of his voice. He met my gaze confidently, and I quickly flitted my eyes away so as not to get lost in his emerald-scarlet depths.

"We'll camp at the bottom of this hill and then journey to the mountain in the morning," Shar ordered.

I urged Diablo down the grassy hillscape and helped the others set up camp in the soft grass. As I walked through the meadow I noticed a couple of wildflowers here and there snuggled beneath the overwhelmingly tall blades. The temperature was warm, and we found that a fire wasn't necessary.

Rouix and I pitched a tent together. Then my focus was broken when I felt someone staring at me from across the camp. I turned around and was surprised to see Dusane's bright blue eyes shining even in the darkness. We looked at each other from across the camp, and I wondered what he might be thinking.

He'd defended me today, yet he'd also said he knew when to give up a fight. I wanted to talk to him, try and understand what was going on in his head. But then he broke my gaze and disappeared into his tent. I inwardly sighed. *When we get to the hidden kingdom,* I told myself, *I'll talk to them both.*

I was suddenly not tired at all and knew that it was going to be another restless night of endless thoughts circling inside my mind. I sighed and peered into the tent to see Rouix already falling asleep.

"I'm going to take a walk," I whispered into the tent. Rouix just muttered a weak reply and I took it as her lack of interest. I left the quiet camp then. Everyone seemed to be in their tents sleeping. Rosen was keeping watch, but he didn't ask me where I was going when I got up to leave. I had been expecting a sarcastic comment, but it never came.

I started for the hill, wanting a quiet place to look out at the scenery and think. When I finally got to the top, it was just as breathtaking the second time as I took it all in.

"Beautiful isn't it?" I heard a voice say beside me. I jumped a little and turned, my body strung for a fight. The adrenaline dissipated when I realized it was just Mid.

He was sitting on the edge of the hill, his arms resting on his knees. The moon was barely illuminating his face enough for me to make out his features.

"Are you following me?" I accused and sat down on the grass several feet away from him. I had walked up the hill to see the view, and I wasn't going to let him ruin it.

"I was here first. Are you following me?" he smirked. I rolled my eyes. When I didn't reply, he chuckled to himself. "I see you still don't find my sarcasm very amusing," he observed.

"I thought you weren't talking to me," I said, while keeping my eyes on the mountains in the distance.

"I'm just waiting till we get back to the hidden kingdom."

I turned to face him, my eyes narrowing. "What do you mean?"

"You said you needed space, so I'm giving it to you. And when we get back, we'll talk," he said easily.

"So you aren't mad about Dusane?" I asked blatantly.

He winced a little, but then chuckled darkly as if to shake off my mention of Dusane's name. "I said I understood what was happening. Not that I was giving up."

I opened my mouth to say something more, but then closed it again unsure how to answer.

"If you think for one second I'm not going to fight for you, well, I'm sorry to say you've been sorely misled." There was an intense determination in his eyes.

"But, you were so upset. . ." I remembered the tormented look on his face when he realized that something was going on between me and Dusane.

His eyes locked on mine, and I could see the fervor in the deep scarlet of his irises, burning like a fire. The words Embrosine said to me about finding my sun came flooding back to me.

"Another man is chasing after the woman I love. Of course I'm upset," he said intensely.

I felt my cheeks go red as he used the word love. I remembered saying that I loved him too at the wedding that seemed so long ago. And I knew that I still loved him. It was hard to ignore the way he made me feel. But now he wasn't the only one that I had feelings for. *Could I have fallen in love with two people at once? And if I had, how was I supposed to measure who I loved more?*

"Mid, there is something else," I suddenly whispered, wishing that I could tell him I didn't want him to fight for me. But something inside of me wanted him to because I was selfish and my emotions were selfish and I wanted both of them in my life, even though I knew that was ridiculous and impossible.

I stretched my arm out, and pointed to the symbol on my arm. He squinted into the darkness, confusion written on his features for a moment, and then the realization dawned. His eyes widened and it was impossible to miss the shock on his face.

"Envorydian," I heard him whisper to himself.

"I understand if it's too much for you," I said, shoving my hand back to my side. I worried with the reputations of the Envorydians that Mid would judge me.

Mid put his finger beneath my chin, and gently lifted my head to meet his eyes.

"I don't care who you've become. I'll take you mortal, Stone-Hearted, princess or Envorydian."

It was a relief to hear him say he accepted me this way. That the decision I'd made didn't alter the way he felt about me.

"Thank you. . . But that's not all that's changed," I whispered, suddenly needing to get the words off my chest. We needed to talk about it, no matter how much I didn't want to.

He sighed and then very gently leaned down to press a kiss to my forehead. When he pulled away he stared intently into my eyes again.

"I know, I can see that. And I want you to have what makes you happy. But I want you to consider that maybe that person is me," he said, "which is why I'm not going to give up."

"You don't deserve being put through this," I started to say.

"I put you through a lot last year." He paused and seemed to struggle to get out his next words. "I should never have flaunted myself with Jasper in front of you. I should have fought harder for us and told my parents about our relationship. If anything, I deserve this," he said and I felt my heart wrench thinking about those memories and just how painful they were still.

"Mid, I was the one that asked you not to tell anyone. I was the one that told you to be with her," I reminded him, a small part of the old Sabeara seeping through the Envorydian that I'd become.

"It doesn't excuse my behavior." I could clearly see that this had tormented him. And I didn't want to see him blame himself.

"I forgive you," I whispered, forcing back tears that threatened.

"I want you to know I told everyone the truth. . ." he added.

"You told them?" An instant pit built in my stomach. I knew the betrothal had been compromised but, I hadn't really considered Mid would admit to our relationship. I nervously waited for his next words.

"They were all more understanding than I expected," he admitted, not quite meeting my gaze. I noticed him nervously fiddle with the sword hilt at his waist. "Also, I made things right with Jasper. And she's happy."

The pit in my stomach dissolved, and a small weight lifted off my chest hearing his words. I didn't realize how much I needed to hear them until that moment. *She's happy.* That was all I ever wanted for her.

"So. . . you and I?" I whispered, not able to finish the sentence. *What did this mean? That I could be with Midennen now if I wanted?*

"We can be together. . ." He looked up again, finally meeting my gaze. "If that ends up being what you decide."

My heart skipped a beat thinking of the possibilities. Possibilities Mid no doubt had been contemplating. But I still had reservations. . . ruling a kingdom was still not something I desired to do. And Queen and King Knadian would one day die, leaving Mid to rule in their stead. . . and then there was. . . cerulean blue eyes filled my head.

"It's not fair for me to ask this of you," I persisted.

"A little competition isn't going to hurt me, sweetheart," he smirked, obviously trying to stay lighthearted despite the heaviness of the conversation.

"All this for a girl you rescued over a year ago?" I whispered, and his smirk faltered a little.

"Am I just the man who rescued you over a year ago?" he countered. And I knew the answer was no. Mid could never just be the man who rescued me a year ago. He was so much more than that.

"It might be some time before I figure out what I want," I warned.

"I can wait," he insisted, but I could see the look in his eyes. The fiery determination glowing behind his expression.

"You aren't going to make this easy on me, are you?" I suddenly blurted out.

"What do you mean?" he asked innocently.

"I don't want you two to fight," I suddenly insisted.

He raised his hands in mock surrender. "I'll behave."

"Why do I highly doubt that," I deadpanned.

He grinned and reached out again to run the back of his hand across my cheek. My skin burned where he touched me. "I promise I'll try and be nice, if you promise me something."

"Depends on what it is," I said nervously.

"Promise me you'll try and remember the good feelings between us," he said gently. But little did he know that I could never forget. They were still fresh inside my head, still pulsing through my body at that very moment. It wasn't a matter of remembering the feelings I had for him. It was a matter of trying to sort through such deep feelings for him—and Dusane—at the same time. And it wasn't fair to either one of them until I figured out what was going on inside of my heart.

"I promise," I suddenly whispered. He smiled and then he leaned in toward me.

"Mid, wait." I pressed a hand against his chest. "When you kiss me, I can't think straight," I admitted.

He grinned but retreated back slightly. "You want me to wait to kiss you until we get back then too?" he asked, his tone only slightly teasing.

I bit my lip. "We should probably wait until I have my feelings sorted out," I said softly, thinking about how much more confusing things got when I kissed the two of them.

"I don't mind being used by you," he smoldered, leaning in again. All of a sudden the devilish prince returned, flirtatious and as fearless as I remembered. I stumbled to my feet, trying to calm my wildly beating heart.

"Mid, please," I begged.

He sighed, pursed his lips, then nodded. "Okay, I won't kiss you. Not until you figure out how you feel," he relented.

"Thank you," I said, blushing furiously.

He stood from the ground. "You should get some sleep. We have to be up early again tomorrow," he said, gesturing back down the hill.

Together we began walking back toward the camp.

"What's it like?" I suddenly asked. "The place where our kingdoms are hiding?"

"Peaceful. Captain Olivine has done well in organizing the survivors and creating a safe place for our people," he explained.

I didn't admit it aloud, but I was nervous to see my family again. It felt like so long ago that I'd seen them. I missed Oli so much that when I thought about him my chest would hurt. I'd left things horribly unsettled with Jasper, and I could only hope she'd be happy to see me when I returned. I missed my father too, despite all the flaws he had. I wanted to see his face again and hug him. I began to feel anxious about the reunion that was bound to happen tomorrow when we arrived.

FORTY-FOUR

The following morning was less contentious. Because I'd talked with Mid the night before, the disdain directed at me seemed to be cut in half. But there still remained the obvious tension between Dusane and me. I knew I'd have to talk things out with him soon enough, and I was dreading having the conversation. I wondered if he'd even talk to me. *Had he really given up?* I'd hoped he wouldn't, because something inside of me felt a sense of dread at the idea of him letting go of whatever was going on between us. The feelings I'd developed for him over the time I'd been in the Courts was something I couldn't ignore. *But would he want to try to figure things out with me too?* It was unfair of me to ask him to wait around while I figured out my feelings, but I didn't see another option at the moment. I was too confused to make a decision.

The sun was high in the sky now, and we'd been traveling across the grassy hillside for several hours. The green terrain seemed to stretch on endlessly. The mountains remained in the same spot in the distance, and it felt as if we were making no progress for a time. I rode beside Rouix and Shar for most of the journey, and it was quiet as we traveled.

"We are coming upon the mountain range," Mid suddenly called up ahead. It was shocking how for so long it had seemed so far away, and then suddenly it was right in front of us. We'd finally reached the large mountains. I gazed in awe at how they appeared to tower over us.

I'd never seen mountains like these. They were twice the size of the mountains that the Aveladon castle used to rest on. These mountains were lush green like the rolling hills we'd just come through with a mix of trees covering the large wondrous structures. At the very tip of the mountains, I could see the faint blanket of snow dusting the peaks. We traveled right up to them and continued on through a path between two of the large mountains in the range. It was a neatly carved canyon. On either side of me, I saw a vast expanse of rocks and trees with a small sliver of blue sky that shined down through the slit between the mountains. The canyon was the perfect entrance to a secret kingdom, and it blended nicely into the mountain range. I doubted anyone would be able to find it if they hadn't known where to look.

We traveled for several more hours. I began to feel the excitement and nervousness prickling my skin. The farther we winded through the canyon, the steeper the path became. Soon Diablo was simply flying gently up the slope, finding it easier than navigating the trees and rocks.

"Stop!" I heard one of the guards call from down below me. I urged Diablo to return to the ground and felt my heart quicken, wondering if we'd hit trouble. But my fear vanished when I realized it wasn't trouble we'd stumbled upon.

A large glistening gate was stationed up ahead. It had a massive structure, similar to the one that used to guard Asmede, only it was made of silver and covered in the foliage of the forest. Beautiful pink wildflowers wound their way through the bars of the gate. Five guards stood out in front guarding it.

The gate was stationed between two large rocks that created an impenetrable wall with their presence. They'd used the mountain side to fashion a wall so they wouldn't have to build one. It was genius using nature to their advantage. I wondered what lay behind the gate, nestled among these tall mountains.

I watched Mid and his guards jump down from their steeds and approach the guards standing at the gate. The rest of us waited patiently while they conversed.

A couple minutes later, Mid and the guards returned to the group. Mid had a frustrated look on his face.

"For safety they've been ordered to contact the king when visitors arrive. The Aveladon king is going to come to the gate himself, and he's bringing some more soldiers. They want to make sure it's really us." Mid seemed to think it was ridiculous to make us wait, but I couldn't blame them for being cautious.

"Then we'll just wait here until the king opens the gate," Shar said while helping Embrosine down from his horse.

"It'll be a good time to rest and eat a little," Embrosine commented.

We all dismounted and waited as the guards at the gate went inside to contact the king. I jumped off Diablo and felt an ache in my thighs from being on horseback for so long. I walked around a little, and the movement helped stretch out the muscles, and soon the soreness subsided.

I sat beneath a tree next to Rouix, and together we ate the

rest of the bread we'd carried on our journey. I was anxiously watching the gate, waiting for it to open again.

"You nervous to see your family?" Rouix asked beside me. I turned toward her and smiled sheepishly.

"A little," I admitted.

"I'm sure they'll be happy to see you," she said encouragingly.

"I hope so," I said quietly, feeling the nervousness increase. *What if they weren't happy to see me?* I forced that thought away. *What a stupid thought. They were my family,* I argued with myself. Then I caught sight of the tattoo on my arm and cringed. *What if they didn't accept me?*

Thoughts of uncertainty continued to swim around in my mind when I suddenly caught sight of Mid near the front of the gates, talking with Embrosine. Confused as to where Shar went, I looked around the caravan to see where he'd gone. The group seemed to be void of not only Shar's presence but Dusane's also.

Just as I started to get worried, I spotted them.

Shar had wandered off into the trees, and I could see his blond hair peeking through the branches about a hundred yards away. I squinted and could see that he wasn't alone. He was talking to Dusane, and it seemed that they were arguing. The rest of the group hadn't seemed to notice they'd disappeared. I stood from the ground.

"I'll be back," I told Rouix. She didn't pay me much attention as I followed after Shar and Dusane into the trees. As I traveled deeper to the place where they were talking together, I began to hear the contents of their argument.

"I can't stay, Shar."

"You can't just go back to the Courts, Dusane. You won your freedom. You really want to become a prisoner again?"

"Look, I don't expect you to understand. But I helped you

find Embrosine, and I helped you find the other token. I think I've done enough here," I heard Dusane respond sharply.

"We need you, Dusane. There are more tokens to be found. The curse isn't over yet," Shar insisted.

"I'm sure you'll be fine without me."

I passed through two pine trees into the small area where they were talking. As I stepped out to where they could see me, both of their heads turned toward me.

"You're leaving?" I asked, and his silence was thick in reply.

For several seconds, Dusane just looked at me, his blue eyes searing with emotions I couldn't name. "Yes, I am," he suddenly stated firmly.

"I'm going to check on the gate," Shar suddenly said, his gaze darkening. He walked past me, and then before going back to the group, laid a hand on my arm. "Ehren, you may have to let this one go," he whispered, before disappearing into the trees behind me.

I clenched my jaw. Anger bubbled up even more inside me as Shar fled the scene. *Let it go? Let him go?* It wasn't an option. I knew he felt something for me too.

"I'm not fighting with you about this, Ehren," Dusane said, turning on his heel and walking farther into the trees. I followed after him, realizing I'd done this once before already.

"What do I have to do to make you stay?" I asked suddenly. He stilled and slowly turned back to face me. His dark black hair was disheveled from the repetitive nights of sleep in the forest. I felt my heart rate increase as something inside of me yearned for him.

"Nothing. I'm not staying."

"Why did you kiss me in Obscurum then?" I questioned.

"I kissed you in the heat of the moment. I didn't know what

was going to happen to us." His words didn't even sting. He wasn't being honest with himself.

"Now that Midennen showed up, you are just walking away from everything? I thought you felt something for me."

"Ehren, for the last time, of course I feel something for you." His eyes looked suddenly pained. "You're irritatingly stubborn and hardheaded. You're dangerously curious all the time, but you're also funny, and smart. You're a great warrior and fighter. You're stunningly beautiful and just about everything I could ever want. But it's obvious that you feel more for him than you do for me."

"I don't know how I feel!" I yelled, suddenly unable to keep my voice down.

"I see the way you look at him! I'm not going to be the fool that fights for a woman who's heart is already won."

I began to feel desperate, horribly afraid he was actually going to leave.

"I want you to stay, Dusane," I said, my voice shaking.

"Don't lie to me, Ehren," he spat. He turned around once more and began walking farther away.

"Dusane, please. Don't go. I need *you.*" I felt tears sting the corners of my eyes. Wishing he could feel the conflict inside me and understand that I felt something for him too. And that I just needed some time to figure out exactly what those feelings were. But I didn't want to lose him in the process.

"Prove it," he growled, turning sharply back toward me.

Then it hit me. I looked down at the amulet on my chest. It glowed the color of Shar's heart. He'd touched me on the way back to the others, and the amulet was holding his ability—to see if someone was lying or not. The amulet was a finicky object, but I was never more grateful for its inconsistency.

My jaw set with determination, and I pulled the amulet up over my head. I walked over to him and could see the confusion in his expression as I neared. I ignored the questioning look in his eyes and then placed the amulet around his neck.

Without stopping to question myself on what I was about to do next, I grabbed the front of his shirt in my hands and crushed my lips to his.

I could feel him go still, obviously taken aback by the suddenness of the kiss. A low groan sounded in the back of his throat, then his lips relaxed against mine. His hand gripped my waist and tugged me closer to him.

It was a much longer kiss than the first one. He didn't hold back. His hands exploring the curve of my hip, then my lower back. His other hand fisted my hair, holding me tightly against him. His lips were just as fervent, pressing against mine with passionate urgency. He scraped his teeth gently across my bottom lip and I felt my knees go weak.

For several minutes, I allowed the blissful moment of our kiss to transport me. When he pulled away, it took me a couple deep breaths to really return to the current realm we were in.

He leaned his forehead against mine, our breathing ragged. I didn't have time to calculate the consequences of the kiss before he leaned in, gently kissing me once more. This time softly, deliberately.

When he pulled away, I looked hopefully into his deep blue eyes. "Now do you see?" I whispered.

He sighed and then a small smile spread across his lips. The unexpected beauty of it made my heart skip. "You really want me to stay."

It wasn't a question, and I simply nodded in affirmation again. "I do." Then I quickly edited. "I want you to stay, so I can figure out how I feel about—" I gestured between us—"all of this," I finished, hoping he wouldn't be upset.

"So you mean to say you want time to think through how you feel about me and your feelings for *him*?" he clarified.

I blushed and looked down at the ground shamefully. "I know it's a lot to ask, but I'm just so confused right now—"

"Okay," he suddenly agreed. I looked up, and felt my whole body flood with relief. "Now that I know your feelings are real, I understand," he said simply.

I bit my lip nervously. "I don't want you to think that I'm doing this to take advantage of you."

"Ehren, don't worry about me. I can handle a little rivalry," he said, suddenly very determined. He leaned in to kiss me again, and I quickly backed away, in a similar way to when I'd backed away from Mid.

"I don't want you guys to fight over me. This isn't some game, okay? And if we're going to do this, I think it's only fair that I don't kiss either of you from now on. Until I can figure this all out," I quickly blurted.

Dusane had a new look in his eyes that I'd never seen. His reserved nature was his natural shown emotion, if you could even call it an emotion. And after that kiss, it was as if his hidden confidence had burst forth. He was suddenly very aware that he was conflicting my emotions just as much as Mid was. My plan to get him to stay had worked far better than I'd intended it to.

"I'll remain civil. As for not kissing you. . . I guess that's fair," he said, crossing his arms over his chest.

"Thank you." I began to feel very anxious alone with him in the trees. "We should head back," I said awkwardly, gesturing toward where the others awaited. I hoped that no one had overheard our fight.

After a moment, he relaxed his stance and nodded. We started back toward the group and together we emerged into the clearing where the gate into the new hidden kingdom was located.

When we arrived, there was a lot of commotion. Everyone suddenly surrounded the gate.

"What's going on?" I asked coming up beside Rouix who was farther back in the cluster.

"The king has arrived, and they're opening the gate," she said, gesturing to where everyone was crowded.

I didn't have time to push my way to the front before the gate swung outwards. I brushed up against Dusane as we were pushed back, feeling abruptly fearful of what was about to emerge on the other side. I could barely see over the heads of the others in our caravan. Then a very familiar voice washed over the group.

"Well aren't we glad to see all of you. Welcome to Knadiel."

EPILOGUE

King Elysian stared at the empty space where the tokens had been only moments before. The amulet had gradually disappeared, along with the hammer—slowly fading until dissolving into nothing.

"Why did you let them get away?" Obsidian was angry. He'd always been emotional. It was a quality he got from his mother. It was that same lack of emotional control that had gotten her killed. Elysian wouldn't be surprised if one day it got his son killed as well.

"If they think they fooled us Obsidian, they will have a false sense of security," Elysian explained to him.

"But how does that help us?" Obsidian growled, clenching his fists at his sides.

Elysian walked to his throne, taking a seat. He threw one leg causally over the arm and gave his son a self-satisfied smile.

"Why would I waste my breath finding the tokens, when they could do it for me?" Elysian asked.

Obsidian's brow furrowed, obviously still confused.

Elysian sighed. "We will get the tokens, this was just an. . . assessment," Elysian said. "Now that we know exactly what tokens they have, we can watch and wait until they have them all."

"And then what?"

"And then we will end this."

PRONUCIATION GUIDE

Dusane: Doo-seyn
Nevrair: Neh-vrair
Conland: Kon-lyhnd
Rouix: Roh-ihx
Rosen: Roh-zen
Theon: Thee-ahn
Vayel: Vay-ehl
Envorydian: Ehn-vohr-ih-dee-in
Envoy: Ehn-voi
Lisle: Ly-uhl
Diablo: Dee-ah-bloh
Elesame: Ehl-eh-seyme
Drego: Dreh-goh
Niuadi: Nahy-oo-ah-dee
Telsiver: Tel-see-vur
Raiel: Rey-ahy-el
Knadiel: Knah-dee-el
Sethen: See-then

ACKNOWLEDGMENTS

I want to thank all that have helped me with Hearted. This was the book that began everything. It has been a long time coming. So I want to thank my father Brent Molen for creating the beautiful maps and for giving me book advice. My best friend Emily Nackos for being so supportive during the entire process. I want to thank my editor Chelsea Jackson for pushing me to be a better writer. I also want to thank the rest of my family and my wonderful husband for sticking by me.

I also want to thank Claire Hansen for making the character art cover for Hearted. You've done such a fantastic job creating the characters from my mind and putting them into something tangible. I can't thank you enough for agreeing to work with me.

I also want to thank all those that have read Granted and urged me to complete this book so you could enjoy more of Sabeara's story. I wouldn't have finished the book without all of you.

ABOUT THE AUTHOR

Kendra Thomas is from Mapleton Utah, a small town pressed against the beautiful Rocky Mountains. Kendra has been an aspiring author since she was in sixth grade. She has a passion for fairytales and fiction books. Along with songwriting, horse riding, and playing the guitar.

Kendra Thomas is a Dental Hygienist by day and a writer by night. She earned her bachelors degree at the Utah College of Dental Hygiene at the young age of nineteen years old. She is also happily married to her best friend, Cade Thomas, who is always pushing her to be ambitious and creative.

Her most wanted dream is for others to love her stories and characters as much as she cherishes them. She hopes to inspire other young authors to pursue their dreams, and to write about the worlds inside their heads as she was once inspired to do as a young girl.

She hopes that the Granted Series might be a place of sanctuary for those seeking a whimsical getaway and a thrilling adventure.

www.ingramcontent.com/pod-product-compliance
Lightning Source LLC
Chambersburg PA
CBHW070838020826
48982CB00021B/1445/J

* 9 7 8 1 7 3 5 0 1 5 3 5 4 *